NEW YORK
STATE OF
CRIME

MURDER ON FIFTH AVENUE
MICHAEL JAHN

LIBATION BY DEATH
DORIAN YEAGER

CLEAN SWEEP
BARBARA PAUL

WORLDWIDE.

TORONTO • NEW YORK • LONDON
AMSTERDAM • PARIS • SYDNEY • HAMBURG
STOCKHOLM • ATHENS • TOKYO • MILAN
MADRID • WARSAW • BUDAPEST • AUCKLAND

A NEW YORK STATE OF CRIME

A Worldwide Mystery/August 1999

Murder on Fifth Avenue and *Libation by Death* were first published by St. Martin's Press, Incorporated. *Clean Sweep* is an original short story.

ISBN 0-373-26317-1

Murder on Fifth Avenue Copyright © 1998 by Michael Jahn.
Libation by Death Copyright © 1998 by Dorian Yeager.
Clean Sweep Copyright © 1998 by Barbara Paul.

Visit us at www.worldwidemystery.com

Printed in U.S.A.

CONTENTS

MURDER ON FIFTH AVENUE

MICHAEL JAHN

For my mother,
Anne Jahn,
who taught me to love books

ONE

"MAKE ME ONE WITH EVERYTHING"

FRIDAY, NOVEMBER 29, the day after Thanksgiving, was brilliantly sunny but very cold. The long line of tourists and other potential customers waiting to get into F.A.O. Schwarz at the start of the holiday shopping season watched their breaths freeze and waft slowly upward in the lifeless air. That very busy corner of Manhattan, diagonally across Fifth Avenue from the Plaza Hotel and Central Park, could be a wind tunnel at times. But on that day no air snaked around the tall office buildings and across the famous facades of such Fifth Avenue stores as Schwarz, Tiffany's, Cartier, and Bergdorf Goodman. Only the murmur of voices (many speaking foreign tongues) and the distant sounds of the season—recorded carols and the tinkling of sidewalk Santas' bells and those rung by assorted beggars—distracted the crowd from the task of getting into the world's most famous toy store. Even the clown posted outside to amuse patrons during the half-hour waits was silent, a mime.

Donovan had forgotten his gloves again—Marcy had threatened to sew them to his cuffs—and as a result his hands were stuffed deep into the pockets of his navy blue greatcoat. He hated to wait in line and as a general rule pulled rank to avoid it. But something about the impending birth of his son made him eager to join the ranks of the other holiday toy buyers, a gleefully anonymous celebrant of the rituals of parenthood. Marcy had been in a bed at Fifth Avenue Medical Center for the previous week, taking medicine to fight off premature delivery and preeclampsia—

high blood pressure during pregnancy. Donovan was on partial leave for a month to keep his wife company while both awaited the magic moment. But there was no reason for Donovan not to wander out to buy his son's first rattle.

He fingered the cellular phone that at any moment could bring the call to rush back to the hospital and watched a sidewalk vendor animatedly explaining a gyro—a Greek sandwich that had become ubiquitous around Manhattan—to a grandmother from somewhere out in the heartland. The smoke of grilled roasting meat curled around the edge of the man's tall aluminum pushcart and hung suspended in the frigid air. The pushcart vendor seemed interesting, a pudgy man of perhaps forty years whose fat cheeks and scraggly beard hung below an immense white turban that completely covered the sides and top of his head. His cart also was colorful, decorated with red, blue, and yellow signs hawking pretzels, hot dogs, sausages, soft drinks, and assorted ice creams. There also was an "Allah Is Great" bumper sticker on which someone had scribbled a street address. Next to it: an aging snapshot of what Donovan recognized as one of the Great Buddhas of Bamiyan was accompanied by a bit of doggerel:

SAID BUDDHA TO THE HOT DOG VENDOR
"MAKE ME ONE WITH EVERYTHING"

By the time the line of customers crept up to the vendor's patch of sidewalk, the grandmother had been talked into buying a soft pretzel and rejoined her family outside the entrance to F.A.O. Schwarz. Donovan eyeballed the turban, having noticed the Eastern ecumenicism—Muslim and Buddhist sentiments back to back—and sensing that beneath the turban lingered someone interesting to talk to. Donovan got the man's eye and asked, "Sikh?"

"And ye shall find," was the reply.

Donovan groaned despite inner gratitude at having found

a conversation. "One clown is enough," he said. The mime was nearby, his impression of Marcel Marceau's man in an invisible box largely veiled by frozen breath.

"You want something?" the vendor asked.

"I want to know where you're from," Donovan replied.

"Afghanistan," the man said, looking around nervously—as if making a joke, or dodging bullets, Donovan thought.

The captain decided to play along. "Then why this kind of turban?"

"It keeps my head warm."

"I thought maybe you were a Sikh," Donovan said, a bit disappointed that no punch line lurked at the end of the turban talk.

"Not a chance. I like their headgear, that's all. They make the warmest turbans you can buy. As for me, I'm a Muslim. I worship Allah. What do you worship?"

"My wife," Donovan said.

Tossing in a disapproving frown, the vendor replied, "You've got it backward. A man's wife should worship him."

"Trust me. There's less argument this way."

The man shrugged. "So are you going to eat or did you just come here to entertain me?" the vendor asked.

"I came to this edifice"—Donovan cocked his head in the direction of F.A.O. Schwarz—"to buy a toy for my unborn son."

"You're becoming a father? For the first time?"

"What are you, a lawyer?" Donovan asked.

"Your wife is giving you a son. No wonder you worship her. Here, have a pretzel on me." He tried to hand Donovan a twisted bit of bread the size of a baseball mitt flecked with rock salt. But Donovan waved it off.

"Too much salt. What do you get for a gyro?"

"For you, five bucks."

"Five bucks?!" Donovan exclaimed. "For half a pita

bread stuffed with lettuce, onions, tomato, and two slices of goat meat?''

''It's lamb, and you get three slices,'' the man said. ''Plus the yogurt sauce.''

''Five bucks is still too much money. And that 'lamb' was last seen eating tin cans outside Kabul. I can get a real gyro anyplace else for three dollars.''

''Such as where?'' the man said, growing combative.

''There's an Israeli joint on Broadway and a Hundred-fifth Street that makes a great one,'' Donovan replied.

''You want to talk about too much salt, you try an Israeli gyro,'' the vendor said. ''Now, the Egyptians don't do too bad. There's this place on Second Avenue.''

''I know it. The Muslim cabdrivers go there. But to be honest with you, the only really good gyro is the Greek one you get in Astoria.''

The man frowned. ''Who has the time to go to Queens to eat when you could eat a perfectly good one here, on Fifth Avenue? Besides, the round-trip subway fare brings you up to five dollars. An Astoria gyro isn't cost-effective. How much is your time worth?''

''I'll have a pretzel,'' Donovan said. ''But I want to pay for it.''

''If you insist,'' the vendor replied, pushing the thing at Donovan again.

''How much?''

''For you…two bucks.''

''Two bucks for a pretzel that a moment ago was free?!'' Donovan exclaimed.

''That's what the price is.''

''I can remember when these things went for fifty cents.''

The man was unimpressed. ''Maybe you can also remember when the Knicks won titles.''

''No one's memory is that good,'' Donovan replied, fishing two bills from his pocket and forking them over. Then he watched the steam from the hot dough freezing in the air, while flicking the salt onto the sidewalk.

The line moved forward by another customer, and Donovan moved with his pretzel to the far end of the pushcart. He assumed that was the end of the conversation, but the vendor seemed to be enjoying the encounter as much as he was. For the man appeared at that end of the wagon, brandishing a can of Coke.

"One buck," he said. "Now, that price has been stable for at least two years. Go ahead; tell me you can get it for sixty cents over at the Korean store on Lexington Avenue."

"I'm not going to drink a cold soda on the coldest day of the year. You're from Afghanistan. Get me a cup of hot tea. Black Russian tea, if you've some left over from those convoys you guys used to raid."

"You're a dreamer," the man replied.

"I'm cold," Donovan said, biting off a bit of pretzel and chewing it while watching the clown duck inside F.A.O. Schwarz to warm up.

Donovan became aware of the fact that the vendor and he were about the only ones talking out loud. The rest of the crowd was silent or talking in hushed tones; whether due to the cold or in respect for the approaching holiday was impossible to tell. The background music—bells ringing here and there and carols beaming from various speakers—seemed that much louder. A wisp of a breeze came up and whisked off the smoke from the grill, just as a jaunty "God Rest Ye Merry Gentlemen" filled the winter air.

Donovan sighed gently and his heart warmed as he thought of Marcy and his unborn son. The trace of a tear appeared in his eye. It was so long in the making, not just the boy but also the very marriage itself, the improbable union of an Irish cop from the West Side and his wealthy, multiracial wife, framed in years of professed love and false starts, coming togethers and breaking aparts, that led up to a family. Within the month, maybe within days, a new child would be born. A new life would enter the world.

Suddenly the air was pierced by screams, screams followed by three shots coming in rapid succession and, Donovan could tell, from a large-bore weapon. There was also the breaking of glass, the ear-piercing wail of a burglar alarm, then more screams. The sounds came from down Fifth Avenue, perhaps a block away. But their immediate effect was to make Donovan's vendor friend jerk his hand inside the cinch holding up his pants.

Donovan saw the glint of black metal on the handle of an automatic. Tossing aside the pretzel, he grabbed the man's hand and immobilized it while shoving a gold captain's badge in his face.

"Are you a cop?" Donovan asked.

The man shook his head nervously. All the color was gone from his face.

"Well, I am, and I'm telling you to stay out of it. And if that's not licensed, get rid of it before I get back."

The vendor was speechless. Donovan sensed it was a rare occurrence. "Understand?" he asked.

The man bobbed his head up and down.

"Happy holidays," Donovan muttered, letting go of the man's hand. Donovan drew his Smith & Wesson and pushed his way through a crowd that parted quickly for him.

TRAFFIC STOPPED DEAD in the middle of Fifth Avenue, the world's most famous boulevard, to watch the scene on the sidewalk. Tourists, many of them European or Asian and babbling in an array of languages, jostled shoulder to shoulder for better views of the carnage. The ten-foot-high plate-glass window of Sarkana, the legendary international jewelers', was shattered. Three monstrous bullet holes—they looked almost big enough to push broomsticks through—sat at the centers of three spiderwebs of cracked glass. The force of the explosions had splintered the "bulletproof"

"I don't think so. She fainted. I never saw anyone faint before," Hargrove replied.

"Have you ever seen anyone shot before?"

"No."

"I think she's OK, Captain!" the patrolman called out.

"Call an ambulance anyway," Donovan said, exchanging his revolver for his cell phone and handing the latter to the officer.

More officers succeeded in pushing their way through the crowds. Donovan had them cordon off both the body and the space outside surrounding the bullet-riddled window. As he worked, Donovan led the still-recovering store manager around Melmer's body to the edge of the display case the man had been standing by when an unidentified assassin with a seriously large handgun sent Melmer to meet his maker.

The display case had a top surface that was flat on the store side but sharply angled on the window side, the latter to allow those outside to peer in at the baubles. The effect also gave shoppers the sense of being celebrities, for anyone rich or merely brazen enough to have a gem taken from that display case was sure to attract a small crowd of gawkers.

"Did you see the one with the gun?" Donovan asked.

"No," Hargrove replied. "I mean I was aware of the window-shoppers, but didn't pay any attention to them."

"All of a sudden there was shooting?"

Hargrove looked out the window at the crowd, which now was pushed back by uniformed policemen and their ubiquitous yellow crime-scene tape. Viewed through the shattered glass, the scene had the surreal quality of something viewed through crinkled cellophane.

"There was a commotion," the manager remembered.

"Like what?"

"Like...I remember now that people moved suddenly. It was as if they were surprised by something."

"By someone pulling out a big gun, maybe?" Donovan suggested.

"That could be," the man replied, excited by the recollection.

"Tall or short, man or woman?"

This time Hargrove shook his head. "I couldn't tell you," he said. "There was a commotion, movement outside, and then the glass exploded and Mr. Melmer was thrown backward. He didn't utter a sound. He just clutched the bracelet and fell."

Hargrove allowed himself a look back at the body, then said, "It's going to be some trick to get the blood off the diamonds."

"It always is," Donovan replied.

Returning his attention to the window, the manager said, "You know, Captain, this window is supposed to be bulletproof. And not just run-of-the-mill bulletproof, but the highest-grade protection. We paid a great deal of money for it."

Donovan reached out and held the tip of his finger near one of the bullet holes, the idea being to gauge its size. "No glass made will protect you from the cannon that made that hole," he said.

"Really? But we paid—"

Donovan took out his Smith & Wesson again and popped a bullet out of the cylinder. He held it up near the hole. "This is a thirty-eight-caliber slug," he explained. "It's a little over a third of an inch in diameter. As you can see, it would fit easily in that hole." He replaced the bullet and gun. "The bullets that made those holes were much bigger, almost certainly special rounds fired from a military weapon."

Hargrove seemed nearly relieved. Donovan recognized what he called the "overwhelming force" syndrome. That is, why feel guilty about something that was way beyond your ability to prevent? Hargrove clearly could go to his superiors and say, "They fired a cannon through the window; what do you expect from me?" And he would probably keep his job.

"The ambulance is en route," the patrolman said, handing back the cell phone.

Donovan nodded but shoved the phone, and a business card, back into the man's hands. "Call the number you see there and tell Sergeant Moskowitz to get up here and bring a team."

"Sergeant Moskowitz," the officer replied, making a note on the back of the card.

"And don't let him give you any guff about it being cold, the Sabbath, or whatever."

"Sure thing, Captain," the officer said, amused at the notion he would order a sergeant around. He went off to find a corner in which to make the call.

Turning back to the store manager, Donovan said, "So you didn't see anyone outside the window."

The man thought for a moment, then replied, "Just the usuals—women tourists, a few men, a Santa's Angels volunteer."

"Ogling jewels? A Santa's Angels volunteer ogling jewels?"

"Dreams are free," Hargrove said.

"Nonetheless, the idea of a uniformed charity worker, nominally here to do the work of the Lord, ogling jewels intrigues me. Male or female?"

"Male...of course."

"Why would a male Santa's Angels volunteer be so interested in..." Donovan looked around, then pointed at the pearl-and-jewel necklace still draped over the dead man's torso. "In that? How much does that cost?"

"For you, one-point-seven million," Hargrove said.

"Jesus, and I thought the gyros were expensive in this neighborhood. Is there any chance you have baby rattles here? Do you have anything under a million? If not, can I postdate a check?''

Hargrove smiled faintly, then said, ''Sure we have baby rattles. Nice silver ones. A hundred dollars. The engraving is free. How does that sound?''

''That sounds good,'' Donovan replied. ''I'd rather shell out the hundred bucks than get back in that line outside F.A.O. Schwarz in this weather.''

The woman who had passed out was stirring, responding to the fanning being given her by salespeople. At the same time, the sidewalk outside was filling up with cops. They had blocked off the two nearest of the five traffic lanes and filled up one of the others with official vehicles. Doing so assured that the everyday gridlock that afflicted Fifth Avenue from Fifty-seventh to Sixtieth Streets would extend up through the Metropolitan Museum of Art on Eighty-second. An ambulance arrived, and the attendants were duly escorted into the store. They put the woman, now jabbering incoherently in German, onto a gurney and wheeled her out. Upon their departure, a morgue wagon pulled up. Blue-jumpsuited attendants stormed into Sarkana and began bickering with the uniformed cops about having to wait until Forensics came and released the body. All in all, the stifling sense of death that permeated the fancy store had been replaced by the refreshing sound of New Yorkers arguing. Following a fatal but brief interlude, life had returned, full tilt, to the city that never sleeps.

Donovan said, ''Places like this videotape everything, don't they?'' He looked around for cameras and found two pointing down at the display case and its adjacent body.

Hargrove's eyes widened. ''Of course! The cameras! You want to see the tape.''

''Are there cameras outside?''

''There's one,'' the man said excitedly. ''We put it there in case someone tried to throw a brick through the window to steal things from the display case. A brick wouldn't make a dent, of course. But a military weapon...?"

"I'll take that tape," Donovan said.

"Can you wait?" Hargrove asked, edging eagerly away from the scene.

"Long enough to buy a rattle," the captain replied.

TWO

"FLAT ON HER BACK TRYING TO REMEMBER WHAT HER FEET LOOK LIKE"

"HERE'S THE CIGARS. You owe me four hundred and eighty bucks." So said Detective Sergeant Brian Moskowitz in handing Donovan an elegant-looking wooden box labeled "Albarron y Gonzalo."

Donovan stood in the cold outside Sarkana and stared blankly at the package. Then he looked down at his assistant—while muscle-bound and tough as a bull, Moskowitz stood several inches shorter than his boss—and said, "What's wrong with this picture?"

"When I got the call to rush up here, no questions asked, I assumed you had become a dad and wanted me to bring the cigars," Mosko replied.

"I want you to handle the investigation," Donovan said. "I'm on leave."

"I can do that, too. So why isn't the baby here yet?"

"It's not even close. Marcy's only at thirty-four weeks. The usual pregnancy lasts forty."

"So what's she doing in the hospital?" Mosko asked.

"Preeclampsia," Donovan said. "Now do you know any more than you did ten minutes ago?"

"What's preeclampsia?"

"High blood pressure during pregnancy."

"How come she has that? Marcy is healthy as a horse."

"She's forty years old," Donovan said.

"She doesn't look it," Mosko replied.

"I guarantee you, right at this moment she feels every year. So tell me about the stiff."

Moskowitz plucked his notebook computer off the hood of his car and looked at the screen. "Erik Melmer was head of Melmer International, which is one of the leading manufacturers of"—the sergeant squinted at the screen—"of contrast media in Europe."

"What's contrast media?" Donovan asked. "A photography thing?"

"No. A medical thing, it says here. Something to do with ultrasound."

"Ultrasound like we've been using to look at the baby," Donovan said.

"Apparently there's a big market for contrast media. That's what the book said, anyway. Melmer was forty-seven years old and divorced. Supported an ex-wife and two kids living in Cologne. His fiancée is—listen to this—Princess Anna of Karlsruhe. They got engaged last August."

"What the hell's Karlsruhe?"

"Beats me. I know it's in the Black Forest…not exactly Moskowitz country, if you know what I mean."

"Is she one of those Eurotrash princesses whose families haven't sat on any throne—except maybe a porcelain one—for two hundred years, yet they still claim to be royalty?"

"Could be. I think Karlsruhe is a former principality. But she lives in Düsseldorf."

"Does this Anna have a last name?"

"Hebbel. Anna Hebbel. She's twenty-seven. Melmer and her had been living together for the past year and were to get married next month."

Donovan shook his head. "Not even Eurotrash royalty deserves what happened to her."

"Yeah, I agree. She's in Fifth Avenue Medical Center under sedation. Maybe Marcy can look in on her."

"Marcy is flat on her back trying to remember what her feet look like. Anyway, she doesn't *Sprechen Sie Deutsch.*

Does Princess Anna have any relatives in this country?'' Donovan asked.

"Not that I'm aware of."

"Put in a call to the German consulate. Maybe they can help."

"You got it."

"And while you're at it, send someone up to get the identification of the Afghan gyro dealer parked outside F.A.O. Schwarz."

"Let me guess. You got agita and want to sue."

"He's carrying a gun and seemed a bit jittery when the shooting started."

"Imagine that."

"Just do it," Donovan said. "I don't want him arrested. I just want to know what his story is. Now, what about the store's surveillance tapes?" Donovan asked.

"Right over here," Mosko said, and led the way to How-ard Bonaci's crime-scene van. The specially outfitted Dodge van contained a miniature crime lab as well as photographic and videotape facilities. Donovan got the city to buy it as an inducement for his old crime-scene wiz to transfer from the West Side Major Crimes Unit. It stood by the curb just outside the inner ring of yellow crime-scene tape, the one that marked off that part of sidewalk where the shooter stood. It was empty now, save for a technician who was poring over the upended Santa's Angels collection tripod.

Moskowitz slid open the side door and urged his boss inside. Donovan unbuttoned his overcoat and complied, squeezing in behind a console that included two monitors and a videotape deck. He sat next to Bonaci. The crime-scene chief's skinny, nervously moving fingers wandered over the pushbutton controls.

"Howard, my son, so good of you to be here this day after Thanksgiving."

"No problem, Boss," Bonaci replied. "The only thing I would get by staying home is more leftovers."

"I love leftover turkey. I could eat it all year."

"Not my wife's you wouldn't. It's tough as rubber and dry as a bone. I got some in the fridge, though, if you want to see for yourself." He reached back and tapped his finger on the pint-size refrigerator that served as repository for fragile evidence as well as for lunch.

"No thanks. I'm still getting over the turkey sandwich I got from the Korean joint yesterday."

"You ate this sandwich in the hospital room?" Bonaci asked, cueing up a tape.

Donovan nodded. "Sitting at the end of Marcy's bed."

"This must have been some Thanksgiving."

"Are you kidding? It was great. I got to be with my wife and child. How much more can a man be thankful for?"

"You got a point," Bonaci said. "Check this out." He pressed a button.

"What are we looking at?" Donovan asked.

"The tape from inside the store. Watch."

Donovan did as he was told. He watched as a camera showed, with relative clarity, Melmer and Hebbel examining jewels as the midafternoon sun streamed in the tinted window. Hargrove stood near her elbow, watching closely. All seemed breezily engaged in a transaction that, to the average man or woman, would represent a lifetime of assets.

Then Hargrove's head seemed to flick in the direction of the window. In that instant, a spray of tiny glass fragments was followed by Melmer wincing. He seemed startled.

"That's bullet one," Donovan said.

Another spray of glass came a split second later. This time all three jerked reflexively, and the woman's mouth opened as if to scream.

"Bullet number two. I couldn't tell if he was hit or not."

Then Melmer jerked backward as the third bullet clearly made a thumb-sized hole in his chest, and lurched forward as the slug, now exiting, made a fist-sized hole in his back.

The man fell backward onto the floor, his fingers in a death grip on the diamond-encrusted bracelet.

"That's three," Donovan said.

"The store manager looked out the window," Bonaci added.

"So he told me. He said he saw a movement."

"He should have seen more than that. Look at the outside tape."

"You got something useful from the outside camera?" Donovan asked.

"Better than useful. We got the perp. Watch."

He switched tapes and pressed a few more buttons. Donovan watched as the monitor showed what appeared to be a normal holiday-season crowd of window-shoppers. They carried green-and-red shopping bags and riotously colored boxes, which they held in arms already fattened by layers of winter clothes. Breath froze in the air, and frost particles clung to scarves. In the center of the crowd, conspicuous in a bright red cape with white fur trim, with collar and cap arranged in such a way as to hide the face, a Santa's Angels beggar stood at the center of the window holding a collection tripod.

"Watch the guy in the center," Bonaci said.

"The Santa's Angels man? Hargrove said there was one in the crowd."

"That's him. Watch him closely."

Bonaci slowed down the tape. All of a sudden the red cape fluttered and a hand flicked into the bucket normally used to collect coins for the poor. When it came out it held a large silvery object. That was when several window-shoppers reacted, lurching away from the beggar. The gun came up and was pointed at the window. Donovan and Bonaci watched as three slugs tore into the glass, which buckled like a tarpaulin buffeted by a gale-force wind but didn't break. Three holes, and the spiderwebbing Donovan had seen earlier appeared in a flash.

Then the crowd fell apart in panic and the Santa's Angels beggar tucked the gun under the cape and fled the chaos, running off in the direction of downtown. The collection tripod tumbled over.

Said Moskowitz, who had been watching over Donovan's shoulder, "We're interviewing as many of the people in that crowd as we can find. So far no one saw where the perp went."

"And there are a lot of Santa's Angels beggars out on the street this time of year," Donovan said.

"At least a couple every block," Mosko agreed.

Donovan leaned back and stretched. "You know, I have the feeling I've been to this movie," he said.

"What are you talking about?"

"Do you remember Andrea Jones?"

Thinking, Bonaci said, "Yes...no, I forget."

"She was using her great-great-granddaddy's navy Colt to leave powder burns on assorted lowlifes around town."

"Where was I when this happened?" Mosko asked.

"It was twelve or thirteen years ago, so more than likely you were working out in gym class at South Shore High," Donovan said to his twenty-something aide.

"Not a chance. I didn't start pumping iron until I got outta college and my hair began to thin. It's a compensatory mechanism for me." He patted the back of his head, where a distinct white glow was pushing through his curly black hair. "So what happened to this Jones woman?"

"Marcy shot her," Bonaci replied. "I remember now."

Moskowitz whistled between his teeth and said, "Boss, I got to say I admire your ability to get along with strong babes. But what's this got to do with Melmer being killed?"

"Andrea Jones once disguised herself as a bum in order to get a point-blank shot at a mob guy," Donovan said.

"Are you suggesting the Santa's Angels beggar who shot Melmer was anything more than a guy who went cuckoo and blew away an innocent man?"

Donovan rolled the thought around in his head, then said, "I would like to know more about Melmer."

"I'm working on that," Mosko replied. "Although, on the face of it, I don't see what there can be about a man who makes contrast media for medical equipment that could get him killed."

"There must be business rivals," Donovan said. "And there's an ex-wife."

Mosko mentioned, "Hey, if you want to kill a guy, you don't wait until he's standing behind bulletproof glass on Fifth Avenue."

"I don't know.... It's a nice smoke screen," Bonaci said.

"I also would like to know more about handguns that fire substantial rounds," Donovan said.

"Now you're in my area of expertise," Bonaci replied, brightening. "There are military handguns that can fire through bulletproof glass."

Mosko said, "But why would anyone need a *handgun* that can fire through glass? I mean if you want to blow a hole in a store window you can use an elephant gun or, for that matter, a damn rocket launcher."

"You can't carry an elephant gun in your Vidal Sassoons," Donovan said. "And a handgun that fires rounds through bulletproof glass is ideal for assassination through bulletproof limo windows."

"Oh," Mosko replied, chastened.

"The only one I could tell you about offhand is the Kammacher seven-point-six-five-millimeter, which fires a round said to be effective through some bulletproof glass at short ranges," Bonaci said.

"That slug is too small to make the holes I saw," Donovan replied.

"Now, that same outfit might have a larger-bore weapon. But the recoil problem would be tremendous."

"That sounds too big for a Santa's Angels coin collector to handle," Donovan said.

"Another problem is where the hell anyone would get a Kammacher," Bonaci added. "It's not only that they're made in what used to be East Germany for sale only in Europe. It's that the Secret Service went nuts the one time— I think it was five years ago—a U.S. company applied for permission to import them. And, interestingly enough, that outfit wanted to sell them to the Secret Service. I tell you, these are big weapons, not like your pocket thirty-eight. I don't see how anyone could smuggle one into America, let alone slip it into New York City."

By way of calling attention to the possibilities that existed for smuggling stuff into New York City, Donovan tapped the cover of his box of Cuban cigars, which sat on his lap.

"Cuban cigars!" Bonaci said excitedly. "Where'd you get them?"

"His Uncle Stanley," Donovan replied.

Moskowitz looked down and kicked a piece of litter across the pavement.

"Uncle Stanley wouldn't also be into illegal weapons imports, would he?" Donovan asked.

"Not that we talk about at the table," Mosko replied, somewhat irritably.

"It seems to me if a man can get a box of—very expensive—Cuban cigars, shipped via Toronto, for a New York City police captain, he can get a damn gun."

"Stop giving me a hard time," Mosko said.

"I wouldn't call a Kammacher automatic a 'damn gun,'" Bonaci added.

"Check and see if any of these substantial firearms are in the U.S.," Donovan said.

"You got it." The crime-scene chief seemed excited by getting an assignment that touched on an area of personal interest.

"If these guns are assassination weapons, that lends credence to the notion Melmer may have been a deliberate target," Mosko said.

"Yes, it does," Donovan replied.

"Maybe there is something about contrast media manufacturing we should know about."

At that moment, a jumpsuited crime-scene investigator came up and handed Moskowitz two plastic evidence bags. They were the size of sandwich bags and contained oddly lustrous, barely deformed pieces of metal.

"What's this?" Mosko asked.

Donovan said, "Only one of the shots hit the target. There were two others."

"This is them, Cap," the crime-scene man said. "We dug them out of a plaster column about ten yards behind the victim."

Mosko thanked the man, who then disappeared back into the crowd of police officers and crime-scene investigators.

Moskowitz, Donovan, and Bonaci took turns inspecting the slugs.

"Nine millimeters?" Donovan asked.

"I'm pretty sure of it," Bonaci replied, his brow more than usually furrowed. "And metal-jacketed, too. This is serious ammunition."

Donovan said, "I'm no firearms expert, but what's with that metal? That doesn't look like any metal jacketing I've seen before."

"You're right. I haven't seen it before, either. And for having gone through the world's best bulletproof glass and an inch or so of plaster these slugs are damned pristine."

"I'll have some tests run on them," Bonaci said. "I'll find out what that metal is. And if they match the one in Melmer—"

"They will."

"Then there's a very big weapon in the hands of a madman," Bonaci said.

"And on Fifth Avenue at the height of the holiday shopping season," Moskowitz added.

Donovan said, "Somebody call up this Kammacher outfit

and see if they have a gun that fits this ammo. Then see if they know how it may have gotten into our country.''

"Boss, it's Friday evening in Germany," Mosko replied.

"Somehow I doubt these German manufacturers of assassination weapons are at the synagogue worshiping," Donovan snapped. "Get them away from the dinner table or wherever they are and ask them what the hell's going on."

"You got it," Mosko said, and left the van.

"Metal-jacketed and some weird kind of metal," Bonaci mused, in respect or awe, holding the evidence bags up and letting the light glint off the bullets.

Donovan got back onto the pavement, checked his watch, and scowled. "It's getting late," he said.

"You wouldn't be giving out those cigars today, would you?" Bonaci asked.

"Not yet. Tell me, Howard, do you think a silver rattle from Sarkana is too ostentatious for my baby boy?"

"Silver? Nah. My grandma got me a silver rattle, engraved with my initials and date of birth. My mom still has it."

"Did you ever use it?"

"It has dents," Bonaci replied with a shrug.

"I have to finish my shopping," Donovan said, and went back into the store.

"THE LINE MUST HAVE been long," Marcy said when Donovan walked into her room. To pose this question she peeked around her belly, which billowed up the white hospital gown as if someone had inflated a basketball beneath a linen tablecloth. To one side was an IV pole. Its several bags were attached to intravenous lines that fed into her arm. Behind it a large electronic monitor sat on a shelf. It beeped at the rate of about 160 beats per minute, the baby's pulse.

He kissed her lips. Then he kissed her belly, saying, "Hi, Danny.... It's Daddy." He touched his fingertips to her belly, awaiting a movement. None was forthcoming. "It would be my luck to get a baby who has nothing to say," Donovan remarked, then sat in a chair and handed Marcy the package from Sarkana.

"I never made it into F.A.O. Schwarz," he replied. "Someone was shot in Sarkana, so I bought the rattle there."

"I thought you're on leave."

"I'm on partial leave. Don't worry. I can keep an eye on things from your side."

She grumbled but said, "Who was shot?"

"A rich German tourist, and I only got involved because it happened a block away. Open the package."

She worked at undoing the wrapping, which included a silver ribbon and a black-on-black gift box. "This is very chichi wrapping to put on a baby gift," she said.

"I work with the tools at hand," he replied.

"Tell me what happened."

"A guy named Erik Melmer was buying jewels for his fiancée when someone pumped a slug into him right through the window of Sarkana."

"Right through the window? Cool."

"Using a high-powered handgun."

"Did you catch the shooter?"

"Nope. All we know is that he was dressed as a Santa's Angels beggar."

"Collecting coins for Christmas, he pulls out a high-powered pistol and shoots a tourist? Talk about holiday spirit. So this was a random act of violence?"

"Maybe yes, maybe no. Anyway, Melmer's fiancée is in this hospital building someplace."

"She's down the hall."

Donovan looked toward the door, then back at his wife. "Excuse me, but isn't this the perinatal intensive care unit?" he asked.

"It is. She's pregnant and they were afraid she might lose the baby."

"She didn't look pregnant fainted on the floor of Sarkana."

"I heard she was at twenty weeks. Not everyone shows as much as I do."

"Credit your exquisite bone structure," Donovan said, kissing her again.

"Thank you," she replied, finally getting the package open. She held up the silver rattle—which was shaped like a tiny barbell—and shook it. The rattle made little tinkling sounds. "I love it," she said.

He was at the door, peering down the hall. When he came back, he asked, "Would her room be where the two suits are standing guard by the door?"

"It would."

"They look like Secret Service agents."

"The nurse tells me they're private cops. What do you want from me? I'm stuck here in this bed. Stop working and sit down by your wife."

He did as he was told.

She said, "I started to get contractions right after you left. Dr. Campagna put me on tributylene and magnesium sulfate."

Donovan peered at the lower of the two electronic lines bumping their way across her monitor. It hovered around 20. "The monitor looks good now," he said.

"It was up to thirty-five a few hours ago."

He held her hand and leaned back in the chair. "Will any of this hurt the baby?"

"No," she replied assuredly.

"That's good," he said, and closed his eyes for a moment.

He lapsed into thoughts of playing catch with his son in Riverside Park, the way his dad had done with him so many years before. But Donovan was roused from this thought by

the unusual amount of traffic in the hall. There were male
voices speaking in German, plus the occasional sound of a
nurse arguing. Donovan stood.

"Can't you relax?" Marcy asked.

"Can you relax with all this stuff going on? I'll be right
back."

"You're going to be a father soon," she snapped. "No
more working. And especially no getting shot at."

"That's not likely to happen in the hospital."

"This is New York."

He went down the hall, showing his badge to a tall and
somber-looking man in a cheapish grey suit that fit him a
bit too tightly. The fellow had given Donovan the eye before
he was within five paces, which signaled extreme jitteriness.

"Captain Donovan, NYPD," he said.

"This is a private room," the man replied with a trace
of a German accent.

"Is this Anna Hebbel's room?" Donovan asked.

The man nodded. He was joined, meantime, by another
security guard, who came out of the room. This one was
shorter and better-tailored but hardly friendlier-looking. Between the two of them Donovan caught a glimpse of the
woman he had seen in Sarkana, but lying in a hospital gown,
eyes open, motionless, being attended to by two doctors, a
nurse, and several other civilians.

"Yes," the first guard said.

"I'm investigating her fiancé's death. I would like to extend my condolences."

"If you would wait a moment."

The two men withdrew and conferred and then got several
others involved in the discussions. After a minute or two,
one of the doctors joined Donovan in the hall. He was a
short man, well dressed. A custom-made sky blue Oxford
shirt shone beneath the usual white coat. A mother-of-pearl
fountain pen decorated the breast pocket.

"I am Dr. Shreffler, Mr. Melmer's physician when he is in New York. May I help you?"

"Captain Donovan, New York Police. I just wanted to extend my condolences to the princess and see how she is."

"She is under sedation—"

"While pregnant?" Donovan asked pointedly.

The doctor sighed, then said, "You are quite right, Captain. No sedation is appropriate. I merely don't want her to get upset—more so than she is, of course—which being interviewed by a police detective would surely do. Is there anything I can ask her for you?"

"No, not right now anyway," Donovan replied, tossing in a shrug. "I just wanted to say how sorry I am. We try to be responsive to the victims of crimes." He handed the doctor a card, then added, "Give her this and ask her to call me in a few days. We'll need to ask her a few questions before she leaves New York. Maybe she saw something that will help us catch the killer."

"I'll do that," Shreffler replied.

"Where were they staying?"

"They have an apartment in Trump Plaza."

"I hope the baby is OK," Donovan said.

"I'm sure he'll be fine," Shreffler replied.

"Tell me, Doctor, can you think of anyone who would have a reason to kill Mr. Melmer?"

"No. He was a lovely man with no enemies that I know of. But I will ask Princess Anna. Now, if you will excuse me..."

Donovan thanked the man and went back to Marcy's room, the two security guards retaking their places by the door and watching him every step of the way.

"Well?" Marcy asked.

"Her baby will be fine," Donovan replied, sitting back down. "Her late fiancé has no known enemies."

"That's very nice, William. Now take off your jacket and

put away your attitude. You're on vacation to attend to your
wife and your unborn child.''

Donovan grumbled but complied. Both of them knew he
had a hard time relaxing and was never entirely off duty—
at least not anymore. At one point not quite a decade earlier,
he gave up drinking, his longtime remedy for the conflicting
feelings of guilt and obligation that kept him up nights. That
problem began with the murder of his father—also a prominent policeman—a crime that remained unsolved.

The older Donovan might still have been alive were his
son, a young patrolman in 1968, not off enjoying the company of his antiwar friends on the Columbia campus one
crucial night. Of course, no one had assigned him to be with
his father that night. The two Donovans weren't even attached to the same precinct. And, if the truth be known,
they didn't get along that well at that point, having parted
company on the subject of Vietnam. But in Donovan's heart
a portion of responsibility for his father's death rested with
him. One day he would solve the crime that had hung over
his heart for nearly three decades. He often sat up nights
pondering decades-old evidence and thinking.

But that only came after he stopped spending countless
hours and many hundreds of dollars each month on scotch.
At midlife, and with the support of Marcy and his friends,
Donovan gave up his bar-brawling days and soon discovered a new ability to get things done. Among them: being
promoted to captain, getting a citywide command, and reac-
quainting himself with books and learning. Gone were the
friends of shabby backgrounds and questionable incomes as
well as the passel of saloons that ran very nearly the entire
length of Broadway.

Donovan began prowling bookshops and patronizing
sidewalk book vendors. He became a computer maven.
Monitors hummed in both his downtown and home offices;
his briefcase notebook computer could download information from his other PCs through a cellular modem. A cell

phone replaced the roll of quarters he used to carry around for use in pay phones or, occasionally in the wee hours of those scotch-filled nights, as impromptu brass knuckles. With his fingers wrapped around it, the ten-dollar stack of coins helped settle many arguments with the pastiche of shady characters—both in and out of uniform—with whom he spent his off-duty hours.

That was Donovan's past. Now, in his early fifties, he had attained something resembling peace. He had financial security and professional respectability—a citywide command as New York City's chief of special investigations, which let him pick the most interesting cases. And in his personal life Donovan had love and family at last; Marcy and he were married after nearly a decade and a half of breaking up and getting back together. And they were about to welcome the baby they had been talking about nearly that long: Daniel Magid Donovan, his son.

"I don't want you even thinking about working until after the baby's born," Marcy said, taking his hand and moving it to her belly.

As he felt the baby move beneath his fingers, Donovan shut his eyes, smiled peacefully, and felt, no doubt about it, very good indeed.

THREE

"START A FAMILY," THE MAYOR SAID

THE WEEKEND slid by. As had become the norm, Marcy's life consisted of watching TV, listening to the monitor beep, and taking occasional walks in the hall to let the creases unfold from her back. On those forays, she and Donovan walked arm in arm, taking turns pushing the IV pole from which dangled her medications. On each trip they passed Princess Anna's room, but after Donovan's first encounter with her doctor the door was always shut and guarded. Late on Sunday afternoon she disappeared along with her entourage. Donovan found her room open and snooped around it for a while, emptying out the personal trash basket kept bedside but finding little of interest: a menu from a Mexican restaurant on East Ninety-sixth Street, a collection of balled-up facial tissues, and several plastic toothpicks. Finally Donovan stole the water glass from her table and slipped it into a plastic bag. Donovan's days were otherwise filled with reading the papers, getting coffee from the cafeteria, and trudging to the Korean place on Lexington Avenue in search of palatable food.

It was on a sunny and warmer morning early in December that Moskowitz showed his face in Marcy's room, bearing his notebook computer and a box of Perugina chocolates.

"Hiya, Sergeant Barnes," he said, amused by the sight of a police sergeant pregnant and propped up in bed.

"Retired sergeant," she replied.

"Whatever." He balanced the box of chocolates on her belly and gave her a kiss on the cheek.

"Thank you for the chocolates. And my last name is Donovan, not Barnes."

"How come a radfem like you didn't keep your last name after you got married?" Mosko asked.

"For one thing, I'm not a radical feminist," she replied, a bit testily. "For another, it took fifteen years to get him to marry me...." She patted the knee of Donovan, who had swiped a semireclining chair from the intensive care waiting room and was leaning back, doing the *Times* crossword puzzle. "Given that, you don't think I'm going to use his name?"

"Morning, Boss," Mosko said, helping himself to a straight-backed chair and setting up his computer atop her food table.

"Hi, Brian." Donovan looked over the top of his newspaper and smiled at his assistant before returning his attention to the puzzle.

"Do you want to hear the daily report now?" Mosko asked.

"Daily report?" Marcy asked.

"Well... I thought that's how he was working his partial leave. He'd get a daily report but otherwise be free to do what he wants."

Donovan put down his paper and tossed his pencil onto the food table. It skittered over the top of the Perugina box and landed in her applesauce. Marcy gave him a dirty look.

"Can I have a chocolate?" he asked.

"No. They're for Dr. Campagna."

"I thought I was buying these for you," Mosko said.

"Are you nuts? Pregnant women can't have chocolate. There's caffeine in it."

He looked at the box, then at the array of intravenous tubes feeding into her long and slender arm. "Are you having fun with this?" he asked.

"I've never been happier," she replied. "Honey...give him the money for the Perugina."

"How much?" Donovan asked.

"Twenty."

He handed over a bill, then grumbled, "This pregnancy is costing me a fortune."

"Insurance covers most of it," Marcy said.

"But not cigars, rattles, and chocolates."

"Think how happy all this is making her...honey," Mosko said.

"Let's hear the report," Donovan snapped.

Moskowitz switched on his laptop, then flipped through assorted screens until he found the one he wanted. "First, the bullets. They were nine-millimeter, all right. And metal-jacketed. Your basic but, in this case, *very rare* assassination round." Mosko gaped at the screen, clearly reading something for the eighth or ninth time and trying to believe it before passing the info along to his boss.

Donovan read his thoughts and said, "Let's hear it."

Mosko cleared his throat and exclaimed, "Would you believe *depleted uranium!*"

Donovan pondered for a moment, then turned to his wife and said, "I really need a chocolate."

"No," she replied tersely.

Mosko said, "That's how the report came back from the lab. The metal jackets on those bullets were made of depleted uranium."

"Isn't that radioactive?" Marcy asked.

"About as much as a glow-in-the-dark watch dial," Mosko said.

"Depleted uranium is used in armor-piercing antitank ammunition," Donovan added. "I never heard of it being used in handgun bullets. For one thing, you would think that the physics of shooting through armor is different than the physics of shooting through glass."

"Wouldn't you consider bulletproof glass to be armored?" Marcy asked, using her sensible tone of voice.

"I suppose," Mosko said. "Anyway, the slugs in the wall matched the one in Melmer."

"I'm surprised that slug stayed in the man."

"Bonaci says an armor-piercing round would lose a lot of momentum coming through tissue."

"And what about the gun?"

"According to Bonaci's source, there's only one handgun in the entire world that fires a steel-jacketed nine-millimeter round that's made of depleted uranium. And that's the Kammacher Stedman."

Donovan offered a quizzical look.

Reading from the screen, Mosko said, "It was developed in the mid-nineteen-eighties for the Stasi."

It was Marcy's turn to look perplexed.

"East German secret police," Donovan clarified. "After the fall of communism and the demolition of the Berlin Wall, the Stasi was disbanded. A lot of them are still being hunted down for cold war atrocities. But what about the gun?"

"Kammacher went private—it was a state-owned company under communism—and tried to sell the Stedman, among other weapons, to the combatants in the Middle East: the Syrians, Palestinians, Iranians, Afghans, and Lebanese among them."

"How did they do?"

"They only made a few—three of them, to be exact, prototypes really—and it turns out there wasn't much of a market. For one thing, the slugs cost a hundred bucks each."

"And close-in assassination ain't the terrorist's thing," Donovan said.

"You're right," Mosko agreed. "Those schmucks like to strap dynamite to their bodies and blow themselves up along with school buses. And Israel, knock wood…" He went to rap his knuckles on her food table but saw it was Formica. Then he looked around for *any* wood that was within reach but found none. So he shrugged, knocking his knuckles against an imaginary piece of wood floating in the air, and returned his attention to the monitor. "…did a great job of keeping the few that were sold outside their borders. So—"

"Kammacher was forced to sell them to a fairly limited black market," Donovan said.

"You got it. They got rid of all three of the prototypes. The Russian mob bought one. We know because a French businessman was shot through the window of his armored limo in Kiev and the perp was caught with the gun. And one weapon supposedly turned up in Kabul as well."

"Afghanistan," Donovan said. "Interesting."

"Why?" Mosko asked.

"How many bulletproof limos do you imagine there are in Kabul?"

"I would think the president, the prime minister, the chief mullah, or whatever they have over there, has one. At any rate, there's another Stedman out there, but no one knows where it is. There's a rumor floating around the Internet that the third prototype was bought fairly recently by an American collector, but no word as to if it got into the country or *what* happened to it. Anyway, Kammacher decided not to put the weapon into full production in 1993 after the State Department slammed the door to America shut."

"Is there any chance the third Stedman got into the country anyway?" Marcy asked.

"Apparently, it did," Donovan said.

"At the moment, I only have hearsay. I didn't have too hard a time getting someone from Kammacher on the phone over the weekend. But the State Department is going to be harder," Mosko commented.

"Why would it be harder to get the U.S. State Department on the phone than a German arms manufacturer?" Marcy asked.

"It's a bigger bureaucracy," Donovan said.

Mosko added, a bit cautiously, "Maybe you can give it a shot."

The reason for his caution was instantly apparent. "He's on leave," Marcy said. "It's one thing for him to take reports from you once a day." She paused, dramatically, then added, talking to her husband, "Once a day. Did that transmission come through?"

"What did you say?" Donovan replied, toying with her. "I didn't hear you."

A bit steamed, she replied, "Earth to Donovan. Did you get that?"

"I got it; I got it," he said. "Calm down or you'll give yourself a contraction."

"It doesn't work that way."

"With you everything is tied into emotions," he said, looking at her monitor to see if the indicators changed. They didn't this time.

"What's all this stuff?" Mosko asked, pointing at her electronics.

"It's a fetal monitor," she replied.

"You look like RoboMom."

"Thank you very much. I find you very attractive, too. Anyway, this man is my husband and about to become a father. I don't want him working. Giving you advice once a day is enough."

"The mayor did say to start a family," Donovan allowed.

What he meant by that remark was that his previous big case, a series of murders in a landmark Broadway theater, got so many headlines the mayor of the city of New York, up for reelection and in need of the ink, begged him to lay low.

"Start a family," the mayor had said. "Settle down," Hizzoner had added as he married the two of them, providing two reclining chairs and a bag of popcorn as an inducement to take things easy. A year later, newly reelected and in an expansive mood, the mayor had the police commissioner grant the city's most famous detective a month's partial leave so he could be by his wife's bedside as she prepared to give birth.

"I just thought that maybe he could use his contacts to get the State Department to open up," Mosko said.

One of Donovan's childhood friends was a West Side Democratic politician who currently served as political adviser to the president. A simple phone call to him could open many doors.

"I'll see what I can do," Donovan said cautiously.

Marcy gave him another dirty look.

"Without getting too involved in this Melmer murder," he added.

He and Marcy exchanged glances, and after a second both smiled. They touched hands.

"I love you," she said.

Moskowitz rolled his eyes. "OK, so you call Washington. Ask them if it's true what Kammacher says, that the State Department went apeshit after Kammacher wanted to sell Stedmans here and if they know what happened to the third one."

"When did this happen?"

"They said '93. That's all I know."

"I'll check it out," Donovan replied.

"On to the matter of witnesses. Nobody we were able to interview could give us a sketch of the guy in the Santa's Angels getup. He pulled the gun; they looked at the gun."

"It's always that way," Marcy said. "Witnesses always focus on the weapon."

"Up to the point he pulled the gun, he was a guy in a Santa's Angels cape and hat. A white guy, maybe in his twenties, and not too tall. That's it. Nobody got enough of a look at him to give us a sketch."

"Did anyone see where he went?" Donovan asked.

"Downtown. He disappeared into the crowd."

"Who would notice him?" Marcy said.

"What about the other beggars—the three in the crowd outside Sarkana after the shooting?" Donovan asked.

"We talked to them plenty. They saw people running away from the site, including one of their own. But they couldn't ID him. Those guys don't all know each other anyway. Most of them are day laborers hired every November."

"How many do they hire?"

Mosko said, "I called the Santa's Angels this morning. They had—are you ready for this?—a total of one hundred people collecting money in the twenty-five blocks of Fifth Avenue between Thirty-fourth and Fifty-ninth Streets."

"That's all?"

"I'm getting a list. The breakdown is seventy-five red-coated beggars with tripods and twenty-five Santas. Three beggars and one Santa per block."

"And the Republicans say the economy is bad. Can we get a list of these people?"

"I'm working on it."

"I don't suppose that Santa's Angels checks criminal records before hiring beggars and Santas," Donovan said.

"I got no idea."

"It is possible to have an ex-con Santa? A rehabilitated drug dealer, for example, out there ho-hoing and waving a bell in the name of God?"

Moskowitz cleared his throat nervously. Donovan was no fan of organized religion, and a lecture on the subject was far from out of the question. The more careful among his men found themselves avoiding topics likely to precipitate tirades.

"What about white-collar criminal Santas, guys who just spent time in the pen for insider trading?"

"I think they hit the college lecture circuit, Boss," Mosko said.

"What about Mafia informant Santas? Maybe the Santa's Angels calls up the Federal Witness Protection Program each Christmas and say, 'Send me over a hundred.'"

"It's possible."

"What about hit-man Santas?" Donovan asked finally.

"Or Santa's Angels bill-collection guys," Marcy said.

"It's not a bad cover to use in stalking and killing someone. What did your inquiries about Melmer get you?"

Relieved to be off the subject of religion, at least for the time being, Moskowitz peered at his screen and said, "Zilch."

"Whaddya mean, 'zilch'?"

"I mean that no one at Melmer International would talk to me. But it was the weekend."

Peeved, Donovan muttered, "I got to make a few calls, honey."

"So call. We have a phone. You know, one thing strikes me here. If you're dressing up as a Santa's Angels Christmas beggar meaning to shoot someone in particular, you're going to have to know his exact schedule."

"Like, 'Melmer will be in Sarkana with his fiancée between three and four p.m. on Friday, November twenty-ninth'," Mosko said.

Donovan nodded. "And you'd have to plant yourself outside Sarkana's window without arousing the ire, or even the notice, of Santa's Angels quality control."

"Say again?" Mosko asked.

"I mean they must have supervisors who walk up and down Fifth Avenue making sure that such-and-such block, say the one where Sarkana is, doesn't have too many collection guys. I can hear this conversation: 'Sorry, Mac, but there are already three beggars and one Santa on this block. You're gonna have to haul your ass down to Forty-seventh, where one of our ex-cons just jumped parole and took off for Mexico, leaving a spot vacant."

Mosko seemed vaguely amused. "I'll check it out."

"Were there any prints on that tripod and bucket?"

"Only about a thousand. It will be hard to tell if any

belong to the perp. Bonaci blew up that piece of videotape and says it looks like the guy was wearing gloves.''

Donovan picked up the Perugina box and turned it over, looking to see if there was a seal on it. If there wasn't, he could get inside later on, when Marcy went to the bathroom. But there was a seal, and she grabbed the box back and put it on the end table on the opposite side of her bed.

"This killer is no madman," he said.

"And why not?"

"Your basic lunatic doesn't go to such trouble to shoot someone. Your average loony buys a cheap gun or uses whatever he has on hand and shoots the first guy who comes along who pisses him off. Some poor slob who reminds him of his father, his mother, his high-school guidance counselor, or whoever he thinks fucked up his life.''

"He doesn't shoot through a store window," Mosko said.

"After donning a disguise and carefully securing one of the only handguns capable of shooting through bulletproof glass," Donovan added. "I have a lot of experience with exotic weapons, and in each case the man or woman using one is making a statement. This killer is telling us something.''

"Melmer was a deliberate target," Mosko said.

"That very well could be. Of course, another possible statement is 'no one is safe, not even behind bulletproof glass.' But that seems a little esoteric and even a bit off the point, considering we don't know much about Melmer yet.''

"Let's try harder to find more about him."

"Check for prints on this," Donovan said, handing Moskowitz the purloined water glass.

"Where'd you get that?"

"His fiancée's room. She was down the hall."

"In the perinatal ICU?"

"The lady is with child," Donovan said. "Twenty weeks. You might also find out where Melmer and his lady were twenty weeks ago.''

"Eighteen weeks," Marcy corrected.

"Right; pregnancy is measured from the first day of the last menstrual period," Donovan said.

"Not from the day you eggulate," Marcy added.

Moskowitz elevated a bushy black eyebrow. "Say again?"

"Not from the day you eggulate," she said.

"Ovulate," Donovan translated.

"Pop an egg," Marcy said.

"I learn so many new words working for you," Mosko commented, making a note. "Do you expect her prints will turn up in the Interpol computer?"

"You never know."

"How do you know she used this glass?"

"Lipstick," Donovan said, pointing out the red smudge below the rim. "She was the only woman in the room today, not counting nurses, who aren't allowed to wear lipstick."

"They let you wear makeup in ICUs?" Mosko asked.

"They do on the day you're being discharged," Marcy said.

"Actually, you can get away with quite a lot around here," Donovan added, retrieving his newspaper and using it to cover an embarrassed but pleased-with-himself grin.

"Such as sneaking into rooms and disappearing with evidence," Marcy said quickly.

"Speaking of disappearing, that's what happened to your gyro dealer," Mosko interjected.

"Gyro dealer?" Marcy asked.

"I asked him to check out an Afghan in a Sikh turban selling gyros outside F.A.O. Schwarz," Donovan said in a voice that indicated he found nothing unusual about that combination.

"I see," she replied. "You weren't planning on eating one of those gyros, were you?"

"Perish the thought."

"You know that lamb is very fatty, and at your age—"

"I'm pretty sure it was goat," Donovan said.

"Goat? You were going to eat goat?"

Mosko said, "In any event, the man was gone by the time we got there."

"Which was?"

"Four o'clock."

"Let me get this straight. Four o'clock on the day after Thanksgiving, the busiest shopping day of the year, and this man up and bolts from his primo spot outside F.A.O. Schwarz? Other vendors could kill for that location. Perhaps literally."

"You said he had a gun. What kind?"

"Black automatic. That's all I know."

"What? Did he *show* it to you?"

"He went for it when he heard the shots," Donovan said. "I was talking to him as a way of passing the time while waiting in line to get into Schwarz—"

"Goat meat," Marcy muttered, shaking her head.

"I grabbed his hand, identified myself, then told him to lose the gun by the time I got back if it wasn't licensed."

"I guess it wasn't," Mosko said.

"So the upshot is the man had an illegal gun and was scared enough of something to feel he had to use it," Donovan commented.

"Scared of what?"

"Of something. Of hearing gunshots. Maybe he flashed back to his days as a member of the mujahideen fighting the Russians outside Kabul. Who knows? Anyway, I told him to get rid of the gun, not take a powder entirely. He could have stuffed it in a garbage can. He could have made that mime outside the store eat it."

"Only you could get the mujahideen and a mime in the same thought," Marcy said.

"Is this guy connected with Melmer, do you think?" Mosko asked.

Donovan shrugged. "He's an Afghan with a gun who

took off after hearing the shots. I'm pretty sure he lives in Queens, by the way.''

"Why do you say that?" Mosko asked.

"He had an address scribbled on a bumper sticker. The address was written by a left-handed man, and he was left-handed. It was Fifteen sixty-two thirty-two seventy-eight Queens Boulevard. Check that out. He also knows the gyro place on Second Avenue where all the Muslim cabbies go."

"Oh, that sure is on *my* route home," Moskowitz replied.

"If it helps, he has a sense of humor," Donovan added. "The man was another New York City rip-off artist, but an entertaining one. He wears a Sikh turban because it keeps his head warm."

"I doubt he's connected with Melmer," Mosko said.

"Me, too."

"But I'll have someone look into him."

Donovan got his pencil out of Marcy's applesauce and wiped it off using one of the napkins that came with her breakfast. He scrutinized the crossword puzzle while Moskowitz shut off the computer and put it in the leather shoulder bag he used to carry all his stuff.

"You know, you ought to bring your laptop here from home in case you want to do things," he said.

"The man is on leave," Marcy replied. "Talking to you once a day is enough of a burden."

"You're cute," Mosko said. Then he leaned forward and touched her belly. "So is this the kid?"

"That's my baby," she said.

"Our baby," Donovan added, without looking away from his paper.

"Danny Boy," Mosko said.

"Daniel," she replied. "He is not named after an Irish song. It's a Hebrew name: Daniel Magid."

"*Magid* means 'storyteller' in Hebrew," Moskowitz said. She knew.

"You realize, of course, that the initials DMD will make people think he's an oral surgeon," Mosko said.

"You're a hideous man to even think that."

"With my luck he'll become a reporter for the *Post*," Donovan said. The captain's battles with tabloid and television reporters were legendary.

"Daniel is going to be a novelist," Marcy remarked.

"I'll be supporting him forever," Donovan moaned.

"In any case, he's our angel," Marcy said. And with that she leaned down and kissed her belly. "I love you, Daniel," she added.

"I gotta get out of here," Moskowitz said.

IT WAS Thursday, December 5. Marcy had been in the hospital for a full week, and in that time Donovan more or less had moved into the private room with her. He put back the semirecliner he had stolen from the intensive care lounge, accepted the gratitude of the nurses for so doing, then went out in the dead of night and stole a full recliner from one of the suites where the residents slept. He packed one of his old L.L. Bean canvas carrying bags with shaving and other stuff as well as changes of clothes. And he brought in a portable CD player and FM radio along with several handfuls of jazz and classical CDs. And reading material, including several back issues of the *Times Book Review* and *New York Review of Books*. (Donovan's shortcut to learning a wide variety of subjects was to read reviews of books about them; he told Marcy his technique was "the *Classics Comics* approach to knowledge.")

The sun was just setting when Moskowitz wrapped up his daily briefing by reaching into his leather shoulder bag and pulling out a brass menorah and a small wrapped package.

"Happy Hanukkah," he said, setting up the menorah on the food table that hovered over Marcy's belly and planting the package atop her outstretched hand.

"Happy Hanukkah," she replied. "What's in the package?"

"It's for Danny Boy," he replied. "For his first Hanukkah."

"His name is *Daniel*," she said firmly. "What's in the box?"

"Open it," he replied. Waving a pack of matches, he said, "Do you want me to light them?"

"No. That's William's job."

"He's not a Jew," Moskowitz said. "He's an ex-Catholic atheist."

"I'm surrounded is what I am," Donovan replied, looking up from an essay on Benjamin Franklin and the American dream. "I'm outnumbered two to one."

"Three to one," Marcy said, patting her belly.

Donovan grumbled and watched as his wife tore open the package and pulled out a large plastic rattle that glowed in primary colors.

"Mickey Mouse," she said. "How quaint."

"I figure the kid will want a rattle he can *use*. Not one to put on the mantel and show to guests."

"Thank you, Brian," Marcy said, beckoning him to bend over so she could plant a kiss on his cheek.

Donovan put away his reading, stood, and stretched. "Today is the first day of Hanukkah, right?"

"You know that," Marcy replied.

"It's also the annual ceremony for the lighting of the Rockefeller Center Christmas tree."

"So?"

"Kind of a coincidence, wouldn't you say?"

Moskowitz offered a quizzical look. "What coincidence?"

"Scheduling the Christmas tree lighting for the first night of Hanukkah," Donovan said. "Both the Christians and the Jews are lighting up on the same night, trees on the one hand and candles on the other. It sounds suspicious to me. We better investigate.''

''I got to be honest, Boss; I don't know what the hell you're talking about. In my book, this don't rank very high on the galactic scale of paranoia.''

Marcy smiled and said, ''What he means is he's bored and wants to get out of this room. Take him to the Christmas tree lighting and buy him a cupcake or whatever his people sell to mark the occasion.''

Donovan plucked his suede jacket off the back of the door and slipped it on. ''Can I get you anything?'' he asked her.

''I don't think there's any such thing as Christmas cupcakes,'' Moskowitz said.

''What you can do for me,'' Marcy said, ''what you can do for your son, is convert.''

''From what to what? From atheism to Judaism? It doesn't work that way. First you're a Jew; then you become an atheist. That's how it works. I can cite you hundreds of examples, and that's just among the guys I grew up with on the West Side. Besides, your father is still a Christian after how many years of being married to your mother? Forty-three? So I'll still be an atheist and glad for it when I'm ninety-five.''

Marcy said to Moskowitz, ''He thinks organized religion is responsible for all the woes of the world since year one.''

''I don't want to get him started,'' Mosko replied, hoisting his bag onto his shoulder and heading out the door. ''I can't take another go-round with the religion lecture.''

''It was you who brought the menorah,'' Donovan said.

''Next time it will be a Christmas cupcake,'' Mosko replied.

A short time later, they walked casually down Fifth Avenue, looking with partial interest at the Santa's Angels and the tourists dropping coins into their buckets.

The Norway spruce stood seventy feet tall, an Everest of a tree, broad at the base and tapering symmetrically to a thin tip crowned by a gigantic white star. Twenty-six thousand lights and ornaments hung silently in the dark, awaiting the moment the mayor would flip the switch to make them glow as bright as the office windows, lit far into the night for the Christmas season, that towered above and enveloped them.

The tree was set in a mammoth pot placed up against the railing that surrounded the Rockefeller Center skating rink. Branches that until the week before had graced a suburban estate sheltered Paul Manship's eighteen-foot-high, eight-ton, gold-leaf-coated statue of Prometheus bringing fire to Earth. On the tree's other side they also sheltered a space, for the dignitaries, that was cordoned off between the spruce and 30 Rockefeller Plaza. Four red velvet ropes enclosed a patch of sidewalk the size of a backyard deck. The mayor stood in it, accompanied by the Roman Catholic cardinal (his childhood pal), and assorted other luminaries, most of them considerably less luminous than the megawattage about to be unleashed in the branches of the sturdy, old, but inexorably dying, tree.

Dozens of blue-clad police officers milled about, separating the big shots from the dozen or so TV crews lined up to immortalize the tree-lighting ceremony. Outside the inner ring of dignitaries, cops, and journalists was the crowd, estimated at ten thousand, that had shown up, Christmas presents and videocameras in hand, to watch the mayor flip the switch that officially started the holiday shopping season.

Donovan and Moskowitz eased their way through the crowd. The smell of Christmas was in the air, as were the sights and sounds. Donovan thought of his childhood and turkey dinners with chestnut stuffing and mashed potatoes smothered with gravy and butter, served alongside a tree surrounded by wrapped packages. He thought of his wife and son and felt good, very good, humming along with "God Rest Ye Merry Gentlemen" and slipping through the crowd in as uncoplike a manner as possible. Moskowitz trailed behind, glancing warily at the gigantic tree and listening with ill-concealed amusement to his boss, the non-believer with the tough-guy past, humming a Christmas carol.

"So what's with Christmas trees anyway?" Mosko asked, wondering if it wasn't time to break the spell.

"It's a nice tradition if you're not allergic to them and don't have cats," Donovan replied.

"I mean what's a tree got to do with Jesus or the Holy Land? I been to Israel a couple of times and I didn't see a single pine tree."

"This is a Norway spruce," Donovan replied.

"I seen even fewer of them," Mosko insisted.

"You want to know what the tree thing is about?"

"Yeah. I figured you would know. Does it have something to do with the tree the Romans cut down to crucify him on?"

"I don't think so," Donovan said dully. "To the best of my knowledge, the Christmas tree is a pagan tradition from northern Europe. They used to bring a tree indoors every year before the snows closed in. It was a ritual to ward off evil and ensure that the trees outside would survive the winter."

"That still doesn't tell me what a Christmas tree has to do with Jesus," Mosko said.

"*Nothing*. What's a gefilte fish got to do with Abraham and Sarah?"

Mosko replied, "The day there's a seventy-foot gefilte fish standing on Fifth Avenue I'll tell you."

"I got a better idea," Donovan said. "Let's ask the cardinal to resolve this." With that, he led his friend off the Fifth Avenue sidewalk and onto Channel Gardens, the slender mews, decorated at that time of year with man-size white wire angels and lined by expensive shops, that led into the heart of Rockefeller Center. At the center's core, the Christmas tree towered over the scores of national flags that surrounded the skating rink with a riot of patriotic colors.

The two detectives eased their way through the masses of onlookers and the knots of uniformed police officers that lingered among them. Donovan and Moskowitz skirted the rink, looking over the railing at the several dozen skaters who displayed their varying skills before a very large crowd in a wholly spectacular setting. Over by the VIP area, the Boys Choir of Harlem was wrapping up "God Rest Ye Merry Gentlemen."

Casting his eyes about, looking over the crowd in search of important faces to wave to, the mayor spotted his favorite detective and waved Donovan over. Then Hizzoner tapped the cardinal on his festive red sleeve to alert him. Both exchanged knowing glances and faint smiles.

Donovan and his family went back many years with both men. While still a parish priest back in the dim recesses of twentieth-century history, the cardinal had heard confession for Donovan's father. Both mayor and cardinal knew Marcy's father when he was district attorney, of course. And Donovan himself hadn't exactly been invisible. He certainly wasn't invisible to another dignitary at the ceremony, Deputy Chief Inspector Paul Pilcrow, Donovan's longtime nemesis.

Pilcrow was Donovan's boss. The captain reported to Pilcrow, but reluctantly so, reflecting a dislike so mutual it came back as if on a tether. In reality, Donovan reported to the commissioner and the mayor, with Pilcrow standing between and finding fault wherever he could. The deputy chief was a man who worshiped at the altar of order. It grated on him that his most brilliant detective was among the world's least orderly persons. But Donovan was too important to fire, at least short of being caught with a smoking gun in his hand. Pilcrow was always looking for one and had proved himself not beneath suggesting that Donovan had fallen off the wagon (his continued sobriety being a condition of the captain's badge). Pilcrow also hated Marcy but, while pigheaded, was not so stupid as to take on a pregnant former policewoman who happened to be the daughter of a media bigwig and a state supreme court justice.

Famous for sucking up to the mayor whenever possible, Pilcrow stood with the dignitaries, his chest puffed out, trying to make small talk, something he was far from good at. Such behavior was part of Pilcrow's long-running campaign to be appointed the city's second black police commissioner.

He saw the captain and Moskowitz approaching and his face tightened. Jumping between Donovan and the mayor, Pilcrow asked, "What are you doing here, Captain? I thought you were on leave for a month."

"Everyone's been pushing religion on me lately," Donovan replied. "I thought this evening's ritual would be a good place to start."

Pilcrow made a noise that sounded a little like a novice driver grinding gears on an old Honda.

"How is your wife?" Pilcrow asked, at last.

"She's doing well, thanks."

"Any day now?"

"Any week now. How's your back healing?"

Pilcrow scrunched his shoulders to indicate discomfort. He had been wounded the year before while butting into one of Donovan's cases. The pain between Pilcrow's shoulder blades was a frequent reminder of the perils of standing too close to Donovan when he was working. This night when all anyone expected was the annual tree lighting, however, Donovan didn't seem to Pilcrow to be working. Even though Moskowitz and he slipped through the red velvet barricade and joined the dignitaries, the captain was looking not at them but up at the monumental tree, which stood massive and dark amid the glittering holiday lights of Rockefeller Center and Fifth Avenue.

He stared at the base of it, then looked it up and down, then finally ducked his head under the lower branches.

When he pulled his head back out, Donovan said to Moskowitz, "This is a good tree for climbing."

"You're a city boy. When did you ever climb a tree?"

"In the park. And at my aunt's house on the Island when my dad sent me out there summers, figuring that the fresh air and clean living would turn me into a Boy Scout or something. I'll tell you; I got to be pretty good at climbing trees."

"My back hurts on cold nights like this one," Pilcrow said, edging the sergeant out of the conversation.

"Generic ibuprofen and hot baths," Donovan replied, patting Pilcrow on the arm reassuringly before walking around him to respond to a beckoning gesture from the mayor.

Donovan hadn't seen the mayor personally in a year, not since the city's top official had married Donovan and Marcy in an impromptu ceremony held in Times Square at the crest of New Year's Eve. Their paths crossed infrequently during the normal course of events, but often in memorable circumstances. In the course of the last one, Hizzoner played justice of the peace at a ceremony that made the front page of the *Times*.

"Maybe the boss wants to check on my progress, how I'm doing as a husband," Donovan mumbled to himself as he left Moskowitz in Pilcrow's clutches and stepped over to where the mayor and the cardinal awaited their turns to speak. Lowering his voice so as not to seem disrespectful to the dignitary currently at the microphone, a fiftyish woman in an expensive fur who was thanking the Connecticut family that had donated the tree, the mayor shook Donovan's hand and said, "You're about to become a father, Bill. Congratulations."

"Thank you, Your Honor," Donovan said, beaming.

"Do you know if you're getting a boy or a girl?"

"I'm going to have a son."

"That's great."

"My blessing on mother and child," the cardinal said, raising his right hand in a saintly manner.

"Thank you."

"You remember Captain Donovan, don't you?" the mayor asked.

"Who could forget? Tell me, Captain, did you enter into a spiritual *paxis in terram* to match the secular one?"

"If you mean did I get religion? Nope. Sorry, still an atheist. Nothing personal, Your Eminence."

"Your father must be turning over in his grave," the cardinal said.

"Why? Because I quit the Church, married a girl who's half Jewish, or stopped drinking?" Donovan replied.

"Take your pick," the mayor said.

The cardinal smiled. "You will see the Lord differently when your son is born," he said.

"There are no atheists in the delivery room, is that it?" Donovan said. He elevated his eyes as if seeking God but saw only a big Christmas tree that sat in darkness waiting for the mayor to flip the switch.

"What brings you here?" the mayor continued. "There's no threat to His Eminence or me, is there?"

"I hope not, sir. Marcy's in Fifth Avenue Medical Center waiting for the baby to come, and I thought I'd take a walk."

"Give her my love," the mayor said, then turned away and to the podium. It was time for him to take over the annual tree-lighting chores. Soon Donovan heard the familiar baritone, so clipped of phrase yet elegant of adjective, intoning that year's version of the annual rite.

It said: "My fellow New Yorkers, we are gathered here this beautiful evening amidst the best tourist season this city has seen in twenty years. More millions of visitors are gracing these streets than ever before. We see them every joyous day, strolling up and down Fifth Avenue, prettily wrapped packages tucked under embracing arms...."

Donovan muttered, not quite to himself, "I hear the relentless hand of commerce ringing the cash register."

"Everything in this life is a reflection of God's love," the cardinal replied.

"You sound like Marcy's rabbi," Donovan replied in a loud stage whisper.

"We have the same tailor," the cardinal replied, touching pudgy, round fingertips to his skullcap.

The mayor's voice boomed on: "We see them every glistening evening, enjoying the dazzling lights of midtown. Last year we saw the beginning of the rebirth of Times Square, whose magical lights spell 'Happy New Year' to the world. This year we celebrate the different magic of Fifth Avenue, the world's most fabulous marketplace...."

The continued talk of money was making Donovan more and more uneasy. So when Mosko sidled over, tilting his head to whisper in his boss's ear, Donovan welcomed the interruption.

"Hey, Boss, I got the tree thing figured out...."

Whatever the punch line was, it was obliterated by a flash of chaos. For the glass-and-concrete canyon that was Rockefeller Center was filled with the deafening roar of large-caliber gunshots. One shot, then another.

Now, when a gun goes off on a New York City street the sound seems to come from everywhere and only the very experienced or the phenomenally lucky can guess in which direction the terror lies. The mayor froze in midsentence, his eyes wild and white and scared with the thought of death. His two-man security detail lurched forward to protect him. But Donovan got there first, coiling his legs and springing to tackle the mayor and hurl him to the pavement, covering his body with his own while wrenching his Smith & Wesson from its holster. At the same time, Moskowitz tossed the cardinal to the pavement and squatted, looking around for the would-be assassin. Mosko's Penzler automatic pointed up at the still-dark tree.

"Where'd that come from?" Donovan yelled.

"Don't know!" Mosko yelled back.

"Is anyone hit?" a security man blurted, kneeling beside Donovan and his boss.

"I don't think so," Donovan replied.

"I'm OK; I'm OK," the mayor stammered.

"Me, too," the cardinal added, feeling along his red-robed body in a search for holes.

There came screaming then, from a block away or so. And a general panic began in the crowd and spread away from the site.

"Those shots sounded like the ones I heard last week," Donovan said, scrambling to his feet and offering a hand to help the mayor up.

"Another shooting?" Hizzoner asked. "What the hell's going on here, Bill?"

"I'll find out," Donovan replied, and ran off. Moskowitz was right behind him.

"I'm in charge here," Pilcrow said then, charging into the scene and sounding like Alexander Haig after the Reagan shooting. As happened in that case, no one listened.

Those in the crowd who didn't run from the shots were gaping at the spot from which they had come. It was at the corner and a bit uptown. A handful of uniformed officers were hustling toward the spot, elbowing past tourists and shoppers whose holiday spirit had been jostled by yet another bloodletting.

As Moskowitz, younger and, despite all Donovan's working out, faster, went on ahead, the captain grabbed one of the cops. To this sergeant he said, "The suspect could be dressed like a Santa's Angel. Stop all you see and check IDs. But be careful."

"Gotcha, Captain."

There were several Santa's Angels around, just standing and gaping like everyone else, for the most part, the sound of tinkling bells having vanished for a time. Four more

Santa's Angels stuck to their posts on the less-crowded east side of the avenue. The sergeant got two more uniformed cops to help him and went off to see whose those red-robed beggars were and what they were up to. Leaving Moskowitz to play front man at the site of what the captain was sure was another killing, Donovan spent ten minutes prowling the edge of the swelling crowd of onlookers, just looking. At one point he watched quietly as the sergeant grilled a Santa's Angel who made the mistake of turning surly and refusing to identify himself. Then Donovan wandered over to Madison Avenue, looking for the route *he* would take were he an assassin escaping his handiwork.

When Donovan got to the edge of the crime scene he found a shoulder-to-shoulder crowd that was jammed against the storefronts and spilled out into the street, bringing the incredibly jammed holiday traffic to yet another standstill. The focal point of the crowd was the festively decorated window of E & J Tuttle, a fabulously expensive store Donovan remembered from his childhood. That was when his mother and aunt took him on their annual window-shopping trip along Fifth Avenue in the weeks between Thanksgiving and Christmas. They never bought anything—much too expensive—although Donovan vaguely recalled a chameleon that he took home in a cardboard box and fed crickets caught in Riverside Park.

As a child Donovan had loved those yearly excursions to wallow in the riches of Fifth Avenue during the Christmas season. Now he gulped hard at the sight of Tuttle's old and famous Christmas display shot up like a target. The gigantic display window—or what was left of it—highlighted an assortment of larger-than-life nutcrackers watching while a gigantic robot Santa rode a fire-engine red sleigh through a starry winter sky behind a team of mechanized reindeer. But now the window was smashed. The robot Santa Donovan had planned on taking his son to see had slivers of glass showered atop its red cap and speckled throughout its white beard. And children were being led away from the scene by horrified parents who were at a loss to explain how precisely assassination helped make it a season to be jolly.

Donovan tucked his Smith & Wesson back in its holster and moved quickly through the crowd. As he did so he met a breathless Moskowitz on the way out.

"Who's dead?" Donovan asked.

"Another Christmas shopper," Mosko said. "Inside the store."

"The same shooter?"

"A Santa's Angels beggar," Mosko reported.

FOUR

A HELL OF A PONTIAC, OR
TWO VOLKSWAGEN BEETLES

"I DIDN'T KNOW IT WAS possible to pay thirty-five hundred dollars for lingerie," Donovan said, looking in the bullet-riddled window—bulletproof, of course—that separated passersby from the extravagant collection of ladies' finery displayed in another display window. In particular, he gaped at a silk nightgown, blood red and edged with gold, that seemed flimsy enough to get the mannequin upon which it was draped arrested for public indecency.

"Me neither," Mosko agreed.

"I can remember when you could get a hell of a Pontiac for that amount. Or two Volkswagen Beetles."

Behind the robot Santa, a handful of exquisitely coifed and dressed salespersons gaped out the window, through the spiderweb of cracks joining and spreading out from the two holes, at the scene outside: a roped-off sidewalk surrounded by police cars, other official vehicles, and hordes of gawkers. Unaccustomed as they were to gore, the fashionable store's personnel looked as one might at a public beheading of the sort the Saudi Arabians favor. The prominent displays of blood and guts—two in as many weeks—were far beyond the pale of their expectations.

"Who's the stiff?" Donovan asked, shifting his gaze downward. A man's body lay bloodied and broken behind the mannequins and a small display case filled with expensive perfumes.

Mosko consulted some notes that were written on the

back of an envelope pending transfer to his computer. "The ID in the pocket reads: 'Terry Seybold.' He's thirty-seven and lived in Southport, Connecticut."

"What did he do for a living?"

"A card in his pocket says he's manager of a stock brokerage office in Westport."

"So he lived and worked in Connecticut. What was he doing here?"

"Shopping," Mosko said, reaching out with the tip of his shoe and touching a white-on-white box from E & J Tuttle.

Donovan crouched down and carefully lifted the top. Inside was a gown identical to the $3,500 one he had been gawking at in the window. It was packed in soft paper that crinkled like pine needles being crushed underfoot on a weekend walk in the woods.

"The man wasn't hurting for money," Donovan said. "Was he married?"

"His ID says no."

"Then who was he buying this *shmatta* for? A girlfriend?"

"Lucky lady," Mosko said.

"Me, I'd rather have the two VWs. But each to his or her own."

Donovan inspected Seybold's clothes, looking at the lining and stitching of his coat and jacket and the leather on his shoes. Then the captain stood and brushed some dirt off his jeans. "He's wearing about five grand himself," he said.

"And that don't count the silk undies. The guy was shot in the chest, which pretty much ruins the togs."

"Pretty much. Can we tell yet what kind of slug killed the man?"

"Are you asking, 'Was it a nine-millimeter fired from a Kammacher Stedman?' It could be. We have several witnesses."

Moskowitz indicated the crowd of onlookers, which if anything was larger than the one that had gathered to wit-

ness the aftermath of the Melmer slaying. Added to it were
several local TV stations' remote vans, hunching up through
the traffic, their saucer-shaped antennae perched atop telescoping antennae that rose from squat vehicles, heavy with
electronic equipment, that seemed always to hum like microwave ovens.

"Including the press, I see."

"Yeah. They just got here. They want to talk to you."

"And me in my civvies," Donovan said, straightening
the old and honorable suede jacket he wore over a black
turtleneck sweater and jeans.

"You're on leave, remember. You were bored, so we
went for a walk. Anyway, the witnesses described a white
male about thirty years old. Average height."

"Hair color?"

"Nobody noticed. They heard two shots—well, one
woman says she heard three shots, but we're downplaying
that."

"Why?"

"There's only two holes in the corpse. There must have
been an echo. Fifth Avenue is fairly narrow, and the buildings are tall."

Donovan led his assistant back out of the store and
glanced up. So did a handful of people in the crowd outside.
One way to get attention on a New York City street was to
stand looking up. Several people would always imitate you.
Donovan always felt that was due to the Big Apple resident's persistent fear of having a suicide fall on him.

"There were a lot of echoes in Dealey Plaza, too," Donovan said.

"Where?"

"In Dallas, where JFK was shot. That's why a lot of
conspiracy theorists think there were two shooters."

"I thought that was because of the Oliver Stone movie."

"You're putting the chicken before the horse, my
friend," Donovan said.

Moskowitz smiled.

"How many bullets did you find?"

"Two. Both in the body."

"So our killer's aim is getting better as he moves downtown," Donovan noted. "What else did the witnesses see?"

Mosko consulted his notes again, then said, "Less than the last time. There were shots. A Santa's Angels guy suddenly was running off."

"I see he didn't leave behind a tripod this time."

"I guess not."

"Maybe Friday's was his only one. Where do you get those things, by the way? Do the Santa's Angels wholesale them or can one of its beggars design his own?"

"I'll ask. The guy wore a regulation cape and a hat, plus jeans."

"Jeans are new. I don't remember them at Sarkana. Was there a videotape of this one?" He scanned the facade of E & J Tuttle, which was polished black marble and stainless steel. "I don't see any security cameras."

"There aren't any," Mosko confirmed. "I guess this outfit doesn't worry as much about smash-and-grab artists." That peculiarly urban brand of robber typically smashed in the front of a store—in extreme cases by driving a stolen car into it—and grabbed as much loot as he could before the cops arrived.

"They go after jewels or TVs or something else anyway, not lingerie," Donovan said. "Where did today's perp go?"

"Downtown," Mosko replied, "in the general direction of Rockefeller Center."

Donovan looked down that way, again leaning over the display case. Several persons in the crowd outside imitated him.

"Maybe he wanted to catch the tree-lighting ceremony," Donovan said.

"Or catch the Christmas show at Radio City Music Hall."

"In any event, he melted into the crowd of shoppers, Santas, and other Santa's Angels coin collectors. I mean *I* didn't see him, and I looked around for where someone might run. Did anyone see the gun?"

"No. Shots. Man on ground. Man running. That's the gist of it."

Donovan was staring off into the crowd, focusing on a familiar face. Then he smiled and waved.

Mosko looked to see who it was, then gave his boss a quizzical look. "A member of your fan club?"

"Are you telling me you don't recognize Paul Duke?" Donovan said.

"The TV guy?"

The anchorman for WTV's *The Morning Show* was one of those impossibly handsome men who only turned up in Hollywood or on television. A regular item on *People* magazine's annual "50 Most Beautiful People" list, Duke was tall and dark, with perfectly coifed black hair and Mediterranean features that were vague enough to allow speculation about Spanish, Italian, Greek, Jewish, or Arab ancestors. His reputation as a serious journalist—serious as television reporters go, anyway—was formed during the war in Afghanistan, when Duke stood atop a mountain ridge not far from Ghazoor and challenged Russian choppers to strafe him. This fearlessness, as much as his looks, got him the coveted morning news job on WTV. Duke's studio, visible from the sidewalk at Rockefeller Center, was a tourist attraction. Each day hundreds, if not thousands, of camera-toting visitors pressed their faces against the bulletproof glass to watch the handsome, debonair, and fearless Duke read the morning's headlines to a nationwide audience counted in the millions.

Duke's path had crossed Donovan's on several occasions. The captain was an occasional guest on the show, usually to comment (or not comment, as circumstances warranted) about some horrible crime he was investigating. Every so often Donovan was put on camera to talk about a faraway homicide. The last such instance came a few years back, when the captain was a regular commentator during the O. J. Simpson trials. It was Donovan's opinion that the LAPD shouldn't have hopped that fence to get into the suspect's estate without a search warrant. "Starting a fire in a garbage can and pulling the alarm always worked for me," he told Duke one time, precipitating a torrent of protest from defense lawyers. In consequence of his many and often colorful appearances on the show, Donovan was a favorite of Duke, who now beckoned him from behind the police barricades.

"I'm going to go talk to him," Donovan said.

"Why?" Mosko asked. "He just wants to ask you about the killings! What can you say?"

"The usual platitudes: 'We will fight them on the beaches, will fight them in the alleyways; we will never give up.'"

"I thought you hated reporters."

"Generally speaking, I do," Donovan said. "But Paul's different."

"He's better dressed," Mosko allowed, after taking another, longer look at the still-gesturing man. "And that haircut must cost a fortune."

"I wonder what he's doing here," Donovan mused.

"He's a reporter."

"No, he's an anchorman. He gets a mil a year to sit there in front of the cameras and pose while reading a story a reporter handed him. He never goes out in the street anymore."

"What about the Afghan war?" Mosko asked.

"That was gutsy to stand up to Russian helicopters, challenging one to fire on him," Donovan said. "But the chances of it happening were really pretty small. Duke traveled with a camera crew, after all, and let's give Russian pilots credit for being able to tell the difference between an

American network TV crew and a mujahideen guerrilla band. Besides, I don't think that Duke is ballsy all the time. In fact, I'm pretty sure he stays indoors for a reason." He drew Mosko's attention back to Duke, who was waving more frantically by way of ignoring two midwestern-looking women who were waving autograph books in his face.

"So what's he doing here?"

"I don't know. Maybe he was coming down Fifth in his limo when this happened and decided to play reporter. Maybe he knows Seybold. They both have houses in Connecticut, if that means anything."

"This is why you want to talk to him—you, a guy who hates reporters? Because it's odd for him to be here and you want to know why?"

"Curiosity is the basis of all learning," Donovan said grandly.

"It also killed the cat," Moskowitz replied.

"Get some uniforms to keep those local TV crews away from me," Donovan said.

Mosko nodded, then added, "I'm going to see what more I can find about this guy Seybold."

The evidence technicians had begun to arrive and were setting up their equipment and staking out their turf. Uniformed officers pushed the crowd back and erected barricades. In addition to the crowd of shoppers and tourists, several very well dressed business types had appeared from the executive offices of other shops and were having a worried convocation in the middle of Fifth Avenue, now gridlocked to a halt once again. Bonaci's crime-scene van was making its way down a side street, fighting the nearly impenetrable traffic.

Donovan left his assistant in charge, went to the police barricade, and slipped out of the protected circle and into the mass of milling bodies excluded from it. He was aware that, well off to one side, uniformed cops were keeping the

TV crews sent to cover the murder from descending on him. They didn't seem happy about it.

Upon seeing Donovan coming, Duke shooed away the admirers and stepped out into the street, finding an open spot between a stalled number 5 bus and a cream-colored stretch limo that, like all the other vehicles, was going nowhere fast.

"Bill Donovan!" Duke exclaimed, pumping the captain's hand.

"Hello, Paul. What in the world has prompted you to leave the studio and walk among the proles?"

"The proles? Oh, the people. Well, I thought I'd pay a visit to my fans." He nodded at the growing group of admirers that gawked at him from the sidewalk.

"Which is why you turned up at a murder scene, risking life and limb from the ladies," Donovan said.

"I heard about it from our news staff," he replied. "You were listed as investigating officer. I thought I'd pay you a visit."

"I'm flattered, but I'm on leave." Donovan indicated his casual attire, which he had augmented by slipping his gold badge onto the outside of his breast pocket.

"On leave? But you're here."

"I was a few blocks up, keeping Marcy company. You met her in the studio a year or two ago."

"Of course. Who could forget the lovely Marcy?" he said.

"You heard we got married?" Donovan asked.

Duke laughed. "Heard? Yes, I would say so."

"We're expecting in the next couple of weeks."

"So you're having a baby? That's great. Congratulations." He shook Donovan's hand another time. Duke seemed genuinely happy for them.

"She's up at Fifth Avenue Medical Center...in the ICU, for a complicated set of reasons."

"Is everything OK?"

"Oh, sure. Just precautions. Her doctor is Mr. Careful."

"You can't be too cautious these days. And Fifth Avenue is a great hospital. A number of my colleagues at the network have been there. Do you know what you're having? Boy or girl?"

"Boy," Donovan said, beaming. "I'm going to have a son."

"Picked out a name yet?" Duke asked.

"Daniel Magid."

"Ma—?"

"Magid."

"That sounds like a family name. After Marcy's mom?"

"No," Donovan said emphatically. "Jews consider it bad luck to name a kid after a living person. *Magid* means 'storyteller' in Hebrew. Marcy wants him to be a writer, like her mom."

"Refresh my memory. Marcy's mom is…"

"Deborah Magid…her maiden name…the editor of *Perfect*."

"The women's magazine. That makes her a powerful woman, doesn't it?"

Donovan shrugged. "She's my mother-in-law, which makes her powerful even if she were a cleaning lady."

"I see your point. And your father-in-law, everybody knows Justice Barnes. Bill, your son is coming into the world bearing a powerful pedigree."

"Yeah, I guess he'll live down my side of the family. So is this your limo?"

The cream-colored limousine they were standing next to began to inch forward as the gridlock eased—at least on the downtown side of the crime scene. The bus also began to move and, showing no consideration for either celebrity or the power of the police, threatened to crush the two men against the big car. They stepped to the back of the latter, with Donovan trying to see through the dark-tinted windows.

"It's mine."

"What kind of mileage do you get on this thing? About the same as on a tank?"

"To be honest with you, I have no idea. But that sounds about right."

"I would think that a limo only attracts crowds," Donovan said. "How many autographs do you have to sign when you step out of it?"

"None. The trick is to keep moving. By the time these tourists have both recognized you and conferred among themselves to make sure it's really you, you're gone."

"And New Yorkers, of course, would sooner give up their rent-controlled apartments than ask a celeb for an autograph," Donovan said.

Duke nodded.

"We like to think there are so many stars living around us that hitting on one for his signature would be like asking the janitor for a stock tip," Donovan added.

Duke looked at the body, then quickly away and up at the store window, then back at Donovan. "Who's the victim?" he asked.

"Is this official? Are you playing reporter?"

"No. Just curious."

"The dead man is a Connecticut stockbroker named Terry Seybold. Know him?"

"I don't think so."

"He looks a bit like you," Donovan said.

"Poor man," Duke replied, with a smile.

"We should all be so unfortunate."

"Tell me, Bill," Duke said, moving closer and slipping into a conspiratorial tone. "Did I hear correctly? Is there a killer out there using a handgun that can shoot through bulletproof glass?"

"It's too early to tell," Donovan replied.

"What's your gut feeling?"

"My gut feeling is that it was done by the same guy. But

we don't have tonight's slug yet—presumably it's in the victim—so you'll have to wait.''

"Is there a gun that can shoot through bulletproof glass? A handgun, I mean?''

"Sure. How's your firearms knowledge? I ask because guns ain't my specialty, really.... People are. I only tell you what was told to me.''

"I know a few things.''

"The Kammacher Stedman will do it. It fires a depleted-uranium nine-millimeter round. That was the weapon used at that killing up at Sarkana. There are only three such firearms in the world, and only one of them is unaccounted for.''

"Why would anyone want a handgun that powerful?''

"Assassination through bulletproof limousine windows,'' Donovan said, nodding in the direction of the limo, which had pulled to the curb near the next corner. "The gun was developed in Europe for that purpose.''

"I see,'' Duke replied, rubbing his chin and falling silent.

Donovan let him have his thoughtful pause, then jumped on it. "Why are you worried about being shot?'' the captain asked.

Duke's reply came in a startled, defensive voice: "I'm not worried.''

"You just left your posh limo, braving autograph hounds, to find out about the presence hereabouts of a gun that can fire through bulletproof glass. And you tell me you're not worried.''

"I'm curious. In covering the Afghan war I picked up an interest in weapons. Exotic pistols in particular. Who could blame me? I was surrounded by them. There were a lot of handguns floating around—all types. I even got one automatic off a dead Russian. But I never heard of a round that could fire accurately through bulletproof glass.'' Duke glanced at the window of Tuttle. "I understand the killer put three bullets in the victim at Sarkana.''

Television reporters, Donovan thought. *They never get things straight.* He said, noncommittally, "He hit the target."

Duke seemed uncomfortable and looked longingly toward the safety of his limousine. At that moment, Donovan found it hard to imagine him standing in Afghanistan, raising his fist at Russian helicopters. *Maybe the man is only fearless about threats he can see,* Donovan wondered. *There's something about the notion of a gun that can shoot through bulletproof glass that chills the soul. You spend six figures on a secure limousine, maybe even hire an armed bodyguard as a chauffeur, and an anonymous crazy can still get you when you pull to the curb to drop off your laundry.*

"It's a crazy world," Duke said at last.

"Paul, who wants to shoot you through your limousine window?"

"Nobody," the man insisted. "Guns are just an interest of mine. You know how it is—I have to maintain my tough-guy image." With that, he gave Donovan a comradely punch on the shoulder, the sort of gesture the captain remembered from his high school days.

"Well, while you're tending your machismo, let me know if there's anything I can do for you," Donovan said.

"Oh, sure, absolutely. I appreciate that. I have your number in my Rolodex. Are you still on Riverside Drive?"

"Yep. Rent-controlled apartment and all. I'm currently preparing to dismantle my home gym and turn it into a nursery."

"You haven't done that yet?"

"More Jewish superstition. Marcy won't buy anything for the baby before he's born."

"Not even a crib?"

"It was all I could do to talk her into letting me buy a rattle," Donovan said ruefully.

"You're going to be one busy fellow the day after your son is born," Duke commented.

"Tell me about it. On my side of the family, we'd have built the Taj Mahal by now. So, are you still living in Southport?"

"Me? Sure. And I have an apartment in town."

"He lived in Southport," Donovan said, indicating the body, now surrounded by a swarm of evidence technicians lorded over by Howard Bonaci. "Are you sure you don't know him?"

"Terry...what did you say his name was?"

"Seybold," Donovan said, then spelled it.

"Sorry." Duke shook his head.

"Want to see what he looks like?"

Duke hesitated but, perhaps sensing his machismo was being tested, rose to the occasion. He followed Donovan to the corpse and looked down on it as a technician uncovered the face. Duke tensed up, then looked quickly up at the store window, as before.

"You didn't see bodies in the Afghan war?" Donovan asked.

"It's different when they're American."

"Funny, but I haven't found that," Donovan said. "I thought you took an automatic off a dead Russian."

"All right, you got me. I bought it from the mujahideen fighter who took it off the dead Russian. I hope you don't blow my cover on that. I told that story to *People*."

"Your secret is safe with me."

"Since I'm being completely honest with you, the mujahideen didn't like me all that much. They expected me, a rich American, to give them millions of dollars for their struggle. When I finally said, 'Hey, I'm a TV reporter just here on business—let's not get carried away overestimating my commitment to the cause,' they were pretty pissed off."

"You had to come down from the mountains posthaste," Donovan speculated, and Duke nodded.

"My visa was expiring anyway," Duke added. After a moment's awkwardness, he changed the subject, and in a predictable direction. Looking at a snappy, rose pink negligee with a $2,500 price tag, he said, "What I like about being single is not having to buy stuff like that."

"Do you know Seybold or not?" Donovan asked.

Duke shook his head. Then he walked away from the body and back in the direction of his limousine. Something in his body language tipped off the chauffeur, who jumped out of the driver's-side door and rushed around the gigantic vehicle to open a back door for his boss. The driver looked beefy and suitably bodyguardish, an ex-marine sort of guy.

Donovan followed Duke to the car, then stuck out his hand. They shook.

"Sorry if that upset you," Donovan said.

"I'm not afraid of bodies," Duke replied, taking a deep breath. "I must be coming down with something."

Donovan decided to allow the man his smoke screen. "Take two generic ibuprofen and take a hot bath," Donovan said. "The single ladies of New York need you healthy."

Duke smiled. The discussion was ending on comfortable turf. Although Duke's reputation as a lady-killer was as legendary as his looks and tough-guy image, he never tired of talking about it. "It's a shame you went and got married, Bill. We could do the town. I know some dynamite babes."

"I'm married to a dynamite babe," Donovan said.

"Of course you are," Duke replied, getting into the car. "My best to Marcy."

FIVE

"IT'S NOT LIKE THIS HAPPENED AT SOME CHEESY SHOPPING MALL"

"THE GUY WAS shopping for his fiancée," Moskowitz said, angling his computer to get the glare from the streetlights off the screen. He had it set up on the hood of a patrol car that was parked near the body.

"Who's she?" Donovan asked.

"One Amy Willets, a graduate student at the Yale School of Drama."

"Wait a second. How old was Seybold?"

"Thirty-seven."

"And the girl?"

"Twenty-five," Mosko replied.

"You mean this guy is thirty-seven and he's going to marry a woman who's—" Donovan caught himself in mid-sentence, sighed, and shrugged. He had just remembered that he was twelve years older than his wife.

Moskowitz smiled. "You were about to say something, Boss?"

"Never mind," Donovan snapped. "Has she been told?"

"Yeah, by the Connecticut cops."

"Try to find out if Seybold had enemies. When was the wedding supposed to happen?"

"In June. They just announced their engagement last month. It was in the papers."

Donovan looked down at the body, then scuffed his left foot idly on the concrete. "Did any of the witnesses notice Seybold before he became a statistic?"

"What do you mean?"

"I mean was he talking to anyone? Did they have words? Or did the killer just march up to the window and shoot through it and Seybold had the bad luck to be standing there?"

"He was talking to the store manager," Mosko said.

"Who's that?"

"Martin Kimble."

"I want to talk to him," Donovan said.

"So do I," Mosko added. "But he ran off to consult with the home office. He disappeared before I could get my hands on him."

"Disappeared as in left the premises?" Donovan asked.

"Ran off. Took a powder. Hit the road."

"Send somebody to find him. In fact, send an army to find him. Tell this Kimble—home office or no home office—that material witnesses who disappear before talking to the cops piss me off."

"I'll put it just like that," Mosko said, calling a detective over and giving him an instruction.

Donovan added, "I don't get this. On Friday, November twenty-ninth, and again this evening, a young guy who's engaged to be married is shot to death on Fifth Avenue while shopping for his bride-to-be. On Fifth Avenue, the world's most famous shopping boulevard. It's not like this happened at some cheesy shopping mall." Looking sharply at his assistant, Donovan added, "Or in Brooklyn, where you might expect violence."

"C'mon; you can get some real good buys on Ralph Avenue and nobody's been killed that I know about."

"They just lost all their hubcaps. Tell me, could there be a connection between Melmer and Seybold?"

"Other than that they were both good-looking young guys who were planning on getting married?"

"Other than that. Did you find out where Melmer was eighteen weeks ago?"

Mosko consulted his computer, then said, "Umh…here, in the city."

"Doing what?"

"Staying in his apartment at Trump Plaza. He was here on business."

"What kind of business?" Donovan asked.

"I dunno," Mosko replied. "The man was in the medical stuff business. I guess he was selling medical stuff."

"Try to be more specific. Call his secretary and ask her."

"Why is this important?"

"It's important if he was meeting Seybold, for example. Our latest victim was a stockbroker. Now, if Melmer was in town on business related to the stock market, we might have a match. Is his firm publicly traded?"

"You mean like on the Big Board?"

"Like that." Donovan nodded.

"I got no idea. But I'll find out. You know, this is the sort of stuff you're good at."

"I'm on leave."

"Yeah, but you seem to be hanging around this case, don't you?"

"I was in the neighborhood, you guys were bugging me about Judaism, so I thought I'd wander over and connect with the tree."

The sergeant said, "Since you're spending so much time sitting next to her while she takes naps or watches TV, maybe you could plug in your laptop and do your Internet thing."

"I can't use the cellular modem in the hospital," Donovan said. "One night I logged on to CNN Online and it set off the fetal monitor. Bell went off at the nurses' station and they came running. They thought she was having contractions."

"So plug it into the wall," Moskowitz replied.

"My laptop is home in my study."

"I'll send a cop to pick it up."

"Marcy will flip."

"She's forty and the size of a house," Mosko said. "Her flipping days are over."

"You don't live with the woman," Donovan replied. "OK, have someone get my computer for me. No, never mind; I have to go home tonight to work on dismantling my gym."

"It seems like only yesterday we got you that," Mosko said ruefully.

"I'm only moving it down the hall to the maid's room off the kitchen."

"'The maid's room.' I love you guys with your big old apartments. Has there ever been a maid in there?"

"Not that I'm aware of, and I've lived my whole life in that apartment. Apart from a few years in the sixties when I was…well, never mind. I'll do my 'Internet thing' for you. But I'm still not officially working. For one thing, these two deaths may not be related—"

"Sorry, Boss, but I think they are," Bonaci said.

"Do we have the same shooter, definitely?"

"I can't give you a definite yes until I get the bullet outta there." He looked down at the body, which was being zipped into a bag. "But I'd bet on it."

"Do those look like nine-millimeter holes to you?" Donovan asked.

"They're big ones, all right. And the descriptions of the shooter match the descriptions of the Sarkana killer."

Donovan said, "The first Santa's Angels killer was first seen ogling jewels in the window he was soon to fire through. Today's Santa's Angels Army killer was seen doing what? Admiring the lingerie?"

"None of the witnesses noticed him until the gun went off," Bonaci replied.

"And then he ran downtown," Donovan said, leaning against the hood of the car and looking in that direction.

"Toward Rockefeller Center," Mosko added. "Where your friend Duke works."

"If I killed someone, I would run away from the crowd, not into the center of it," Bonaci added.

"When a tree wants to hide, it goes into the forest," Donovan said, thinking once again of the gigantic Norway spruce. It had been lit by then, the mayor and cardinal having recovered sufficiently to complete the ceremony. "Did you have any luck reaching the Santa's Angels people?"

"I have a guy making calls to find out where they come from," Mosko reported.

"We need a roster of volunteers and paid workers—the names of everyone they have on Fifth Avenue this season. Also the names of supervisors, if any. How do those cloaks, hats, and tripods get distributed? Where and when do they turn in the day's receipts? Is there a mustering point?"

"You mean like a union hiring hall?" Mosko asked.

"Yeah, like that. Do Santa's Angels guys show up at the hiring hall every morning at seven to see if there's work for them? And, more to the point, is it a place where we can check IDs and videotape their faces?" Donovan said.

"Friday's tape wasn't good enough to compare faces, if that's what you have in mind," Bonaci said.

"No, but you might get a match with the eyewitnesses. You guys find out where the mustering point is and any other details you can. Like how many of tonight's Angels were also on duty November twenty-ninth. And get ahold of the names of those supposed to be working this block."

Donovan looked across the street, in the direction of a ringing bell. There were Santa's Angels volunteers—two red-cloaked beggars and a Santa—working the sidewalk. "I asked a uniformed sergeant to talk to those guys," Donovan said. "Track him down and see what he got."

"You got it," Mosko replied.

"And while you're at it, find out if anybody knew Seybold's schedule ahead of time."

"I got that already," Mosko replied, consulting his computer. "He had on his calendar that he was driving into the city. His secretary knew about his plans."

"Did anyone else?"

"No. She said he told her he was going to buy a surprise for his fiancée's birthday."

"When is that?"

"Sunday," Mosko replied.

"Seybold had a cell phone in his pocket," Bonaci said, producing the plastic bag that held the device.

Donovan took it and looked it over. The digital phone was one of the small, expensive ones. "Get the record of calls made on this for the past week," Donovan said.

"For the past week? Wouldn't for today be enough?"

Donovan gave his assistant a withering glance.

Mosko said, "No, of course it wouldn't be enough. I can tell you, though, that he didn't call in before he died. The secretary said he left the office late and drove straight here."

"Do you think the killer knew his schedule and was waiting for him?" Mosko asked.

Donovan tossed up his hands.

"Do you think the killer was lying in wait for Melmer?"

"I think I need more information before thinking anything," Donovan said at last. "I'm hungry. You don't happen to have a sandwich in that fridge of yours, do you?"

Bonaci shook his head. "I got a container of strawberry yogurt and a knish."

"What kind of knish?"

"Cheese. But it's left over from Saturday."

"Forget it," Donovan said, pushing away from the hood of the patrol car and looking around for the telltale smoke of a sidewalk vendor. On a nearby corner, a black man in a chef's hat was serving up fajitas and burritos.

Donovan said, "Maybe I'll get a... Hey, what about my gyro vendor?"

Moskowitz switched screens on his computer, then said,

"Gyro vendor...gyro vendor, let's see. Oh, the Afghan you met the day of the first killing. The guy with the automatic who split. I checked out Fifteen sixty-two thirty-two seventy-eight Queens Boulevard. It turns out to be one of those Muslim meat shops."

"Muslim meat shops?" Bonaci asked.

"Where they sell the stuff prepared according to the Islamic kosher laws, or whatever they are," Donovan said. "They call it *halal* meat."

"That could be his supplier," Moskowitz said. "Now, we just can't walk in there and ask if they know this guy. At least, I can't go in and ask. I'm trying to find a Muslim police officer who can do it for me. In the meantime, I have someone checking with the city bureau that licenses sidewalk vendors to see who was assigned that spot in front of F.A.O. Schwarz."

"That's a primo location," Donovan said. "These guys fight over less important corners. The name and address of the guy I talked to must be on record somewhere."

"I'll find him, Cap."

Bonaci asked, "Why are you so interested in this street vendor? I mean, he can't have been the Sarkana shooter—he was arguing with you at the time."

"We were having a discussion," Donovan said.

"Most likely he ran because that gun was unlicensed. Maybe he also has green card problems."

"You know I don't like guys who run away from me," Donovan said. "They switch on my gene for pursuit. My pal from Afghanistan did that when he took off after I spotted his gun. And Kimble bolted after witnessing a murder."

"We'll find both of 'em," Mosko said.

"Do it fast," Donovan replied.

NOT TOO LONG LATER, Donovan walked into his wife's hospital room to find her on her back with the head of the bed elevated halfway. Her robe was pulled up, exposing her huge, perfectly round belly to the early-afternoon light. She was getting ready to inject herself in the upper thigh. Her doctor stood on the far side of her bed, near the window, eating a Perugina chocolate and scanning the last several hours' worth of printout from the fetal monitor.

"Skin-popping heparin again, huh?" Donovan asked, sliding into his chair and unfolding the brown paper bag that held his dinner.

"It's subcutaneous injection," she said sharply. "Not skin-popping."

"I know what I see," he replied, watching as she pinched a fold of skin and slipped the short, slender needle under it. A few seconds later, the anticoagulant was spreading through her system; in the time since she had begun the successful pregnancy Marcy had learned that it was clotting in the womb, not bad luck, that had caused the earlier miscarriages. Those were the tragedies that had put so much stress on her relationship with Donovan.

Then she pressed an alcohol pad on the site and handed the detritus of the operation—the needle and its wrapping—to him. "I hate it when you hand me your garbage," he said, but nonetheless walked across the room and deposited the needle in the red sharps container on the wall. On the way back, he snagged a chocolate from the Perugina box and popped it into his mouth before she could notice.

"Good afternoon, Captain," said Dr. Campagna, folding the six-foot strip of printout into a manageable size and slipping it into a folder.

"Doctor," he replied, chewing and swallowing.

"She's doing very well. The baby is doing very well. You should be proud of both."

"I am. How is her coagulation status?"

"It should be all right. I'll check the newest figures in a moment. I would say, though, that if you don't let her get stabbed or shot she won't bleed to death."

"I won't let that happen," Donovan replied.

"He's said that before," Marcy commented, giving him a look. In fact, she had been shot, and in the stomach, a decade and a half earlier during an undercover operation that he ran. Only the fact that he, too, was wounded saved the relationship.

"What about bleeding during delivery?" Donovan asked.

"I'll stop the heparin well before. Also the tributylene and mag sulfate. And the baby aspirin."

"What about the insulin?" Marcy asked. To an already full palette of pregnancy complications had been added gestational diabetes, which, like the rest of the problems, would probably go away after she gave birth. But four injections a day—two insulin and two heparin—had left her tummy and thighs black and blue.

"That you'll take right up until you deliver," Campagna said. "Of course, the baby will have to go into an incubator for a few days as a result."

"Why?" Donovan asked.

"To stabilize his blood sugar. Don't worry. It's just temporary."

"Will I be able to nurse him?" Marcy asked, looking sad.

"Sure. But you'll have to do it in the nursery, not in your bed."

"At least it's something," she said, leaning back and pushing her gown into place.

"How long will it be before her bruises go away?" Donovan asked.

"Several weeks. The combination of anticoagulants and all those injections make the bruising worse."

"I'm afraid if anyone sees her I'll get hauled off for beating my wife," Donovan said.

"As if you would," she said, taking his hand.

"As if I *could*," he added, thinking of her black belt in kung fu.

Marcy asked, "Can you tell me yet if I'm going to have a vaginal delivery?"

The doctor looked down at her and smiled enigmatically. "All I can say is I like to deliver babies on Saturdays," he replied.

"What's that mean?"

"You're going to have a C-section," Donovan said.

"Do you have any Saturday in particular in mind?" Marcy asked.

Campagna thought for a moment, then said, "Two weeks more, at least."

"Two weeks!"

"Maybe three."

"Three weeks will be Christmas," she protested.

"I live alone and have no family, so Merry Christmas," the doctor replied. "Or Happy Hanukkah. Whichever you celebrate."

"In our family we celebrate both," Donovan said.

"Which are you?" the doctor asked the captain. "The Christian or the Jew?"

"I'm the atheist," Donovan said.

"Captain, I assure you that will change after your son is born."

Donovan harrumphed, and the doctor smiled at him. Donovan liked Campagna. He was a character, a short and driven man who delivered three hundred babies a year at an average, the captain had discovered, of $7,000 per. Even Donovan's barely remembered high school math yielded an income of $2.1 million. Some of that was spent, it turned out, on a passion for soccer that took the doctor around the globe to see World Cup events. Campagna himself was hardly an athletic figure. He was pushing seventy and smoked filtered cigarettes, a pack of which always was jammed into his shirt pocket. And smoke figured into one of the great stories about this man, who was the chief of maternal and fetal medicine at Fifth Avenue Medical Center.

One time, huffing and puffing as he pushed a sonogram cart down the hall at three in the morning, Campagna tripped on the newly washed floor and hit his head on the back of the cart. He was rushed unconscious into a treatment room, where the attending physician looked at the doctor's age and pack of cigarettes and assumed he had fallen as the result of a heart problem. When Campagna woke up he had a pounding headache and a case of nicotine withdrawal that was made considerably worse by the sight of the myriad wires sprouting from sensors on his chest. He stripped them off and, clutching his smokes and holding his gown about him, scurried down the hall. Frantic hospital personnel found him on a fire escape, puffing away and stamping his bare feet to ward off the bitter cold of a February morning. The yarn became a centerpiece of the Campagna legend, along with his threat to quit medicine and open a pizza parlor the day a managed-care cost cutter tried to tell him how to treat a patient. As a result of his fame as a leading authority on high-risk pregnancies such as Marcy's, couples came from around the world to have their babies under his care.

Campagna walked across the room to a small grey metal desk that sat next to a pint-size refrigerator like the one in Bonaci's van. That was where Donovan stored the yogurt, fruit, and seven-grain bread he bought for Marcy to pick at during the night. Campagna left the folder on the desk and went to slip the box of chocolates into the fridge. He stopped in midmotion and waved for Donovan to come get a piece.

The captain did just that, braving a look from his wife. "How many of those have you had?" she asked.

"Just one."

It was her turn to harrumph.

Donovan picked up a hazelnut chocolate that was wrapped in gold foil and unwrapped it while the doctor switched on the computer monitor that sat atop the desk. He tapped in a password and, after consulting the folder, Marcy's Social Security number. A row of numbers presently appeared on the screen.

Donovan bent over to look at them. "Lab results?" he asked.

Campagna nodded. "And the rest of your wife's medical history, going back ten years."

"Is anything wrong?" Donovan asked.

"No. I just wanted to recheck her clotting status."

"How is it?" Marcy asked from across the room.

"Good."

The doctor switched off the monitor.

"I think I might like being a doctor," Donovan said.

"We have our uses, I guess. Do you have any other questions? I have to go."

Donovan said, "Is Gicana going to re-sign with Italy?"

His eyes widening, Campagna said, "Roberto Gicana is a soccer genius. If he doesn't, it will be the end of the world. I cannot even consider the possibility of an Italian team without him."

Campagna shook Donovan's hand, then went and took both of Marcy's hands and squeezed them. "Have a restful night," he said.

"How can I rest when the baby is hiccuping every half hour?" she asked.

"How does he feel?" Campagna asked, grinning.

"He makes me giggle. But sometimes I wish he would stop."

"You cannot tell the baby what to do," Campagna said.

When the doctor was gone, Donovan sat back next to his wife.

She said, "So tell me about it."

"Tell you about what?"

"About the second murder. About how you threw the mayor to the ground and covered his body with your own. It was on the news and the nurses were talking about it."

Donovan took her hand and said, "I heard shots. I reacted. There was no serious chance of my getting hurt—if the killer was shooting at the mayor he could have killed him by then—except maybe that Pilcrow might have tripped over me trying to get attention."

"Was *he* there?" she asked.

"Unfortunately. Anyway, the party turned out to be around the corner. A guy was shot inside E & J Tuttle."

"Fancy," she said.

"And, until this evening, a pretty safe place to shop."

"Who was killed? The TV didn't say."

"A stockbroker from Connecticut," Donovan said.

"Through the window like the one a week ago?"

"Yep. I'm not sure if the perp was celebrating the first night of Hanukkah or the lighting of the Christmas tree."

"Same perp?" she asked.

"Probably."

"You're not going to be able to stay out of this investigation, are you?" Marcy said.

"I'm going to try," he replied, leaning back in his chair and closing his eyes.

They held hands silently for a long time, then switched on CNN and watched the coverage of the disrupted Christmas tree lighting. Nurses came and went, taking readings off the fetal monitor and checking Marcy's IVs. The baby moved off and on and hiccuped some, and when those things happened she pressed her husband's hand against her belly. For a while, when the nurses were gone, Donovan rested his cheek against her bare flesh, which was hot and ripe.

Later on he took a cab home, where he spent an hour taking his Universal gym apart and lugging the pieces down the hall to what once was the maid's room. The new layout of the Donovan apartment was shaping up: master bedroom, baby's room, study, living room, dining room, maid's room (soon to be the exercise room), kitchen, and two and a half baths. All this in a white turn-of-the-century Federalist-style building, the lower floors of which were laced with ivy.

At midevening Donovan showered and put a load of laundry into the wash. He dressed and packed his laptop into his briefcase along with a file full of printouts that Moskowitz had sent to the apartment. These were the day's reports, part of the price Donovan had to pay for spending most of the month in his wife's hospital room. When he got back to Fifth Avenue Medical Center, Marcy was asleep, lying flat on her back with one arm curved around her head, her face aglow even while dreaming, her café au lait skin glistening in the light from the fetal monitor.

Donovan unpacked his briefcase quietly and was about to crank up the laptop when he thought, *The hell with the case; I'm off.* Unless told otherwise, he would let Mosko handle it. Better to spend the time staring at Marcy. He eased himself into the recliner and turned so he could see her face. Donovan lowered his head onto a pillow and, before too long, fell asleep dreaming, like her, of babies.

SIX

MELMER'S BLACK FOREST COOKIE

IT WAS TEN the following morning, the first Friday in December, and Marcy had moved far enough to her right to let Donovan squeeze onto the bed alongside her. Her head was nestled against his shoulder, and she had one leg hooked over one of his to keep him from falling off. The head of the bed was cranked halfway up and they were watching a travelogue about Tanzania when the door flew open.

Deputy Chief Inspector Pilcrow straightened his jacket and strode into the room, clearing his throat into his hand as a way of announcing his arrival.

Moskowitz came through the door behind him, flashing Donovan a palms-up "What could I do?" look.

"Don't get up," Pilcrow said as Donovan lurched toward unwrapping himself from his wife.

Donovan sank back down against the pillow. "Deputy Chief," he said, resigning himself to his fate.

"Good morning, Bill. Hello, Marcy."

"Hi," she said flatly.

"Boy, you're really coming along. How long will it be now?"

"Two or three weeks," she replied.

"And it's a boy, I hear. That's great. Congratulations to you both."

He extended his hand for both to shake but pulled it back when he saw the array of IV lines sprouting from Marcy's free arm. Instead, he grasped Donovan's left hand and gave it a mushy squeeze.

"What's up, Paul?" Donovan asked, although he knew quite well what it was. Pilcrow only made personal appearances to deliver bad news.

"I'm afraid I'm going to have to cancel your leave."

Marcy squeezed her eyes shut and looked away.

"This is about the two murders on Fifth Avenue?" Donovan asked.

"It is."

"What about these two killings is important enough to get you up here in person?"

"You know that they're related?" Pilcrow said.

"It seemed that way as of last night," Donovan replied.

"Well, they definitely are. We've gotten a message. Sergeant Moskowitz can give you all the details, but basically, at seven-twenty-seven this morning the Midtown Merchants Association—"

"The sort of chamber of commerce for all these swanky stores along Fifth Avenue."

"Correct. It received an anonymous note that took credit for the two killings and threatened a continuing campaign of murder that would be sure to destroy the Christmas shopping season."

"How much does he want?" Donovan asked.

"Ten…million…dollars," Pilcrow said, spacing the words out to lend weight to them.

"Is that a lot these days?"

"It's enough to get your leave canceled. The mayor wants this madman caught ASAP."

"I saw the mayor last night and he didn't say anything," Donovan said.

"You mean looking up at you from the sidewalk where you threw him?" Pilcrow replied.

At that point, Marcy looked back in Pilcrow's direction, her eyes blazing. She was about to speak when Donovan beat her to it. "My wife is expecting our first and maybe only child. She needs me by her side. I worked hard for this leave of absence...this *partial* leave, during which I still get daily briefings on active cases."

"I understand that," Pilcrow said.

"And ten million dollars doesn't seem like that much for an association made up of stores that pay a hundred grand a month each in rent. Why don't they just pay it?"

"They will if need be."

"Frankly, Paul, I don't see why I should do anything that would hurt my wife and child just to save the bottom lines of—"

"The Midtown Merchants Association."

"—a bunch of multimillionaires who don't need the extra dough," Donovan argued, pulling his arm out from around his wife and sitting up on the side of the bed. "And what about you? You're an African-American with three generations in Harlem. How much do you really care if E & J Tuttle makes a few million less this fiscal year? That store isn't even owned by an American, let alone a New Yorker. It's owned by a billionaire Japanese businessman."

"How do you know that? I haven't seen that in the papers."

Donovan shrugged. "I plugged in my laptop in the middle of the night and poked around the Internet. Something is bothering me about these murders."

"You got that off the Internet?"

"Yeah. It's not the be-all and end-all, but it's a good research tool."

"I thought you didn't care about the Midtown Merchants Association," Pilcrow said.

"I don't. It's the puzzle that intrigues me."

"Well, the mayor and the commissioner, your old pals *and protectors*"—he spit out the last two words—"care about the Midtown Merchants Association. And that means I care. Now you care as well. I'm sorry this is eating into your personal time, Captain, but I'm making it official. Your leave is canceled."

With that, Pilcrow turned and stalked out of the room. Furious, Donovan scrambled off the bed to go after him, but found himself caught in Brian Moskowitz's brawny arms.

"It ain't worth it, Boss," Mosko said, holding Donovan back.

"Yes, it is. Getting fired. Sued. Thrown in jail. It's worth every bit I would have to pay."

"You're becoming a daddy. You can't go around punching out superior officers."

Donovan relaxed, and Mosko let him go. "Maybe not, but it sure would feel good to throw one more right cross before I get too old and lose the ability forever," Donovan said.

"So you're going back to work?" Marcy asked.

"You heard the man," Mosko replied.

"I am and I'm not," Donovan said. "He can put me back on the job, but he can't tell me how to do the job."

"What do you mean?" Marcy asked.

"I can conduct this investigation from right here," he said, patting her bedside.

"How can you do that?"

"I'll be here when I'm not on the job," Donovan said. "When I'm on the job, I'll most likely be just a few blocks away. This is Fifth Avenue Medical Center, I mean."

"You can do that?"

He nodded. "Call me on the cell phone if you need me and I'll run right back. I'll only go back to the apartment when I absolutely have to."

"Such as to take showers," she said.

"Campagna will let me use the residents' quarters for that, I suspect," Donovan replied.

"I love you," Marcy said, reaching out for him.

He leaned over and kissed her on the lips. "I love you, too."

Mosko tapped his foot on the floor.

"But don't get fired over me," Marcy added.

"It's not just you."

"Over Daniel and me."

"He can't just fire me. He would have done it long ago if it were that easy."

"I hope you're right," Marcy said.

Donovan sat down in his recliner and gestured for Moskowitz to pull up a chair.

"The man wants me to work," Donovan said. "Let's work. What have you got?" he asked.

Mosko said, "You have a meeting in half an hour with the Midtown Merchants Association."

"Is this necessary?" Donovan said.

"What do you think?"

"Of course it isn't. They'll just tell me the same thing Pilcrow told me: 'Please, Captain Donovan, save our bottom lines. Stop this grinch before he ruins Christmas.'"

Marcy smiled.

"They do have the ransom note," Mosko said.

"They didn't make you a copy?"

"They want to make a presentation of it, I guess."

"Oh, God, this is going to be worse than I thought. They'll glad-hand me and offer all the help in the world. But they'll make it clear they contribute millions to the city's economy and, if my luck runs true to form, to the mayor's soft-money fund as well."

"There could be a little pressure." Mosko smiled.

"I should have just decked Pilcrow and taken my chances," Donovan said.

"I don't know how it was in the neighborhood you grew up in," Mosko replied, "but in Canarsie it ain't a good idea to beat up deputy chief inspectors."

"As attractive a proposition as that may be," Marcy said.

"Easy for you to say, having done it," Donovan noted.

It was about two years earlier that Marcy had kung-fued Pilcrow onto his ass in order to prevent his interfering with Donovan while the captain was hot on the trail of a killer. She had claimed—successfully, she thought—that it was an accident. But since that event Pilcrow's dislike of her—stemming from her half-Jewish parentage—had turned to out-and-out hatred.

"Where's this meeting taking place?" Donovan asked.

"At the Wolf studios in Rockefeller Center," Mosko replied.

"Why there?"

"Your friend Duke? He's in on this, too."

"How so?"

"It seems he's on the board of the Midtown Merchants Association and has volunteered to help them catch the grinch."

Donovan grumbled, "Standing foursquare in the middle of Fifth Avenue, no doubt, shaking a fist at the heavens and defying the killer to come and duke it out with him. Same as he did in the Afghan war."

"Exactly who are we maligning now?" Marcy asked.

"Paul Duke," Donovan said.

"Oh, he's *cute*."

"He's cute on television. They make him up to look like a million bucks. In person he's just another guy."

"William," she said with a smile, "I believe you're jealous."

"I am not," Donovan insisted.

"And I did meet him. Remember that last time you appeared as an authority on police procedure? During the second O.J. trial? I was in the studio with you."

"Oh, that time. I remember now."

"Paul came into the greenroom. I'm sure he was flirting with me."

"Well, you're a mother-to-be and in no position to be

flirted with by TV stars,'' Donovan snapped. ''Besides, he's my friend.''

''Your friend whose cottoning up to you last night seems suspicious given today's turn of events,'' Mosko said.

''It was suspicious then.''

''You didn't tell me you saw Paul Duke last night.''

''I figured why trouble you?''

''Thank you very much.''

''He showed up, limousine and all, asking questions about the murder weapon.'' Donovan turned to his assistant and asked, ''Was Seybold killed by the same gun as Melmer, by the way?''

Mosko nodded. ''The results came in late last night. It was a Kammacher Stedman. The slugs matched.''

''Yesterday Duke seemed nervous about the possibility of being shot through the window of his limousine, although he denied it. Today he wants to be the spokesman for the murder investigation. What do you think gives?''

''I don't hobnob with celebrities,'' Mosko said. ''You figure him out.''

''Something's wrong,'' Donovan replied. ''The man is afraid of something and is dealing with it by snuggling close to the cop on the beat.''

Marcy shrugged. ''That shows a basic intelligence at work.''

''And of course the ransom note will be featured prominently on his newscast, if it hasn't been already.''

''It hasn't,'' Mosko said. ''I asked.''

Donovan stood and straightened his pants. ''When did you say we have to be there?''

''It would be twenty-five minutes now,'' Mosko replied, checking his watch.

''What's the weather like?'' Donovan walked to the window to see. He opened the blinds to reveal another brilliantly sunny day, crisp and very Decembery, falling over Central Park. The smoke from dozens of furnaces made cottony lines in the sky over Central Park West, on the other side of the park.

"Cold but not too bad. We can walk. Look; there's more news for you to chew on en route."

"Such as?"

"We got prints off that water glass you stole from Princess Anna's room and ran them through the NCIC and Interpol computers." Moskowitz read from a window on his notebook computer. "The lady's clean in the States."

"But in Europe—"

Mosko smiled while saying, "Princess Anna reveals herself to be Anna Fritsch, shoplifter and check kiter extraordinaire."

Donovan brightened, his face taking on a glow not unlike that on a fox who has just spotted a hare. "So, Melmer's Black Forest cookie has a past," he said.

"And there's more. Does her real name, Fritsch, ring a bell?"

Donovan thought for a moment, looking at Marcy, who shrugged, and then staring out the window. "No...yes, it does, but it's a long-ago and faraway bell."

"Think 1968," Mosko said.

"My favorite year," Donovan grumbled. "Fritsch. Yes...the Fritsch-Haegler gang. Those bombings of American-owned businesses in Stuttgart and Frankfurt."

"Stuttgart and Düsseldorf," Mosko corrected.

"Anna wasn't even born yet in 1968."

"No, but her mother was," Mosko said triumphantly.

Donovan brightened even more. "Kirsten Fritsch," he said. "The American-raised woman who led an adjunct of the Bader-Meinhoff gang. They did antiwar bombings and other stuff in Germany during the Vietnam era. She must be my age, if not older. I thought she was in jail for having blown up a GI."

"She was," Mosko verified. "She was in the West

German lockup at Karlsruhe. That's where she gave birth to a baby girl. The year was 1971."

"Princess Anna."

"Yep. Mom got out of the slammer in 1979 and promptly dropped out of sight. No sign of her. No record of who the father was. Nothing in the record about the daughter until she scored her first shoplifting bust. That was in Berlin—West Berlin, then—in 1984."

"When she was thirteen. Whatta girl."

"Like mom, like daughter," Mosko replied.

"Bearing children under adverse circumstances also seems to be a familial trait," Donovan said. "Where's Mom now?"

"I got no idea."

"And where's Moll Flanders?"

"Who?" Mosko asked.

"What, they don't carry *Masterpiece Theatre* in Brooklyn?" Donovan asked.

"We got laws against the classics. Except maybe classics like professional wrestling and *Married with Children*."

"Never mind. Presenting culture to you is like trying to teach a monkey to play the oboe."

"Hire a lawyer and sue me," Mosko said.

Donovan asked, "Where's Princess Anna?"

Moskowitz shrugged. "You saw her last."

"Let's go hunting," Donovan said.

THE WOLF TV studios were designed specifically to be a tourist attraction, with on-air personnel sitting in front of gigantic windows against which the noses of tourists were perpetually pressed. Overlooking the skating rink itself, the centerpiece of Rockefeller Center, the spanking new WTV studios were so surrounded by glass and gawkers as to resemble a fishbowl, a high-tech one awash in blinking lights and flashing monitors. Donovan always felt a little vulnerable in it, as if being on national TV didn't make you feel naked enough by itself.

With Moskowitz by his side, he followed the production assistant who met them at the security door. They walked through *The Morning Show* set—a collection of pastel brown-and-blue chairs and sofas set off by maple desks and coffee tables, augmented by several high-tech pedestals bearing monitors—which was empty following the day's broadcast. They wound their way through the production facilities and editing suites to an elevator—also glass and overlooking the skating rink—that rose through the skin of the building to the third-floor executive offices. Eventually they were shown into a large conference room dominated by a crescent-shaped maple table at which sat Paul Duke and a woman.

She was fiftyish and very expensively dressed in a grey Bardosi suit and silk blouse, the same woman Donovan had seen helping officiate at the tree-lighting ceremony the night before. A contrasting silk scarf rode wrinkle patrol around the neck, which supported a once-killer face grown a bit gaunt and predatory with age. But she had auburn hair that, for the most part, hid the grey roots, and large brown eyes that roamed over Donovan; admiringly, he thought, despite his inappropriate jeans and suede jacket. Duke introduced her as Claudia Hummitz, executive director of the Midtown Merchants Association.

"I'm sorry to take you away from your wife," she said, adding, "figuratively speaking, of course."

He nodded. "Sorry I'm not dressed."

"Oh, don't worry about that. We just want to get this terrible business cleared up."

"Me, too."

"Captain, I can't stress too much what this tragedy is doing to business on Fifth Avenue. Did you notice how much thinner the crowds are today than they were a week ago?"

He hadn't. "I don't know how to measure that," he said.

"We do. We have a laser people-counter mounted on the corner of Fifty-third Street. Foot traffic is down twenty-five percent from last Friday."

"That was the day after Thanksgiving, the busiest shopping day of the year," Donovan said.

"Even allowing for a certain falloff, today's crowds are less. Everyone is afraid of being murdered."

"Not so long ago a madman of my acquaintance thought he could wreck a Broadway show by killing people in the theater. Attendance skyrocketed."

"That was Times Square," Hummitz sniffed, "not Fifth Avenue."

"Well, maybe blood doesn't sell on Fifth Avenue during the holiday season," Donovan said. "People are in the mood for chocolate and stuffed bears—"

"And Christmas cupcakes," Mosko added.

"So, you called the mayor and the mayor called me."

"He is an honorary member of our board and a great supporter of midtown merchants."

"I know. When we got married he bought us two recliners and a bag of popcorn. Maybe the popcorn came from a corner deli, but I'm sure the recliners were straight out of Bloomingdale's. Not Fifth Avenue, but close enough."

She seemed surprised, but pleased, to hear that Donovan also knew the city's top official. From his point of view, it was helpful to register a protest, however slight, at having his head gone over.

"Can you help us?" she pleaded.

"Let's see the note."

She pushed a maroon folder across the table. He opened it and found himself looking at a single plain sheet. In unremarkable type, it read:

GIVE TEN MILLION DOLLARS IN ONE-KARAT
GEM-GRADE DIAMONDS AND SAVE YOUR

HOLIDAY SEASON. WE WILL CONTACT ABOUT DELIVERY. BETRAY US OR CALL AUTHORITIES AND KILLINGS CONTINUE. NO ONE IS SAFE.

"Who's seen this?" Donovan asked.

"My secretary and me. I put it right in a folder afterward."

"And it came in when?"

"Actually, the call came in at seven-twenty-seven," she said.

"Call. What call?"

"You didn't mention a call," Mosko said.

"I didn't?" Hummitz replied. "I'm sorry. I got a telephone call at seven-twenty-seven this morning. The man said that he left an important message beneath the Rockefeller Center Christmas tree."

"Beneath the tree," Donovan said dully.

She nodded. "And that if I wanted to stop the killings on Fifth Avenue I should go get it."

"What was this like, a present? Wrapped in red-and-green paper and tied with a ribbon?"

She shook her head. "It was folded over and taped to the back side of a fence post. Have you seen the tree?"

Donovan nodded. "You might say that," he said.

"It's surrounded by a waist-high white picket fence," Duke explained, gesturing out the window.

Donovan went to look outside. A large crowd of tourists had already surrounded the tree, obscuring all but an occasional glimpse of the fence.

"He was right outside my window, Bill," Duke added, using the tone of voice anchormen employ for somber news. "I can look over my shoulder and see the tree."

"So what did he look like?" Donovan asked lightly.

"I didn't see him," Duke snapped. "I'm trying to work in there. Besides, the tree isn't that close. Only a few hundred yards." He left the impression that was quite near enough, thank you.

"Where's the tape?" Mosko asked.

"My secretary threw it out, I guess."

"We'll need to go get it," Donovan said. "There may be fingerprints on it. We'll also need your fingerprints and your secretary's."

"That will be fine," Hummitz replied. "We'll cooperate fully."

"You were at work at seven this morning?" Mosko asked.

"Every day."

"What hours do you guys work?"

"During the holidays it's seven in the morning to nine at night. But that's only for a month."

"What, will sales stop if you go home?" Mosko asked.

"No, but I like to give that impression," she said with a smile. "My members appreciate it."

Donovan sat back down at the conference table and asked, "What did the voice sound like?"

"It was changed. You know, like they do sometimes on *60 Minutes.*"

"Electronically altered. You go into one of those spy stores and you can buy gadgets that will do it."

"Yes, like that. I remember this interview with a man in the Federal Witness Protection Program. His voice had that electronic sound."

"I don't suppose you taped the phone call," Donovan said.

She shrugged. "Sorry."

"So you got this call. What did you do?"

"I ran down to get the message, of course."

"I'm trying to picture this. You're sitting at your desk at the start of your fourteen-hour day. You're having your first cup of coffee. You get a call about the murders."

"Yes, just like that."

"Who answered the phone?" Donovan asked.

"Why, my secretary, of course."

"What did the caller say?"

"He told her, 'Put me through to Claudia Hummitz. I have information about the killings.'"

"So he asked for you specifically."

She nodded. Then, seeing the quizzical look on Donovan's face, she asked, "Is there a problem with that?"

Mosko replied, "I'm a mad killer. I'm striking out at Fifth Avenue stores. I call the switchboard at Tiffany's."

Donovan nodded. "Logically, you would call the most famous store on Fifth Avenue. Or the Associated Press, which is who terrorists usually call to take credit for stuff. But he called you."

"I'm not getting your point," Hummitz said.

"He knows who you are," Duke interjected.

"Oh," she replied, apparently taken aback. She had been squeezing a piece of facial tissue into a tiny ball with the palm of her right hand. It was an ad hoc worry bead, and Donovan noticed three or four like it around the Filofax and soft leather bag that sat on the table in front of her.

"And he knows what the Midtown Merchants Association is," Donovan said.

Casting about for an explanation that would let her sleep nights, Hummitz said, "I was in *The Wall Street Journal* a few weeks ago. A story about the upcoming holiday season."

"I have a vision of this terrorist reading *The Wall Street Journal* while polishing his weapon," Donovan commented.

"Maybe he's a Republican," Mosko added.

"This is New York. Anything's possible. Did you say anything to him?"

"What, this morning? Why, I said, 'Who is this?'"

"And he replied?" Donovan asked.

"He said, 'This is the Mountain Brigade.'"

Donovan gave Duke a hard look. "Recognize that name?" the captain asked.

"No," Duke replied after a moment's consideration.

Donovan thought that maybe the man was trying to look like he had the faintest idea of the answer. "When you were standing there in on that mountain ridge, daring the Russians to fire at you, you never tripped over the name of one of the major guerrilla organizations fighting the Russians?"

Donovan swore that Duke went pale. *That won't look good on tomorrow's newscast,* Donovan thought.

"You mean...this madman is after *Paul?*" Hummitz exclaimed.

Donovan shook his head. "Not necessarily. After all, if he was after Paul, he knows where to find him."

Duke cleared his throat uncomfortably. Donovan sensed the man was thinking of that big "bulletproof" window that his back was nearly pressed up against two hours a day, five days a week. That glass was all that protected him from an assassin in the crowd outside.

"Bill's right," Duke said suddenly, his chest puffing up. "The involvement of a terrorist group—"

"Alleged involvement," Donovan corrected.

"—with supposed ties to Afghanistan has nothing to do with me. Except that maybe the captain will let me assist him in his investigation."

Hummitz smiled and gave the anchorman an admiring look, the way a woman will sometimes do when a man in her life is acting gallant. It was the look Nancy Reagan always used staring at her husband when he was president.

Moskowitz gave Donovan a distressed look. This was the look he used whenever an unavoidable complication entered a case.

"I may be able to lend my expertise to the matter," Duke said.

"The New York Police Department always appreciates the assistance of the public," Donovan replied flatly.

"What does this Mountain Brigade do, other than hate America?" Mosko asked.

"I don't know the specifics, but I can find out on the Internet. All I can tell you now is they operate in Afghanistan, Pakistan, and Malaysia, and supposedly are bankrolled by Iraq."

Moskowitz scowled out the window in the direction of the Christmas tree. "So they come here to wreck the holiday shopping season? Does that makes sense?"

"They're striking out at the heart of capitalism," Hummitz said.

"I suppose," Mosko replied.

"We'll check them out," Donovan said. "In the meantime, tell me if you saw anyone while you were retrieving that note. For one thing, how did you know which post to look behind?"

"He said, 'Near the Wolf TV studio where the people gather.'"

Duke went a shade paler.

"This killer knows where the Midtown Merchants Association is, and he knows where the TV station is," Donovan said. "He's an observant man."

"Everyone knows about those crowds outside my window," Duke said.

"I agree," Hummitz replied. "There was a large crowd even at eight in the morning, waving placards at that idiotic weatherman...."

Duke chortled. George Halloran was rumored to be a nasty drunk and not at all like his down-home, rib-tickling, homespun-humorist image. Seeing Duke's reaction to her calling Halloran idiotic made Donovan think there might be something to the rumors.

"Other than the weatherman, who did you see?"

"You mean in the crowd outside Paul's studio?"

Duke cringed.

"No, I mean around the tree."

"Just a security guard. And three Japanese tourists taking one another's pictures."

"Check out the guard," Donovan said to Mosko.

"You got it."

"See if he saw anyone loitering around the fence." To Hummitz, Donovan said, "What about in the crowd outside the studio? Did anyone stand out there? Were there any Santa's Angels people?"

"I just remember people with placards. 'Green Bay, Wisconsin,' or, 'Bozeman, Montana.' All those places, you know."

Donovan shook his head. "Anything west of the Hudson River is a mystery to me," he said. "I've heard stories about a place called California but can't verify that it exists."

"I've seen movies about it," Mosko added.

"No one stood out," Hummitz said.

"I could pull the tapes," Duke added helpfully.

"What tapes would those be?" Donovan asked.

"Why, the master shots made with camera two, of course. Those are the head-on shots they use when I read the news. They show everyone...all those hundreds of people, pressing their faces against the bulletproof glass behind me."

"Relax, Paul," Donovan said, reaching across the table and patting Duke on the hand. "We'll get the SOB before he can get you."

SEVEN

"TOMORROW I'M TALKING TO TEN MILLION PEOPLE AND THIS WRINKLE LOOKS LIKE THE GRAND FUCKING CANYON"

"THAT'S NOT what I mean," Duke replied quickly.

"Sure it is," Donovan said.

Duke pulled himself up—he had been slouching in his chair—and asked, "Can we talk about this privately?" Then he gave a sideways glance to Hummitz, who flashed a little smile back at him. Donovan felt that, despite the admiring look she gave him earlier, she was enjoying the embarrassment suffered by the man. He clearly was taking some body blows to his macho reputation.

Donovan decided to change the subject. "Pull the tapes and make dubs for me," he said. "All those shot this morning a half hour before and after nine o'clock."

"Do you really think the killer is on them?" Hummitz asked.

Donovan shrugged. "I'll say this about Fifth Avenue: There are a lot of videocameras around. Eventually our man will turn up on one."

"Let's hope it's on mine," Duke said.

"I'll need to get into your phone records," Donovan added. "Chances are that call you got was made locally and not on record anyplace, but maybe he called long-distance."

"Like from a mosque in Teaneck," Mosko said.

"Now, now."

"Or from a gyro-supply shop on Queens Boulevard."

"What's this about gyro supplies?" Duke asked. "Do you mean gyrocopters?"

"Gyro sandwiches," Donovan said. "They're an obsession of his." He nodded at his assistant, who replied by frowning.

"I'll gladly give you permission to access our phone records," Hummitz said. She checked her watch, then added, "If there's nothing else—"

"Sure, you can go," Donovan said. "And thanks for your help."

"Any time, Captain." She stood, straightened her suit, picked up her briefcase, and walked to the door. There she turned for a moment and asked, "Do you think I have anything to worry about from this man?"

"Who, him?" Donovan asked, nodding at Duke.

"No. I *know* about him." She shot the man another loaded glance. "I mean from the killer."

"No. He's after shoppers and tourists."

Duke also was on his feet but had gone to the window. There he looked out at the growing crowd, assessing, Donovan thought, the likelihood that one of those people was his would-be assassin.

Donovan added, "But just to be safe, I wouldn't spend too much time window-shopping. And I would be very careful about going into dark alleys with Santa's Angels guys."

"I don't go into dark alleys," she said.

"Anymore," Duke added, turning and smiling.

Her face turned hard, but she smiled and said, "Have a nice day, Paul; you, too, Captain," and walked out.

"Take it easy," Donovan replied.

The heavy conference-room door slid closed with a whoosh and a barely audible click. Mosko looked at the door, then at Duke, and asked, "Friend of yours?"

"We go back a long time," Duke said, still looking out the window.

"And into some dark alleys?" Donovan asked.

"Is this germane?"

"Probably not. But I'm curious."

Duke turned around, stuck his hands in his pants pockets, and said, "Can we talk alone, Bill? Nothing personal, Sergeant."

"No problem," Mosko replied. "I got things to do anyway." He got up from the table and hefted his shoulder bag.

Donovan said, "See if you can track down the little princess."

"I'll do that and a few other things," Mosko said, following Hummitz out the door by about a minute.

"Who's 'the little princess'?" Duke asked.

"A movie I'm renting."

Duke's brow furrowed, in either disbelief or astonishment.

"Hey, I'm becoming a dad," Donovan said. "I have to bone up on these things. How much do you know about diapers?"

"Not a damn thing."

"No kids? Not one little heir left behind on the road to fame and fortune?"

Duke returned to the conference table and knocked on it. "Just a string of broken hearts," he said. He sat back down and resumed slouching.

"Including Claudia Hummitz's?" Donovan asked.

"Why do you say that?"

"The two of you exchanged a few barbs."

"You can't break what you don't have," Duke said, adding a faint smile.

"It must have been a hell of an evening," Donovan replied.

"Three of them, actually, on consecutive Saturdays."

"Before or after you became the spokesman for the Midtown Merchants Association?"

"After. We were working late on a proposal last September and went out for a drink. One thing led to another."

"It's amazing how often it does," Donovan said.

"All was fine until I had too much to drink that third night and blabbed on about this woman I had had a fling with over the summer. Claudia freaked out on me. Strange. She's our age. But I guess not everyone who came up in the sixties is a sixties person, if you know what I mean."

Donovan knew what he meant.

"You should hang out with me some night," Duke continued. "No, you're married. Forgive me."

"Who do you want to talk about privately?" Donovan asked.

"You mean you're not really interested in what went on between Claudia and me?"

"Does it have anything to do with these murders?"

"Oh, God, I don't think so. There wasn't even a husband involved for me to outrage."

"I understand you've done quite a bit of that," Donovan said.

"You've been reading *People* again."

"I got my hair cut the other day and there it was, at the barbershop. Your pretty face right on the cover alongside Brad Pitt...whoever that is. How does it feel to be one of the fifty most beautiful people in America?"

"Tiring," Duke said with a sigh. "It gives you too much of a reputation to live up to."

"Not to mention tells all those outraged husbands where to find you," Donovan said.

"Yes!" Duke exclaimed. "And that's what I want to talk about."

Donovan's eyes widened. He said, "So there's some truth to the notion the killer I'm chasing is really out to get you?"

"That's what I'm worried about," Duke replied, looking down at his hands, which were clasped atop the table.

"Why didn't you tell me this yesterday?"

"I wasn't sure then."

"Now you are."

"I'm not the expert on homicide—you are. But it sure looks that way."

"What changed your mind?" Donovan asked.

Duke said, "The call Claudia got this morning. The one from the Mountain Brigade."

"At last count, Mountain Brigade was not an outraged husband."

"I'll get to that. Just hear me out."

Donovan folded his arms and stared at the man, imparting as much sympathy as was possible given what was being said.

Which was: "When I reported on the war in Afghanistan, I said a lot of things that infuriated the Russians."

"So did Dan Rather," Donovan replied.

"Dan Rather didn't wave his fist at their troops and defy them to shoot," Duke said.

"That was pretty gutsy of you," Donovan replied.

"I was drunk," Duke admitted. "It was like a frat-boy prank. I can't imagine why I did it."

Donovan said, "If Boris Yeltsin or whoever wanted to kill you, why wouldn't he just do it? In my opinion, governments that send assassins to kill their enemies don't involve themselves in a whole lot of rigmarole about store windows and Santa's Angels volunteers. The guy Stalin sent to kill Trotsky went straight for the target."

"But the CIA tried to poison Fidel Castro's mouthwash or something like that," Duke argued.

"Meaning?"

"Meaning that the Russians are trying to break me . . . to humiliate me, before killing me. The way I humiliated them."

Donovan shook his head. "Maybe I'm getting dense," he replied, "but I don't see how shooting shoppers through store windows is meant to humiliate you."

"They want me to sit there on national television looking over my shoulder waiting to be shot and having a nervous breakdown," Duke said, slamming his fists on the table before getting up and returning to the window.

"*Quos vult perdere Jupiter dementat,*" Donovan replied, in extraordinarily bad Latin.

"Huh?"

"'Who God wants to destroy he first makes crazy.'"

"You're a Latin scholar?"

Donovan shook his head. "I read it in the paper this morning. In a book review about the Dreyfus affair. When stuck in a hospital room for weeks on end you do a lot of reading."

Duke fell silent. Donovan stared at him for a moment. When no further words were coming, the captain said, "You were going to tell me about the outraged husbands."

Duke smiled bitterly. "You know my reputation."

"According to *People*—"

"They're polite," Duke interrupted. "You should read what the *Enquirer* says."

"I would sooner have my flesh ripped by demons," Donovan said, using his favorite phrase for dealing with intolerable situations. "According to *People,* your affairs with married women have caused enough scandal to keep you in the news without getting you fired."

Again Duke smiled bitterly.

"But your highly publicized liaison with...what's her name?"

"Sandra Block."

Donovan continued, "The young wife of the Hollywood studio head—"

"Martin Block," Duke reported.

"Got you a warning from your bosses at WTV—keep your private affairs private or lose your million-a-year job."

"It's a million-five," Duke said, expelling a huge gush of air.

"Congratulations," Donovan replied.

"A lot of good that money will do me if I'm dead. Do you see the problem now?"

"I see several problems," Donovan admitted. "One of them is keeping your pants on, a lesson I would have thought you had learned by now in this age of AIDS. And another is paranoia."

"What do you mean, paranoia?" Duke asked.

"I think you're overreacting," Donovan said.

"Look at those people out there, standing around the Christmas tree," Duke replied. "And here...look down.... Come and look down."

Donovan walked around the table, went to the window, and looked down. He could see part of the crowd outside the studio windows, which at that time of day offered only taped segments and other modest attractions. The star was off camera, upstairs in the conference room discussing his nervous breakdown.

"Nice crowd," Donovan said, hoping to sound agreeable.

"Any one of them could be my assassin."

Donovan patted his friend on the back. "You know, Paul, I've been shot at a couple of times in my life. Often enough so that my wife routinely tells me to avoid it, if possible, in the future."

"Smart woman," Duke said, still refusing to make eye contact.

"And each time it happened it came like *that*." Donovan clapped his hands. "There were no rococo warnings, no cryptic threatening phone calls...just 'Jeez, there goes the bullet; thank God it missed.' And then I would shoot back, and all of the time so far my aim has been better than his."

"You don't sit with your back to a window for two hours every morning while a madman is out to get you carrying a gun that can shoot through bulletproof glass," Duke said, at last turning around.

Donovan again looked out the window and straight down,

this time pressing his forehead against the glass to get a better glimpse of any potential assassins.

"I don't know, Paul. I see a lot of grandmas in that crowd."

"Two people were just shot to death by Santa's Angels volunteers," Duke said, his voice rising slightly.

"You have a point," Donovan acknowledged.

"Through bulletproof glass," Duke said. His voice had entered the plaintive register.

"Two points."

Donovan took the man and led him back to the table. The two of them sat on the edge of it, looking out at the gigantic tree.

"I can't take it anymore, Bill. My nerves are shot. I can barely concentrate on the TelePrompTer. All I can think about is a bullet crashing through that window and going into my back."

"Can't you draw the curtain or something?"

"Don't you think I thought of that? No, my producer won't let me. 'The people want to see you,' she says. 'And ratings go down when the folks at home can't see the crowds in Rockefeller Center in the background,' she says."

"Fire him," Donovan replied.

"Her. Are you nuts? Fire a producer? She could fire me. They'll never close the curtain or the set. I heard that Matt Lauer over at NBC got sick of having tourists gawk at him every morning while he worked and tried to get the set closed. But no-o-o. Do you watch *The Today Show?*"

"I can't stand commercials, so I listen to *Morning Edition* on National Public Radio," Donovan replied.

"Jesus…an intellectual cop. What's the world come to?"

"This is New York, my friend," Donovan said. "Even the schmucks have Ph.D.s. So who's trying to kill you—Boris Yeltsin or Martin Block?"

"Yeltsin may be, given this morning's phone call."

"How can I say this politely, Paul? You're delusional."

Duke ignored the remark. "As for jealous husbands, it's not Block I'm worried about so much as Valery Koslov." Duke jammed his hands back into his pockets.

Donovan's eyes rolled. Valery Mikelovich Koslov was a multimillionaire Russian émigré with links to a faction of the Russian mafia suspected of extorting millions of dollars out of legitimate Russian businessmen and sports figures who made it big in the United States. Koslov's nefarious business made the headlines when a Russian-born professional hockey player had his arms broken for failing to pay a reported $10,000 a month in protection money. Following indictment for extortion and manslaughter—an unrelated charge—Koslov dropped out of sight.

"The Brooklyn DA wants him to surrender, but word is he doesn't trust anyone in a uniform," Donovan said. "It seems that in the old Soviet Union the cops would occasionally create shortcuts for what passed for courts in those days. So maybe Koslov is hiding out in the wilds of Brooklyn someplace or maybe he's beat it back to Mother Russia."

"I'm trying to tell you, Koslov is gunning for me," Duke insisted. "That's what the bloodshed on Fifth Avenue has been about."

"Please, tell me you didn't sleep with Valery Koslov's wife," Donovan said.

Duke looked away. "I'm not as strong as I seem," he replied, sighing loudly, apparently too embarrassed to face the captain.

"Strong ain't the problem—horny is," Donovan said.

"Gina Koslov is a beautiful woman, Bill, hard to resist."

"How old is she?"

"Twenty-four."

"And him?"

"Fifty-something."

"So you not only slept with a Russian mobster's wife;

you slept with a Russian mobster's *young* and *beautiful* wife.''

Duke tossed his hands up.

''You're a dead man,'' Donovan commented.

Duke turned paler yet. After a second he said, ''Wow…just what I wanted to hear.''

''Paul, I have to be honest with you: I don't know how much of this to take seriously. Frankly, I doubt any foreign assassins are on your trail. Judging by recent terrorist acts in this country''—a group of Arabs had recently been convicted in Federal District Court downtown for conspiring to dynamite bridges and tunnels leading into Manhattan— ''their MO is blowing stuff up—and that doesn't include shooting holes in the windows of fancy Fifth Avenue stores.''

''Egyptian fundamentalists are killing tourists as a way of stopping tourism,'' Duke said. ''Why can't it happen here?''

''Because Fifth Avenue ain't the Valley of the Kings and Tiffany's ain't the Great Sphinx,'' Donovan replied. ''Here the terrorists put a car bomb in the basement of the World Trade Center. Maybe flame an airliner. I advise you to forget that drunken night in the mountains of Afghanistan. Nothing you did over there is coming back to haunt you.''

''I wish I had your confidence.''

''On the other hand, Valery Koslov has shown himself unimpressed with star power and willing to avenge himself.''

''That hockey player,'' Duke said.

''The same.''

''What should I do? I'm afraid if I keep sitting with my back to that studio window someone is going to put a bullet in me. But if I come out in the open and ask for police protection, I'm going to get fired. They made it perfectly clear after the Sandra Block episode—'One more fuckup and you're gone.' ''

"I know somebody I can ask about Koslov," the captain said, taking out a ballpoint pen and making a note on the back of a parking-garage receipt fished out of the depths of his back pocket. "If anyone can help me find him, this guy can."

"You're a pal," Duke replied.

Donovan scratched his chin and said, "Not to take the issue of firing too lightly, but aren't you rich? And at your level, don't they have to throw money at you to get rid of you? So they kick your horny little ass down the stairs. Don't they also have to toss another million or so along with you?"

Duke shook his head. "I'm tapped out. There's no golden parachute in my contract. I have huge expenses. And I know for a fact that I'm considered unhireable due to my legal problems."

"You're a good-looking guy who's popular with the women," Donovan argued. "Fox would hire you in a flash."

"Not true. I've already sniffed around there. I tell you, Bill, this job is my last chance. Lose this and I'm hosting an all-night cable show for peanuts—if I live long enough to tape the first installment, and you're telling me I probably won't."

"I'm telling you that while it's true you've made enemies, building up to an assassination by taking target practice on Fifth Avenue store windows is a pretty weird way of doing business."

"Which is another reason I'm appealing to you," Duke said. "You specialize in unusual crimes and exotic weapons."

"My main requirement of life is that it be interesting," Donovan replied.

"I'm begging you—tell me what to do."

"Hire a bodyguard. Can you afford it?"

"My chauffeur is also my bodyguard. He didn't want me to get out of the car to talk to you."

"Take his advice. No more wandering into crowds outside Fifth Avenue stores, even if you do happen to see me in them. No sitting next to the window in your car. Go straight from your limo to the studio to your home. If you need to eat, send out for Chinese. And no fooling around with strange women."

"They're the most fun," Duke protested, smiling. He was lightening up a bit, perhaps seeing a light at the end of the tunnel.

"Who'd you hear that from, Dick Morris? No one is safe now that supermarket tabloids are waiting to throw money at any hooker who manages to snag a celebrity. For God's sake, lay low and take cold showers until I catch whoever is behind these crimes."

"Koslov...I'm sure of it."

"We'll see," Donovan said. "In the meantime, I'm going to have a man in that crowd outside your studio window beginning at eight a.m. tomorrow."

Duke brightened a lot. "Can you do that? That's great."

"When you're on the air, he'll be outside the window. In fact, I'm going to have a lot of men outside a lot of store windows starting tomorrow."

"Wow. What a great story."

"Too bad you can't report it without getting yourself fired," Donovan said. "If you want me to help you, play ball. I'll give you an exclusive when I catch the bum. Now, can we go get those tapes?"

To Donovan, walking through a TV station after the day's business was done must be like walking through Mission Control right after a rocket launch. A lot of very expensive equipment blinked at no one. Few eyes remained to gape at the rows and rows of monitors, which in some places were stacked to the ceiling. Few feet remained to trip over the cables, some secured with duct tape, others strewn like yesterday's noodles across the grey industrial carpeting. Here and there a worker toiled in a corner. Following Duke through a maze of control rooms and postproduction facilities, Donovan noticed an old man adjusting color bars on a monitor and a raven-haired beauty fiddling with a drawing of Woody Woodpecker displayed on a video graphics machine. Neil Diamond sang "America" from a small candy-colored boom box.

"How'd you miss her?" Donovan stage-whispered to the star after they passed.

"What makes you think I did?"

"She didn't look up when you walked by."

"You don't miss much yourself, do you? She's saving herself for her husband," Duke muttered, his tone indicating he might be speaking of someone in the nineteenth century.

"Lucky man," Donovan said.

Duke led Donovan up a flight of metal steps, around a corner, and into Master Control, which looked down on *The Morning Show* set through a window that sprawled from one wall to another. A sickle-shaped hickory control panel sat below it, its back edge curling around six high-backed executive swivel chairs. Two of the latter were occupied: a woman of thirty or so years, with close-cropped red hair and an impish smile, sat next to the weatherman Duke had been maligning earlier. She had her hands outstretched to encompass three or four buttons and a small joystick.

"What is this, the bridge of the *Enterprise?*" Donovan asked, looking at the rows and rows of buttons, dials, and small monitors.

"This is Master Control," Duke said. "It's where they run my life from. There are six hundred and two buttons on this console. I sat here one morning and counted them."

"Do you know what they all do?"

"They all give me agita," Duke said. "Every single one. Hi, Rose. Hello, George."

The woman looked over and gave the two of them a smile. But George, being George Halloran, had a more complex reaction. Upon seeing Duke he scowled and the muscles in his thick neck tightened, causing a roll of pink skin to puff out. But when Donovan's face hove into view, Halloran popped into his public persona.

"Hi there," he said, jumping up and extending a plump hand. "George Halloran, and you are...I know you, don't I?"

"Bill Donovan, New York Police."

"Of course. It's been a year, hasn't it?"

"About that."

"What are you here for, the O.J. civil appeals verdict?"

Donovan shook his head. "I don't get scale for this appearance," he said. "I'm here to pick up a tape."

"This morning's master shot from camera two," Duke said to the woman. "I asked Rose to run a dub for me."

She reached under the console, where a soft brown leather carryall bag was propped against a stanchion. She plucked from it a black cassette and handed it to the captain.

"Here you go, Captain," she said.

"Thank you." He turned the tape over in his hand. It was without a label.

"Rose Waucqez," she announced, sticking out her hand. They shook.

"Good to meet you," Donovan said.

"I'm an assistant director of *The Morning Show*."

"She rules my life and does an admirable job," Duke said.

"You need occasional guidance," Donovan commented, in a friendly sort of way.

"This is true," Duke replied.

"If you're not here to tape a segment on the O.J. appeal, what are you up to?" Halloran asked.

"I'm investigating the murders on Fifth Avenue," Donovan said.

"And our camera two can help you?"

"I'm interested in seeing faces in crowds outside Fifth Avenue windows," Donovan said. "I'm curious to see who was there during this morning's show."

"Speaking as someone who did two stand-ups—I went outside and shot my weather sequences while standing in the crowd—there were a lot of regular folks from around the country. Grandmas and grandpas and Little Suzies from the Heartland." Halloran was on a roll and moved closer to Donovan. That was close enough for the captain to get a whiff of alcohol stench, the smell that oozes from the pores of a confirmed boozer. Reflexively Donovan stepped back, clumsily backing into a chair and making a noise that called attention to what he was doing.

The jolly weatherman facade stiffened, then crumbled like yesterday's graham cracker. "Of course," Halloran said, fumbling for words, "it was cold out there and Little Suzie's Boston terrier peed on my foot."

"Be grateful she doesn't like Saint Bernards," Donovan said agreeably.

"Yeah," Halloran muttered, returning to his seat and lowering his three-hundred-pound, six-foot-three frame into it.

"Can I keep this or do you need it back?" Donovan asked the assistant director.

"Keep it. We have tons of tapes. But do we have a news item on how your investigation is going?"

Duke shook his head. "In return for an eventual exclusive I promised him to keep it off the air for the time being."

Waucqez frowned slightly, then shrugged. "I don't suppose there's much of a story in your wanting to see who was in the crowd outside our window," she said.

"Not much of one, no," Donovan agreed.

"What kind of a gun was used in those killings?" Halloran asked. "Do you know?"

"Most likely a Kammacher Stedman nine-millimeter."

"Oh. The assassination handgun. That's a nice piece of work, that weapon." The weatherman brightened considerably upon hearing a line of conversation that interested him.

"You've heard of it?" Donovan asked, also interested.

"Last year I was with a bunch of guys who could talk about little else."

"Where was this?"

"In Montana. What town was that, honey?" He nudged Waucqez with an elbow.

"Moose Horn. A little burg about an hour from Bozeman," she replied. "Don't call me honey."

"The two of you went together?" Donovan asked.

She pretended to scratch her forehead so she could roll her eyes without Halloran seeing.

"I was doing a setup at the Moose Horn Billiards Tournament, and Rosie came along to manage the crew."

"Don't call me Rosie," she said.

"Oh, c'mon, darling; have a heart. You're dealing with a sensitive old man who just is lookin' for a friend." Halloran was back in his cornpone public persona and living it up. Duke was nonplussed by this turn of events, but Waucqez seemed irritated.

"Turn it off, George," she snarled.

He shrugged and leaned back in his chair. The springs groaned under his weight as he began to swivel from side to side.

"Was it easier to do the weather from Moose Horn, Montana, than it was from Fifth Avenue?" Donovan asked.

"Easier. No Little Suzie in Montana."

"But lotsa moose."

"I never saw so much as a hoofprint. At that time, the state was full of reporters doing Unabomber stories. The moose were hiding in the hills. Anyway, I took…Ms. Waucqez…along to protect me. She's a crack shot, you see."

"Crack shot?" Donovan asked.

"It was beginner's luck," Waucqez said.

"Where did you shoot?" Donovan asked, taking a quick look at Duke to see if he was reacting. He wasn't.

"The town was also hosting a firearms exposition," Waucqez said. "George wanted to drop in on it, because George is a redneck who likes to drink shooters and beer and talk guns with the rest of the extra-chromosomal former marines."

Halloran seemed pleased with that description. He fairly glowed.

"My dad used to hunt deer with a handgun," Waucqez said. "He showed me how. Of course, I would never kill anything."

"What did you shoot?" Donovan asked.

"Oh, just a run-of-the-mill Wilson Combat Automatic," she replied, with a shrug.

"Just whose gun was this?"

"One of the rednecks at the exposition. Ask *him*." She tossed her red hair in the direction of Halloran.

"Well?" Donovan asked.

"One of the boys. A dealer, I think. I don't know the man. But what do you care about Wilson automatics? You're looking for the legendary lost Kammacher Stedman."

"The one that's unaccounted for. Do you know who owns it? And is it in this country?"

"One hears rumors about a rich Montana survivalist. A guy who's somewhere to the right of Hitler. Would never set foot in New York City—thinks it's ground zero of the international conspiracy of Jewish bankers who want to take over America and destroy traditional values. You know what I mean?"

"Sure I do," Donovan replied, rocking back and forth. "My wife took me to one of their board meetings last year. Go on."

"In any event, I don't know his name. I suspect I don't want to know his name. But for you, I'll ask around."

"I'd appreciate that," Donovan said. He handed Halloran his card.

"I'll give you a call if I hear anything."

Waucqez asked, "Is that all, Captain? 'Cause if it is, I have this segment I'm blocking out for George." She swiveled back to the control panel.

"What on?" Donovan asked.

"The Utah Snow Festival," Halloran said. "I'm flying there tomorrow. I'm thinking of doing my weathercast from the ski lift."

"Have a ball," Donovan said, shaking the man's hand.

"I will. Nice meeting you, Captain. See you tomorrow, Paul."

"Yeah," Duke replied.

"Stay cool," Waucqez said over her shoulder.

"I'll try," Donovan responded.

She added, "Paul...if you're on your way out, stop in and see June first. She wants to talk to you."

Duke said, "OK," but Donovan saw him grimace.

As they were walking out, the captain said, "That would be June Lake?"

"Regrettably," Duke replied, leading the way back down the stairs and through the studio.

"*People* says you two are—"

"No," Duke said sharply. "My coanchor and I are *not* involved."

Donovan, surprised by the strength of Duke's reply, said, "That was what we in the cop trade call an emphatic response."

Duke tossed up his hands and replied, "This is an old story. She's always been after me. I want to say to her, 'What is it about no that you don't understand?'"

"But being polite—and politically correct—you don't," Donovan said.

With Duke walking faster than usual, they reached that point where a corridor led straight to the exit. Through the glass panes on the door Donovan could see a handful of fans gathered outside. Beyond them, Duke's white limo idled by the curb. Moskowitz lurked just inside the door, talking on the phone.

"What about you and Rose?" Donovan asked Duke.

"Never! You must be nuts."

"Why? She's as cute as a button. I would think you'd flip for her."

"The woman is a director," Duke said. "Never sleep with one of those."

"Why not?"

"She has the power of life and death over me. See this wrinkle?"

He pressed a fingertip against a small crow's-foot on the side of his right eye.

"I see it," Donovan replied.

"If I get her mad at me, tomorrow morning I'm talking to ten million people and this wrinkle looks like the Grand fucking Canyon. You got it?"

Donovan got it.

"Directors can do that to you. It's better to stay away. But you're right; she *is* adorable. And *very* smart. I wish her well in love and life. Let's talk tomorrow, Bill. I have to go and see if June wants what I think she does."

"From what I can see of your life, there's only one thing that could be," Donovan said.

"That's the *last* thing that will happen," Duke replied. "Though it's not for lack of trying on her part. I'm not interested."

"On the other hand," Donovan said, "this *is* a TV studio. Maybe she just wants you to go out on a shoot with her."

Duke offered a mocking laugh. "On location? June Lake, the Heartland princess, set foot outside the carpeted studio? Actually go out on location with a camera crew and risk breaking a nail? My friend, June Lake has *never* gone on a shoot. She does everything in the studio, where expert camera work can make sure that the famous perkiness looks the same on Tuesday as it did on Monday.''

"I'm sorry I asked," Donovan said.

When Duke had gone back into the studio, Moskowitz came over, storing his phone in his pocket as he walked.

"News?" Donovan asked.

"Guess who we found?" his assistant replied.

EIGHT

A VIKING WARRIOR WHO RECITES POETRY, THAT'S WHO

THE WINDOW TRUCK was getting to be a familiar sight on Fifth. Au Bon Pane, the company that supplied most of the glass panels to avenue merchants, had again parked its flatbed at the curb in front of a famous store. Atop the truck, six tinted glass panels were held not quite vertically, in such a way as to resemble a very narrow (but extraordinarily deep) church spire.

"Donuts and biscuits," Donovan said, looking at it solemnly.

"Say again?" Mosko replied.

"My dad's little Catholic joke. His way of saying, 'Dominus vobiscum.'"

"What's that?"

"I think it means 'the Lord be with you.' But since I haven't set foot in a Catholic church since 1962, you'll have to ask your old Irish mom. Doesn't that collection of glass look like a church spire?"

"Yeah. Our Lady of the Flat Trajectory. Can we go inside the store? We've got your chump."

E & J Tuttle was half-repaired. Four workmen were laying putty around the new bulletproof panel while two more installed a security camera. The blood had been cleaned up, and the myriad splinters of glass had been vacuumed from the floor. To change the mood, new and more cheerfully colored nighties decorated that part of the display window not taken up by Santa. Calming pastels had replaced smoldering reds and pinks. The price tags remained much the same, however.

"I wonder if sales dipped while they cleaned up the blood," Mosko said.

"Somehow I doubt it," Donovan replied. "I don't know what Hummitz and company are worried about. Death sells. Even on Fifth Avenue."

It was then that he spotted the chump he had come to meet. Martin Kimble was thirty-fiveish and thin, wearing an Armani suit and an expensive haircut. He smelled of cologne and perspiration, however, and his pale skin had gone pallid with fear. No doubt that was caused partly by having been on the lam for twenty-four hours and partly by the stoic-looking detective who watched, arms folded, as the young man sat in an upholstered chair and fidgeted.

"Is that Kimble?" Donovan asked from a score of paces away.

"That's him. We found him at his mom's house in Litchfield. That's in Connecticut."

"I know. I have a friend there."

"You? A West Side Democrat has a society friend in Litchfield?"

"This one drives a van for a living. He's a moving man; specializes in moving harps."

"Harps," Mosko replied.

"Delicate musical instruments. It takes a special skill to schlepp a harp. So, Kimble was at his mom's house? Is that where he lives?"

"Nope. He lives on Seventy-fifth and Second."

"He lives in the city but went home to spend the night with Mom in order to recover from a homicide in his store. This is fascinating. Introduce us."

After the introductions Donovan said, "Store manager, eh?"

"Harvard MBA," the man replied, summoning up a credential in an effort to compose himself.

"It must be a big deal, being manager of a top Fifth Avenue store."

"I would say so, yes."

Donovan said, "You know, Mr. Kimble, I figure I go into five stores a week."

"Five stores."

"So I would say that, in my life, I have been into—let's see—thirteen thousand, seven hundred and eighty stores. Not counting a few unpleasant afternoons at the Garden State Mall and a positively disastrous two hours with a young nephew at Chuck E. Cheese."

Kimble was smart enough to sense that a punch line, perhaps a nasty one, was coming. He tensed up.

"In all that time, I think I've talked to three store managers. And you know what? In each case there was a body laying there and I was investigating a homicide."

"I'm not sure what you're getting at," Kimble said cautiously.

"I'm getting at the fact that a big shot Fifth Avenue store manager with a Harvard MBA doesn't talk to just any customer. Maybe he talks to a big shot customer when he's alive and the homicide cop who's mopping up after the guy is shot dead."

Kimble shifted his weight nervously from foot to foot.

"What the hell were Seybold and you talking about?" Donovan asked. "And don't tell me you were offering to gift-wrap that nightie he bought."

Kimble sighed. It was a big sigh of relief. He said, "This is because I went to call the home office."

Donovan imitated the man's sigh but did it better. "I'm a cop, Mr. Kimble, but I'm a New York cop. That means I'm open to any number of possibilities that, out in the sticks, would put you under immediate suspicion if not earn you a fast trip to the hoosegow. Do you know what I mean?"

Kimble shook his head.

"For example, I can understand—and forgive—a man who might want to talk to his therapist after witnessing a murder. Who might want to tell his boss that there's a big mess on the floor. Who might also want to consult an attorney before talking to a cop. Who might even want to have a few drinks."

Donovan gave Moskowitz a little smile.

That man said, "What the captain means is he ain't never heard of a grown man running home to talk to his mommy before answering a few simple questions from the police."

"Such as what you and Seybold were talking about," Donovan said.

Kimble sucked in his breath, then replied, "Actually, we were talking about that…nightie…as you call it. But you're quite correct that Terry wasn't just any customer."

"Now it's 'Terry,'" Donovan said.

Kimble nodded. "We knew each other quite well. It was Terry who brokered the sale of E & J Tuttle to Osamu Hirai."

Donovan smiled. "That being the Japanese billionaire I've heard about."

"Yes. I had to call his office to let them know what happened. Mr. Hirai doesn't like to hear bad news through the press."

"And how did he react?"

"Well, I didn't talk to him personally, of course. But the chief of his retail division handled the news well."

"And how did Mommy react?" Mosko asked.

Kimble looked around uncomfortably. The guest chair in which the detective kept him was placed next to a rack of baby dolls. Those nighties looked like they might have come from the Frederick's of Hollywood catalog were it not for the $700 price tags. In looking around to see if any employees could overhear the conversation, Kimble found himself staring into a C cup. It did nothing for what remained of his Harvard dignity.

"This is more complicated than you imagine," he said at last.

"Like I said, I'm a cop, but I'm also a New Yorker," Donovan replied. "Nothing is easy."

"Let's hear it," Mosko added.

Kimble sighed again. "Terry and I grew up together along with members of the Tuttle family."

"*This* Tuttle family?" Donovan asked. "As in, those who owned the chain of stores?"

"The same. It was a family enterprise, family and friends."

"The Tuttles owned it. The Kimbles and Seybolds worked for it."

"Correct."

"But the market took a bad turn and the family had to sell."

"The market wasn't that bad," Kimble said. "It was the Tuttle family that took a bad turn."

"Please explain."

"For generations, E & J Tuttle was handed down from father to son. Occasionally from father to daughter. But always to a family member."

"But no longer?" Donovan prompted.

"No longer. There was the problem of Tom."

"Tom?"

"Tom Tuttle. Uh, Thomas Hastings Tuttle."

"Who's that?"

"He was in line to inherit the presidency of the chain."

"Let me guess," Donovan said. "He moved to Vegas, supported himself by playing piano in a lounge, and married a stripper."

Kimble shook his head. "He would be better off were that true. Tom graduated from West Point and went into the Gulf War as a lieutenant. He was gassed—or whatever happened over there, poison or nerve gas or something else."

"I think it was a neurotoxin of some sort," Donovan said.

"Anyway, poor Tom had a breakdown, I guess you would call it. He dropped out. You know how, in the sixties, people would 'drop out' of the system?"

"I heard the expression," Donovan replied.

"The upshot is that he had some problems and the family no longer could count on him to run the company. So with no heir to assume the mantle of leadership it decided to take up Mr. Hirai's offer and sell out. It insisted, however, that they keep current management. Including me. And, as you know, Terry brokered the sale."

"And what of Tom?"

"We've lost touch with him. I know he wanted to be a novelist. The last I heard from him was a year ago. He was looking for a place in Alphabet City and planned to write a book."

"Does he have the money to support this habit?" Mosko asked.

"Not that I'm aware of. He went through his trust fund pretty quickly paying medical bills."

"And the family doesn't give him anything?" Donovan asked.

"They would if he would speak to them. But he cut off all contact after the sale went through to Hirai. Tom was pretty upset about that sale."

"Upset enough to make him kill his old friend Terry?" Donovan asked.

Kimble looked down into his hands. He was squeezing them until the knuckles went whiter than usual. But he kept silent.

"I think the man just answered you," Mosko said.

Kimble looked up and stated, "We're worried about him."

"Who's 'we'?" Donovan asked.

"My family and his. The Kimbles and the Tuttles. Yesterday when Terry was murdered, I called the home office—

the new one, in Tokyo, not the old one, in Providence. But then I went home to talk to the families.''

"You suspected that Tom might be the killer," Donovan said.

Kimble nodded.

"Did you see him outside that window?"

"No. I was talking to Terry about that negligee he bought. In our business you quickly learn to ignore the people looking in the window. They're like wallpaper…always there.''

"So you didn't see anyone?" Mosko asked.

Kimble sighed and said, "I did see the Viking. He was out there when the shots were fired."

"Viking?" Mosko asked, shaking his head. "What Viking?"

"He's talking about the guy who replaced Moondog," Donovan said.

"Moondog? Moondog?" Mosko turned from Donovan to Kimble and asked, "You got another chair? 'Cause sometimes in this business you gotta sit down."

"In my business, too," Kimble replied. But he didn't offer to get up or send for another chair.

Kimble said, "There's a man who, since March, has stood ten, twelve hours a day at the corner dressed as a Viking warrior reading poetry and panhandling. He's over six feet tall—without the Viking horns. Over seven feet with the horns and all. Rather hard to miss."

"And of course you know him," Mosko said to his boss.

"Nope. I just read the item in the *Times* mentioning him," Donovan replied.

"Is this guy homicidal?"

"He's a Viking. What do you expect he does, play checkers? Brian, I have no idea if the man is homicidal. He recites poetry…not his own. He's memorized what I suppose you would consider classics.… Poetry ain't my field."

"Glad to hear something isn't."

"And he collects coins from tourists who think it's cute to give quarters to poetry-reciting Vikings on Fifth Avenue. Nobody knows who he is, and to make sure of that he wears a kind of leather mask. And he never speaks."

"So who was Moondog?" Mosko asked.

"A blind composer of music who stood on the corner of Fifty-second and Sixth dressed as a Viking," Donovan said. "He died a few years ago, and when this new guy replaced him there was a hue and cry in certain quarters. True New Yorkers demand authenticity. So, Mr. Kimble, did Moondog Two look in the window?"

"I just caught a glimpse of him, but I think he was looking in the window."

"Maybe he was looking for an Xmas gift for the little lady," Mosko said.

Donovan said it was possible. "So he might have seen the shooter," the captain added.

"He might have been the shooter," Mosko said.

"Not at his height. Besides, it's hard to hide wearing Viking horns. Anyway, Mr. Kimble, let's get back to your old friend Tom."

"Oh, yes," Kimble replied, a bit disappointed that the diversion had ended.

"Do you know if he came out of the army with a special interest in weapons?"

Kimble shrugged. "Weapons I can't say. Death interested him, though."

"In what way?"

"He fancies himself a serious novelist. Wants to write literature. Do you know what I'm saying?"

Donovan knew.

"He has this fancy theory about death being the door to another reality. I can't connect with the logic."

"If anyone can, it will be the captain," Moskowitz said.

Donovan smiled. "Do you have a phone number for this guy Tuttle? Any idea how we can get in touch with him?"

Kimble fished a bit of paper from the pocket of his custom shirt. Torn off the end of a fancy envelope such as high-society invitations come in, it bore a number in the 212 area code.

Donovan took the paper and looked at it. "This in Alphabet City, isn't it?" Donovan said.

"I think so," Kimble replied.

Mosko looked over his boss's shoulder and said, "How do you know that the six-seven-three exchange is on the Lower East Side? It's a numerical exchange and not a letter code like Murray Hill eight or something."

"I guess you never ordered take-out from Sammy's Famous Roumanian Restaurant," Donovan said.

"Do they have a take-out menu?"

"They do for me."

Kimble stood, straightened his suit jacket, looked down at the workman who was trying to scrub the chalk outline off the floor, and said, "Terry was a good man. He was good people. And his fiancée is a wonderful girl. I feel so sorry for her. If it turned out that Tom is responsible..."

Donovan asked, "Does the name Erik Melmer mean anything to you?"

"No. I don't think so."

"He was the man killed last week in Sarkana."

"Was that the name? I'm sorry; I didn't pay that much attention. I thought it was a once-in-a-lifetime tragedy." Kimble laughed bitterly.

"He was CEO of Melmer International in Düsseldorf. Is there any chance that Terry knew him?"

"I doubt it," Kimble replied. "Terry didn't hobnob with CEOs as a rule. He was the manager of a suburban stock-brokerage office, not a Wall Street investment-banking firm. He only got involved in the Tuttle sale because of his family ties."

"Thanks for your cooperation, Mr. Kimble," Donovan said. "We'll be in touch."

WHEN THEY WERE out on the sidewalk again, Donovan
looked up and down Fifth Avenue. He couldn't be sure, but
it seemed that the number of shoppers was indeed down, as
Hummitz had said. In the thick of the normal holiday season, the Fifth Avenue sidewalks between Rockefeller Center
and the Plaza were shoulder-to-shoulder. It could easily take
three minutes to walk a block. (Normal walking time, as
Donovan reckoned it on an average city street, was a shade
under a minute a block.) But today not only could you take
a step without bumping into a package-laden tourist, but you
could also hear the bells of the Salvation Army volunteers
that much louder. Fewer fur coats were out there to absorb
sounds.

Moondog II also was gone. He was nowhere near his
familiar corner. The words of Tennyson and Keats and the
clinking of coins in his old brass pot were not heard that
morning.

Donovan bought a bag of chestnuts from a street vendor
and cracked one open, tossed the shell into the gutter, and
nibbled at the meat while looking to see which of those
holiday shoppers might be a killer. Moskowitz leaned
against a no parking sign, answering a long cell phone call
from headquarters.

When the sergeant was done he waved the phone at the
facade of E & J Tuttle.

"What's the story?" Donovan asked.

"Our underwear heir has a rap sheet, as you suggested."

"How long?"

"Ever been in a traffic jam on the Long Island Express-
way?" Mosko asked.

"That bad, huh? OK, let's hear it."

"Thomas Hastings Tuttle, age thirty-two. Born Newport,
Rhode Island. Graduated West Point. Commissioned in U.S.
Army. Served in Gulf War as leader of a sniper group."

Moskowitz interrupted the narration with a pause that was
more pregnant than Marcy could ever be.

"Go on," Donovan said.

"Got medical discharge. Treated at Veterans Administration facilities in Portland, Cleveland, and Hartford. Alleged to be suffering from Gulf War Syndrome. Arrested for assault, aggravated assault, and attempted murder."

"What happened with that last one?"

"It was plea-bargained down to simple assault after he paid the victim's medical bills. Tuttle also was picked up for vandalism, malicious mischief, vagrancy, and destruction of property. He became a one-man wrecking crew notorious for busting up neighborhood bars."

"How did I miss running into this guy?" Donovan asked.

"My guess is that he started drinking after you stopped," Mosko said.

"That would do it."

"Also, you were a West Sider. Tuttle was a menace mainly on the Lower East Side. One of his arrests was for trying to bust up the Shining Path Poets Cafe. They wouldn't let him read the stuff he wrote."

"I thought they encouraged violent revolutionary acts at that joint," Donovan said.

"They probably like their little *banditos* to take their chaos elsewhere," Mosko replied. "Anyway, that's it for Señor Tuttle."

"What's his current status with the law?"

"He has a parole officer—more fallout from the attempted murder—but failed to report last week."

"What day?" Donovan asked.

"Friday...the day the killings started."

"We need to talk to Tuttle. Do we have a current address?"

"Yeah, one that matches the phone number Kimble gave you. But the parole officer went there yesterday and the guy had cleared out."

"Cleared out?"

"Yeah, scooped up his futon, his CDs, his typewriter—"

"Typewriter?" Donovan asked.

"So the man is a troglodyte. The point is he took off, leaving no forwarding address."

"Find the parole officer," Donovan said. "Have him meet us this afternoon at the last-known address. Where is it, by the way?"

"On Avenue C, down the block from the Shining Path Poets Cafe," Mosko said.

"We'll go there."

Donovan handed Moskowitz another chestnut and cracked open one more for himself. The captain looked up and down the block again, hoping to spot Moondog II. But the Viking was as missing as Tuttle.

"That was a long call you took a moment ago," Donovan said. "Was there anything else?"

"Yeah. I finally got more from Melmer's secretary as to what he was doing in New York eighteen weeks ago."

"Which was?"

"Ever hear of the Diagnostic Equipment Manufacturers Association?" Mosko asked.

Donovan hadn't.

"They had their summer convention here last July, August. Melmer's company had a booth."

"In other words, he was here to sell contrast media," Donovan said.

Mosko nodded. "Medical diagnostic equipment is his main market. But last week Melmer and his fiancée were in New York strictly on personal business—buying holiday gifts and getting ready for their marriage. And Melmer's company isn't publicly traded. He didn't know Seybold. I had the office ask."

"Short of the possibility that they met at the sequined-bra counter at Bloomingdale's, I guess the Melmer-Seybold connection never existed," Donovan said.

"I guess not."

"Did Anna Fritsch ever call us like I left a message for her to do?"

Mosko shook his head.

"Call her apartment and make an appointment for me to talk to her," Donovan ordered.

"Why? Seybold and Melmer weren't connected. There's nothing she can tell you."

"Maybe I want to know what Eurotrash royalty is like," Donovan said. "I'm telling you, there's something wrong with her, and I want to know what it is."

"You just want some inside dope on her mom," Mosko replied. "This has something to do with those three years in the sixties that you won't talk about."

Donovan frowned and made a dismissing sort of motion with one hand.

"You're beating a dead horse, Boss," Mosko said.

"It's my bat," Donovan replied. "In the meantime, while you set up an appointment with her for me, let's go check out Tuttle's East Village pad."

"Do you want to do Alphabet City and Trump Plaza in the same day?" Mosko asked.

Donovan nodded. "One before and one after lunch," he said.

"Where would you like to eat?" Mosko asked.

NINE

ONE CHE BURGER TO GO, WITH FRIES

THE BATHTUB was an old clawfoot model, one leg of which was duct-taped to the tub to keep it from falling off. Rust stains ran down the sides of the tub, mixing with soap scum to form a reddish grey abstract painting that mirrored a similar artwork on the ancient linoleum floor. The bathtub was a freestanding one, sitting not quite in the middle of the kitchen just to the left of the apartment door and across from a four-burner gas stove that dated to World War II.

Two tin pots sat atop it, a small one to heat water for coffee and a larger one whose most frequent use was betrayed by its contents: petrified glop that a few weeks earlier had been macaroni and cheese. A small refrigerator was as ancient as the stove; its condenser was on top like an exposed engine of a Ford trimotor airplane. Donovan opened the door cautiously, and for good reason. The inside was filled with rotting vegetables and moldy bread. A jar of hot Russian mustard had been left open. The stench assaulted both Donovan's stomach and his eyes. He slammed the door shut.

"Having been gassed in the Gulf War, you would think that Tuttle would be more careful about the atmospherics," Donovan said.

"The guy didn't have a much better pantry," Mosko replied, examining the cabinet whose doors, stuck permanently open by too many years of repeated painting, swung above the stove. "A copy of the Sunday *Los Angeles Times* from last July, a moldy box of vanilla wafers, and, hey, look: two cans of vegetarian baked beans. Tuttle at least *thought* of eating healthy.''

''How much sodium?'' Donovan asked from across the room, where he was going through the mail.

''Five hundred and sixty milligrams a serving,'' Mosko replied, after examining the label.

''He ought to think again.''

''There's also half a bottle of Richard's Wild Irish Rose wine, the stuff alkies drink.''

''Check it,'' Donovan said.

''What for?''

''I never knew a drunk to leave liquor behind when making a getaway. Silverware, yes. Booze, never.''

Moskowitz uncapped the bottle and sniffed the contents. ''Oil of some kind,'' he said.

''Any idea what type?''

''I have to ask Bonaci to be sure, but I think it's the stuff you use to polish the stock of a fancy gun.''

''What kind of handgrip does the Kammacher Stedman have?'' Donovan asked.

''Walnut. I'll bring this with us.''

Donovan sat down at the folding card table that served to eat on, toyed with some cigarette burns in the vinyl top, and said, ''There's nothing in the mail except a sale flyer from Stern's, an overdue notice from the public library, and a notice from the Shining Path Poets Cafe.''

He handed his assistant the overdue notice. ''Tuttle absconded with a copy of the annotated *Finnegans Wake*,'' Donovan said. ''No wonder the poor man's deranged.''

''I'll check and see if heisting Joyce is an indictable offense,'' Moskowitz said.

Tuttle's parole officer, one Harold Armis, lingered by the door, looking embarrassed and awaiting the moment he would be called on the carpet. He was a sixtyish man with pallid skin and a small amount of black hair that was combed laterally across his otherwise bare scalp, creating the impression of a football gridiron. His silver wire-frame glasses were perched at the end of a skinny nose.

"So, Harold, where's our boy gone?" Donovan asked at last.

In relief, the man expelled a lungful of air. "I wish I could tell you, Captain," he said. "Frankly, I was feeling proud of myself for checking up on him after he missed only one weekly meeting with his parole officer."

"You're a conscientious man."

"Most POs have such heavy caseloads—you know, ever since the mayor ordered the arrest of everyone who panhandles too loudly or pees on trees in the park—that they don't check on someone until after he misses two or three meetings."

"Which brings me to my next question," Donovan said. "Why did you check up on Tuttle? I mean the guy sounds more or less like a registered fuckup with literary pretensions. I've run across a few in my life. One of them actually published books. Was it the attempted murder?"

"Tuttle was just like you said—most of the time," Armis replied. "He drank too much, maybe dropped a couple of pills—he liked painkillers, I'm pretty sure, though he denied using them—and once in a while got into a fight in a bar. So far this is nothing you would call Perry Mason over. But Tuttle was wound as tight as a drum. He was capable of snapping—the way he did when he tried to kill Mr. Harachi."

Donovan spun around to face Armis. "Since he tried to kill who?"

"Whom," Mosko said, sticking his head out of the trash-strewn living room.

"I'm talking about Tomio Harachi, the victim in Tuttle's attempted-manslaughter plea bargain."

"'Harachi' as in Japanese?" Donovan asked.

"You said it. A tourist in the city for a week. He dropped in at the Shining Path Poets Cafe after seeing an article about it in *New York* magazine. This was a night Tuttle was in there drunk, and not only drunk but in the process of being tossed out by the manager. You would expect under such circumstances that Tuttle would turn on the manager. No, he attacked Harachi, and out of nowhere, too. I mean the man was just sitting there eating his flan."

"There was no provocation?" Donovan asked.

"None whatsoever. Apparently, Tuttle hates the Japanese."

"When did this happen?"

"In February," Armis replied.

"That would be a month after the sale of E & J Tuttle to Hirai went through," Mosko said, appearing from out of the living room and announcing his arrival partly by kicking a Wendy's bag in front of him. Mosko flicked a bit of paper onto the table in front of Donovan. "That's a receipt from a theatrical costume shop in Times Square," he added. "Maybe Tuttle was trying to disguise himself as a normal person."

"He told me he was mad at his family and that it had something to do with the Japanese," Armis said.

"Did he give you the details?" Donovan asked.

"No. He gets mad when you press him too hard. And since, technically speaking, I'm his PO and not his psychiatrist, my only interest is in how well he's living up to the conditions of his parole."

"Which is not too good," Mosko said.

"That's right," Armis agreed.

Donovan stood, kicked the Wendy's bag back into the living room, and said, "Here's what I want you to do, Mr. Armis. Get a warrant for Tuttle's arrest on grounds that he broke parole."

"You got it," Armis replied, making a note on a piece of lined paper.

"Hopefully that will keep the press from finding out we

want to talk to him about the murders on Fifth Avenue,''
Donovan said.

"Do you really think that Tom gunned down those two
people I read about?"

"I would say he's a suspect. He has motive: He needs
money and he has a grudge against the Japanese, who
bought his family firm. I can't say if he had opportunity.
Certainly his whereabouts are unaccounted for at the times
of both killings. And God knows the man has the firearms
knowledge to have pulled this off. Tuttle is a suspect, sure
enough—"

"A damn good one," Mosko added.

"Yeah, but one thing I've learned is that the guy who
seems more obvious to have pulled the trigger is seldom the
one who really did it," Donovan said. "Tuttle is far from
being the only suspect. I don't want his name to get into
the papers and let the others think they're off the hook. Can
you help me with that?"

"I'll do my best," Armis replied. He folded the piece of
paper into his jacket pocket and edged toward the door. "If
you have no further need for me, I'll get on that warrant."

"You don't happen to know who owns Sarkana, do
you?" Donovan asked.

"You mean the jewelry store where the first murder took
place?" Armis asked.

"The same."

"I have no idea. I take care of all my jewelry needs on
Canal Street."

"Never mind," Donovan said, and waved as the man
slipped out the door and pushed past the several Hispanic
tenants who loitered out in the grimy hall, eavesdropping
on the police investigation that suddenly had cropped up in
their midst.

"I can't find anything else of use here, Boss," Mosko
said. "The guy lived like a pig. What connection this has
to literature is beyond me. But then, I mainly read the *Post*."

"Three years with me and the man hasn't learned," Donovan moaned. "Come on; let's go read some poetry."

The Shining Path Poets Cafe sat in the middle of a block off Avenue C, nestled between a small locksmith shop and an even smaller bodega, the window of which held a box of Tide, a box of Pampers, a six-pack of Corona beer, and a display of hex-removing candles. The latter were tall votive candles in transparent red or blue jars that were painted with images of Christ and the Virgin Mary as well as with symbols of Santeria, the Cuban Christian-African spiritual mix. Donovan liked folklore as well as colorful candles. He occasionally had bought one of the spice-scented hex-removing candles from an equally old bodega on Amsterdam Avenue and 107th Street and lit it in the kitchen to see if it would scare the cockroaches. Then Marcy had married him and hired an exterminator.

Still, Donovan ducked into the shop and came out with a red-and-yellow candle that smelled of lilacs even through the brown paper bag in which it lurked.

Moskowitz eyeballed the bag. "A fifth of Ripple to have with lunch?" he asked.

Donovan showed him the candle. "To burn in Marcy's hospital room to make sure the baby is OK," he said.

"Do you really think this stuff works?"

"You can't be too careful," Donovan replied.

He led the way into the cafe, which smelled of cigarettes, red wine, pastry, and cinnamon-scented coffee. Donovan breathed deeply, expelled a goodly volume of air, and said, "Takes me back to some sixties book parties."

"When were you ever at book parties?" Mosko asked.

"I have lots of literary friends. Such as—"

"That meshugah music critic who used to lurk around Times Square before it got respectable," Mosko said.

"I was thinking more of some old beat friends of mine. Early sixties, son. Before you were so much as a gleam in your mammy's eye."

"Among them Kirsten Fritsch?"

"I never met the lady...that I know of," Donovan said.

"I don't understand your interest in her," Mosko replied.

"My instincts are good and you know it. Trust me."

The cafe was empty save for a thin man of sixty-some years who was poring over a copy of *Wired* while sipping scented tea. Otherwise, the small round tables sat with their shakers of Mrs. Dash salt substitute, their Jamaican hot sauce, and their fishnet-covered candles undisturbed by patrons. It was morning. Donovan walked along a plain wall made of cheap tongue-and-groove pine boards that had been whitewashed and used as a bulletin board for management and customers to tack up whatever fancied them. Among the items: a contemporary reproduction of a sixties Che Guevara poster, a Puerto Rican flag and accompanying broadside advocating independence for the island, a movie poster for *The Pancho Villa Story*, pages from a World War I army ordnance manual, pages and pages of handwritten and typed poetry, and a still photograph of John Wayne from his movie *Rooster Cogburn*.

Mosko stared at the latter. "Am I missing something?" he asked.

Donovan tossed up his hands. "Perhaps it's symbolic of anarchy, which is the essence of revolution."

"And what does any of this have to do with poetry?"

At that point a woman came up dressed in tight, faded, worn-at-the-knees jeans with a black leotard and a canvas vest of the sort photographers sometimes wear. Those are the vests that sport many small pockets in which to keep handy items like film, coins, batteries, and, depending on the mileu of the photographer, bullets or cocaine. Perched precariously atop her curly black hair was a red beret.

She stuck out her hand. "You must be Rachel Baez," Donovan said, grasping it.

"Good to meet you, Captain. Sergeant Moskowitz."

"Hello...Rachel Baez," Moskowitz said, looking at her red beret with a faint smile on his lips.

"Your office said you'd be over. What can I do for you?"

"We want to talk about Tom Tuttle," Donovan said.

She rolled her eyes. "Oh, that loser. I had a feeling the cops would come for him for one fine day."

"Here we are," Donovan replied jauntily.

"Who did he kill? How *many* did he kill?"

"One, two, or none. Where can we find him?"

"Look under rocks," she replied.

"Ain't too many on Avenue C. Mainly garbage cans."

"Look under them. Did you try his apartment?"

"He split," Mosko said.

She shrugged. "The guy was always moving around. Probably to avoid bill collectors. Hey, is it true he used to be rich?"

"Yep. He still could be again, if he only let his family help him."

"He was running from them. Said they stifled him."

"Regardless, Tuttle was pretty mad when they sold the family business—the one he expected to inherit—to the Japanese."

"Tell me about it," Baez said. "That idiot nearly took the head off a Japanese customer one night. Got sent to Riker's Island for it, too. Funny."

"Why funny?" Donovan asked.

"'Cause we run an outreach program there. You know, poetry seminars for the prisoners."

"Revolutionary poetry," Mosko said.

"That's right," she replied.

"What the hell's revolutionary about poetry?"

Donovan held up his hand. "The explanation would be longer than you and I have time to hear," he said.

"You're right," she agreed.

"But it has something to do with raising your fist and trying to sound like Charles Manson," Donovan concluded.

"You're a tough man, Captain Donovan," Baez said. "If not entirely original."

"You're an interesting person, Rachel Baez," Mosko added.

"You should stay for a reading. There's one tonight. A guerrilla performance artist from Guatemala."

"What does he do?" Mosko asked.

"She."

"The sergeant doesn't want to know," Donovan said. "Look; I wonder if Tuttle left anything here. A guy who spends so much time in a club—plus moved in down the block to be near it—might leave behind a trace of his pitiful existence."

"That was very poetic of you, Captain," Baez replied. "He did, in fact, leave something behind. Something weird. Just yesterday morning, in fact. I wasn't here or I never would have let him in the door. Let me go get it for you."

The two policemen tapped their feet and looked at a menu while she slipped into a dark area, at the rear of the club, that served as an artists' mustering room. When Baez returned she carried an old canvas backpack with the stencil U.S. Army on it. A bit of horn peeked out from under the canvas flap. "You know what was so weird about this guy?" she asked.

"Beyond trying to destroy East Side bars and kill Japanese tourists?" Donovan asked.

"Yeah. He wanted like all the world depended on it to read his poetry here. And guess what it was?"

"Tennyson and Keats," Donovan said.

Her mouth fell open. "How could you possibly know that?" she asked.

"Is that a Viking helmet in that bag?" Donovan asked.

"Why, yes. Yes, it is. I told you the guy was weird. What he wanted this for I can't imagine." She pulled it out into the light. The Viking helmet looked like an old artillery shell onto which someone had glued cow's horns.

"Moondog?" Mosko asked. "Tuttle is Moondog?"

"Who's that?" Baez asked. "Not the blind composer who died a few years back."

Donovan shook his head. "The man who, since last March, has been imitating him, standing a few paces from the facade of E & J Tuttle."

"The famous store? You mean that Tom Tuttle is related to those people?"

Donovan nodded. "He was due to inherit it, but he flipped out after being gassed in the Gulf War and decided that his true calling was reading versions of Tennyson and Keats in the East Village."

"Sounds revolutionary once you put it that way," Mosko said.

"But you guys wouldn't have him, his family sold the chain of stores to the Japanese, and Tuttle punched out a Japanese tourist right here where we stand."

"Actually, it was over there, beneath the Che poster," Baez said. She pointed at the likeness of the old revolutionary.

"And after that he moved his Viking act up in front of his onetime inheritance and stood there, spouting poetry and collecting coins," Donovan said.

"But really staking out the joint waiting for one of the new Japanese owners to show himself," Mosko added.

"I wonder why Kimble didn't recognize the SOB, costume or no," Donovan said.

"Yeah! They were old friends."

"But it was Kimble who put us on to Moondog, and why would he do that if they were old friends?" Donovan scratched his chin and added, "What time yesterday did Tuttle drop this off?"

"Around eleven," Baez said. "He told the waitress he wouldn't need it anymore."

"We'll need her name."

"Sure, but she doesn't know anything."

"There is nobody on the planet who knows nothing," Donovan said grandly. "The least of us has a tiny piece of the puzzle."

"You're way beyond me," Baez said.

"Life can be very confusing," Donovan told her. "Forget what the revolutionary tracts say about policemen. Some of us are stumbling around looking for the truth like everyone else."

Donovan looked especially sincere when he said that. As a result, Baez looked at him warmly and said, "You have a way with words, Captain. You should come down here more often."

"Let me see the menu again and I'll consider it," he replied. She waved for someone to bring one over.

The captain scanned both sides of the single sheet, which was printed on coarse recycled paper. Then he said, "I'll take a Che Burger to go, with fries and a Coke. And my partner will have…?"

"A Shining Path Burrito. I don't suppose you have Dr. Brown's Cel-Ray Soda?"

"Not a chance. But if you want to go over to Gem Spa, the egg cream place—"

"I know what Gem Spa is," Mosko said, clearly offended at his knowledge of Lower East Side eating spots being underestimated.

"You can get one there," she finished.

"I'll take a Coke, too."

Baez wrote up the order and handed it to a waitress, who appeared wearing camouflage pants and a black rhinestone-studded bustier. She scurried off while Donovan watched her with considerable amusement.

"Where are you guys going to eat this stuff?" Baez asked. "In the subway?"

Donovan shook his head. "At Trump Plaza, where else?"

DONOVAN AND MOSKOWITZ sat hip to hip on the Louis XIV settee, balancing their lunches on their laps. Mosko also had his computer on one knee, which made for an especially tricky balancing act. Between the odors from the burger, fries, and burrito, and the scent of lilacs from the hex-removing candle that sat in its bag at Donovan's feet, the two policemen were a blight on the afternoon of George Bliley, the valet. Impeccably dressed in a deep blue Savile Row suit and speaking in a carefully schooled voice that only an equally schooled ear could tell was more Manchester than West End London, he hovered nearby holding an Edwardian wicker wastebasket. His gaze shifted back and forth from the food to the Persian carpet, nervously awaiting the catastrophe of a dropped french fry.

"Your office said you would be calling, Captain," Bliley intoned, "and I'm most regretful that I was forced to keep you waiting."

"No problem," Donovan said. "We had to eat someplace. So this is Trump Plaza."

"This is Mr. Melmer's—forgive me, the late Mr. Melmer's—suite in Trump Plaza. They're all individual."

"No gold bathroom faucets in this one, eh?" Donovan said, munching a fry.

Looking pained, Bliley replied, "Indeed there are. Mr. Melmer changed many aspects of the decor, but not that one. He found it...entertaining."

"So would I."

"And, I must say, they never tarnish."

"That's the whole appeal of gold, Mr. Bliley. The only tarnish it collects is on your bank account. So tell me, who owns this place now that Melmer is dead?"

"His fiancée, I believe. Mr. Melmer took quite good care of her, even though the wedding had yet to occur. Would you like some napkins from the kitchen?"

Donovan had been fishing around for something to wipe a ketchup smear onto. At last he found a handful of paper napkins folded into a back pocket.

"No thanks. Who have you been taking instructions from lately?"

"Why, from his fiancée, of course."

"The princess," Mosko said.

"That is quite correct. I have been taking my instructions from Anna Hebbel, the princess of Karlsruhe," Bliley said.

"Do you like her?" Donovan asked.

"I don't have to like her or dislike her. She is the lady of the house." Bliley sniffed and waggled the wastebasket as Mosko crumpled up his burrito wrapper and looked about for a place to throw it.

"Oh, come on, Bliley," Donovan said. "This is New York in the nineteen-nineties, not London in the nineteen-twenties. You're not Jeeves the Butler and she's no goddamn princess."

"I beg your pardon," Bliley said, his shock apparently genuine.

"Ever hear the name Anna Fritsch?"

Bliley hadn't, so Donovan filled him in on the recently widowed woman's genealogy. As the details unfolded, so did the valet. All the starch went out of Bliley's carefully practiced stiff spine until he was as limp as the wrapper from Mosko's Shining Path Burrito.

"Are you telling me that my mistress is a cheap hustler with a criminal record?" Bliley said, stepping backward and sitting rather abruptly on a Regency love seat. He put the wastebasket at his feet and seemed to forget it.

"No," Donovan said. "I'm telling you that she's a cheap hustler with a criminal record whose mom was—*is,* since, failing evidence to the contrary, she's still alive—a convicted murderess."

Bliley lowered his head and shook it. "I paid five thousand pounds for the training that got me this bloody job and they told me I'd meet royalty."

"You still got gold faucets in the throne room," Mosko remarked.

Donovan balled up his hamburger wrapper and tossed it across the room, hitting the wastebasket perfectly.

"Three points," Mosko said.

"There couldn't be some mistake?" Bliley asked, looking up.

"Show him," Donovan said.

Mosko carried his computer to the man and showed him the screen. It displayed Fritsch's complete criminal record, which included a mug shot that was unmistakably hers. When he was done looking at it, Bliley said, "Princess Anna. Cheeky."

"So where is she?" Donovan asked. "I sent a message I wanted to talk to her."

"She bolted," Bliley said. "Took off this morning. Said she was going to spend some time with her mother in Germany and got a limo to take her to the airport. She said she's not coming back to this place that reminds her of the tragic death of her dear fiancé."

"With her mother?" Donovan echoed. "Where are they meeting, at a halfway house? At the annual barbecue of Adult Children of Felons?"

"I overheard her on the phone making reservations for a flight to Bonn."

"She was on the phone?" Donovan asked. "Pregnant and bereaved, she still had the wits about her to make her own plane reservations? How come she didn't ask you to do it?"

"I was packing all her things," Bliley replied. "I assumed she was being considerate."

"What time was the flight?" Mosko asked.

"The one o'clock Concorde out of JFK."

"It's left already," Donovan said, after checking his watch.

He stood and brushed some crumbs off his lap and onto the Persian carpet. He was about to apologize when Bliley looked up and muttered, "Oh, fuck it. I guess I'm out of a job anyway."

"Wait and see if she comes back. Once cheap hustlers become real ones they still need servants, no?" Donovan said.

"I suppose that's possible."

"Did Princess Anna leave anything behind?"

Bliley shook his head. "Not a bloody thing. I cleaned the entire house this morning. You're welcome to look."

Donovan nodded, and Mosko went off to do it.

"Except, of course, her rock."

"Her rock?" Donovan said patiently.

Bliley went to the mantel and took from it a round rock, brownish with white speckles, about ten inches in diameter but quite flat. It looked like something that had been poured into a mold.

Bliley handed the thing to Donovan, who hefted it. "It's light. Is it volcanic?"

"Yes, a souvenir of Princess Anna's disastrous vacation."

"Tell me about that."

"Mr. Melmer was here on business, as often happened. She was bored and decided to go off for a week by herself in the Caribbean."

"And booked a hotel room in Carricola," Donovan said.

"How could you know that?" Bliley asked.

"It's the only Caribbean island to have a volcanic explosion this summer," Donovan said, as if it were the most reasonable thing in the world for him to have known. But since it wasn't, he added, "I read a lot."

"I'm impressed."

"When was she there? When to when?"

"Oh my, this must be important, although I can't imagine why. I can tell you exactly. She was scheduled for July twenty-first through twenty-eighth."

"But the explosion cut off the island for nearly three weeks," Donovan said. "Several hundred tourists—all of them in this one hotel that became isolated near the eruption zone—were finally rescued by the Coast Guard.''

"Yes indeed. She was one of them. Mr. Melmer was very upset about not seeing her for three weeks. But she assured him in frequent phone calls—I mean when the phones were working, that is—that there was plenty of food and good company.''

"Especially the latter,'' Donovan said.

"She finally got out on that Coast Guard boat,'' Bliley concluded. "August fifteenth it was. She flew right back up to New York. And it was just a week or two after that they announced their engagement. They must have missed each other terribly.''

"Terribly,'' Donovan said.

"And this rock is her only souvenir of her adventure.''

"Not quite,'' Donovan stated.

"What do you mean?''

"She'll always have her memories.''

"Yes. I see that you're a sentimental man.'' Bliley sighed and added, "Even if she is a cheap hustler, she deserves to have a man to be father to her unborn child. Would you like to take the rock? I mean she said she's not coming back.''

Donovan thanked the man, arranging the rock next to his candle on the floor. It was then that Mosko came in from another room, bearing a broad grin as well as a thin leather folder.

"You know the good thing about these antiques from a cop's point of view?'' he asked.

Bliley shook his head.

"The boards on the bottoms of the dresser drawers separate over time. Stuff falls through the cracks.''

"What did you find?'' Donovan asked.

"Princess Anna's passport!'' he announced triumphantly.

Bliley looked astonished. Donovan was delighted. "No passport, no Concorde.''

"She couldn't have gotten on the plane."

"She's still in New York," Donovan said.

"But she said she was going to spend time with her mum," Bliley objected.

"Surprise!" Donovan said. "Mum's in New York, too."

TEN

"I HAD TO GIVE UP DRINKING," DONOVAN MUTTERED

"IF YOU WANT TO BE a doctor, Captain, come learn about ultrasound," said Marcy's doctor. Donovan peered over his shoulder at the tiny black-and-white screen and the keyboard below it.

"I like gadgets," Donovan replied. "And I like to see my son."

It was miraculous, the little picture. As Campagna ran the transducer over Marcy's undraped belly, the screen lit up with a tiny photo of a tiny life. Seen looking down from over his head, Daniel seemed a perfect little boy ready to pop out of his mother's womb and begin causing trouble, in the grand tradition of his father. Already he opened and closed the fingers of his right hand, which floated in amniotic fluid that appeared as clear as water. Far below, his umbilical cord twisted off to its attachment point on the wall of Marcy's womb.

"He has your nose," Marcy said, happily squeezing her husband's hand. "Isn't it perfectly adorable?"

Campagna looked at her, then back at the screen, and replied, "Your nose is lovely, Mrs. Donovan. The baby's nose looks more like yours."

Donovan smiled.

Seeing her husband's reaction, she said, "I had it done."

"Pardon me?" the doctor asked.

"I went to the wizard on Park and Seventy-third."

"A plastic surgeon?"

"He got it broke," she said, indicating Donovan.

"I think you're telling me more than I need to know."

"I don't mean that he broke it. I'd kill him if he ever laid a hand on me in anger. I mean that a long time ago, when I was an undercover policewoman, he sent me out on an assignment that resulted in my nose being broken."

"Really," Campagna said.

"The city paid for the nose job," Donovan added. "But, in fact, she had a beautiful nose before. And it wouldn't have been broken if she hadn't decided to duke it out with a man carrying a two-by-four."

"What was I supposed to do?"

"Shoot him," Donovan said.

"I wish things were as simple for me as they are for you," she replied, sighing.

Donovan reached out with a forefinger and touched the bottom of the screen. "What's 'DOC' mean?" he asked.

"Date of conception," Campagna replied.

"That's when Marcy got pregnant?"

"You mean you don't remember the night?"

"I remember every minute," he said quickly. "But it was an afternoon."

Mollified, Marcy smiled and once again squeezed his hand.

Campagna twice pressed the button that made Polaroid snapshots of the baby, then pushed the ultrasound cart a few feet away from the bed. He wiped the lubricant off Marcy's belly with paper towels and pulled the gown back down. When the photos appeared from a slot on the side of the machine, he handed one to each parent.

"You're a miracle worker, Dr. Campagna," Marcy said.

"No. You work the miracles. I merely stand by in case I can be of assistance."

Donovan patted the ultrasound machine and said, "Interesting gadget. I think I'll get one."

"What on earth for?" Campagna asked.

"Until my medical degree comes through, I can use it to check hard-boiled eggs to see if they're done," Donovan replied.

"I suppose it would work for that."

"Does this thing store data and for how long?"

"This is the newest model. It knows everything about the baby—all pertinent data. It keeps records for all the patients on the floor for a week. Then the technician downloads the data into the mainframe, where it becomes a part of the patient's confidential medical record." With that, he switched off the machine.

After a few pleasantries and another trip to the box of Perugina chocolates, the doctor excused himself. When he was gone, Donovan closed the door and went back to the ultrasound machine.

"What are you up to?" she asked.

"I want to see if Anna Fritsch had an ultrasound while she was in that room down the hall," Donovan said. He switched the machine back on.

"Honey, those medical records are confidential," she argued, but with a wry smile.

"And so they are."

The screen came up blank save for a menu asking the operator for his password.

"And the machine is password-protected."

"And so it is," Donovan replied, typing in "Gicana" and hitting the Enter key.

The screen came to life. "How did you get Dr. Campagna's password?" she asked.

"I looked over his shoulder. Roberto Gicana is the name of a prominent Italian soccer player. I saw Campagna using it the other day. It works to get into the medical records computer, too."

"This is highly illegal," she said, but seemed impressed all the same.

"And unethical. I'm trying to catch a killer."

He fiddled around with the menus for a time, trying this and that, occasionally muttering to himself. Such as: "She's German and doesn't have a Social Security number, which is how most medical records are stored, so let's try the name and see if we get lucky."

Donovan tried "Fritsch" and got nothing. But "Hebbel, Anna," earned him a couple of beeps and a bright sonogram of a tiny infant.

"Got her," Donovan said proudly.

"Does it give the sex? Boy or girl?" Marcy asked, craning her neck in that direction.

"Girl. Twenty weeks. Cute little thing, too." But, in fact, the image showed little more than one blur that resembled a head and another that looked like a leg. "Maybe Danny would like to meet her."

"Any babe that tries to lay a hand on my boy is in big trouble," Marcy said, petting her belly reassuringly.

"I thought you were going to be a progressive mom," Donovan commented.

She shook her head. "I want Daniel to be a virgin when he marries."

"The second half of my life is going to be a challenge, isn't it?" Donovan moaned.

"What was the first half of your life, a walk through Disneyland? You're a New Yorker: you like aggravation. When was the baby conceived?"

Donovan peered at the data displayed alongside the image. "Date of conception was August fourth," he said.

"And where were the parents then?" Marcy asked.

Donovan said, "The baby was conceived on the Caribbean island of Carricola while Melmer was manning his booth at a trade show at the Javits Convention Center."

"Anna…what are we using for a last name?"

"Let's settle on Fritsch."

"Anna Fritsch gets pregnant by God-knows-who and flies

to New York, where Melmer and her promptly announce their engagement. Do you think he knew?''

"My guess is 'yes,'" Donovan said.

"I agree. People are pretty sophisticated these days."

"*Technology* is pretty sophisticated these days," Donovan added. "Once upon a time a girl could talk a guy into believing that somebody else's kid was his, but no more."

"Melmer was a good man," Marcy said. "I think we can assume he loved her despite her carrying someone else's baby. But whose?"

Donovan shrugged. "I have to get my hands on the manifest of that Coast Guard boat."

"That assumes she wasn't made pregnant by a houseboy at the resort hotel," Marcy said.

"True," Donovan admitted.

"How important to the case is this information?"

"Melmer was killed by an unknown man," Donovan said. "The fiancée he left behind carries someone else's child. Maybe the real father is the murderer."

"Why would someone do that? To leave her with no option but to go back to him? And then what of Seybold? Why kill him? And who's behind the extortion demand? It makes no sense."

"Not at the moment, anyway. I need to know more. Including who was booked into that hotel on Carricola."

"How can you get that?" Marcy asked.

"There are ways," Donovan said, pressing the button that turned the sonogram on the screen into a Polaroid photo.

"What's the photo for?" Marcy asked, taking it from his hand and scanning it.

"To give to the father when I find him," Donovan said.

"William...what if this is a run-of-the-mill lovers' triangle that has nothing to do with the murders on Fifth Avenue?"

"That's too much of a coincidence to even think about. It's related; I just can't tell you how."

He shut off the ultrasound machine, then picked up the piece of volcanic rock and sat on the edge of the bed, tossing the rock into the air and catching it.

"You're just mad because she ran away," Marcy said. "You see suspects fleeing and you get this incredible testosterone surge. I can feel it from here." She laid her hand on his arm and continued, "You're hot."

"You, too," Donovan said.

"I mean that your blood is up. Isn't that how the Irish put it?"

"Since I stopped drinking and married a Jewish girl I've pretty much forgotten what the Irish do about anything," Donovan responded. "And on the subject of fleeing, they're all on the lam: Kimble tried running; Tuttle, Fritsch, and my Afghan friend actually did it."

"That last one would be the gyro guy," Marcy said.

"Yeah. Moskowitz can't find him. He even sent a Muslim police officer to talk to the owners of that halal shop on Queens Boulevard."

"Nothing came of it?"

"Nada," Donovan replied. He turned to his laptop, which purred away atop Marcy's food service table. He flipped through a few screens before finding the information he wanted. Then he continued, "And the city agency that licenses street vendors says only that the spot in front of F.A.O. Schwarz goes to one Saihaj Bahador, a Sikh immigrant who has worked there every day for the past two years."

"Every day? The guy doesn't take off?"

"He works seven days a week, from eight in the morning until seven at night," Donovan said. "I guess he's one of those immigrants the Republicans say come here to get on welfare and poison the fabric of America. According to the agency, Bahador has an impeccable record and supports a large family."

"So where was he last Friday when Seybold was shot?"

"A good question. I think I'll ask him. He's back at work today." Donovan got up and stretched. "Time for a snack," he said.

"You're going out again? You just ate."

"I'm hungry."

"No more junk food. Please. You've slipped recently."

"At the worst I'll get a pretzel."

"Get one with no salt," she replied. "You're going to be a daddy soon, and I need you to live forever?"

"Well, that doesn't put me under too much pressure," he said, bending over and kissing her.

"You know how you always said your guiding principle as a cop was that good people should live forever?"

"I said that?"

"Often. And you said it offended you when crime prevented that from happening."

"Melmer sounds like he was someone who should have lived forever," Donovan said. "And Seybold wasn't a bad guy, either. I'm gonna get whoever killed them."

He walked across the room and plugged a tape into the VCR he had hooked up to the standard-issue hospital television. Then he tossed her the remote.

"Watch this for me," he said.

"If this is another of your Learning Channel documentaries, I'm not interested in Clovis points, Paleo-Indian burial mounds, or the attack formation Nelson used at Trafalgar," Marcy said, clicking the VCR on.

"You lucked out. This is two hours of your basic heartthrob, Paul Duke, reading from the TelePrompTer. It's the master tape from his show the day the extortion demand was left beneath the Rockefeller Center tree."

"Cool," Marcy said. "What am I supposed to be looking for? The guy leaving the note?"

"I don't know if the tree is in the shot," Donovan replied. "I'm hoping that maybe the killer wandered over and stared in Paul's window."

"I don't know what he looks like," Marcy protested.

"Look for Santa's Angels volunteers, seven-foot-tall Vikings, or mujahideen freedom fighters," Donovan said.

"Those people out there every day are grandmas from Iowa," she said.

"So look for an angry one," Donovan replied, slipping out the door.

As he headed down the hall, he heard her call out, "I'm retired! And pregnant!"

THE LINE OUTSIDE F.A.O. Schwarz was shorter than expected and didn't reach all the way to the sidewalk where the gyro vendor had set up his cart. As a result, this man catered to his regulars—office workers on late lunch breaks and cabbies who pulled to the curb, blocking the usually fierce midtown traffic just long enough to snag hot dogs.

Both cart and vendor were different. The cart was newer and without decoration. The one Donovan had seen on November 29 was plastered with stickers and other adornment, including the jokey Buddha snapshot. This cart was immaculate and frequently polished. A blue Windex bottle sat atop it, alongside a roll of paper towels. The only advertisement was a neatly printed wooden sign listing prices. (Gyros were $4.50, Donovan was gratified to see, and pretzels were $1.50, both cheaper than on the day after Thanksgiving.)

November's phony Sikh had been forty and fat, with a scraggly beard. This man was fifty and thin, with a magnificent beard that was carefully groomed and parted in the middle. He wore a black turban.

Getting his attention, Donovan smiled broadly and said, "Make me one with everything."

The man offered a polite smile. "I beg your pardon?" he asked. "May I get you a hot dog?"

Donovan shrugged. "I was fishing for a joke, but I'll take a pretzel."

"I do not understand," the man replied.

"One with no salt."

Donovan gave the man money and showed him his badge. At that, the vendor finally cracked a smile. A formal one. As he handed over the pretzel, he said, "You are a policeman. Is there something I can do for you?"

"I would like to know about the man working this spot on the day after Thanksgiving," Donovan said.

"There was no man working here that day," the vendor replied, raising his voice slightly to be heard over a chorus of "Deck the Halls" that suddenly blared over the store's outside loudspeakers.

"How would you know, Mr. Bahador?... You weren't here."

"This is my spot. No one else can work it."

"I assure you that someone was right here. I bought a pretzel from him. For two dollars."

Bahador seemed interested in the high price Donovan had paid but said nothing about it. Instead, he said, "On that day I went with my wife to see the doctor. We are expecting another baby."

"Who are you using?"

"What do you mean?"

"What doctor?"

"Levy, at Columbia Presbyterian."

"Congratulations on your baby," Donovan said.

"Thank you very much. Who was this other man?"

"An Afghan pretending to be a Sikh. Do you know him?"

"As I told you, Detective, no one should have been here. If someone was, it was an interloper. If you have his name I will report him to the authorities."

"I was hoping you could give me his name," Donovan said.

Bahador shook his head. "It is possible that a vendor from one of the other corners took advantage of my absence."

"Where do you keep this thing anyway?" Donovan asked, pointing to the cart.

"I rent space in the Lexington Trader Garage, as do most of my colleagues."

"And where is that?"

"On the north side of Sixty-fourth Street between York and First Avenues," Bahador replied.

"How many of your colleagues use that facility?" Donovan asked.

"At least one hundred. Why don't you go over there and look? Will you recognize the man?"

"Yes. And his cart as well. Where do you buy your meat?"

"My halal meat, you mean?"

"Yes."

"In Paterson."

"New Jersey? Why there?"

"I live in Fort Lee."

"So you commute to the city to run a pushcart?"

"That is correct," the man said proudly.

"Times have changed," Donovan replied.

"I drive in, park my car in the garage, then push the cart from the garage to here. I support my family."

Donovan nodded.

"Have I done something wrong?" Bahador asked.

"Not if you don't know the man I spoke to," Donovan said.

"Did he do something wrong, may I ask?"

"Well, if you don't know him then it doesn't matter, does it?" Donovan said.

Customers waiting for service were beginning to get agitated, so Donovan excused himself and walked off briskly. But he didn't go far. He slipped around the corner and stood where he could remain unseen while keeping an eye on the vendor. That man served the customers on line, then took advantage of the first free moment to pull out a cell phone and make a call.

Donovan did likewise, telling the detective on his staff who answered the phone, "There's a suspect, Saihaj Bahador of Fort Lee, New Jersey, making a cell phone call from the corner of Fifth Avenue and Sixty-first Street. Get his cell number and find out who he's calling."

That done, the captain watched while Bahador spoke with increasing agitation to whoever was on the other end of his line. When the vendor hung up his phone, Donovan called his wife to say he would be out a bit longer than expected. Then he walked to the corner of Madison Avenue and caught a cab across town to Sixty-fourth and First, where the entrance to the Lexington Trader Garage was as dingy and urine-soaked as the entrance to any side-street parking tenement. A four-foot white sign, stained by rust, dangled over the entrance. It read: "Early birds, $7, 8 a.m. to 6 p.m." That much of a bargain could only come with serious problems. Among them: a stench that was overwhelming even in the frosty winter air, a dark and narrow driveway that plummeted steeply into a shadowy abyss lit only by a solitary bare bulb, and a screeching alarm that jarred Donovan's teeth when he set it off by breaking an invisible beam placed a few paces down the path.

A 1970s-vintage transistor radio blared Arab music. Its long-torn-off telescoping antenna had been replaced by a rusty coat hanger that someone had tried to twist straight. But only Donovan was there to hear the music, or so it seemed. There was no attendant; whoever was in charge of that garage had gone wherever Donovan's suspects had gone. The captain pulled out his Smith & Wesson and flipped his badge onto his jacket pocket. He thought of his unborn child and of Marcy and how he had promised her to avoid situations involving guns.

The attendant's booth had a fly-specked window made of glass in which chicken wire had been embedded to discourage breakage. A mouse hole big enough for money to pass through was at the bottom, along with a sign made of shirt cardboard listing the monthly prices. Among them: "Car, $250; Cart/car, $350; payable in cash on 1st." Another bare bulb hung limply at the end of ancient cloth-covered wire. It cast its yellow glare on a strip of flypaper that curled from the grimy ceiling, bearing hundreds of tiny corpses.

The door to the booth was ajar. Donovan nudged it open, then swung inside with his revolver in front of him. The booth was empty, although a half-eaten falafel sandwich was still warm atop the counter. The spice lightly scented the booth. The radio blared on from its place, on a shelf, next to an old black rotary phone. Donovan switched off the music.

The echoes faded from the gloomy dark. In their place was the distant rumble of traffic and the occasional blare of horns as well as a persistent hiss from an overworked radiator. Donovan lifted the telephone receiver and dialed a number. When a detective answered, the captain said, "Yeah, Donovan again. Is five-five-five, four-seven-five-eight the number that guy called before? Too soon to tell? OK, well, get a patrol car over to the parking garage at Nine-seven-four East Sixty-fourth Street. I may have a bad situation here."

"You got it, Cap," was the reply.

"And tell Sergeant Moskowitz to get his buns over here, too."

Donovan was about to hang up the phone when he heard a sound, a rusty wheel, such as on a street vendor's pushcart, turning. He shot a glance out of the booth but couldn't see much at all, the window was so dirty. Mainly he could see some light coming down the steep driveway from the street and the glow of the other bulb, which hung halfway down a row of parked cars interspersed with sidewalk vending carts.

The detective on the other end of the line reacted to the silence. "You got a problem?" he asked.

"Hang on," Donovan said. Realizing it was too easy for someone outside to see him, he reached up and pulled the string to shut off the light in the booth.

In the instant he did so, there was the shriek of splintering glass followed a split second later by the roar of a nine-millimeter. He threw himself down onto the floor of the booth as the window—chicken wire or no chicken wire—exploded inward in a thousand fragments. The roar of the gunshot echoed throughout the dingy garage, and when his ears cleared he could hear a voice saying, "Captain! Captain!" over the phone.

Donovan scooped up the receiver and mumbled, "I'm under fire." Then he dropped the phone again and squirmed around until he could see out the door, his cheek pressed against the concrete floor, which was cold as ice and filthy from decades of spilled coffee, ground-in cigarette butts, and gum.

"I *had* to give up drinking," Donovan muttered, and worked his Smith & Wesson out in front of him, the stubby muzzle pointing down the row of cars and carts.

The hissing of the radiator seemed louder than before. Donovan kept quiet for ten, maybe twenty seconds. Then he pushed the door open a few more inches and yelled, "Police! Throw out your weapon and come out with your hands up!"

There was a muzzle flash down in the darkness and another roar. There was no more glass in the booth to break, and the echoes didn't sound as loud to him, lying as he was with one ear against the concrete. Donovan fired three quick shots in the direction of the muzzle flash. Before the echoes came he heard one impact on metal and another on glass; a windshield, he thought. After the echoes of the gunshots came the sound of heavy shoes running away.

Donovan scrambled to his feet and gave chase, running

down the aisle of cars and aluminum carts, keeping close to them in case he had to dive for cover again. The sounds of the shoes stopped, and he ducked behind an old Chrysler. This time he heard only the sound of a metal door that had been thrown open. Its hinges screamed and then it crashed into what sounded like a basement corridor.

Donovan saw the rectangle of light where a door now stood open. Beyond it wasn't a corridor, but an alley. He got out from behind the Chrysler and jogged cautiously toward the door, his revolver out in front. The sounds of the street—engines, horns, and, in the closing distance, sirens—grew louder. But the sound of a man running away was gone.

When Donovan got to the door he flattened himself against the wall, then dropped to a squat and pivoted around the corner. He found himself staring into a basement-level alley flanked by brick buildings and marked on the far end by a black cast-iron fence and a wide-open gate. Garbage cans from both buildings lined the walls, on one of which an artistic janitor had meticulously painted a life-size rendition of a red 1959 Cadillac.

Donovan found himself alone in the alley. He walked briskly to the far end and went through the gate. A set of cast-iron stairs led up to street level. He climbed them and walked through a stone gate, the one the janitors used to take the garbage to the curb for twice-weekly pickup. The sidewalks on Sixty-fifth Street were empty save for a solitary woman pushing a baby in a stroller. But traffic had ground to a halt on First Avenue, and the reflections of flashing red lights were everywhere.

ELEVEN

A HANDFUL OF HOTDOGS,
WRINKLED LIKE LAST YEAR'S PICKLES

THE GARAGE WAS FULL of cops and their equipment. Several tall light stands flooded the underground chasm with white light that was blinding at times. Long shadows snaked across the dirty walls and over the rusted steam pipes that sweated orange water onto the hoods and roofs of cars. Radios crackled and cell phones beeped. Moskowitz had set up his notebook computer atop a newish aluminum hot dog stand. Its cellular modem was busy downloading files and e-mail from the office.

Donovan poked around the selfsame hot dog cart with whose owner he had exchanged idle banter just a few days earlier. It didn't seem to have been used in a few days. The propane grills and steam trays were cold as ice trays, and a handful of Sabrett hot dogs languished, wrinkled like last year's pickles, in a vat of frigid water. The fat bubbles that had congealed atop that water picked up the cops' lights and shone like dirty pearls floating in an ice bath.

Halfway down the side of the cart, a .38-caliber bullet hole punctured the aluminum skin. It came from Donovan's gun, as did a similar hole in the driver's-side window of a 1992 Chevrolet.

Donovan glowered at the Great Buddha of Bamiyan.

"'Make me one with everything,' my ass," Donovan said. "The sonofabitch who owns this cart tried to make me one with the floor of the attendant's booth."

"So much for your trying to achieve enlightenment

through Eastern religions," Mosko said over his shoulder, his main focus remaining on the computer. "Forget their alleged quest for nirvana. Experience the religion that brought the world weekends, Moses, Sigmund Freud, Barbra Streisand, the captain and first officer of *Star Trek,* half of Goldie Hawn, and, if you insist on counting the guy, Jesus."

"I heard of him."

"He's not normally on those lists we keep of prominent Jews, but it's wrong to forget the guy entirely. I mean he had an impact. In time he got to be as big as, well, as John Lennon."

Donovan poked around the assorted drawers and cubbyholes found on the sidewalk cart. "What *are* you doing on Christmas?" he asked.

"We usually have a Jewish Christmas—two movies and a Chinese restaurant. There's nothing else to do in town."

"Last year Marcy took me to Ratner's," Donovan said. "The year before that it was Sammy's Roumanian. Before that, *Schindler's List.*"

"What a warm and cuddly Christmas," Bonaci said, breezing past en route to supervise an evidence-gathering crew working out in the alley.

Donovan found nothing of interest in the cart and stepped back from it and folded his arms. "The bum tried to kill me," he muttered.

"Who, Steven Spielberg?"

"No, the Afghan in the Sikh turban. I guess his head got too hot and fried his brains."

"How do you feel?" Mosko asked.

"Incredibly pissed off."

"I think you're entitled."

"Marcy doesn't know about this, does she?"

"Nah. I called and told her you'd be a little longer yet, that's all. Now, if she just doesn't listen to the radio—"

"Damn! She turns on National Public Radio every day

at five to get *All Things Considered.* They could carry the news. I'm in big trouble.''

Laughing, Mosko said, ''My friend, if you're more worried about what your wife thinks than about being shot at by a lunatic Afghanistani hot dog vendor, you're Jewish already. Make your wife and unborn child happy and convert. I'll call a rabbi for the bris.''

''Leave me alone about religion,'' Donovan replied, squirming and crossing his legs. ''I'm an ex-Catholic practicing atheist.''

''How do you practice atheism?'' Mosko asked.

''You don't believe in anything. For example, I don't believe you have a salary review coming up in three weeks.''

''Oops,'' Mosko said, deciding in that instant to give full attention to his boss and the matter at hand.

''Did we get prints off this thing?'' Donovan asked, kicking a tire.

''Only a million. But there's one that occurs more than the others. Assuming it belongs to the owner, we should be getting results soon. I faxed the prints to the database administrator, who will patch them into the FBI data bank and e-mail me the results if we get a match.''

''When will this happen?''

''Any time now.''

''Is this cart registered to anyone?'' Donovan asked.

Mosko nodded. ''It belongs to the owner of this garage, one Walid Maroofi.''

''That name sounds Afghan.''

''It is. Maroofi is a naturalized citizen and, get this, runs a service that gets jobs and places to live for newly arrived central and southern Asians, especially his countrymen.''

''Including, possibly, jobs as parking-garage attendants,'' Donovan said.

''The thought occurred to me,'' Mosko replied.

''Haul his ass down here,'' Donovan snarled.

"I have men on the way to his apartment now," the sergeant said proudly.

"Where does he live?"

"Across the river. In Queens. Not far from that halal shop, in fact."

"Considering that I'm against everything that Archie Bunker stands for, it amuses me that his home borough is rapidly becoming Little Asia. You drive down Northern Boulevard and it's like taking the milk train east from Istanbul. Every stopover is another Asian ethnic enclave."

"True," Mosko replied.

"Does this Maroofi have anything to do with the Mountain Brigade?"

"The guys who sent the extortion note?"

"Allegedly," Donovan replied.

"I'll find out. I have a request in to Immigration."

Donovan fished a pencil and a Post-it notepad from his pocket and scribbled something, leaning on top of the cart. Then he pulled the top note off the pad and handed it to his aide.

"Who's Jerry McGinty?" Mosko asked.

"FBI, antiterrorist section," Donovan said.

"Where do you know him from? An old case I don't know about?"

Donovan shook his head. "A bar on Third Avenue. That you also don't know about. It's not what you think, though. I helped his cousin, just off the boat from Ireland, get a job there three or four years ago."

"Whatever works," Mosko said with a shrug, and got on the phone.

Donovan stuck his hands in his pants pockets and wandered back out to the alley door and from there made his way back to the street. It was getting near the end of the day, and the uptown commuter traffic on York and First Avenues was bumper-to-bumper. The side street was blocked by official vehicles, which had the predictable effect on the avenues. Horns blew nonstop, and with the arrival of each new green light came the roar of engines and the screeching of tires as drivers drag-raced the handful of yards allowed them.

Donovan walked to York and bought a cup of decaffeinated coffee from the Te Amo—a chain tobacco, candy, newspaper, and snack shop. He carried it across the avenue to a bench in front of Rockefeller University, where he sat and watched the Manhattan skyline. He called Marcy on the cell phone and managed to tell her what had happened without revealing that he had been shot at. She was sufficiently preoccupied with the results of the day's tests to avoid hard questions about what he had been doing, and for that he was grateful. He also was glad to hear music playing in the background. As long as she skipped the news, his secret was safe.

When it got too cold to stay, he walked back to the garage. Most of the technicians had cleared out, leaving Moskowitz and Bonaci supervising a handful of detectives. Two of them stood guard over a thin and extremely nervous-looking man—Maroofi, beyond a shadow of a doubt—who chain-smoked and alternated between gaping at the ceiling and the floor.

Donovan tossed his coffee cup into a trash can and let himself be drawn aside by Mosko, who pointed at a smiling face on a passport-type photo displayed on the computer monitor.

"Mojadidi," he said. "Yama Mojadidi."

Donovan bent over and squinted at the somewhat fuzzy photo. Then he smiled faintly. It was the pudgy fortyish man with the scraggly beard with whom Donovan had had that brief conversation just before being interrupted by the murder of Erik Melmer.

"This is the hot dog vendor I talked to," Donovan said.

"The one with the nine-millimeter?"

"That's him. His name is...what did you say?"

"Mojadidi," Mosko replied.

"Who is he?"

"He's a forty-three-year-old guy who came here on a visitor's visa a couple of months ago. He overstayed his welcome and disappeared into the underground. His last known address is in Long Island City."

"Another Queens boy," Donovan said.

"Yeah. In the shadow of that big Citibank building. I got guys headed over there now, but I wouldn't count on him still being there."

"What do we have on him before he came to the U.S.?" Donovan asked.

"Not too much. He listed his occupation as air traffic controller. That was in Kabul."

"How much air traffic does Kabul get, other than incoming missiles?" Donovan asked.

"I guess enough to need guys watching radar screens," Mosko replied. "Anyway, Mojadidi came here by way of Karachi—"

"Coincidentally, perhaps, the same route a couple of the World Trade Center bombers took."

"And stayed out of sight until running into you the other day," Mosko said.

"Did you get Jerry McGinty on the phone?" Donovan asked.

Mosko nodded. "He never heard of either Mojadidi or Maroofi. He has heard of the Mountain Brigade, of course, but has no idea if this Afghan guerrilla group operates in the States. He's a little mystified by that possibility. As far as he knows, they don't have a worldwide agenda; they're just a local bunch of freedom fighters."

"What the hell is Mojadidi doing in this country?" Donovan asked.

"Ask Maroofi," Mosko said, nodding at the thin, chain-smoking man.

"That him?"

Moskowitz nodded.

"How'd he take to being brought here?" Donovan asked.

"He's scared. One minute he's running a seedy parking garage; the next minute he's surrounded by detectives. You know how these immigrants tend to be scared of authority."

"Which is why they came here, generally speaking," Donovan said. "Bring him over."

Moskowitz went to the man, introduced himself, told him who Donovan was, then returned with his muscular arm around the man's shoulders. Maroofi was fumbling for another cigarette when Donovan replaced Mosko's arm with his own and steered the by-then trembling Afghan toward the attendant's booth.

"Did my associate tell you who I am?" Donovan asked.

"He said you are an important man," Maroofi replied, flicking his thumb nervously at a Bic lighter—a souvenir one carrying a picture of the Statue of Liberty—and nearly dropping it before managing to light his smoke.

"He lied," Donovan said.

Caught off guard, Maroofi looked around at the muscular Moskowitz. "He lied? I don't understand."

"I'm not an important person," Donovan said. "I'm a nobody. But I'm a nobody whose wife loves him. You are an important person, because you have it in your power to find the man who tried to make my wife a widow. Don't you agree that it would be sad should my wife become a widow?"

"Yes. Yes." Maroofi bobbed his head up and down, his long and skinny nose slicing the cloud of smoke that Donovan could tell was a permanent fixture in front of the man's face.

Donovan led the man to the attendant's booth. The shattered window still lay in myriad pieces on the floor. The bits of glass crunched beneath their feet, the noise amplified by the concrete walls of the garage, which were painted dark grey years before but had turned to black following much neglect.

"I came down here looking for a hot dog vendor with a sense of humor, and look what happened to me," Donovan continued. "A man shot at me. I presume it was the same man I came to see."

From the corner of his eye Donovan could see Moskowitz staring intently at an e-mail coming in on his notebook computer.

"Fortunately, he missed. I shot back and, unfortunately, I also missed. Had this exchange of gunfire taken place out in the open—say on Fifth Avenue during the holiday shopping season—the two of us could have gunned down half a dozen bystanders."

Maroofi continued bobbing his head up and down, puffing furiously. Now and again Donovan waved some smoke away from his face.

At that point, Mosko waved to get his attention. Donovan said, "What?"

"You wanted to know who Saihaj Bahador made that cell call to?" Mosko called back.

"Who?"

"Him," was the reply.

Donovan's assistant pointed at Maroofi, who, hearing the conversation, coughed sputteringly and threw his half-smoked cigarette down onto the floor. He said, "I am a workingman. I am an honest workingman. I came to this country—"

"Not to get involved with these characters, certainly," Donovan interrupted.

"I helped get them jobs and this is how they repaid me," Maroofi said. He fumbled for another cigarette.

"Who shot at me today?" Donovan asked.

"That must have been Mojadidi," the garage owner stammered, lost again in the struggle to light up.

"Tell me what happened."

"He is my attendant here. I also allow him to take a cart out and use a spot when it becomes temporarily vacant. As happened the day after Thanksgiving. Your assistant told me of your interest in that date."

"So this guy Mojadidi was out, using Bahador's prime real estate in front of F.A.O. Schwarz making a few extra bucks selling hot dogs, when I happened along and spotted his gun."

"I don't know anything about a gun. I don't associate with men who carry guns. He only told me he fled that day after a policeman questioned him. He has overstayed his visitor's visa, and Immigration is looking for him. So it made sense to me that he ran."

"I can understand the fleeing part, but why was he carrying a gun?" Donovan asked. "Fifth Avenue is hardly the O.K. Corral, if you know what I mean."

Maroofi didn't.

"You're not generally in danger of being gunned down there," Donovan explained.

"He must have been worried about being robbed, but as you say, that doesn't happen on Fifth Avenue," Maroofi replied.

"Having a gun—I assume it was an illegal one, since Mojadidi now is an illegal alien—is bad enough," Donovan said. "But using it to fire at a policeman is worse. To me that means that we're dealing with something more than a guy who's afraid of being sent back to Afghanistan. Is Mojadidi a member of the Mountain Brigade?"

"You mean the political party in my country?"

"If that's what they call themselves."

"I have no idea. I don't think he is political, especially. He is a Muslim, but not a fundamentalist. He doesn't have strong opinions about religion or politics. I don't know why he shot at you, but I am very sorry that he did."

"What do you know about him?" Donovan asked.

"He's interested in flying. I don't know much about him.

He answered my Yellow Pages ad. I have a listing for my placement service.''

"Does he have family?"

"Mojadidi told me once that his wife was killed in the fighting."

"Which fighting? Against the Russians or the current civil war?"

"Against the Russians. His daughter also died tragically, I know. Mojadidi was very bitter about that. But he wouldn't talk about it much."

Donovan thought for a moment, then said, "You said he's a Muslim. But he had a snapshot of the Great Buddha of Bamiyan pasted on that cart. Unless you put it there, of course."

"Oh no, that belongs to Mojadidi. I am sure of it. He took that photograph himself years ago. He is from the Hindu Kush Mountains, which is where Bamiyan is located. I don't think he keeps the photograph out of religious devotion, however. He is, you know, Muslim."

"Just a souvenir of the old hometown, huh?" Donovan said, turning and leading the way back to the hot dog cart. Maroofi followed him, and together they leaned over and squinted at the yellowing snapshot.

Donovan had read about the Great Buddhas of Bamiyan. Massive sculptures—one is eighteen stories high—carved into the sandstone of the Hindu Kush Mountains seventeen hundred years ago, the Buddhas look down into the Bamiyan Valley upon the invasion route taken by Genghis Khan on his conquest of Asia. The gigantic statues also witnessed the battles by the mujahideen against the Russians and continue to watch the civil war, an antiaircraft battery sitting atop one of them.

A tiny imprint at the bottom of the photo showed that it was taken in March 1993. Standing proudly at the feet of the Buddha and nearly invisible to the casual onlooker was a pretty girl, twenty-something, with straight black hair and huge, coal black eyes. She was barefoot and wore a light grey robe.

"Who's the girl?" Donovan asked.

Maroofi shrugged. "A tourist, I guess. The Great Buddhas were big tourist attractions for centuries. Not since the fighting, though."

"Mojadidi took her picture. She must be important."

Squinting even harder at the photo, Maroofi said, "Perhaps he was photographing the guns and the girl just happened to be there."

Donovan watched as the Afghan pressed a pointy fingertip against the antiaircraft emplacement, which was just barely visible, resembling a few wild strands of hair, over Buddha's head.

"Perhaps," Donovan said.

"I wish I could be more helpful," Maroofi responded, lighting his third cigarette in ten minutes.

"You could stop blowing smoke at me," Donovan replied.

The man flung his cigarette onto the ground and stamped it ferociously.

"So Mojadidi worked for you. Every day?"

"Yes."

"How did you pay him? By check?"

"I paid in cash," Maroofi said.

"And, of course, you couldn't file withholding on him 'cause he's an illegal. So I guess I'll have to get the IRS involved in this," Donovan said.

The man looked even more uncomfortable than before.

"I mean, so far I only have you down as harboring an illegal alien and complicity in the attempted murder of a police officer."

"Me? What did I do?"

"You own the phone line that Mojadidi was tipped off on. Bahador called to warn Mojadidi that I was on to him, and the sonofabitch took a shot at me."

"What they did is no fault of mine," Maroofi protested.

"Not true. You gave safe haven to a known illegal alien who carried an illegal gun, and he used it to try to kill me. Frankly, I think we may have to hold you in custody and shut down your garage for a few days while we sort all this out."

The thin man looked panicked and reached for another cigarette. But Donovan waggled a finger at him, and he jammed his hands together nervously and squeezed them. "You cannot do this to me," he said.

"Watch me," Donovan replied.

"You cannot shut down the garage. My customers need a place to store their carts."

"No problem. We'll padlock the joint after the carts are stored for the night."

"But my customers won't be able to get them out the next morning," Maroofi protested.

"Is that so?" Donovan replied.

"They will be furious."

"And, from what I've seen, armed. If I were you, I would hop on the first flight back to Kabul. It may be safer for you there."

The Afghan walked away from Donovan, downcast, thinking. Mosko watched him carefully, lest he bolt. But the man merely paced back and forth for a moment. Then he returned to Donovan and said, "Maybe I can help you find the man who shot at you."

"I had a feeling you could," Donovan replied.

"Mojadidi has an apartment in Long Island City," Maroofi said.

Donovan called his assistant over, then asked the Afghan, "Where in Long Island City?"

"On Twenty-first Street."

"Been there," Mosko said, shaking his head. "Tried it."

"Which one did you go to?" Maroofi asked. "The old apartment near Jackson Avenue?"

Mosko nodded.

"He gave that one up a few months ago. He moved down a few blocks to Hunters Point Avenue. I will write down the address for you."

He did so, using one of his business cards and the stub of a pencil.

"This address is right alongside the Long Island Rail Road yards," Mosko said.

"The rent is reasonable," Maroofi replied.

THE BUILDING STOOD three stories high, its fake-stone facade barely rising above a mountain of used automobile tires that occupied a lot adjacent to the Long Island Rail Road's Sunnyside Yards. The building's ground floor bore a hand-lettered sign reading: "Flats fixed." But the shop was boarded up; the boards were plastered with eviction notices. One or two such papers also adorned the door that led to the apartments on the second and third floors, that part of the building where the linoleumlike exterior peeled off in slabs that reminded Donovan of skin peeling off a sunburned forehead. The day had grown late and the sun was setting behind the Manhattan skyline. Its accompaniment was the buzz of rush-hour traffic leaving the city and the occasional rumble of a subway train rattling along the elevated line. The mountain of used tires smelled even in the depths of winter.

Donovan got out of his Buick and stood with his hands in his pockets, watching as Moskowitz directed the platoon of detectives that surrounded the building, flak jackets on, weapons drawn. Gesturing with a walkie-talkie, Moskowitz looked like a baseball manager moving his outfielders around. When all were in place and there was no way out of the building except for rats and roaches, Mosko walked over to his boss.

"You want a part of this?" he asked, drawing his Penzler automatic.

Donovan shook his head. "I got shot at once today. That's my quota. In fact, that's it for me for all time. From now on, I manage. *You* get shot at."

"Hey, I really like you; you know that," Mosko said.

"Go get him," Donovan replied, and watched while the sergeant tried.

Two men broke down the door, which was locked. Three more, toting shotguns, followed them up the stairs. Not all that eager to get shot at, either, Moskowitz brought up the rear. At the same time, cops trained guns on the ground-floor windows and the solitary fire escape. The passing of another subway train bound for the far reaches of Queens drowned out sounds from within the building. After a minute, Mosko's round face appeared in a third-floor window, peeking out from between the shreds of a yellowed window shade.

Donovan looked up at his assistant, who gave him the hands-up signal of futility.

"He ain't here!" Mosko yelled as soon as the subway was gone.

Donovan pushed away from the Buick, walked across the street, and went into the building and up the stairs. They were wooden and old, worn down by the decades until each step had twin scoops where the feet landed. The walls had been painted once but now were marked by graffiti and streaked by rust stains from plumbing that leaked when it worked at all. Far atop the stairwell, a small square skylight was coated with pigeon droppings.

"No gold faucets in this place," Donovan said, stepping into a one-bedroom apartment that was dirty and claustrophobic, the latter coming from low ceilings and linoleum that had turned brownish yellow with age.

A queen-size mattress sat atop a metal frame. Atop a recently draped white sheet was a paper shopping bag from the Sloan's supermarket down Jackson Avenue. In it: an economy-size bag of Snickers, two tins of hummus, a Spanish onion, a half-pint of extra-virgin olive oil, and a pint of plain yogurt. Donovan touched the latter with the backs of his fingers, carefully avoiding leaving prints.

"It's still cold," he said.

"We missed him again," Moskowitz observed. He was using the tip of a pencil to open a copy of the December issue of *Aviation Week & Space Technology*. Other detectives pored over the squalid quarters, peeking behind the nonworking radiator, sniffing the fumes coming from a Sears kerosene heater, looking in almost-empty closets, and checking a bottle of generic aspirin found in the medicine cabinet.

Donovan went to a window, raised the shade, and looked out over the mountain of tires. A commuter train had just filled up at the Hunters Point Avenue station. Three hours later, the old diesel engine would deposit a few hardy resort denizens at Montauk Point. At the moment, though, it rumbled and rattled across the spider's web of intersecting rail lines that was the Sunnyside Yards.

Donovan opened the window and shut it again after catching a whiff of the used tires. "A rickety train. A mountain of used tires. Add a Kalishnikov assault rifle or two and we could be in Kabul," Donovan said.

"Maybe that's why Mojadidi rented the place," Mosko commented. "It reminded him of home."

"Did we find anything of interest?"

"No. Apparently the guy wasn't here very long."

"Apparently he's either the luckiest SOB in the world or else the best-informed," Donovan said.

"Well, we'll keep looking," Mosko replied, his voice halfway plaintive.

Donovan frowned at the useless comment. "I'm going back to my wife," he said.

"You want to bring her some Snickers?"

"No. Do you need me to drop you back in the city?"

Mosko shook his head. "I'll catch a ride with one of the guys," he replied.

TWELVE

"WHO HASN'T PAUL DUKE SLEPT WITH?"

DONOVAN SHOOK his head in amazement when he stepped inside Marcy's room. Sitting by her side were the two anchors of *The Morning Show,* Paul Duke and June Lake. With them was a full network camera crew. It had set up three light tripods as well as an umbrella reflector that softened the light shining on Marcy's face, which was glowing with all its pregnant radiance. She had her bed cranked up and was snuggled between pillows. Most strikingly, she wore a stunning white-on-white nightgown on the sleeve of which was stitched the logo of E & J Tuttle. Wearing jeans and an Irish sweater, Duke sat back a bit and watched while June Lake, dressed to the nines in a beige suit and silk blouse, wrapped up an interview with the mom-to-be.

Dr. Campagna stood behind her, resting a paternal hand on her shoulder. He looked as pleased as the cat that caught the canary.

A woman carrying a clipboard spotted Donovan and gestured to him to be quiet. He crossed his arms and listened to Camapagna deliver a litany of advice on the subject of high-risk pregnancy until the camera and lights flicked off.

"We're taping a medical segment," the woman with the clipboard then snapped at Donovan. "Who are you?"

"The sperm donor," Donovan replied. At which she looked quizzical, then annoyed, then turned away.

"Hi, honey!" Marcy called out, able to see her husband now that the blinding lights were off. "I'm going to be on television."

Donovan walked to her side and kissed her. "That's great," he said.

"Where were you all day while I was being interviewed for national television?" Marcy asked.

"Out getting shot at," Donovan replied.

She laughed, then winked at Lake. "This is my husband William. He likes to kid around."

The woman got up from her chair, pressed her skirt back into place, and took Donovan's hand as Paul Duke introduced them. She was about five-seven, Marcy's height, with lots of wavy black hair, black-pearl eyes, and a four-alarm smile that inevitably was accompanied by a cocking of the head, Miss America-style, to one side. Marcy generally hated the beauty-contest look, Donovan thought. His multiracial wife had long ago perfected the aura of the ethnic goddess and generally despised the Barbie look. But that dislike apparently had been put on hold long enough to get on television.

"I'm always glad to meet Paul's friends," Lake said. "He has such good taste."

Donovan gave Duke a glance. The man shrugged.

"So what's the occasion?" Donovan asked.

"I'm doing a report on high-risk pregnancy. Since Dr. Campagna is the world's authority—"

"You're very kind, June," Campagna said. He had moved off the impromptu set and was fiddling with the medical records computer.

"—and your wife is so beautiful—"

Marcy glowed brightly enough to blind someone.

"—I thought I'd make them the centerpiece of my report," Lake concluded.

"How'd you hear about them?" Donovan asked.

"Oh, from Paul, of course. But I know Dr. Campagna from a shoot I did years ago. I'm sorry you got here too late to be a part of it. If we have to reshoot to add more material I'll be sure to get you in."

She gave him the look you give children you expect to be disappointed. But Donovan said, "I have no need to be on television. Thanks anyway."

"Bill was an expert commentator during the O.J. trials," Duke explained.

"Of course. Captain Donovan. That's where I've seen you. You were in the studio with Paul." Lake looked at him again, more appreciatively this time, as if he were a fellow celebrity. "I loved it when you said you would have gotten onto the O.J. estate by starting a fire in his garbage pail. You were kidding, weren't you?"

Donovan gave her the palms-up sign of ambiguity. Then he added, "In retrospect, I would have torched the whole place."

Lake sighed and said, "Ah, yes, dreams die hard, don't they?"

The camera crew was busy packing its gear into a handful of aluminum trunks and loading the latter onto a dolly. The woman with the clipboard was on the phone getting her voice-mail messages. Campagna was done with the computer and was eating a Perugina chocolate and gazing idly at the yards-long strip of printout from Marcy's fetal monitor. The inches-wide paper curled onto the floor and piled up in bouquets.

Donovan felt the fabric of his wife's new gown. "Where'd you get the rags?" he asked.

"From Paul," she said proudly.

Duke looked away.

"Well, I have to tell *Paul* that you can't keep it."

"I can't?" she said, her voice a mew and her mouth a pout.

"And you know why."

Of course she did. That meant Paul was a suspect. In something, if not in shooting shoppers on Fifth Avenue. But in replying Marcy said, "You're a captain now and can't accept gifts."

"As if I ever did," Donovan replied.

"I seem to recall a few beers," she said dryly.

"Ancient history. This is a thirty-five-hundred-dollar nightie and it will have to go back."

At that point, Duke chimed in, "It's not like I paid for it, Bill."

Lake added, "E & J Tuttle was delighted to 'lend' us this gown for use in the piece. Think of what it would cost them in advertising dollars if they paid to have one of their gowns—with their logo on the sleeve—displayed on *The Morning Show*."

"Big bucks," Duke agreed.

"Nonetheless, you'll have to take it back," Donovan said.

"Whatever you want," Duke replied.

"Can I at least wear it until the baby comes?"

"Give it back before your water breaks," Campagna replied, looking up from the printouts.

Marcy grimaced and said, "I'll put it back in the box when I get up for my shower later."

Donovan smiled and squeezed her hand. "You're very understanding," he said.

"What's this about getting shot at?" she asked.

"I was kidding around, just like you said. Did you get a chance to look at the video?"

Marcy nodded. "Paul and June watched it with me."

"That must have been hard," Donovan said, speaking to them. "I don't think I could sit through watching two hours of me doing my job."

"It wasn't bad," Lake replied. "Paul and I know where the crowd shots come, and we helped your wife fast-forward to those spots."

"Did anyone stand out?"

"Yes," Marcy said proudly.

"Who?"

"Your Viking friend," she replied.

"He was there?" Donovan asked. "Let me see."

The *Morning Show* camera crew had moved out of the room, so there was a clear view of the room's TV screen. Donovan flicked on the VCR and handed Marcy the remote. She, in turn, handed it to Duke, who pressed a button. The tape had been wound to the spot where "Moondog II," aka Tom Tuttle, was seen in freeze-frame gaping in the window of the Rockefeller Center TV studio. At least, Donovan thought he could be Tuttle. For the head was covered with the horned helmet Donovan had picked up at the Shining Path Poets Cafe and the face was hidden behind a leather mask. But sprigs of mustache stuck out from the slit left for the mouth, and a certain angry fanaticism burned in the steel-grey eyes. The imposing figure, which looked very nearly seven feet tall, was draped from shoulder to calf in a forest green cloak big enough to hide an infantry regiment.

Tuttle was right at the front of the crowd, staring deep into the studio, his eyes ablaze.

Nervously fingering the remote, Duke said, "He's only there a minute. Then he takes off. Look! Look!"

He pressed a button and they all watched while Tuttle suddenly jerked his head, then all his body, away from the window and lurched through the crowd. Grandmas from Iowa jumped to either side to escape being trampled by the gigantic raging figure.

"So much for the power of poetry to soothe," Donovan said.

Duke shut off the tape, and the monitor on the wall reverted to showing CNN.

"Is that the killer you're after?" Lake and Duke asked, almost simultaneously.

"He's a suspect," Donovan replied.

"I never heard of this Viking," Duke said.

"Sure you did," Lake interjected, momentarily and lightly resting her fingertips on Duke's forearm. "Don't you remember we watched that piece about him on *CBS Sunday Morning?*''

Duke tossed his hands up, then brought them together and rubbed them nervously. She patted him reassuringly on the back, then pulled back her hand.

''I know his identity and I want to talk to him,'' Donovan said. ''We're looking for him now. At what time of morning was this piece of tape shot that we just watched?''

Duke checked some notes he had made and answered, ''We shot that segment between eight-fifty and nine.''

''That day's killing occurred at nine-fifteen, so our Viking pal could have done it,'' Donovan said.

Campagna was done with the printouts and dropped them back onto the floor. The paper strip continued to flow from the machine, a thin glacier coated with chicken scratches. He packed up the folder containing Marcy's medical record, walked to the door, and stuck it in the plastic holder on the outside.

He said, ''I'll stop by later tonight if I get a chance, Mrs. Donovan.''

''Do you have another delivery?'' Marcy asked.

''The quads are coming tonight,'' he replied.

''The ones whose parents flew in from Saudi Arabia?'' she asked.

''Yes. My third set of quads this year. I should get an award.''

''You're wonderful, Dr. Campagna,'' Marcy gushed.

The physician smiled, then reached through the little crowd by Marcy's bed and shook hands with Duke and Lake. To her he said, ''Good to see you again, June.''

She smiled back and waved as he walked out of the room and into the hall, brushing past the woman with the clipboard, who took advantage of eye contact with Lake to tap a fingertip against her watch.

''The crew has to go,'' Lake said.

"I'll see you tomorrow at the studio," Duke replied. He held back as she angled toward the door.

But she took him by the arm and pulled him with her, saying, "For God's sake, let's leave this happy couple alone."

"I'll never be alone now that I'm having a baby," Marcy stated.

"Marcy, you can ship the nightgown back to me when you get a chance," Duke said. "Or just ask your husband to drop it off at the store."

Donovan nodded. Then he asked, "How'd you get here? Walk?"

"God, no," Lake said. "I won't let him set a foot outside the studio without his bodyguard."

Duke blushed. "She's mothering me," he replied sheepishly.

"We came in Paul's limo," Lake continued. "The poor man has been made a nervous wreck by all these terrible killings. For some reason, he's taking them personally."

"The killer was standing three feet away from me," Duke said tersely, indicating the TV monitor.

"The glass is bulletproof," she said.

"He has a special gun," Duke replied.

Lake smiled and made a dismissive gesture. "You will catch the killer, won't you, Captain? Before Paul has a nervous breakdown?"

"I always have in the past," Donovan replied.

"I'm sure you're as good as your reputation," Lake responded. And after a few pleasantries, she managed to pull Duke, who was shrugging and giving in to the inevitable, from the room. They joined the camera crew, a rattling caravan pushing aluminum boxes on heavy dollies, and followed it down the hall.

Donovan closed the door, then gave Marcy a long hug and a handful of kisses. After that he stole one of Campagna's chocolates and sat on the edge of the bed.

"What did you make of that?" he asked.

"I have to call my mother and tell her I'm going to be on TV," Marcy said, reaching for the phone.

Donovan caught her hand and held it. "I mean why do you think June told us they spent a Saturday night together?"

"When did she say that?" Marcy asked.

"When she pointed out that they watched *CBS Sunday Morning* together. That show comes on at nine a.m. Don't tell me they were in a conference room at work."

Marcy thought for a second, then replied, "I guess she likes him. I guess they slept together."

"Who *hasn't* Paul Duke slept with? Beyond Benazir Bhutto and Mother Teresa, of course."

"Didn't you tell me he was ducking June?"

"Yeah. When I went to the studio to pick up the tape you watched today. He acted like she was carrying the plague."

"Maybe they made up," Marcy said.

"Clearly."

"She *is* mothering him."

"He seriously needs direction of some sort," Donovan said. "Interesting that she knows what a nervous wreck he is. And he swore me to secrecy on that point. Said it would be the end of his career should anyone at the network find out. Oh, well, a man tells everything to the woman he sleeps with, I guess."

"I hope so," Marcy replied.

"In which case we can only be glad that Duke isn't carrying the codes that fire the nuclear missiles. Oh, well."

They rested and watched CNN for a while; then around ten Marcy drifted off and Donovan pulled his computer into his lap and logged on to the Internet. Ten minutes later he had followed a logical series of searches and links to produce, in sinewy tones of walnut and steel, a remarkably plain-looking nine-millimeter automatic, the barrel of which was etched with the words "Kammacher Stedman." The photograph came from the on-line catalog of Weber and Augsberg Classic Arms, the Zurich arms merchant that was among the few European weapons manufacturers that hadn't quite got around to apologizing for selling arms to the Nazis during World War II, despite the hoopla that arose half a century after that conflict's last bullets were fired.

The catalog showed three views—from the side, from the front, and from the top—as well as half a page of glowing reports about the weapon's armor-piercing ability. Donovan found the look of the thing to be unremarkable, a bit like the Glock nine-millimeter that some New York police officers had begun carrying. He was no authority on guns but realized that whatever the Afghan gyro vendor had been carrying, it wasn't a Stedman. That man's weapon was relatively slender, more like a Wilson.

What did catch Donovan's eye was a fact hidden in the glowing description. Only three Stedmans were ever produced, that was true. Moreover, only 100 *rounds* were ever manufactured. Most of those, 75 in all, were accounted for with the first two guns. Of the 25 bullets sold with the third, "lost" Stedman, 17 were fired in the course of its history as a collector's item. According to Weber and Augsberg's Web site, eight depleted-uranium slugs remained. But, Donovan noted, that site was last updated before the two murders on Fifth Avenue. In them, the killer used first three, then two bullets.

"There are three still out there," Donovan muttered, switching screens on his computer to begin searching for information on what the survivalists in Montana were up to.

THIRTEEN

"EACH X MARKS A SANTA'S ANGEL; EACH Z MARKS THE BIG GUY HIMSELF"

A STEEP AND NARROW stairway—wooden and old, and creaking like a pair of angry crows, led to the second-floor office labeled SSA. The gold-leaf lettering struggled in vain to lend respectability to a weary old suite of rooms that would not have been out of place as the headquarters of a cheap import-export business. There was no need to push the door open. It opened and closed more or less constantly, syncopated like a grandfather clock, as Santa's Angels, some reeking of alcohol, others of tobacco, came and went, little slips of paper clutched between fingers more often than not twisted by age and arthritis.

Donovan and Moskowitz paused as an especially corpulent gent, his red cloak stretched over a genuinely plump belly, squeezed himself out the door and ventured down the narrow stairs, earning the glares of those who had to wait while he clogged their vital artery.

"What does 'SSA' stand for?" Donovan asked, pondering the gold leaf on the door.

"Seasonal Staffing Associates," Mosko replied.

"Do they handle just the Christmas season or is there more?"

"There's *lots* more. Bunnies at Easter. Remember the white fuzzy Easter bunnies that were begging coins outside St. Pat's and other local churches last spring?"

Donovan shook his head. "Marcy was eggulating at the time. I was busy getting her pregnant. The only rabbits I saw were the half dozen that died in the course of the impregnation.''

"Oh, *that's* when she was eggulating. Say, they don't really kill rabbits anymore, do they? I mean it's just a saying, right? 'The rabbit died.'''

"To the best of my knowledge, they only kill a couple of chemicals," Donovan said.

Moskowitz led the way into the office, stepping in the door before the flow of Santa's Angels could resume and block the passage again. The room was large and square and smelled of 1947, something about cigar smoke and hissing radiators and a tiny AM radio playing the Andrews Sisters. A sixtyish man whose waistline bore the cumulative strain of too many egg, cheese, and bacon sandwiches was wedged between a rust-stained wall and an ancient oak desk chicken-scratched with penknife and dug-in ballpoint pen marks that indicated prior service in the local public school. Initials, hearts, and the customary obscenities were partly hidden by a huge vinyl desk calendar. On it, amid coffee stains and phone numbers, was a grid that showed Fifth Avenue from Thirty-fourth to Sixty-second Streets.

Donovan looked down on the grid and waited while the proprietor of the desk—one Walter Huncke, according to a plastic sign that sat next to a battered brass ashtray filled with cigar butts and spent matches—finished a phone call.

"You guys got experience?" the man asked without looking up.

"How much experience do you need to ring a bell and beg coins?" Donovan replied. "What is it, corporate downsizing has finally reach the nth degree—now a man needs a *résumé* to become a panhandler?"

"Who are you?" Huncke said, a flash of irritation in his eyes, finally lifted from the desk and telephone.

"Bill Donovan, New York Police. This is Sergeant Moskowitz."

"Oh, yeah," Huncke said, looking at Moskowitz. "You

called. What can I do for you ossifers?'' He smiled at his little joke.

''One of your red-cloaked little beggars may have blown away a shopper on Fifth Avenue,'' Donovan said.

Huncke's smile faded, ground out into the ashtray with his cigars. He looked at the three hopefuls seated on wood-slat folding chairs across the room. What before had seemed like a trio of life's losers grasping for a few weeks' income now had the look of hit men. Huncke waved a fat forefinger at them. ''Would you guys mind waiting out in the hall till I call you?'' he said. ''Close the door and don't let nobody in and you all got jobs through New Year's.''

The trio complied happily, flush with new authority— control of a door being one of city life's power basics—and the promise of dough.

When they were gone, Huncke said, ''This would have been that thing on Thanksgiving?''

''The day after,'' Donovan said.

''One of *my* guys did it? You got any idea which one?''

''If we did, he'd have been drawn and quartered by now.''

Mosko said, ''We need a list of Santa's Angels, along with everything you got on them.''

''You want all of them?'' Huncke asked.

''Every last wino,'' Mosko replied.

''Hey, some of 'em ain't that bad. The Santas, for example. All of 'em are clean as far as records go. I even do things I don't have to do to make sure they stay clean.''

''Like what?'' Moskowitz asked.

''Each Santa got to shave every day,'' Huncke replied proudly.

''Seems like a waste considering the beards they got to put on,'' Donovan said.

''Just like I told you. I go that extra mile to make sure this is a merry and authentic Christmas season for all the children who see my Santas,'' Huncke responded.

"What else do you do?" Mosko asked.

"Each Santa gotta bathe at least twice a week. No one wants to give money to a Santa with BO, you know what I'm saying? That's even though it's so cold and windy out you can't smell nothing, not even dog shit."

"I'm sure that the tourist board appreciates your efforts," Donovan said agreeably. "Now, let's have a list of employees. And I'm interested in Santa's Angels, not Santas."

Huncke nodded and pulled open the wooden file drawer built into the side of his desk that lay to the right of his fat legs. There, carefully rested atop a jar of Maxwell House instant coffee and a large box of Sweet'n Low, was a crisp new manila folder. Donovan sensed that the man put the folder atop his personal food stash to make sure he could find it. Huncke transferred the file to the top of his desk and opened it gingerly. He said, "When the sergeant here called, I asked the girl to xerox the job application forms." He indicated a small metal desk, vacant save for a comb, a mirror, several tubes of Revlon lipstick, and an old AT-style computer. The desk was crammed into a corner of the room but near the window.

Huncke added, "I put Doris's desk closer to the window than mine because I smoke. This way she can stick her head out and get some air."

"That's thoughtful of you," Donovan said.

"Like I said, I take care of my people. Anyway, Doris is out getting her nails done."

"If I knew thirty years ago that it would be possible to make a living selling ultraspecialty items—nail jobs, cookies, socks—I would have gone into another line of work," Donovan said.

"Selling what?" Mosko asked.

"I haven't thought it out. Indulgences, maybe. So, Mr. Huncke, are there any serial killers in this batch?"

Donovan used his thumb to flip through the one hundred or so pages in the folder.

"Nah. A couple of guys who been through the school of hard knocks, maybe. But they're harmless."

"How about you letting us be the judge of that," Mosko said.

"Name them," Donovan ordered, tapping the pile of papers.

"The top three," Huncke said. Proud of his effort on behalf of justice, he took a fresh stogie from a weary old humidor and tamped it down on his desk calendar.

Donovan scrutinized the top application. "'Jack Swain,'" he read out loud. "Fifty-seven. Lives in Bensonhurst. So who did he kill that you singled him out?"

"He didn't kill nobody. He did three years at Danbury for running a sports book."

Donovan shrugged. "No big deal. My old *paison* Gaetano did three at Danbury for running a numbers joint. Now he drives a limo during the day and in the evenings eats pepperoni and watches professional wrestling with his mom. They live together, in Bensonhurst, now that you mention it. He's harmless."

"Maybe your Danbury con knows his Danbury con," Mosko speculated.

"It could be. Danbury grads think of themselves as belonging to 'the club.'"

"Howard Klempert is harmless too, I think," Huncke said. He clipped off the end of the cigar and began fumbling around in his top desk drawer for a match. "He lives in Long Island City."

"'Hunters Point Avenue,'" Donovan read off the second application.

"Above a butcher shop. I think he shares with another guy. I feel sorry for the slob—he's warmhearted and hardworking—and so I give him two tokens a day so he can get to work and back."

"What did *he* do?" Donovan asked.

"He did time for armed robbery a while back," Huncke said.

Moskowitz's eyes widened.

"What did he hit and when?" Donovan asked.

"A 7-Eleven in Union City. In the sixties."

"I think I better check this guy out," Mosko said.

"Do you know any more about it?"

"He told me he carried a gun at the time but didn't shoot nobody. He also said he did five years."

"Where?"

"Someplace in Jersey, I guess. Anyway, the guy is in his fifties now and, like you would expect for a guy that age, is in no shape to do anything physical."

Mosko smiled, earning himself a scowl from his boss.

"Did he say what kind of gun he used?" Mosko asked.

"He called it a 'popgun,'" Huncke said. "I don't necessarily believe everything these guys say. You know, they're applying for bottom-of-the-barrel jobs. Still, I have to check 'em out. I think Klempert is probably harmless. But you said you want to be the judge."

Donovan nodded. "What about Walter Tillis?"

"Now, *there's* an angry man. I mean one who's got a bee in his bonnet about *something*—I couldn't tell you what."

"His application says he's sixty-five and a Korean War vet," Donovan said. "That's way too old to be stalking people on Fifth Avenue."

"You would think so, but he bragged about being a two-time pistol champion. And I thought that might interest you."

"Really," Mosko said.

"Champion of what?" Donovan asked.

"His army unit," Huncke replied. "He's pretty proud of that."

"That's nice. He's got something good in his life to think

back on. So what did he do that was so bad? Why are you fingering him?''

"He didn't *do* anything," Huncke said. "It's his attitude. The man is ready to boil over."

"And you have no idea what he's pissed off about?" Mosko asked.

"I don't have so much as a clue. Didn't you ever see these time bombs in bars? Tell me, Captain, did you ever spend an afternoon in a Blarney Stone?"

"Never," Donovan replied, rolling his eyes.

"Three Our Fathers and three Hail Marys," Moskowitz said, sotto voce.

"Well, if you had you'd know the type of guy Tillis is," Huncke went on. "Sits there hour after hour, staring into space and looking *mad*. Every so often swears at something on TV or growls at a guy who sits too close."

"I get that way in the subway," Moskowitz replied.

"If we arrested every guy who was pissed off we'd have to turn the Bronx into a jail," Donovan remarked.

"Isn't it one now?" Mosko said.

Unable to find a match, Huncke looked forlorn and tossed up his hands. "Can you guys help me out here?" he pleaded.

"We don't smoke," Donovan replied.

"Cops who don't drink or smoke. What's the world coming to?"

"Its senses, maybe," Donovan said.

With difficulty, Huncke pushed away from the desk, stood, and lumbered over to his secretary's work space. From her top drawer he plucked a matchbook. Then he went back to his desk and lit up as he lowered himself, grunting, back into his complaining chair.

Huncke carefully blew the smoke away from the detectives. He flipped the matches onto his calendar. Donovan noticed that the pack had red lettering on a yellow background and was subtle as a "Stop—Biohazard" warning. It read: "Sunnyside Tavern."

Donovan pointed at the calendar and asked, "Is this how you keep track of how the troops are deployed?"

"You got it," Huncke replied, leaning back in his chair, the tobacco giving him the glow of the newly addicted. "I got each man's post marked...see?" He jabbed the cigar at the corner of Fifty-fourth and Fifth. "Each X marks a Santa's Angel; each Z marks the big guy himself."

"How do you know everybody is in the right spot?" Donovan asked. "Do you have a supervisor who goes up and down the avenue checking?"

"You're looking at him," Huncke said, pointing at his chest with the cigar and spilling ashes onto his lap. He gazed down at them, deciding if it was worth the effort to clean up. Apparently he decided it wasn't. He shrugged and looked up at the captain.

"You do it?" Donovan asked.

"I'm the man," Huncke said. "Every morning at nine. Every afternoon at three. Again at seven in the evening."

"That's a long day for you," Mosko commented.

"It's a big responsibility, taking care of Santa's Angels," Huncke said proudly. "There's a lot of guys goin' out on the job every day. There's a lot of money coming in."

"How much?" Donovan asked.

"Come on now, Captain. That's a trade secret. Is it important?"

"I guess not. But how do you know it's all going to God's good work? Given the backgrounds of some of the guys you hire, don't you worry that a lot of money is being diverted to the corner liquor store?"

"Yeah," Mosko agreed.

"Two things," Huncke said. "One is actuarial data. That's what I call it, anyway."

"Actuarial data?" Donovan asked.

"Let me explain it this way. I know how much bread

should be collected by a guy standing in a specific spot. After years of watching trends, you know?''

"*Trends* in panhandling? Christ, everything is data-specific these days. OK, I'll bite. Where are the best and worst spots to glom cash on Fifth Avenue?''

"I can tell you without even having to look it up," Huncke said. "The best is in front of Tiffany's and Cartier. The worst is in front of F.A.O. Schwarz.''

"Explain," Donovan said.

"It's simple. In front of Tiffany's and Cartier you got shoppers who have no prayer in this man's earth to buy anything they see in the window. But they can make themselves feel better by dropping a quarter in a bucket.''

"That makes sense. And what about F.A.O. Schwarz? I can tell you one thing—that not many people can afford the gyros the guy out front sells.''

"That I can't help you with," Huncke said. "The issue here is toys, not food. People who are thinking toys are thinking affordable, and they're already thinking happy thoughts, so there's no subconscious impetus for them to give to charity.''

"None of this would ever have occurred to me," Donovan commented.

"That's why the world needs experts," Huncke said in a self-satisfied sort of way.

"You said there were *two* things that made you sure you weren't being robbed," Donovan said.

"I check up on them," Huncke replied.

"How? Except for the three times a day you check locations, you sit here, right, ministering to the parade of guys coming through the door?''

"Right. Sorry. I meant to say Doris does it. She goes undercover for me, if you will.''

"Undercover," Mosko said.

"'Cause the guys know what she looks like. So she puts on a wig and changes her clothes—''

"Changes her nail color," Donovan said.

"Yeah, that," Huncke agreed. "And then walks up and down Fifth Avenue looking to see if she can catch someone stealing from the Lord."

"We'll need to talk to Doris," Donovan said.

"She's at the nail parlor, like I told you."

"Which one?" Mosko asked.

"Kim's Beautiful Nails, two blocks uptown on the right. The Korean nail place, not the Spanish one around the corner."

"Koreans have nail shops now?" Mosko asked. "Is there anything they aren't into in this city?"

"I haven't seen them riding to the hounds yet," Donovan replied. He closed the folder and handed it to Moskowitz. "Go talk to her."

"Will do," Mosko replied.

"Just two other things, Mr. Huncke," Donovan said. "Where do you keep the Santa's Angels outfits? Where do you keep the tripods?"

"That's easy. I got the tripods from a wholesaler of surveying tripods. I painted them and hung buckets. The outfits I got from a theatrical costume shop in the Garment District. I keep both in there." He hooked a fat thumb in the direction of a back room.

"What I want you to do is count them both and let Sergeant Moskowitz know if the numbers of outfits and tripods matches up with the number of Angels."

"Whatever I can do," Huncke replied.

Moskowitz tucked the folder in his bag. Then the two of them exchanged a few more words of small talk with the proprietor of SSA before slipping out the door and walking down the narrow and creaking stairway past the line of men waiting all along it.

At the corner, Donovan bought a bag of chestnuts and cracked one open while watching traffic chug dutifully deeper into midtown. Mosko watched the cars full of Christmas shoppers from New Jersey, Pennsylvania, and Connecticut, the people all eager to walk the famous mile in front of the famous shops and absorb what holiday spirit was left following the depravations of a mad killer. Then he said, "This time tomorrow Fifth Avenue will be lousy with cops. Every corner. Every window. Every goddamned Santa's helper will have a cop watching him. We'll get the sonofabitch this time, Boss."

FOURTEEN

STALER THAN A CHRISTMAS CUPCAKE IN MARCH

BUT THEY DIDN'T, in fact, get the sonofabitch. In fact, two weeks later the investigation was staler than a Christmas cupcake in March. On December 21, the NYPD was no closer to finding the Fifth Avenue killer than it was to halting illegal parking or curing the common cold.

None of the Santa's Angels leads checked out, not even Tillis, the one said to be a ticking bomb. He turned out to have been harassing passersby, who complained to the police, at precisely the times of the killings. And while Huncke's inventory of equipment came out that nothing was missing, a cop checking a Dumpster at a construction site on Fifty-third and Park came up with a sort of imitation that may or may not have been the prop used by the killer. No useful fingerprints graced its exterior; there was nothing traceable about it at all.

As for the other suspects, whatever hole Tom Tuttle had crawled into to hide, he had pulled the walls in on himself and disappeared utterly. No one could find him, not the police, not the parole authorities. So, too, with Anna Fritsch. An even more extensive search failed to turn her up. She didn't show up at the other end of that Concorde flight; there was no second passport. Neither did the woman, now twenty-two weeks pregnant, reveal her presence to the FBI, Immigration, the German consulate, Interpol, or anyone else. Donovan's men, try though they might, could turn up no clues to her whereabouts by badgering her doctor, who professed ignorance and had the lawyers to back it up, or by polling other local obstetricians.

The Mountain Brigade, after its dramatic extortion attempt and demand for ten million dollars' worth of diamonds in exchange for a cease to terror, appeared to have gone back into the mountains—whichever mountains they hailed from. And as for Yama Mojadidi, the New York City Afghan community appeared to have absorbed him down to the last fiber of his fake turban. When an entire ethnic community, especially a newly arrived and still struggling one, wants to hide one of its own, that man might as well be vacationing on Pluto. Once he disappeared from his hovel on the rim of the Long Island Rail Road's Sunnyside Yards, Mojadidi was gone absolutely.

Despite the apparent disappearance of those who had made so many headlines threatening it, the holiday season on Fifth Avenue remained in dire straits. Though the perpetrator or perpetrators had apparently disappeared, the tabloids remained full of gory details about the two murders and the weekly newsmagazines all carried cover stories about what one of them called "the grinch that shot Christmas." And, of course, the late-night talk show hosts were ablaze with bulletproof window jokes.

And so it came to pass that Donovan spent the first part of the seven a.m. hour of December 21 by sitting in bed with his wife watching *The Morning Show* as June Lake introduced the taped segment about high-risk pregnancy. There Marcy was, in all her dusky beauty, wearing the Tuttle gown, speaking glowingly of her unborn child and the doctor who was to deliver him just a few days away. Then came the phone calls from family to discuss how beautiful she looked and how wonderful the pregnancy was and how proud Donovan must be to become a father at his age.

Half an hour later, Donovan held his laptop, appropriately enough, in his lap while doing the latest in a long series of computer searches, requests for information, and correspondences with his many friends in the worldwide law enforcement community. This work session came after he shaved and showered and got a cup of coffee from the staff cafeteria in the subbasement and eavesdropped on a diagnostic consultation that was being conducted in one of those interminable rides on the medical-staff elevator.

Marcy had just got out of the shower—which she had taken, given her size and late-term lack of equilibrium, while sitting down on an aluminum chair that the nurses had placed in the shower stall. She was sitting on the edge of the bed naked, a towel around her hair, rubbing moisturizing cream onto her belly. Suddenly a ripple of hard flesh, a bump that moved, appeared in her skin and shifted an inch or so to the left. That happened to be the side on which Donovan was sitting.

"Ooh," she said, and pressed her palm against it.

"'Ooh' what?" he asked, barely looking up from his laptop.

"That's the back of Daniel's head. He's moving toward you, honey."

"How can you tell that's not his bottom?" Donovan asked, reaching over and feeling the bump, moving her hand aside for an instant.

"Because his tush is up here," she said, patting that part of her belly that curved in to form a shelf atop which rested her breasts.

"I don't know how you can tell."

"Because he's supposed to be in that position, given how far along I am, and because I can feel every little bit of him, and because I saw the sonogram."

Donovan looked at the mammoth belly that soon would produce his son. "Isn't he supposed to be lower at this point?" he asked, pointing to the spot he had in mind.

"Yes. He hasn't dropped."

"Dropped?"

"His head should be down against my cervix, and it isn't."

"You're not due for four days yet," Donovan said, looking at his watch.

"It doesn't matter. Something is preventing him from dropping."

She put away the moisturizing cream and began to pull on her panties and bra.

"Is there a problem?" Donovan asked.

"If he doesn't drop, it will mean I definitely will have a C-section," she said, a bit ruefully.

"That's all it means? You were expecting that anyway."

"I know, but it would be nice to feel him being born."

"Can I still be in the room if you have a C-section?" Donovan asked.

"Of course. They just put a sheet up so you can't see the operation. They don't want you to see blood."

"It's happened before, on rare occasions," Donovan said.

"Not the same thing. When it's your wife, it's different."

"What do I do, then, sit there?" he asked, his eyes flicking back and forth from her to the monitor—more to the monitor as a particular screen got his attention.

"You hold my hand," she said.

"Easy enough," he replied, then added, staring full-time at the monitor now, "Whoa!"

"'Whoa' what?" Marcy asked, leaning forward to see.

"It seems that I'm not the only dad-to-be among our recent acquaintances," Donovan said.

"Who's the lucky guy and why is this information being displayed on the Internet? Is it Brian?"

"Mosko has enough kids," Donovan said, shaking his head. "Guess who was among the guests trapped on the island of Carricola last summer with Princess Anna."

A smile crept across Marcy's lips. "It would have to be Paul Duke."

"Bingo."

"Otherwise it wouldn't rate a mention on the 'Net."

"No wonder he's so interested in this case," Donovan said. "It's not just that somebody—maybe—is trying to kill him."

"It isn't him who's the target of the killer," Marcy said. "It's her."

"Or her and him."

"You're not thinking of June Lake," Marcy said. "America's sweetheart? The only woman who's thought of as being perfect?"

Donovan coughed into his hand. "Stranger things have happened," he said.

"Can she even shoot?"

"Like you said, she's perfect," Donovan said.

"It wasn't me who said it. It was a thousand magazine covers. Look at any newsstand. Where was she when the killings took place?"

"I'll have to find out."

"The notion of June Lake being a killer seems very weird to me," Marcy said. "It's so Hollywood, the idea that a woman would *really* kill to get a man."

"Even if that man is America's premier hunk, now that Mel Gibson hasn't taken his shirt off in a movie in ten years?"

"I guess." Marcy swung her legs back into bed. "I also guess this kills the theory that the killer is trying to extort ten million dollars from Fifth Avenue stores."

"I never liked that theory much," Donovan said.

Marcy looked at the door and asked, "Where's the nurse with my breakfast?"

The phone rang. Marcy answered it saying, "Daniel's house." Then she frowned and listened and said to her husband, "It's your office."

Donovan took the instrument and said, "What?" into it. He listened for a while, then said, "Okay," and hung up.

"Tell me they're sending up bagels," Marcy said.

"Sorry. There's been another note from the Mountain Brigade."

"Oh. Maybe there *is* something to it."

"They want their diamonds delivered today."

"You are *not* making the delivery yourself," Marcy said firmly. "It's way too dangerous and you could be a daddy at any moment."

"Don't worry," he replied. "I have no intention of getting involved. The whole line of investigation is a fool's errand, and I'm not the fool who wants to waste time on it. However, I've been wrong before."

"Not when you married me," she said.

"And I do want to talk to Claudia Hummitz again, and she's the one who got the extortion call."

"What do you need her for? She's only the one who picked up the telephone when it rang."

"No one is only what they seem in this case," Donovan said.

WHEN DONOVAN GOT to the office of the Midtown Merchants Association, Claudia Hummitz was sitting at the black leather banquette that sat across the room from her desk, wrapping around a glass coffee table, staring at her Filofax and an array of glossy catalogs from the Fifth Avenue stores that paid her salary. Her expression was blank, and she balled up a piece of tissue paper in the palm of her right hand. Three or four like it were clustered meticulously, tiny Kleenex cannonballs, next to the appointment book.

Her desk had been taken over by cookie-cutter young men, all thirty or so, wearing crisp Macy's suits and talking in clipped tones into cell phones. One of these, jacket off and folded carefully, was at work installing a fancy electronic device of one kind or another on the office telephone.

When Donovan got inside the office he was stopped by one of the men. This one, perhaps forty but dressed like the others and comporting himself just as crisply, as if he were on an eternal job interview, flashed a leather-bound ID in Donovan's face and said, "FBI."

"My condolences," Donovan responded, producing his badge. "Bill Donovan, chief of special investigations, New York Police." Having detected a hint of a Carolina accent in the man's speech, Donovan tossed in, "How are you boys doing here?"

"Very well, thank you, Captain. I've heard a lot about you. This is your case."

"You're welcome to a piece of it," Donovan said agreeably.

The man smiled and introduced himself as Dan Clark, special agent in charge. That name was, Donovan thought, one of those names that come up more often in Tom Clancy novels than in the ranks of real-life law enforcement officers. But this fellow seemed to be real enough, if a bit starched, and Donovan was delighted to work with him.

"What's going on?" Donovan asked.

"We were called in by the Midtown Merchants Association and have been in touch with your Deputy Chief Pilcrow," Clark said.

"My favorite people."

"The merchants group was of the opinion that the resources of the NYPD were being stretched a little thin trying to pin down the Mountain Brigade."

No, Donovan thought, *Pilcrow just wants to embarrass me; so be it.* "Our experience with mountains is limited," he said. "And, in my opinion, certain investigations have to follow a certain course and time line no matter what the professionals do or the amateurs think."

If Clark caught that insult to Pilcrow, he showed no sign of it.

Donovan continued, "Go ahead; jump in. Who *is* or *are* the Mountain Brigade?"

"We have been following two lines of investigation. One

is that they're an Afghanistani guerrilla group that is part of the coalition fighting the Taliban.''

"The Islamic fundamentalists who seem to be winning the civil war over there," Donovan said.

"Oh, you follow affairs in that part of the world?" Clark asked.

"I read the papers. And I have a certain fondness for Islam these days.''

"Oh, why?" Clark asked, raising an eyebrow.

"It's the only major religion—other than Buddhism, of course—that hasn't tried to convert me recently. Go on.''

"We have been getting reports that the Mountain Brigade has a wing in the U.S., here in New York City, soliciting money from members of the Afghan community so their brothers can continue the armed struggle back in the mountains of their homeland.''

"I took note of those reports this morning," Donovan said.

"Where did you get that information?" Clark asked, his otherwise-neutral expression turning slightly in the direction of suspicion.

"They have a Web page," Donovan replied.

"Of course," Clark said. Donovan was certain this was the first the man had heard of it.

"Everybody has a Web page these days," Donovan said. "Even fund-raising American arms of foreign guerrilla groups. I'm thinking of getting one myself. Do you have any names for me? Such as of specific Afghans in New York?"

Clark shook his head.

"Ever trip over the name of Yama Mojadidi?"

"Who's he?" Clark asked, requesting the spelling and calling a crisp-suited aide over to write it down.

"A Queens lad originally from Afghanistan who took a shot at me a few weeks back. I'm still pissed off about it.''

"No doubt. Got an address on him?"

"If I did—"

"Right, Captain. Now, the idea that the Mountain Brigade is trying to extort ten million dollars from Fifth Avenue merchants is attractive to us."

Of course it is, Donovan thought. The Feds always suspected the foreign-born first. Especially if the suspects were Muslims who could also be suspected of trying to throw a monkey wrench into the Christmas season at the same time.

"Striking at both God and country," Donovan said.

"I see you agree."

Donovan shrugged.

"On the other hand, the men behind this extortion attempt could be the Montana survivalist group under the leadership of Harlan Deaver. We've had our eyes on them for some time."

"Normally those guys just run check scams to raise money. And file phony liens against their enemies to foul up their credit ratings."

"You *do* keep up with things outside your turf. That's good."

"Nothing is outside my turf," Donovan said. "Because eventually everyone comes to New York."

"The story on these guys is that they will do anything to get money and screw the system. The notion of getting big bucks out of Fifth Avenue stores—"

"Particularly ones owned by Japanese billionaires," Donovan interjected.

Clark grinned for the first time during the conversation. "I see we *are* on the same wavelength," he said.

"If the Mountain Brigade is, in fact, behind these killings—"

"And the extortion attempt."

"A motive beyond getting the money to finance their secessionist campaign would be to strike at the foreign investors who are buying up American real estate."

Clark bobbed his head up and down.

"Do you have a problem with the idea that the group would never set foot in New York?" Donovan asked.

"No. They adjust when they have to. They say they hate the court system and don't recognize its authority, but they can spend hundreds of hours in courts filing false liens."

"True," Donovan admitted, looking over at Hummitz, who seemed to be growing bored with the FBI takeover of her office.

"I understand you're interested in the Stedman," Clark said.

Donovan said that he was.

"We traced it as far as Montana."

"Did you?"

"We learned that Deaver wanted to buy it and had an agent looking. And we heard that the weapon actually made it as far as Montana. But that's all we know."

"That's more than I have," Donovan said.

"Can we agree to share information?" Clark asked.

"You bet."

They shook on it.

"Who are at the top of your list?" Clark asked.

"The same guys you and I have just been talking about are right up there," Donovan replied.

"Any others?"

"One or two, but not developed to the point where I could talk about them."

"Can I give you a tip?" Clark asked.

"I'm always interested in what the FBI has to say."

"Take a closer look at George Halloran," Clark said, lowering his voice conspiratorially.

"Why him?"

"Just vague suspicions," Clark replied.

"He made my list, too."

"Good. I see we're *really* on the same wavelength."

"So what's your plan for today?" Donovan asked. "Tell me about the extortion note."

"It's a tape," Clark replied. "Made on her machine."

He nodded in the direction of Hummitz, who was watching the two men talk. She waved in a cursory sort of way at Donovan, adding a grim and fleeting smile. He returned a half-wave.

"It came in at seven-twenty this morning. Let's listen to it."

Clark snapped his fingers and one of his men—this one blond and especially young-looking—pressed a button on a hand-held tape player. An electronically altered voice said, "This is the Mountain Brigade. If you want the killings to stop so you can resume the course of your yearly plunder by rich corporations, leave ten million dollars in uncut diamonds beneath the elevated subway line at Thirty-seventh Avenue and Northern Boulevard at three o'clock this afternoon. You will notice that the plate covering the electrical circuits at the base of the northeast stanchion is held by only one screw. Remove that plate and put the diamonds inside. Replace the plate, leaving it as it was. We will retrieve the diamonds within twelve hours. Do not call the authorities. Any attempt to do so or to interfere with us as we pick up the diamonds will result in further bloodshed along your most gilded boulevard."

Clark said, "You can keep this copy of the tape." He took a cassette from his associate and handed it to the captain.

"Thanks."

"As I'm sure you know, that drop-off point is in a neighborhood with many Afghanistani residents."

"Asian, anyway," Donovan said.

"So we are, of course, most interested. And we will be making the drop. You don't want to do it, do you?"

Donovan shook his head. "My wife won't let me," he said. That remark earned him funny looks from the several FBI agents who were within earshot.

"Your wife must be a very strong woman," Clark said, a bit awkwardly.

"And a better shot than me, too."

"We'll be watching to see who picks up the jewels. We'll have extensive surveillance, of course. You're welcome to join us."

"Nah, you guys go it alone," Donovan said. "I'd only be in the way. I can tell you one thing, though. The Mountain Brigade guys—the Montana ones, that is—would stand out like moose in that neighborhood. Unless, of course, they have Asian allies."

"Not Deaver, never. He's too right-wing."

Donovan said, "Hitler had Asian allies, and it's tough to get farther to the right than him. Well anyway, have a ball. Are you about done here?"

"Jim?" Clark called to the fellow in shirtsleeves who was working behind the desk.

"The device is installed," the man replied, zipping up the cover on a small leather tool kit that he then slipped into his jacket pocket on the way out of the office.

Clark and Donovan exchanged business cards, with the man from Washington saying, "I'll give you a shout later on today. Where will you be? At the hospital?"

"Oh, you know about that?"

"We *are* the Federal Bureau of Investigation."

Donovan thought, *Pilcrow told them.*

"I'm very aware of your reputation," Donovan said.

"This is your first child?" Clark asked.

"Barring someone unforeseen tumbling off the Greyhound from Tucson, our Christmas baby will be my first," Donovan said. "Our first."

"The baby is due on Christmas? That has to be good luck. Does that mean you will be at the hospital this afternoon?"

Donovan thought, *This man is more than casually interested in my schedule.* "Absolutely," he replied.

"Good. I'll call you there, then."

A few minutes later, the FBI had cleared out, leaving Donovan alone with Hummitz. He smiled at her and—his hands jammed deep into his jeans pockets as a way of showing the woman, who looked more than a little beaten up on, that he was being loose and casual—said, "So, how goes the revolution?"

Her eyes flashed up at his and they met in an exchange of…something…a kindred spirit, perhaps, a shared caustic outlook on life, before she looked back down at the table. She said, "So much upheaval."

Then she sighed and her day-to-day personality clicked on and she said, "Captain, I imagine you don't think that I should pay the money these extortionists and murderers are demanding."

"Not for a second," he replied. "Pay away. Pay *twice*. Indulge yourself in a little redistribution of wealth. Why should I care? The way I see it, your members can write off the loss and the money is going from folks on Fifth Avenue who don't need it to folks in Queens who do."

Hummitz looked slightly amazed, but before she could respond Donovan went to the table, plucked the Tuttle catalog from among those arrayed in front of her, and opened it to the page showing the $3,500 nightie that Paul Duke had borrowed for Marcy to wear for her TV interview.

"Tell me," he said. "Is this rag worth thirty-five hundred dollars?" He handed her the catalog.

She looked at the page, then replied, "*I* wouldn't pay it. But I'm old enough to know better." She sighed and said, "About lots of things. But if someone can, who cares?" She handed the catalog back to Donovan, who folded it inside a pocket.

"Where are the diamonds coming from?" he asked.

"I'm getting the note from the bank at nine," she said, glancing at her watch. "And one of our members is supplying the diamonds."

"Done as a tiara or as a brooch?" Donovan asked.

She smiled. "Loose stones in a small sack," she said.

Donovan noticed that Hummitz had softened in the weeks since he first saw her. Or maybe she had aged. She looked predatory no longer. And she had forsaken the scarf that previously hid the wrinkles around her neck. She looked her age.

She also opened her hand long enough to release another tissue ball. When she noticed him watching, she smiled sheepishly. "An old habit," she said.

"I noticed," Donovan replied.

"I do it when I'm nervous or hungry."

"I play with my car keys," Donovan said, sticking a hand in his pocket and illustrating. "Which are you now, nervous or hungry?"

"Both. I didn't get the chance to order breakfast before you-know-what hit the fan."

"Do you like Mexican?" Donovan asked.

"I *love* Mexican," she said, brightening.

"I know this place, but it's uptown."

"Which side?"

"East."

"I live uptown—Ninety-sixth and Second. The Beresford Towers."

"My wife and I looked at a two-bedroom there once, before deciding we could never be pried away from the West Side," Donovan said.

"I thought you looked like a West Sider," Hummitz replied.

"But while looking on East Ninety-sixth we found this good neighborhood Mexican restaurant."

"Not Paco's?" she asked, eyes agleam with the thought of tastes and sounds far removed from the sterile glitter of Fifth Avenue.

"That's the place. You know it?"

"I eat there all the time," she said.

"Marcy thinks that the chorizos are salty," Donovan said.

"Chorizos everywhere are salty," Hummitz replied. "That's part of the appeal. God, I could use a breakfast burrito right now. How could you do this to me, Captain?"

"I'm a beast," he said.

"I doubt that very much."

"As I was telling my wife just a little while ago, no one I've run into recently is exactly what they seem."

"You included?" she asked with a coy smile.

"Me especially," Donovan replied.

She looked at Donovan for a long moment, at the end of which he sensed there was something she wanted to say. But it passed. Hummitz stood, sighed, and said, "I guess I have my desk back. And there's lots to do."

She walked over and sat behind it.

"Seen Paul lately?" Donovan asked.

"Paul." She laughed bitterly. "Oh my, *Paul*. No, I haven't seen him. As far as I'm concerned, he disappeared."

"It's been all the rage lately."

"Has it? I doubt that Paul will ever change. I hope, for his sake...for a lot of people's sakes, that I'm wrong."

"Maybe he will," Donovan said. "Fear of being shot at is a powerful motivator."

"Actually being shot at is an even stronger one," Hummitz replied, opening her desk drawer and then slamming it shut with a resounding bang.

FIFTEEN

"THAT AND FIVE MILLION DOLLARS' WORTH OF ATTORNEYS WOULD HAVE GOTTEN YOU OFF," DONOVAN SAID

"YOU REALLY AREN'T going out on the FBI surveillance this afternoon?" Marcy asked, finishing the bagel he had brought her after leaving Hummitz's office.

"I'm really not."

"I expected a fight from you."

"Let the Feds go and spend a pleasant afternoon and evening under the el in Queens," Donovan said. "They won't find anything."

"Why not?"

"Because nobody will come to pick up the diamonds. This is a fool's errand, I tell you. Not even he's interested in going."

Donovan had nodded in the direction of Moskowitz, who replied, "And a Merry Christmas to you, too, Boss." The sergeant sipped a cup of coffee brought up from the cafeteria.

"What are you going to be doing?" Marcy asked her husband's assistant.

"I got a lead on the gyro guy. I heard he's working in a pet shop in Queens, on Northern Boulevard."

"Where on Northern Boulevard?" Marcy asked.

"As if you would know anything about Queens," Mosko replied. "You never been outside Manhattan except maybe to visit your parents in... What's the name of that place? Crouton-on-Hudson?"

"Croton-on-Hudson," Marcy replied.

"Yeah, there. So what difference does it make where on Northern Boulevard the pet shop is?"

"OK," she said, a trace of exasperation in her voice. "*How far* is the pet shop from the drop site?"

"About fifteen blocks. A mile and a half."

"And you don't see a connection?"

Mosko did that thing that New Yorkers do by way of saying, "Maybe." He held his hand out flat, palm down, and waggled it from side to side.

"Where *do* the Afghans live in this town?" Marcy asked.

"All over," Donovan said. "But many live in Queens, along Northern Boulevard."

"So? There you have it. The Mountain Brigade *is* Afghan, they *are* behind the killings and the extortion attempt, and they *will* be there this afternoon, probably heavily armed, to pick up the diamonds. That's why my husband isn't going."

"Isn't it cute, the way she protects you?" Mosko said to Donovan. The sergeant leaned forward and, pretending to knock on her belly, said, "So what's going on in there? Police! Come out with your hands up!"

"Stop it," Marcy snapped, slapping his hand away.

"Daniel isn't moving much the past couple of days," Donovan said.

"It looks like it's getting cramped in there," Mosko replied.

Marcy said, "And you should stay away from the surveillance, too. What would your wife say?"

"My wife would say, 'Honey, what can I make you for dinner?'"

Marcy sighed and scrunched back into her pillows, nestling herself in and holding her belly proudly.

Donovan pulled an evidence bag off the end table where the phone was kept. The bag contained the Tuttle catalog he had got from Claudia Hummitz's office. Donovan gave it to Mosko, saying, "Send this downtown and have it checked for prints. Especially the page that shows the thirty-five-hundred-dollar nightie."

"You got that catalog this morning from Claudia Hummitz," Marcy said. "You're running prints on *her?*"

"You bet," he replied.

"Why? You *know* who she is."

"Oh, I know who she is. I just want proof."

"Who is she?" Mosko asked.

Donovan raised a finger admonishingly. "You keep running two paces behind me and you're never going to see that Christmas bonus. Aren't you two interested in why I'm so sure that nobody will pick up the diamonds this afternoon?"

"'Cause this case isn't about money," Mosko said.

"I think it *is* about money," Marcy disagreed.

Donovan shook his head. "Sorry, honey, but you're wrong. The person who's behind these killings—"

"Note he said 'person,' not 'persons,'" Mosko said.

"—isn't in it for the loot. So the diamonds will just sit there, all ten million dollars of them, in the base of that stanchion under the el, until Clark and the rest of his FBI boys realize that their surveillance is colder than J. Edgar Hoover's pink taffeta party dress."

"Why the diamonds, then?" Marcy asked.

"To get the investigating team away from Fifth Avenue. To give us something to obsess on while he—the killer—does something. Probably kills Paul Duke."

Marcy's eyes widened. "What time is the drop?" she asked.

"Three or after," Mosko replied.

"Which means you'll be with Paul," Marcy said.

"No. But I left a message on his machine telling him to stay indoors and with people he trusts," Donovan replied. "I'll be talking to George Halloran at three. For one thing,

I want to be with him at three o'clock. But first I have to go to Brighton Beach.''

"Koslov?" Marcy asked. "The Russian mobster whose wife was seduced by Paul? You're going to talk to Koslov?''

Donovan shook his head. "Mdivani.''

"Who?''

"Georgi Mdivani. You and I weren't talking at the time, so you never got to meet him. Too bad, 'cause you would have liked him.''

"Which time that we weren't talking was it?" Marcy asked.

"The last. He's a former diplomat from a former Soviet Central Asian republic—''

"Anywhere near Afghanistan?" Mosko asked.

"Don't they teach geography in Brooklyn?" Donovan asked.

"You know what Brooklyn geography is?" Mosko replied. "How to get to Kennedy Airport without going through East New York or Brownsville.''

"Pamiristan is right near Afghanistan, now that you mention it," Donovan said. "Maybe I should rethink the Afghan connection. Anyway, Mdivani these days is a prominent bookie working in the Brighton Beach Russian émigré community. And I hear he bought into one of the nightclubs there.''

"What's he going to do for you?" Marcy asked.

"Tell me about Koslov. At least he said he would.''

"If you're going to be in that neighborhood, bring me something to eat.''

"Not bagels from the place under the el. It went out of business and now is an Italian deli.''

"Just what Brooklyn needs, another Italian deli. OK, how about a pint of decent borscht and a portion of chicken Kiev?''

"There's too much salt in chicken Kiev," Donovan said.

"Almost as much as there is in chorizos. Think of your blood pressure."

"Isn't it cute how he's always protecting you?" Mosko asked her.

"Right," she said to her husband, making a sad face.

"I'll get you the borscht. What about a bottle or two of that Georgian mineral water? Didn't you say you liked that?"

"That stuff is vile, William," she replied. "What *were* you thinking about?"

"My case," he replied.

She shut her eyes and, clearly daydreaming, said, "I'm going to have a baby in four days."

"Merry Christmas, honey," Donovan said.

She made a growling sound. "I called the hospital's Jewish chaplain," she informed her husband. "The rabbi will stop by and talk to you before the baby is born."

"I'm not talking to any rabbi," Donovan said firmly. "I just blew off the cardinal, who also was trying to save me from the clear light of nonbelief. Why should I bother talking to a man—"

"Rabbi Weiss is a woman," Marcy said.

"God, a politically correct rabbi. It just gets better and better, doesn't it? From this point on, my mantra is 'Farther my God from thee.'"

Donovan got up, brushed some bran muffin crumbs from his lap and into a tissue, then balled up the tissue and left it on the end table, next to the telephone. He patted his laptop, which rested there quietly while the battery recharged.

"Wonderful invention," he said. "I'd be lost without it these days."

DONOVAN TOOK his knish out into the bitter cold wind that was blowing sand across the boardwalk from the broad white strip that prevented the Atlantic Ocean from swallowing the garlicky take-out restaurants, gone-to-seed highrises, and aging bungalows that lined Brighton Beach and neighboring Coney Island. He held the knish between cupped hands, nibbling on a corner while using the steaming pack of fried potatoes as if it were a hand warmer. The steam sifted between his fingers before whipping away in the morning wind that smelled of salt water and seaweed.

Donovan walked across the boardwalk to a bench that faced the sea. An ornate old cast-iron lamppost, painted black of course, rose from one side of it, the top of the stanchion curved around like a shepherd's crook, the bulb still burning despite the blinding December sun. There was a man on the bench, a barrel-chested man about a decade older than Donovan, huddled in a full-length suede-and-sheepskin coat worn beneath a black Russian hat the earflaps of which were turned down. He alternated furious puffs at a cigarette with sips at a cup of hot coffee that steamed like Donovan's knish, only hotter.

Donovan eased himself onto the wooden slats next to the man. "Hello, Georgi," he said, extending his hand.

"Good morning, Captain," the man replied, taking it. Georgi Mdivani's voice was thick and gravelly, the result of decades of bitter cold coffee-and-cigarette mornings spent toiling as a Communist Party apparatchik in Soviet Central Asia. Those days of the old Soviet Union also had given the beer-bellied former tractor-factory manager turned minor diplomat and, most recently, émigré entrepreneur operating on the fringes of the law in New York City, an attitude that was as callused as his hands.

A black tanker, its hold weighted down by a full load of number two home heating oil from Dhahran, chugged slowly and, as seen from a mile away in that morning of perfect visibility, silently toward the mouth of the Hudson.

"It is a bitter morning to be staring out to sea for a man of my age," Mdivani stated.

"I like Coney Island and Brighton Beach," Donovan said. "Where else can you see the sea, have a knish, talk to a Russian friend—"

"Georgian," Mdivani admonished.

"I know where you're from. I was teasing you, knowing your fondness for Russians."

Like many émigrés from the breakaway republics of the old Soviet Union, Mdivani claimed loudly and often to hate those members of the ethnic group that included many of his former masters. But his hatred didn't keep him from associating with many of them, particularly the criminal elements who were fast making Brighton Beach as famous in 1990s crime as Cicero, Illinois, had been in 1920s crime.

"As I was saying, where else can you have this scenery and talk to a *Georgian* friend?"

"The old country has its scenic points," Mdivani said expansively. "The Black Sea resorts are not so bad."

"If they were so good, you would still be there."

"There are too many Russians, even these days," Mdivani said, gesturing at the sky. "You know, when the ancien régime collapsed, we all thought, *That's it; the bastards will go home.* But, no, they stay on and on, like a bad toothache."

"They have no place to go in their own country," Donovan replied. "No job. No apartment. Nowhere to hide from the mafiosi who are shooting at each other across each street corner."

"Which brings us to the subject of your visit."

"Valery Koslov."

"Ah, yes, a Russian." Mdivani rolled his tongue around that *R,* his way of imparting extra meanness to the word. "What can I tell you about him? I know the man, of course. He comes into my club from time to time, insulting one and all with his arrogance and lack of manners. Me, since I left my country's service, I eke out a marginal living as a provider of gaming information to gentlemen."

"You're a bookie," Donovan said.

"I run a modest sports book."

"Now it's 'modest'? Three years ago you told me it was 'small.'"

Mdivani shrugged. "A man must seek to improve himself."

"And I hear that you bought the Gemini."

"My club? Sure. I got a deal on it. This is the land of opportunity, even today. Who do you think will be in the Super Bowl this year?"

"I couldn't care less," Donovan replied.

The Georgian seemed surprised. "Don't all Americans love the Super Bowl?" he asked.

"Should the opportunity present itself," Donovan said, sighing and settling into a parable, "a grown man will make love to the woman who rejected him when he was a boy. But the event is nearly always a disappointment. For both of them."

"Sad but true."

"To answer your question, in a month if there is nothing else to watch and nothing to read, I will watch the Super Bowl. An event notorious for failing to live up to expectations, formed when you were a kid and sports mattered to you. Now, about Valery Koslov—"

"I told him of your generous offer to preside over his surrender to the Manhattan district attorney. I told Valery Mikelovich that a man of your stature—who personally knows the mayor—would not let some staged catastrophe befall him on the way to the arraignment."

"Say what you will about America, it remains a nation of laws," Donovan said. "Thus O. J. Simpson is a free man."

Mdivani grunted and sipped his coffee. Then he pushed the cup in Donovan's direction, saying, "Take some…. It will warm your soul."

"What's in there?" the captain asked, taking the cardboard cup and sniffing suspiciously at the wedge-shaped opening in the white plastic cover.

Mdivani tossed his cigarette over the boardwalk railing and down to the frozen sand below. "Triple espresso. Four sugars. Two shots of vodka. Have a taste."

"You're a madman," Donovan said, handing the cup back.

Mdivani smiled. "We'll see who lives longer, the man who knows how to live life to the fullest or the man who gets shot at for a living."

"I want to talk about Valery Koslov," Donovan insisted.

"*He* is a madman. So why are we sitting here, freezing our asses, to save his? Because we are gentlemen, that's why."

Donovan said, "You're doing it because I cleared you of suspicion in the murder of Paolo Lucca. You owe me."

"I was innocent," Mdivani replied, jabbing the air with his hand.

"That and five million dollars' worth of attorneys would have gotten you off."

"God himself proclaimed my innocence," Mdivani insisted.

"Maybe. But it helped to have me rubber-stamp the document," Donovan replied.

Mdivani seemed to accept that notion. "I am grateful," he said, with a nod.

"I need to know where Koslov was the morning of November twenty-ninth and the evening of December sixth," Donovan said.

"In the first instance, he was at an associate's house in Coney Island all morning. I know because he placed bets with me several times. I was on and off the phone with him the whole time that German was killed at that store. And since *I* called Koslov several times, I know for sure he was there. You can check my phone records. On the second date, Koslov was slapping his wife around. Sent her to the emergency room at Coney Island Hospital, too, to have the bruises covered up. You can check that as well."

"Why'd he hit her?" Donovan asked.

"Why else? For sleeping with that TV pretty boy. You can ask her if you like. He left her. A man does these things when his wife is unfaithful. Slaps her around."

"Not when his wife has a black belt in kung fu," Donovan said. "Tell me, do you think Koslov would try to kill Paul Duke?"

Mdivani laughed heartily.

"I agree," Donovan said.

"The man faces a minor charge from the Manhattan DA. Nothing his lawyers can't handle. At the worst, they will delay and delay until he is safely back in Saint Petersburg. As you said, this is a nation of laws. And nobody knows how to get around laws better than Russians. I will give the bastards that much."

"So Koslov was accounted for at the times the killings occurred. He could just as well have ordered someone to do the dirty work for him."

"This is something Valery Mikelovich would not do," Mdivani said. "Were he to kill someone for revenge, he would want to do it himself. Besides, it is absolutely ridiculous to think that a professional man—even a professional thug, as some people might describe my friend—would destroy a rival by scaring him. Shooting tourists and businessmen to make him worry about his own health. Preposterous."

"It sounds nuts to me, too," Donovan agreed. "But I have heard stranger things."

"But not from a Russian. Think about why the Soviet Union collapsed. A Russian solves a problem by throwing numbers at it. The Soviet Union competed with America not by being clever but by throwing numbers at it—numbers of troops, tanks, ships, planes, and everything else—until at last they could not pay for the whole thing and the entire system fell apart. In the same way, a Russian thug will get rid of an enemy by gunning him down on the street corner or in his car in a hail of bullets. That is the Russian way. Not by trying to drive him mad first.''

"Paul Duke is convinced that someone is trying to make him crazy before killing him," Donovan said.

Mdivani shook his head vigorously. "An Englishman would do that. Or a woman. But never a Russian."

Donovan thought for a moment, then said, "I'll need to have someone check what you told me about Koslov's whereabouts when those two men were killed."

"Of course you will. Have that man call me. What's his name? The weight lifter.''

"Sergeant Moskowitz."

"Ah, yes, interesting man."

"My favorite kind," Donovan replied.

"Now, on to the other business. Koslov has agreed to surrender himself to you like we talked about, but he wants to do it on Christmas Day."

Donovan laughed. "What does he think he is, a gift from the Magi? Why can't I just walk him into Manhattan Criminal Court?''

"I am merely repeating what the man said," Mdivani replied. "Perhaps he believes that the importance generally attached to the day will protect him."

"Well then, he'll have to come to the hospital," Donovan said.

"You're not sick?" Mdivani seemed genuinely concerned.

Donovan said, "I'm becoming a father sometime in the next few weeks."

"Congratulations!" Mdivani replied, twisting his body toward Donovan and pumping the captain's hand. "A son, of course."

"Of course."

"Your first?"

Donovan tossed his hands up.

"I can remember my first, though it's been many years. And I can remember my seventh, my eighth—"

"You have been blessed."

"I have been blessed that I am still healthy—despite some of my habits," Mdivani said, finishing the last of the concoction in his paper cup and tossing the empty vessel over the rail and onto the sand below. "And that I can still work to pay for it all. Three of them are in college now."

Donovan groaned at the thought.

"So, it is done. Koslov will go to the hospital on Christmas Day. The district attorney will be there?"

Donovan said he would arrange it. "Tell Koslov not to show his face without something for the baby," Donovan added.

"I will make a special note of that. You will tell me what hospital and where and it shall be done. But tell me, how do you know that Christmas is the day the baby will come?"

"It *is* Marcy's due date," Donovan said.

"How did you arrange that?"

Donovan shrugged. "I needed something different to do on that day. The past several Christmases were washouts."

"You are a man of many talents," Mdivani replied. Then, glancing out to sea, he added, "Do you see that tanker over there?" He pointed at the black tanker that was moving slowly and silently up into the harbor, the smoke from its long stack whipping away, driven by a fierce and bitter wind.

"What of it?" Donovan asked.

"I will bet you anything, right now, that there are three illegal aliens aboard her."

"Only three?" Donovan said.

"Each one wants his crack at America. You know, streets paved with gold."

"Tin, a lot of the time."

"But, you see, tin is worth something to a starving man.

Certainly it is worth more than the dirt and mud that paves the roads where they come from. Do you see what I'm saying?"

Donovan nodded. "You're trying to tell me that, in this country, even Valery Mikelovich Koslov can thrive. Despite the district attorney and his petty concerns."

"Exactly," Mdivani said, slapping his knee with his right hand. This gesture caused his newly lit cigarette to go flying onto the boardwalk, where it quickly blew over the edge and fell to the sand to join the others. "Just what I am saying, that Koslov has no need to kill this pretty TV star. And he certainly has no need to shoot up store windows on Fifth Avenue. To the very best of my knowledge, he is not the man you're looking for. Now, I have told you everything I know about the man. There is no more."

"You are a good friend," Donovan replied, then finished his knish in silence. He balled up the bit of waxed paper it came in and tossed it up and down, trying to figure out whether to stick it in his pocket for eventual transfer to a trash can or to toss it over the railing, as Mdivani was doing with his garbage. A weather-beaten seagull stood nearby, hoping for a handout.

Suddenly Mdivani laughed. "I will tell you something funny," he said.

"I could use a good laugh," Donovan replied.

"You ask, does Valery Mikelovich plan to kill Paul Duke? I tell you, Valery Mikelovich is afraid of assassination himself."

"I know that. He's afraid of the cops summarily executing him on the way to the station house for arraignment. That's why I get to spend Christmas overseeing the process."

"That's not what I'm talking about. What I mean is that he is afraid that one of his rivals in the Russian mafia will shoot him through the window of his bulletproof limousine. And for that reason, Valery Mikelovich"—Mdivani laughed heartily, then slapped Donovan on the leg—"paid a lot of money to buy the only pistol capable of doing the job."

Donovan tossed the balled-up piece of litter over the railing and onto the pristine white December sand of Brighton Beach. The seagull took to the air and dived after it.

"Koslov bought a Kammacher Stedman?" he asked.

Mdivani bobbed his head up and down. "The only one on the market," he said, and laughed again.

"Where is Koslov now?" Donovan asked, standing.

"Don't you want to know what's funny?" Mdivani asked, standing also.

"Where's Koslov?" Donovan said again, more insistently the second time.

"At one of his apartments, I suppose. He has several. I can only point you at two of them. But I doubt he is there. Most certainly he is hiding out at a safe house that is nearby but well concealed. Why is this so important?"

"A Kammacher Stedman is the gun being used by the guy who's shooting up Fifth Avenue," Donovan replied.

"Oh. That's interesting, but I already pointed out how Koslov couldn't have committed those crimes. But what's funny," Mdivani said, "is that Koslov bought the gun so no one else could have it. Then, guess what?"

"What?"

"Someone stole it."

SIXTEEN

"MAYBE MRS. KOSLOV WANTED TO DRIVE HER HUSBAND CRAZY BEFORE KILLING HIM," MOSKO SAID

THE SECOND apartment that Mdivani took them to was like the first, a Russian mobster's version of American wealth, 1950s style. The colors were exaggerated, with reds and gold predominating, and nearly everything made of fabric seemed to have gold and silver fibers in it. The furniture was the best the chain furniture stores had to offer. A hot pink velvet sofa, with wood trimming that had been covered in gold leaf, sat below a mural oil painting of Gina Koslov. She was beautiful, all right. Blond, of course; whether born that way or created from a bottle, Brighton Beach wives were necessarily blond. In Gina Koslov's case, the hair was piled high in an elaborate series of symmetrical waves the likes of which had gone unseen in most of the rest of America for several decades. Around her neck was a glittering diamond necklace; below it, a push-up bra and a skintight gold lamé dress created a brand of sexiness that Ann-Margret might have been comfortable with on a Las Vegas evening in 1962.

"I wonder who gets the painting when this happy couple finally divorces," Donovan mused, scratching his chin.

"Maybe Paul Duke can pick it up cheap," Mosko replied, staring at his notebook computer, which he had set up atop the gold-flecked Formica bar.

"Where is she, still at Coney Island Hospital?" Donovan

asked Mdivani, who had decided to plunk himself down on the couch and was puffing away at a Chesterfield.

"I hear that she's living with her mother," Mdivani said.

"Where's Mom?"

"Fair Lawn, New Jersey."

"Send somebody out to talk to her," Donovan said.

"You got it," Mosko replied.

Donovan picked up a chunk of polished glass, the size of a large eggplant, an anonymous artist had created to emulate an undulating patch of water. It was crystal clear save for a gold figure of a nude swimming woman that floated in the middle of the sculpture. Donovan put it back down where he had found it, atop a silver-and-glass coffee table also adorned with a fiber-optic flower burst. Its hundreds of illuminated strands waved gently with every blush of breeze stirred up by a passing detective, casting an electronic glow onto the deep-pile purple-and-gold carpet.

Donovan stared at the fiber-optic flower. "I'll bet if you play 'Raindrops Keep Falling on My Head' on the stereo this thing will move in synch," he said.

"Want to try it?" Mosko asked.

Donovan didn't. Instead, he looked back up at the oil painting. "I guess if you got rid of the hairdo and the Ann-Margret outfit that would be a beautiful woman," he said.

"She is," Mdivani replied. "She is."

"Are the rocks real?"

"Do you mean the diamonds? Of course they are. Valery Mikelovich buys only the best."

"So I see. Like the Kammacher Stedman."

"Like that. He is a man who likes to cover all bases, to use your American baseball metaphor. When that gun went on the market last year, he outbid all others. In secret, of course. He made a joke of the purchase, as if he wasn't really afraid that it otherwise might be used on him. But he was afraid, all right. I am sure of it."

"Where'd he keep it?" Mosko asked. "There's no gun

cabinet in this apartment or in the other one you took us to.''

''He kept the Stedman right here, in a walnut box on the cocktail table.'' Mdivani leaned forward and tapped a finger against the glass. ''He used to call it his insurance policy.''

''What happened to it?'' Donovan asked.

''It was at last year's Brighton Beach Days festival. You know, where the chamber of commerce runs a big promotion to drum up business for local stores. Hires bands. Invites the press. The usual.''

''Every ethnic neighborhood in New York has one of those street fairs,'' Donovan said.

''The press came. Somebody pulled a string—I think I know who—to get network television down here to do a story on the new rich of Brighton Beach.''

''Who pulled a string?'' Mosko asked.

''I'll bet that Gina Koslov pulled Paul Duke's string,'' Donovan said.

''Right you are, Captain,'' Mdivani confirmed.

''She wanted a videotape of this apartment and that painting on the TV news,'' Donovan said.

''The woman saw herself as the Marla Trump of Brighton Beach,'' Mdivani said.

''I hope she has a better prenuptial agreement. So down came Paul Duke with a TV crew to photograph this austere little love nest, among other things.''

''On this point you are *almost* right,'' Mdivani said. ''Paul Duke did not come here personally.''

''That would have been too obvious, even for him,'' Mosko said.

''Who did he send?''

''The Irish weatherman. What's his name?''

''George Halloran,'' Donovan replied. ''He specializes in trivial broadcasts from local celebrations. He also happens to be a gun nut.''

''Now, what happened after then is a little uncertain,''

Mdivani went on. "Valery said the gun was stolen. But my suspicion is that Gina gave it to the weatherman to get it out of the house. Lest it be used on her."

"Or so that it could be used on her husband," Donovan mused. "Remember what you said before, Georgi? A Russian wouldn't try to drive a man crazy before killing him. But an Englishman would...or a woman."

"Maybe Mrs. Koslov wanted to drive her husband crazy before killing him," Mosko said. "After all, she knew he was afraid of that gun."

"Valery thought of all that, I assure you," Mdivani added. "And that is when the real trouble began between the two of them. Eventually he found out she was sleeping with Duke. But by then the marriage was over."

"All but the battering," Donovan commented.

Mosko broke away from the conversation to take reports from several detectives and make a call on his cell phone. When he came back to Donovan and Mdivani, he said, "There's nothing to help us here or in the first place we looked at, the apartment on Beach Fifth Street. There's no sign of Koslov. But George Halloran called you. Says he has some information."

"About time."

"Frankly, I don't think we're gonna have any more luck finding Koslov than the Brooklyn cops did."

"And you swear you don't know where he is," Donovan said to the Georgian.

"On my mother's grave."

"How do you contact him?"

"He calls me at my club. But always from a different pay phone, so tapping my line won't help you. I promise you, though, that he will show up to surrender on Christmas Day."

"Tell him not to bother with the bulletproof limo," Donovan replied.

Mosko looked up from his computer and said, "Here's

how things look. Last year's Brighton Beach Days were June seventh through tenth. Halloran was here with a crew. The Stedman disappeared. Last year's Moose Horn Billiards Tournament—''

''Moose Horn Billiards Tournament?'' Mdivani questioned.

''Was June twenty-fourth through thirtieth. Halloran is reported to have been discussing the Kammacher Stedman with a bunch of Montana gun collectors.''

''Yeah, one of whom Halloran described as being a rich Montana survivalist who is somewhere to the right of Hitler. Halloran was going to dig up his name and get back to me, but he never did. Maybe that's what he wants to talk about now.''

''Why would this jolly pudgy weatherman take this famous gun from Gina Koslov—gift or no gift—and give it to the guy in Montana?'' Mosko asked.

''If that's what happened,'' Donovan replied.

''And how did the gun get from Montana back to New York and in the hands of someone shooting Christmas shoppers?''

''It's a puzzlement.''

''Could this mean that some right-wing survivalists from Montana are the ones claiming to be the Mountain Brigade?'' Mosko asked.

Donovan shrugged. ''Well, when the name 'Mountain Brigade' came up we all sort of assumed the mountains in question were in Afghanistan,'' he said. ''Maybe we were getting ahead of ourselves.''

''Maybe.''

''They have mountains in Montana, don't they?'' Donovan said.

''I think they're called 'the Rockies.'''

''I've got to talk to Halloran,'' Donovan replied.

SEVENTEEN

WHAT'S IT LIKE IN ARKANSAS IN AUGUST WITH COW CHIPS FLYING EVERYWHERE

DONOVAN DIDN'T GET into many bars in the years since he stopped drinking, but this one had the look and feel of an old friend. Hurley's was made of dark wood and leather and smelled of brandy and good cigars. It was an expensive smell, the scent of money. That was because Hurley's was the watering hole for the well-paid personnel of the NBC and Wolf networks.

George Halloran was hunkered down at the end of the bar, flicking cigar ashes into a brass tray conveniently placed adjacent to the rows of single-malt scotch. He wore clothes of the sort chosen by a man who can afford to go casual in style—a custom-made plaid shirt with equally expensive khakis fastened over his considerable girth by a Venetian leather belt. His hiking boots were brand-new and highly polished, as if the only trail they would ever see was the well-worn one to the automated teller machine. He was staring blankly at the brass ashtray when Donovan walked in the front door, but upon spotting the captain broke into a broad show-biz grin.

"Bill Donovan! Sit your weary bones down and have a drink."

"I'll sit," Donovan said, taking off his jacket and draping it over the back of the stool next to him before sitting.

"You're not a drinking man, my friend?"

"I'll have a Kaliber," Donovan said to the bartender, who sidled up wiping his hands on a towel.

"What is that, a brandy?" Halloran asked.

"Nonalcoholic beer."

"I like the sound of the name."

"It's made by Guinness," Donovan said.

"That, too."

Across the room, someone slipped a dollar bill into the jukebox and pressed some keys. Sinatra came on, singing "I've Got the World on a String." As Donovan's dark glass bottle was produced and poured, Halloran sipped a Johnnie Walker Black Label and asked, "Has this been as busy a week for you as it's been for me?"

"I've had worse. What have you been up to? How was the Utah Snow Festival?"

"Vertical and cold. Have you ever been on a ski slope?" Donovan shook his head. "I'm a New Yorker. Going down a mountain at sixty miles an hour, standing on two planks, was never my idea of a fun time. How did your broadcast go? Did you do it from the lift?"

"Yeah, I went through with it. It was harder on my crew than me. I just sat there shivering and talked into a wireless mike. They had to pack into the chair after me and try to focus while swinging back and forth in a blizzard."

"I thought TV crews like challenges," Donovan said. "You know, offering to shinny up a flagpole to get a shot of a pigeon laying an egg."

Halloran nodded. "Yeah, but I think I wore my guys out last August shooting a remote from the Arkansas cow-chip-throwing championship. Do you have any idea what it's like in Arkansas in August with cow chips flying everywhere?"

"Sorry. My childhood playing in Riverside Park offers no parallels. So, my sergeant tells me you called. Do you have something?"

Halloran plucked a business card from his shirt pocket and handed it over. On the back, written in bold strokes that tilted precipitously to the right, was the name Harlan Deaver. Sinatra had begun singing "South of the Border."

"Ever hear the name Harlan Deaver?" Halloran asked.

"I read about him on the FBI's Web site," Donovan said. "He's the real-estate guy who became a multimillionaire by selling ranch land to rich Hollywood types of the Robert Redford and Jane Fonda ilk, then bought himself a thousand-acre parcel and set up a militia organization."

Halloran nodded. "Their main beef being that too much of Montana was being taken over by rich people from New York and California," he said.

"Does the word *chutzpah* come to mind?" Donovan asked.

"I was thinking of an earthier term. Anyway, the man has put out a lot of smoke about being dangerous, so the FBI says he is. His henchmen have roughed up a couple of marshals who came out to serve him with papers regarding nonpayment of taxes. Deaver has declared that his parcel of land is an independent nation no longer subject to the laws of the United States."

"And he's set up a kangaroo court and handed down death sentences upon a whole lot of people he doesn't like," Donovan said. "Of course, if they don't cross the border into his 'free and independent nation,' they're safe. The FBI has his parcel surrounded and is watching him, hoping to pick him up if he drives to the 7-Eleven for beer. But that's unlikely to happen, too. Deaver's militia—"

"He calls them 'the Mountain Brigade.'"

"—runs errands for him. George, I have to ask you a question."

"Shoot."

"Did you steal the Kammacher Stedman automatic from Valery Koslov's apartment and give it to Deaver? Or sell it to Deaver?"

Halloran looked surprised. Then he took a bolt of scotch and smiled. "No, no, and no," he said.

"You didn't steal it?"

"The dear woman gave it to me, and that's the God's honest truth."

"She gave it to you."

"Sure as the day is long. Gina was afraid that her husband would shoot her with it…would shoot her with any gun he might have in the house, so she got rid of the only one he had. It turns out that it was a famous one."

"Did you know she was having an affair with Paul Duke?" Donovan asked.

"*Everybody* at the network knew that. It was before management handed down its keep-it-in-your-pants ultimatum. Paul asked me to go to Brighton Beach to cover their little shindig because he was afraid that Koslov might have found out."

"He was afraid that Koslov would kill him."

"I suppose he was. Anyway, I do these kinds of festivals all the time. Sometimes five days a week I go to shoot my weather report at—"

"Little Suzie and Aunt May's Crawfish Festival and Cake Bake-off," Donovan said.

"Yeah, like that. This is how I got to be three hundred pounds. Anyway, I did it as a favor for Paul and because I can do it in my sleep. So Gina—she knew that I knew—asked me to ditch the gun for her."

"What do you think of the possibility that she gave you the gun hoping it would find its way into the hands of a rival who would use it on her husband?" Donovan asked.

"How might that happen? Through my exquisite set of contacts in the Russian mafia? Look at who you're talking to. A good-old-boy, ex-marine, all-American yahoo."

"Who's better acquainted with the Montana Mountain Brigade than the Afghanistan Mountain Brigade," Donovan said.

"Does Afghanistan have one, too?" Halloran asked.

"I feel pretty sure the two groups are unrelated. Why didn't you tell me all this the last time we spoke?"

Halloran sighed, then said, "We in network TV live a precarious existence that depends on public approval. We all have to be squeaky clean...or damned good liars. Paul isn't a very good liar. He likes women and makes no bones about it. It may get him fired yet. But me, it's easy for me to be squeaky clean, or at least pretend that I am. I drink. You see before you my one and only vice."

Halloran waggled the empty glass at the bartender, who came running with a bottle. "Something Wonderful Happens in the Summer" was on the jukebox.

"But if it got out that I knew something about—in fact, held in my hands—the gun that's doing all the killing on Fifth Avenue, management would fire me in an instant."

"And your golden parachute is no better than Paul's."

"Everyone's is better than his," Halloran said. "The man spends money like there was no tomorrow. Even now. But I still don't want to be fired. Nobody likes to be fired. It's no good for the reputation. You lose little perks, like lucrative endorsement deals."

"What did you do with the gun?" Donovan asked.

"Well, I heard that Deaver wanted to buy it but, as you can imagine, had even less of a likelihood of knowing someone in the Russian mob than I do. And, I think I told you, he wouldn't set foot in New York."

"In fact, can't run up to the 7-Eleven for beer."

"You got that right. So I made some calls and connected with the man. Sorry I lied to you about that. I arranged to bring him the Stedman when I was in Moose Horn covering the billiards tournament."

"How much was he going to pay you for it?" Donovan asked.

"Pay me? Nothing, of course."

Donovan's eyebrows arched toward the ceiling.

"The price I wanted for the gun was an exclusive interview with the man. You see, Captain, I'm as sick as you seem to be of this jazz with me always covering the catfish festival. To be absolutely, one hundred percent honest with you, if I have to do one more stand-up from a cake-baking contest I'm gonna toss my cookies."

Donovan smiled.

"I saw this as being my chance to be taken seriously as a reporter," Halloran said. "It's important to me."

"So you brought the gun to Montana."

"And therein hangs a tale. It disappeared from my hotel room."

"Wait a second," Donovan said. "The gun was stolen from *you?*"

"I assume one of his henchmen did it, so he wouldn't have to do the interview. That was the last I saw of the thing. I never even got to shoot it. Not that I would have at a hundred bucks a round for those fancy depleted-uranium bullets. Even I don't like spending money that fast."

Donovan had about finished his Kaliber and spent a moment peering into the near-empty glass. Then he asked, "Who was working with you in Montana? Besides Rose Waucqez."

"Just my crew. But one of them couldn't have done it. I've known these guys for years. Who else was there? The girl who books our flights. I can't even think of her name. And June dropped by for an afternoon on her way to San Francisco to interview the mayor. And Rose was there. But if you're thinking of Rose, forget that, too. She's as honest as the day is long."

"And a good shot," Donovan added.

"I'm gonna tell you a secret, and I hope you take it alright. I *like* Rose."

"I'm not so sure it's reciprocated."

"Oh, you mean her dumping on me? That happens all the time. I know what it means."

"What's that?"

"It means she's sweet on me. Weren't you ever a kid?"

"Sure I was. In the sixties. Things worked differently then."

"Well, I'm older than you and remember a time when a girl kidded and teased you if she wanted you. I'm sure that Rose *really* likes me but can't bring herself to admit it because she thinks I'm a... What was that she called me?"

"'An extra-chromosomal former marine,'" Donovan replied.

"So I want to do something to impress her."

"Like get an exclusive interview with the leader of the Mountain Brigade: Harlan Deaver."

"You got me cold. Well, as you can see, I blew my chance. Somebody stole the Kammacher Stedman from my hotel room."

"And after that happened, you never heard another word about the gun?" Donovan asked.

"Not until you brought up the subject," Halloran replied.

"Why didn't you tell me this before?" Donovan asked. "Why did I have to wait all this time to hear how the Stedman got from Brighton Beach to Montana?"

Halloran looked embarrassed. He smiled and said, "Like I told you, guys in my line of work have to be squeaky clean. You have two murders to solve. And here I am, the man who last saw the murder weapon. With the exception of the killer, of course."

"Who knows about Gina giving you the gun?" Donovan asked.

"Well, let's see. The guys in my crew. The boys in Montana—like Rosie says, 'the rest of the extra-chromosomal former marines'—I told them. But *after* the gun was stolen. Oh, and June."

"June Lake? You told her?"

"She's a good egg and a great listener. Been kicked around some in her life. Doesn't show it."

"You weren't worried about her telling on you to network brass?" Donovan asked.

"Nah. She's a true-blue friend. Everyone confides in her."

"Paul has."

"Yeah. I guess you know they had a thing for a while. Not that it means anything. Paul had a thing with everyone. Everyone except Rose, of course."

"Of course," Donovan responded.

"I have to ask one question," Halloran said.

Sinatra began singing "Here's That Rainy Day." Normally, that was one of Donovan's favorite songs. But the first verse wasn't out before Donovan's cell phone rang. He plucked the instrument from his pocket and said, "Either this is someone about to be born or someone who just died." And he brought the phone to his ear.

"Donovan," he said.

He listened in silence and, as he did, the lines in the corners of his eyes flattened and deepened. With his free hand he reached for his car keys—an old habit—and jingled them in his pocket. Then he said, "I'll be right over."

Halloran read him perfectly well. If the weatherman was lacking in intelligence or sensitivity, it didn't show at that moment. He said, "That wasn't a birth."

Donovan laid a five-dollar bill on the bar and stood, slipping on his coat.

"I just got a report that Paul Duke was shot to death in the back of his limo."

"My God," Halloran said, making the sign of the cross over himself.

"When did this happen?"

"Ten minutes ago."

"Where?"

"On Fifth Avenue, half a block from the studio."

"I'm coming with you," Halloran said, abandoning his drink and, with a grunt, lifting himself off his bar stool.

IT WAS MIDAFTERNOON and once again a death had stopped traffic on Fifth Avenue. Blue police barricades and yellow crime-scene tape were just going up when Donovan finished hurrying, in a sort of half-jog, down the short block from the Avenue of the Americas. Halloran huffed and puffed along behind, great clouds of hot and weary breath coming from his lungs and crystallizing in the frosty air four days before Christmas.

Packed-in motorists honked their anger at the bumper-to-bumper traffic. Sirens converged on the scene, on the periphery of Rockefeller Center, from far and near. Already, a shoulder-to-shoulder crowd of tourists and shoppers surrounded Duke's white limousine, which was parked neatly against the curb between a posh boutique jewelry shop and the Brazilian Tourist Office.

With Halloran in tow, Donovan pushed his way through the crowd and squeezed between two blue sawhorses. Two uniformed cops approached, hands up, then recognized the two men and, blushing and smiling, backed away. The right rear door of the limo was open. The window was rolled up. A single neat hole had pierced it.

While holding Halloran back with one hand, Donovan stuck his head in the open door. What he saw was Duke's bodyguard and driver, lying on his left-hand side, a solitary hole piercing the side of his skull above and in front of his ear. The man wore the same blue uniform Donovan had seen on him a few weeks earlier. His white cap was in the front seat, though. At his feet were two paper bags, each holding a bottle of liquor. Johnnie Walker Black Label was in one, Jack Daniel's in the other. And there was a bag of supermarket ice propped up beneath the sliding Plexiglas door of the minibar.

Donovan pulled his head back into the afternoon air.

"Paul...?" Halloran said.

Donovan shook his head. "Paul's driver," he replied.

"Thank God. I mean...Jesus, man, you know what I mean."

Donovan knew.

"Apparently he was sitting in the rear on the right-hand side restocking the minibar when he got hit," Donovan said. "The back door was closed. The killer must have mistaken the guy for Paul. Through that glass you can make out the outline of a head and maybe tell if it belongs to a man or a woman, but not who it is."

Donovan beckoned to the two cops who had come over a moment before. One of them, a sergeant, hurried up.

"Yeah, Captain?"

"Anybody see the perp?"

"Nobody we talked to," the man replied. "The closest we got to a witness is a couple from Pennsylvania who heard the shot and looked over."

"What did they see?" Donovan asked.

"They saw a whole lot of people running away. But ordinary people, mind you."

"No Santas or Santa's Angels."

"No, nothing like that. I specifically asked them that question."

Donovan thanked the man and told him he had done a good job, but nonetheless told him to introduce the couple to Moskowitz when he arrived. Maybe his aide, whose talent for friendly badgering had wrung additional memories out of many eyewitnesses, could do better.

Donovan's eyes were drawn to the storefronts where the driver had left the limo standing—in a No Standing Zone, of course—while waiting for his boss and setting up the bar.

"Why did the guy pull up here?" Donovan asked.

"Why not?" Halloran replied.

"Why here, in front of the Brazilian Tourist Office, and not back there?" He pointed up Fifth Avenue to the spot, near the entrance to Channel Gardens, where he had seen the car waiting for Duke before.

"Because this is where Paul gets picked up every day," Halloran said, checking his watch. "Just about this time."

"Why not back there, where it's a quiet walk across the plaza?" Donovan looked around again, then spied the plain grey door with a buzzer and a peephole on it tucked away between the two stores. Were that a block zoned for apartments, the door would have led to several upstairs flats. "Is that a stage door?"

"You got it," Halloran replied. "That's our not-very-secret entrance."

"Who knows about it?"

"All the people at the network, although only the talent is supposed to use it."

"The talent?"

"The anchors and reporters and, of course, the weatherman. And the paparazzi know to wait out here if they want pictures of us. Not too many fans know about that door. They look in the studio window, as you know."

A clamor in the crowd heralded the arrival of several field detectives and Moskowitz. He spotted Donovan standing by the shot-up limousine and exclaimed, "Oh, no!"

"Not Duke," Donovan said. "His driver."

"And bodyguard, right? So much for half his talents."

"He's also parked in a no standing zone," Donovan said dryly. "What happened at the pet shop?"

"You were complaining that I'm two steps behind you? Well, Mojadidi remains one step ahead of *us*. He did work at that pet shop but cleared out abruptly this morning."

"*This* morning? Interesting."

"Yeah, he got himself hired as Christmas-season help, then quit four days before Christmas. Coincidentally, on the same day the extortion attempt and the attempt on Paul Duke's life were going down. I don't know, Boss. I think Mojadidi is at the top of the list. Maybe he's the one who demanded a payoff as a way of getting the attention shifted to Queens long enough to take a close-range shot at Duke."

"You're suggesting that having cops on every corner dressed as Santa's Angels has helped," Donovan said.

"Well, it sure didn't help the bodyguard none," Mosko replied.

"I guess not."

"Say, what is it with hippies and pet shops? Every time I go into one there are these guys with long hair and rock-and-roll T-shirts gawking at the guppies."

"That's entertainment in their quadrant of the galaxy," Donovan replied.

"It's got to be," Mosko said, shaking his head.

Halloran appeared to be growing eager to get in on the conversation, so Donovan invited him over. "You didn't get to meet George Halloran, did you?" Donovan introduced them.

"Have you warmed up yet from that thing on the ski lift?" Moskowitz asked.

"Have you ever been skiing?" Halloran asked.

"They don't have it in Canarsie."

"Well, I'm still cold despite the liberal application of antifreeze."

Moskowitz peered in the back of the car and said, "One shot. Our boy's aim is improving. A good thing, too, 'cause he only has a handful of slugs left."

"Two, now," Donovan replied.

"So I guess this answers the question of whether Duke is the target or not."

"It would appear to."

"Damn, I hate when he does that," Mosko said.

"Does what?" Halloran asked.

"Says 'it would *appear* to.'"

"Oh, you mean that the captain is entertaining other theories."

"*Entertaining?* The captain has a whole senior prom's worth of suspects and theories going on in there." Mosko pointed at his boss's head, then asked him, "Has anybody seen the perp this time?"

"Not so's I can tell, but talk to the uniformed sergeant over there." Donovan pointed out the man, who stood by his pair of witnesses looking as eager to please as puppies. "He's got a couple of eyewitnesses who saw people running away. No Santa's Angels, though."

"Maybe I can get more out of them."

"I was hoping you could," Donovan replied.

Mosko went off to do it.

Another clamor—this one of sirens and blaring horns—announced the arrival of Bonaci's van. Soon the crime scene was filled with technicians and the uniformed cops were relegated to controlling the still-growing crowd.

"So Paul leaves every day at this time," Donovan said, returning his attention to the weatherman.

"He's late today," Halloran replied, again checking his watch. "Lately, he walks out this door and into the back of the limo."

"The driver holds the door open for him?"

"Yes. Paul hops right in."

"How do *you* get home?"

"By cab, most of the time."

"No limo?"

"I don't want to spend the money. Besides—"

"Half the time, Paul drops you off," Donovan said.

"How'd you know that? Did he tell you?"

"No. But he has a bottle of Black Label in there. That's pretty strong stuff."

"When you're a guy my size, nothing is too strong," Halloran said. "But you're right; Paul often drops me off at my place."

"Which is where?"

"East Sixty-fourth. Park and Lex."

"And Paul lives at…"

"Seventy-seventh and Madison."

I sleep with. I got chlamydia once, ten years ago, but I took some pills and it went away.''

''What about a bullet?'' Donovan asked. ''Are you going to take pills that stop bullets? One way or another, my friend, your lifestyle is going to kill you.''

He pointed at the limo, where a police photographer was taking snapshots of the corpse. That seemed to get through to Duke, the starkness of it, the made-for-TV reality of a man taking photographs of the body. Duke appeared to re-alize that he might actually be the target of the killer's rage. Duke gaped at the body of his bodyguard and the blood in the back of his white limo and the shot-up window. And it sank in that he, Paul Duke, could have been the one lying there with a bullet in his skull. He began to pale.

He said, mumbled rather, ''I mean before all this stuff started happening I used to walk home. Not every day, but often. I walked right up Fifth Avenue. Then *People* called me 'the sexiest man alive' and, a while after, bodies started dropping.''

After spotting the corpse and hearing June scream, Duke, Donovan figured, had been moved to play the tough guy. It seemed to come naturally to him, and that was how Duke had come to be famous, for shaking his fist at Russian hel-icopters. His stance was one actors take, a pose that was not backed up by any real backbone.

By the time he made his mumbling admission, however, Duke had got paler, a bit corpselike himself, same as he did a few weeks back when he was forced to face the prospect of a violent end. His knees seemed to weaken and his mouth fell open a crack and he breathed harder to get more air into his lungs.

''Brian!'' Donovan shouted to his assistant while slipping an arm about Duke's waist to hold him up in case he keeled over.

Moskowitz came running and got a well-muscled arm

around the anchorman just as his eyes rolled back into his skull and he fainted dead away.

June Lake screamed Duke's name. She, too, ran over, Halloran right behind, his grizzly-bear frame towering over her.

"What happened? Is Paul all right?"

"He fainted," Mosko told her.

"Stricken with grief at the death of his friend and bodyguard," Donovan added, charitably and diplomatically, in case any reporters were within earshot.

"Let's get him to the hospital," Halloran said, trying, unnecessarily, to get a hand in to help the other guys in holding Duke up.

"I don't think he needs that, much as my wife would like to see him again," Donovan replied. "He just needs to lie down."

"We'll take him to my place," Lake said. "I'm close."

"How close?" Donovan asked.

"Central Park South."

"That will do."

"We need a car here!" Mosko bellowed, to no one in particular but in his best Brooklyn accent, the one sure to get results. Within a minute a squad car was through the crowd with its door flung open. Already Lake had her house keys out of her purse and jingling in her hand.

Efficient woman, Donovan thought, as he helped load Duke into the back of the car and got in along with him and his coanchor.

EIGHTEEN

NO TV, NO RADIO, NO MORNING-AFTER PILLS

WITH MOSKO'S HELP and the connivance of the doorman, Donovan got Paul Duke's emotionally drained and temporarily inert body into the elevator and up to Lake's nineteenth-floor apartment overlooking Central Park. The apartment was shiny and modern, oddly sterile, all white Formica and stainless steel save for the occasional modern art flourishes that broke the monotony of eggshell-white walls. And since Lake appeared to admire the minimalists, those paintings tended to series of white-on-white or grey-on-grey or, in the case of an immense mural hung behind the white leather couch, a series of beige-on-beige triangles.

They laid him on the couch in Lake's office, a tufted-leather affair set across a smallish room otherwise furnished with a glass-and-stainless desk, several file cabinets, and a wall unit that held tapes, a TV, and a VCR. Once on the couch, Duke stirred and opened his eyes, a bit like a hatching chick peeking warily from the shell. They flashed around the room, seeking orientation.

"Where am I?" he asked.

"In June's study," Donovan replied.

"In her apartment?" he groaned, rubbing his eyes.

"I'm here for you, Paul," she said, sitting on the edge of the couch, her thigh touching his, her skirt riding up her legs with a swoosh of panty hose.

He lowered a hand from his eyes and left it where it was convenient for her to pick up and cradle in both of hers.

"My life is over," he said.

"Not when you compare it with Tony's," Donovan replied.

Duke shook his head and momentarily scrunched his eyes shut but otherwise ignored the remark. "I'll lose my job. They'll definitely fire me now. I have nowhere to go."

"I'll take care of you, honey," Lake replied, squeezing his hand for emphasis.

"I feel sick."

"Do you want a doctor?" she asked.

"God, no. Just time to rest and think. This is *awful*. Can I get a glass of water?"

"Sure."

"No, coffee."

"Anything."

"The way I like it," Duke added.

Lake stood, adjusted her skirt, and said, "You guys watch him while I go into the kitchen."

"Sure," Mosko replied, taking her place on the edge of the couch but farther down, by the stricken man's feet. She walked out of the room, leaving the three men.

"How *do* you take your coffee...honey?" Donovan asked, sticking his hands in his pockets and strolling over to her desk.

Duke groaned again, said, "Light, one sugar," and scrunched his eyes shut. When he opened them, he said, "The network will wait until after Tony is buried. They'll wait until after Christmas. Then they'll fire me. I'm ruined."

"It's beginning to look like you have an angel who will take you in," Donovan noted. "I hope you like the decor."

"This place is outstandingly warm," Mosko said, looking up at another painting, a beige circle inside a darker beige icosahedron. "It reminds me of this girl I dated before I met my wife. She was a weight lifter from Sheepshead Bay. Thirty-three and buns of steel. Lived in a one-bedroom apartment a block from the el. She had this bedroom set she bought from a place on Ralph Avenue. It was grey Formica.''

"Sexy," Donovan said.

"Battleship grey. And on the matching vanity table she had this hockey puck she used to keep papers from blowing from the fan she had stuck in the window.''

Donovan was fiddling with some papers on Lake's desk.

"I used to call this place 'the Winter Palace,'" Duke said, forcing a smile. "But listen; June is really a very warm and feeling woman. I've been horrible to her in the past.''

"What did you do?" Donovan asked.

"She wanted a long-term relationship. I didn't.''

"She wanted to marry you?"

"I've always had a problem with that word," Duke said.

"Me, too, until two years ago," Donovan replied. He had found a neatly stacked pile of financial records and was unable to resist prying.

"She also thought it would be good for our careers. You know—and this was her idea, not mine—June wanted the network to bill us as the married anchors, 'Duke and Lake.'"

"Sounds like the name of a prizefighter," Mosko said.

"'Dukin' Lake.' Look, Cap; if you're done with me—"

"Take off," Donovan said.

"I'll get back to the stiff. So long, Mr. Duke.''

"'Bye.''

With a handshake and a shouted "Good-bye!" to the woman in the kitchen, Moskowitz disappeared through the living room and out the apartment door.

Duke said, "Maybe the way you did it is the right way. I'm over fifty, too. Maybe it is time to settle down with the right woman.''

"June?" Donovan asked.

Duke sighed audibly enough to be heard across the room. He said, "I'd kind of like to have a kid. A little rug rat running around. A son to whom I can, someday, teach everything I know.''

''I would pay to sit in on that lesson,'' Donovan said.

Duke frowned. ''I want a son,'' he said nonetheless.

''But June is our age,'' Donovan replied. ''The battery has run out on her biological clock.''

''I'm a wretched man who deserves to be sent to the poorhouse alone and without a family,'' Duke said, perhaps realizing his misery, his voice rising into the plaintive range.

Donovan pulled a rectangular slip of paper from the pile he had been perusing and held it up. It was an old pay stub. ''She makes thirty-eight thousand, four hundred sixty-one dollars, and fifty-four cents in take-home pay? How often do you guys get paid? Monthly?''

Duke shook his head, looking embarrassed, then proud. ''Every two weeks,'' he replied. He held up two fingers in what looked like a *V*-for-victory sign.

''She makes more money in a month than I made in a year until recently,'' Donovan said. ''What's *your* paycheck like? Are you in this league?''

''My friend, I *invented* this league,'' Duke answered proudly. ''I make more than she does.''

''How can you get a check like that every two weeks and still be broke? What do you spend it on? I don't recall seeing anything in the papers about mansions or yachts.''

''I have houses in L.A. and East Hampton, an apartment here in town, and a pied-à-terre in London,'' Duke replied.

''Well, I guess that could eat up a buck or two.''

''And I put money down on a little spread in Montana last year, but—''

''Where in Montana?'' Donovan asked. ''In Moose Horn?''

''Not far from there. But I changed my mind and got my money back.''

''How come?''

''Call it bad vibes. I spent a few days out there last year, when George and some other people I know were singing the praises of Montana real estate, and came back to New York with the distinct feeling that the natives were unfriendly.''

"Some of 'em are, I hear," Donovan said.

Duke looked pensive for a moment, then sighed and pulled himself into a sitting position, pausing to straighten his pants and tuck his shirt back in. "So that's where I've been spending my bread. Then there are the cars and..." He looked around to see if Lake had come back into the room. "And then there's the women. I guess I spend more than I should on them."

"How? Fur coats?"

"Sometimes."

"Jewels?"

"Definitely."

"Trips to Paris for lunch?"

"It's been known to happen," Duke replied.

"And what does June feel about all this?" Donovan asked.

Duke stretched and yawned. "She's a good friend these days. I'm sorry I didn't live up to her expectations for me. Now if I can just find some way to save my career."

"You're sure that Wolf will dump you?"

"As sure as the day is long. But maybe I can pick up something on cable. I'm not a bad-looking guy, even after all I've been through. Maybe I can sell stuff on the Home Shopping Channel."

"But kiss the big paydays good-bye, eh?" Donovan said, surreptitiously folding up Lake's old pay stub and slipping it into his pants pocket.

The rhythmic swooshing of panty hose announced the return of June Lake, bearing two mugs of coffee. If a tragedy had just befallen her TV family, such didn't show on her face or in her demeanor. The Barbie sheen was back and in full bloom.

Upon seeing Duke sitting up, she beamed and said, "You're up! How do you feel?"

"With my fingers," Duke replied, wiggling those on one hand.

"Your sense of humor is coming back. That's good. Here's your coffee."

She handed one mug to him, a plain white mug, and gave another to the captain. "You take milk and one sugar, don't you?" she said.

"That's fine. Thanks." Donovan had a sip and put the mug on the desk next to the stack of financial records.

Lake was back sitting on the couch next to Duke, one hand resting lightly on his leg. Her fingers were splayed out, delicately, like those of a harpist.

"What were you two doing in the costume room before?" Donovan asked.

"I don't know…talking," Duke said. "We were both running in and out,"

"Talking about what?"

"Is that important?" Lake asked—a bit defensively, Donovan thought.

Donovan said that it was.

"I don't know…stuff," Duke said.

"I was trying to pry him away from the city for the holidays," Lake added with a sigh.

"Christmas."

"The week between Christmas and New Year's. I was hoping to get him to come to the islands with me. I have to make reservations, so I wanted to pin him down today."

"Any island in particular?" Donovan asked.

"I have a villa on St. Bart's," she replied.

"God, you people sure know how to spend money. The last beach I spent any time at was Brighton Beach."

"I'm never going back to the Caribbean after last summer," Duke said.

Donovan smiled faintly, then commented, "When a volcano blew up and stranded you on Carricola for three weeks before the Coast Guard came and got you out."

"Oh, you know about that? Funny. I traveled incognito, with a beard, and it never made the papers. Except for a little mention when I was one of the Americans rescued."

"That little item remains on the AP Web site," Donovan said. "What did you do while you were down there?"

"God, what can you do *anywhere* for three weeks when you have only a few changes of clothes? I cooled my heels on the veranda with the other guests and ate too much. I put on five pounds." Duke patted his tummy. Then he added, "Dammit, I should have called my personal trainer and canceled."

"Did you hobnob with any royalty while you were in Carricola?" Donovan asked.

Duke hesitated for a second, and his eyes flashed to Donovan's, then away. "Oh, *heaps,*" he replied, a bit too flippantly.

"You *did* have a horrible time last summer," Lake said then. "So, let's not go to St. Bart's. Let's go to Rio."

"Rio at Christmas?" Duke asked, interested.

"It will be totally different, and you need a change of pace to help settle your nerves."

"I'm not sure I can afford it, since I'm going to be losing my job."

"I have plenty enough money for both of us," she said.

Duke picked up her hand and squeezed it. Yet again she cupped his hand in both of hers.

"Remember when we talked—in the costume room, come to think of it—after that German man was murdered. You told me about your 'desperation plan,' you called it."

"Desperation plan?" Donovan asked.

Duke's face took on a nearly childlike look that combined fear and helplessness. "I told June"——he held up her hands so Donovan could see, out in the open now, the bond between them——"that if the network ever seemed on the verge of firing me, I mean actually doing it and not just leaking threats to *Variety,* I would bag it and quit.''

"To do what? It seems to me we had a discussion along these lines and you didn't know how you would pay for everything," Donovan said.

"I'd dump everything," Duke replied. "Sell the houses and cars. Live a simple life."

"We'd get married," Lake said, tossing in the part of the plan Duke had neglected to mention.

Duke bobbed his head up and down, a bit like a two-year-old promising Mommy he would be good. "I'd write my memoirs. You know, *Tales of a TV Tough Guy.*" He laughed bitterly.

"Where would you live?" Donovan asked.

"Here, I guess," he said, looking around in a cursory manner.

"I have a country house, too," Lake added.

"I need to be straight on something," Donovan said. "You want this guy to be a househusband? To go from being TV's biggest hunk to being totally dependent on you?"

"I could keep an eye on him that way," she replied, her voice and expression tending to regard Duke as a scamp who was, nonetheless, adorable.

"I see," Donovan said. He walked away from them and to the window to look out at Central Park. The city's most famous patch of green was veiled behind fine snowflakes that had begun falling within the previous few minutes. They also floated down in front of Fifth Avenue Medical Center, off to the right across the corner of the park. For a moment Donovan tried to guess which of the dozens of windows was Marcy's.

Then Duke said, "That's it. That's what I'll do."

"I'm so proud of you," Lake responded.

"I'll call right now and quit—before they can fire me. Then I'll call my press agent and have her make the announcement. Then I'll call my lawyer and tell him to put everything I own on the block. I'll take a few days to arrange stuff. We'll have a quiet Christmas together and then get married in Rio.''

The happy couple embraced, arms entwined, then kissed so passionately that Donovan wished he had a camera, knowing that such a snapshot was worth half a million dollars to the *Globe*. Duke and Lake: he dependent on her, helpless; she wearing the pants in the household. As fond as the captain was of strong women, having married one, the match he saw developing in front of him was too bizarre to be true. And not just because Duke had been ducking Lake only a few weeks earlier.

Donovan folded his arms and said, ''I'm sorry, but you two aren't going anywhere.''

''What?'' they exclaimed, more or less in unison.

''You're not leaving town—certainly not leaving the country—till I find out who's killed three people, so far, on Fifth Avenue.''

Lake bristled. No gloss covered her demeanor now. Instead, a hard edge, a frustrated and angry one, presented itself. ''You can't stop us,'' she said.

''Watch me,'' Donovan replied.

''What's this about, Bill?'' Duke asked. ''Don't tell me I'm a *suspect*.''

''Everyone is a suspect at this point.''

''But I was with June when Tony was killed.''

''Did you hear the shot?''

''No.''

''So you don't know when it happened. And June doesn't know where you were at the time your bodyguard was killed.''

''You can't hear anything that goes on in the street when you're inside the studio,'' Duke said. ''The walls are insulated to make sure you can't.''

"So each of you doesn't know where the other one was when Tony was killed," Donovan stated.

Duke appeared to be astonished. "Well, now that you mention it—"

"Did anyone else see you guys in that room? Going to that room? Leaving it?"

Duke shook his head. "That corridor by the costume room is empty in the afternoon. You see, the whole studio is dedicated to *The Morning Show*. It shuts down a few hours after the show airs. Our typical day runs from five in the morning to noon. A few of us stay longer, mainly June and me. Sometimes George. And Rose, often."

"The redhead in Master Control. The one whose father taught her how to hunt with a pistol."

"Do you suspect her?" Duke asked.

Donovan shrugged.

Lake was still seething quietly, glaring at the captain while tightening her grip on her newly caught man.

Donovan said, "Let's talk about Carricola last summer."

Duke sighed, and then Lake and he exchanged glances. "He knows," Duke told her.

June softened then, the hard edge dissolving in favor of what seemed like a look of relieved honesty. Relieved at being able to tell the truth at last. Or was she acting? Donovan wondered.

She said, "I want you to know, Captain, that I know all about Paul's past. And I don't care. I truly don't."

"That's very modern of you," Donovan responded. "If it's true, then you won't mind listening while Paul and I talk about Princess Anna."

"I already know the story. Paul was trapped with this woman at the hotel in Carricola. They had an affair. Big deal."

Duke said, "Anna Hebbel seemed like a nice young woman. She was down in the islands having a final fling before getting engaged, getting married, and settling down.

She chose me to have it with. She's European royalty. She could have had anyone. I was flattered. And, of course, in the hotel during the time we were trapped, there was nothing else to do. No TV. No radio."

"No morning-after pills," Donovan said.

Duke's eyes whitened and broadened. It was the deer-in-the-headlights look that Donovan knew so well. It was hard for the captain to avoid gloating.

"You don't know about the baby, do you?" he said.

"Baby?" Duke stammered.

"Your child. Daughter, to be accurate. Count back twenty weeks—well, twenty-three or so now—to Carricola, and you are the father-to-be. Congratulations, Dad."

Duke sort of laughed and shook his head. Then he caught a glimpse of Lake, who was not amused, and the glimmer of a smile vanished from his lips.

"Did she sleep with anyone else down there?" Donovan asked.

"No. Just me. I'm sure of it."

"She flew back to New York to be with Melmer, and very soon they announced their engagement. I suspect he knew about the baby but didn't care. Apparently, he was as 'modern' as you are." Donovan nodded in the direction of Lake.

"I had no idea about this baby, but it changes nothing," Lake said. "I still want to marry Paul. And Princess Anna didn't."

Duke added, "She's royalty. They cover up things like this."

"Wrong," Donovan said. "She's not royalty. Her real name is Anna Fritsch, and she's a penny-ante European scam artist who was born in prison, the daughter of a notorious sixties radical."

Duke had the deer look again. Donovan was less certain about the extent to which Lake was startled by the information.

And it was Lake who spoke. "What you're saying is, she'll be back," she said. "If she's a crook, no matter where she's gone, she will be in touch with Paul looking for money. In fact, I wouldn't be surprised if she slept with Paul deliberately to get pregnant."

Duke looked at Lake then, as if he was about to disagree. Donovan sensed a man about to stand up for the honor of the mother of his child. But the moment passed.

Donovan said, "If I'm not mistaken, Melmer had more money than Paul does, did, or ever will."

"He died before marrying her," Lake replied.

"This is true. Paul, she doesn't happen to be staying at one of your residences, does she?" Donovan asked.

"With me? No, of course not. I didn't even know she was missing."

"But you did show up at that second murder scene, not out of general curiosity, but because you wanted to see if I would spill some information about her," Donovan said.

"I was concerned about Anna, that's true. Her fiancé had just been murdered. And like I told you, I was afraid that someone was gunning for me. Don't you see? I was right all along. It makes more sense now. Whoever is gunning for me must have thought that Melmer was me. I was supposed to be that first victim. God, I hope Anna is all right."

Lake looked sharply at him, and Duke said, "Just...you know...because she's been through so much."

"When you put the Lamborghini on the block, maybe you could give her a hubcap," Donovan remarked.

"I'm sure a payoff of some kind will be in the offing," Lake said. "Never mind. I can handle this...*princess*. Nothing will come between Paul and me now, certainly not some cheap hustler who got lucky and seduced my man when both were trapped in a hotel."

This time Duke said nothing but instead let his head roll to one side until it rested lightly atop hers. Then he began petting the back of her hand.

A short while and a few meaningless conversational exchanges later, Donovan excused himself and walked back to the crime scene. There he found that the body had been probed, prodded, and deemed fit for travel, then zipped into a body bag and driven the two dozen blocks south to the morgue. Traffic was moving again, though down to two lanes and creeping along. TV remote vans were everywhere, their telescoping antennae making the stretch of Fifth Avenue in front of the Brazilian Tourist Office resemble an asparagus patch.

Donovan found his aide sitting in the famous costume room, staring fixedly at a largish plastic evidence bag that he had placed next to the coffeemaker. Donovan couldn't see what was in it, there were so many labels printed or otherwise affixed to the parcel. But from Mosko's seriousness, Donovan felt he wasn't looking at lunch.

"I take it that's no prune Danish in there," he said.

"It's the Kammacher Stedman," Mosko responded, looking up in pride. "We found it under the car."

"Really? That's it, there? Amazing." Donovan was genuinely surprised, too. In his considerable experience, killers who went out of their way to acquire exotic weapons generally were separated from them only by deadly force. "You found it where?"

"Under the car, I told you."

"Where exactly?"

By way of reply, Moskowitz got to his feet, walked to the coffeemaker, formed his hands into a gun, went, "Pow," and pumped an imaginary bullet into the twelve-cup carafe. Then he flipped his right hand back and down around in a semicircle, as if to chuck a gun below the smallish table atop which sat the coffee machine.

"Right under the body?" Donovan asked.

"About where the head rested." Mosko sat back down.

"So the killer is right-handed."

"How do you figure that?"

Donovan said, "He shoots through the window. He yanks the door open. Sees the body. Chucks the gun. Left hand is on door. Splits. It's midafternoon on Fifth Avenue four days before Christmas and he needs to get away before the panic wears off and people start to remember things."

"I guess this means that Duke can stop being afraid of being shot through the window," Mosko said.

"His fears are over anyway," Donovan replied. "The man is quitting as of right now."

"What's he going to do? Open a gyro cart? The guy has some Greek blood. I'm sure of it."

Donovan shook his head, then filled in his assistant on the part of the conversation he had missed by leaving Lake's apartment.

When Donovan was done, Mosko said, "So Duke will have to sell the Lamborghini. Poor baby."

"I pretty much conveyed that sentiment to him."

"Did he listen?"

"Not that I noticed. You know, he said he's going to be flat broke and fully dependent on June Lake."

"Which is what she wants, you told me."

"She caught him.... She says she accepts him, warts and all...and she means to keep him."

"Seems to me I've heard of this happening before. A guy chases women and spends money until he wears himself out doing both. Then a good, simple woman comes along and takes him in, warts and all, like you say, and he's so grateful he stays forever."

Donovan nodded. "And it's not like Duke will be flat broke the way you and I might be flat broke."

"You've got plenty of money," Mosko said.

"I'm OK now. I wouldn't say I have plenty of money."

"Ever since you made captain and married Marcy—come on, admit it—her parents' money has been trickling down to you."

"My friend, captains make pretty good money these days,

and my apartment is still on rent control," Donovan said. "So let's just say that, wherever it comes from, I can afford butter with my toast these days."

"You're saying that Duke will be able to afford butter *and* jam with his toast."

"At the very least, and good-quality jam, too. Even if he declares bankruptcy, those laws let you keep a house and a car. Maybe you get to keep a Honda, not a Lamborghini."

"Poor baby. Duke has a Honda?"

"Beats me. And anyway, he's going to write his memoir, *Tales of a TV Tough Guy.*"

Mosko snickered. "He won't be doing it for free."

"No, he wouldn't. But if I read my June Lakes correctly, he sure won't be spending what money he may have on other women. Do you want to do something for me? Just for the hell of it? The Stedman fires depleted-uranium bullets. Is this depleted uranium radioactive?"

"You're asking me a science question? I got no idea, Cap."

"Me either," Donovan said.

"So what do you want me to do?"

"Get a guy with a Geiger counter and send him around this building. Send him around all the dressing rooms— Duke's, Lake's, and Halloran's—and around Master Control where Rose works. Send him to Tuttle's apartment in the East Village and to Koslov's apartments in Brighton Beach. Send him to that garage where the gyro guys park their carts and to Mojadidi's apartment in Long Island City. And let's not leave out the offices of the Midtown Merchants Association."

"What's he looking for?" Mosko asked.

"Radiation, of course. I doubt he'll find any, but that's really beside the point. Have the guy act like he's hot on the trail. Have him take lots of notes and look concerned but say nothing."

"Have him put on an act," Mosko said, getting it.

"And he needn't hide his activities from the press, either," Donovan added.

NINETEEN

STORIES THAT TAKE YOU FROM RAGS TO RICHES BUT REQUIRE THIRTY YEARS TO GET THERE

ROSE WAUCQEZ WAS in Master Control, editing a taped segment that had something to do with canoes and a swamp, when Donovan eased himself down into the chair beside her.

"Captain Donovan," she said pleasantly, without quite looking up.

"Ms. Waucqez, how are you today?"

"It's 'Rose,' and you know it's a sad day. That poor man. And poor Paul. I suppose he'll be leaving the network now."

She hadn't taken her eyes off the monitor except to acknowledge Donovan's arrival, so he said cheerily, "The Great American Canoe Festival, I guess?"

"Wrong. The Okefenokee Catfish Festival. It's going on all next week. This tape is from last year."

"Who's covering it?" Donovan asked.

"Who do you imagine?"

"George, but I don't think he'll be squeezing into a canoe without sinking it."

That got her to turn away from the monitor. "The man is a pig. And fat enough to sink the *Titanic,* if it hadn't already been sunk by that iceberg. Did you come here to ask me about George Halloran? Is he a suspect? If so, haul him off, lock him up, and throw away the key."

"He thinks you like him," Donovan said.

"The man is delusional. They let him stand in for the

anchors a couple of times and he imagines he not only can fill Paul's shoes, he can wear his pants.''

"George, stand in for the anchors?"

"Don't you watch the show?" she asked, looking Donovan up and down. "No, of course you don't. You have the look of a Public Television viewer."

"Thank you," he replied. "Why does the network let George stand in for the stars?"

"Because, in their reductionist vision, George is the wave of the future for them."

"Reductionist as in lowest common denominator?" Donovan asked.

"See; I was right about you. George has that slob-level appeal that the MBAs that run Wolf like. It's an open secret that we appeal to the Tonya Harding, professional wrestling, tractor-pull crowd to begin with. Adding a gigantic drunken ex-marine who waggles his eyebrows and leers at women is just their idea of the next network news superstar."

"I guess you don't like him much," Donovan said.

Waucqez reached over and shook Donovan's hand. "I guess I like you, Captain," she replied. "I'd go for you in a big way if you weren't already taken. The truth is I'm a committed feminist whose standards in men are so high I might as well move into a convent. Me go for George Halloran? I'd sooner go for George Wallace. And isn't he dead?"

"So much for Halloran's ability to guess what women are thinking," Donovan said.

"What did I tell you? He has the sensitivity of a kidney stone."

"Tell me this. Are you in any way suggesting that George might want to see Paul Duke lose his job?"

"Ha! *Might* want to! Would *love* to, that's more like it. But if you're thinking that George might kill to get the job, no, as much as I want to think ill of the man, I doubt it. He's a slob and an opportunist, but not a killer. Besides, how would you pack that fat body into a Santa's Angels costume?''

"You have a point," Donovan admitted.

She smiled and turned back to the screen. A few seconds later, the canoes, formerly seen sharply, were paddling off through the swamp, bathed in a misty glow that suggested early-morning fog. She said, "We're trying to tell a story about fog, and there wasn't any on this tape. So I just added it. The Wolf network. Integrity in journalism. George Halloran, future anchorperson."

"You're awfully hard on the network that pays your salary," Donovan said.

"And you never criticize the NYPD?"

"The other night, Marcy and I were watching *20/20* on ABC."

"Now, that is network news as it should be," Waucqez said.

"Is it? They ran a piece on a woman who gave up her wealthy lifestyle and her family to marry a convicted murderer currently residing on death row."

"I saw that; classic journalism."

Donovan shook his head. "In prime time and narrated by Barbara Walters, it looks classic. But run the same story at three in the afternoon on *Jenny Jones* and you have something like 'Men on Death Row and the Women Who Love Them.'"

"What are you trying to tell me? That Wolf Television isn't so bad? Or that all television is bad?"

"I'm telling you that there's a reason I read a lot," Donovan said. "I like information. Such as on dates and times. How are you on those?"

"You mean like when the murders took place?" she asked, turning back.

"Like then," he replied.

"Well, I keep track of all the comings and goings around

here, so yes, I can help you. You want to know where George was?''

''I want to know where all three of them were.''

''The other two being Paul and June?'' she asked, a little thrown by the possibilities.

''Yep.''

She thought for a moment, then said, ''Well, that is a shocker. The police want to know if Paul Duke and June Lake—''

''Dukin' Lake,'' Donovan said.

''—have alibis for the times of the murders. Let's see. As I recall, the first killing, where a man was shot through a store window, happened right after we went off the air, right?''

Donovan nodded. ''Shortly after the stores opened. Nine-fifteen.''

''And the date was?'' She was calling up a screen on one of the half-dozen monitors in front of her.

''Friday, November twenty-ninth, is when Erik Melmer was killed,'' Donovan said. ''Thursday, December fifth, is when Terry Seybold was murdered.''

''That was the one at night.''

''Right in the middle of the tree-lighting ceremony. At eight-seventeen. And the third murder, as you know, was about an hour ago. Around three.''

''It's all right here,'' she said, smiling at the screen and her own record-keeping ability.

''Well?''

''Does the word *bupkes* resonate with you?'' she said.

''If Marcy's mom is right, and I'm not going to be the one to argue with her, it means 'goat turd' in Yiddish.''

''In other words, nothing. They have no alibis.''

''You're sure of that?'' Donovan asked.

''On November twenty-ninth we closed the show at nine a.m. Paul and June, as they always do, repaired to their dressing rooms. Which means that nobody saw them. Every

day they do the same thing. They go to their rooms to unwind, lay down, kick the furniture, whatever they do in
there. The point is, they are alone. Unless they happen to
be with one another, and as you must have surmised, they
don't get along that well. What happened before, by the
way? I heard the rumor that she took him to her place?''

"She certainly did that. And I think she's keeping him,
too."

"My, my. As Dorothy Parker said, 'Read a book, and
sew a seam, and slumber if you can. All your life you wait
around for some damn man.' Anyway, the corridor where
the stars' dressing rooms reside is off-limits to all but the
exalted themselves. So, in short, no one saw them on that
day. And no one saw them at the time of the second killing,
either."

"But that one was at night," Donovan said.

"Yes, but we were on the air that night, covering the
tree-lighting ceremony. In fact, we preempted the *Marlboro
Classic Monster Tractor Mash* to do so."

"What a shame."

"Yeah. You should have seen the letters. Paul and June
introduced the personality who was covering the tree-
lighting, then repaired to their dressing rooms per usual. So,
once again, no alibi."

"Who covered the ceremony?" Donovan asked.

"George. So he's in the clear, at least for that murder.
For the first one, he was in his dressing room. Which is on
a different corridor but just as secluded. I heard that George
was with you an hour ago when Paul's bodyguard was shot.
So I suppose that the gigantic sot is off the hook for two-
thirds of your murders. And as the poet said, 'two out of
three ain't bad.'''

"Dorothy Parker again?" Donovan asked playfully.

"Meat Loaf," she replied.

They were interrupted by the ringing of Donovan's cell
phone. He put the device to his ear and had a brief conver-

sation, at the end of which he imagined that a smile must have crept across his lips. For Waucqez looked over at him and said, "You ought to bottle that look."

"Which look is that?" he asked, his mind swimming with entertaining possibilities.

"The cat-that-ate-the-canary look. I don't suppose you can tell me what fascinating tidbit you just learned."

Donovan shook his head. "I suppose you read *Moll Flanders,*" he said.

"Many years ago."

"I love stories that take you from rags to riches but require thirty years to get there," Donovan said.

"Doesn't everyone?" she replied. "But what has that got to do with the murders?"

"Everything and nothing," he said, and headed for the door.

IT WAS ABOUT seven in the evening when Donovan, having planted a suggestion at breakfast time, saw it come to life during the dinner hour. All he had to do, really, was be there to intercept the shipment. Consequently, it was Captain Bill Donovan of the NYPD, and not Jaime the delivery boy, who carried a sack of take-home food from Paco's Mexican Restaurant to a two-bedroom apartment in the Beresford Towers.

He rang the bell and, a moment later, heard Claudia Hummitz's voice, mellower than at any other time since he first heard it, say, "It's dinner, honey." And then footsteps approached the door.

She swung it open and, when her eyes met his, Donovan said, "Chorizos, anyone?" He held aloft the bag.

It was an awkward moment, at best, that could have led to tears or violence if the captain hadn't read the personalities correctly. But he had, and after a fleeting, surprised silence Hummitz laughed, shook her head, and laughed again.

"Damn, you're good," she said.

"Nah, just persistent. You aren't going to shoot me or anything, are you?"

"I haven't killed anyone in thirty years," Kirsten Fritsch replied. "What gave me away? I know; you got my fingerprints off that catalog."

"That and your habit of balling up tissues and leaving them all over the place, including your daughter's hospital room. Can I come in? I brought enough for three. How is your daughter? She is here, isn't she?"

"Of course she is. She came right to her mama after her fiancé, the only man who ever treated her with true love and absolute respect, was murdered. And she's been here ever since. Anna?"

The young woman was sitting on a floral print couch, her legs primly tucked under her, her pregnancy at last showing. She looked radiantly beautiful, but like an orchid does when it's slightly damaged. She had been through a lot, and looked up at Donovan with cat's eyes, full of fear. She said, tentatively, "I remember seeing you in the hospital. Your wife is multiracial, isn't she?"

"African-American and Jewish," Donovan replied.

"So you're not an ordinary policeman. Is my mom under arrest?"

"Not if she hasn't killed anyone in thirty years," Donovan said, helping himself to a seat on the couch next to the young woman. He put the bags on the coffee table, which was an old ship's hatch cover that a clever artisan had restored and converted. Claudia Hummitz—Kirsten Fritsch, that is—sat on his other side.

"Am *I* under arrest?" Anna asked.

"What for?" he replied.

"Running away?"

"It isn't illegal to run away from someone who's trying to kill you," Donovan said.

"Then it's true," Kirsten said. "What Anna and I have

been assuming. That the madman who's killing people on Fifth Avenue wants her dead."

"I think she was one of the targets," Donovan replied.

"And the other target? Paul?"

"Definitely. That is Paul's baby, isn't it?" He waved a bag of food in the direction of Anna's tummy.

Anna nodded. "We had an affair in Carricola. Paul is very charming...and very attractive."

Kirsten looked away, but when her gaze turned back to Donovan it had an ironic smile.

Anna continued, "I didn't want to get pregnant, at least not by Paul. I slept with him, I don't know, out of boredom but also as the last gasp of my single days. I was going to get married, and here was my chance for a final fling, and with the man they're calling 'the sexiest man alive.'"

"And is he?"

"He'll do," Anna said, with a girlish giggle.

"What do *you* think?" Donovan asked her mother.

"Paul isn't bad for a man his age," she replied, shaking her head. "Do you know how *mad* I got at him when I learned?"

"I think I can imagine."

"There we were, in bed together, comparing notes about our love lives, when I found out he had slept with my daughter. Not only that, but he was the father of her unborn child. And he didn't even know it. The man sleeps with so many women he isn't even aware of getting one of them pregnant."

"Did you tell him that Anna is your daughter?" Donovan asked.

"No. I was afraid he'd do something to fuck up her engagement. But I was still mad enough to throw him out of my apartment at four in the morning." She laughed and added, "I think that's the first time any woman threw him out."

"Well, he still doesn't know you two are mother and

daughter. Only that he's going to have a child,'' Donovan said. ''I told him.''

''What did he say?'' Anna asked.

''He seemed pretty amazed. My sense is he's giving that fact plenty of thought right about now.''

''My God, a spark of decency,'' Kirsten said.

''Maybe more than a spark.''

''I was mad enough to kill him, but like I said, I don't do that anymore. And I paid dearly for the one death I caused, over in Germany so many years ago.''

''Just for the record, where were you on November twenty-ninth?'' Donovan asked.

''When poor Erik was killed? I was in my office, with my secretary.''

''On the evening of December fifth you were helping officiate over the tree-lighting ceremony. And this afternoon at three?''

''In my office, taking a call from that idiot FBI agent. God, can you believe it? The FBI trying to help *me?* What a fucking hoot. I only wish that J. Edgar Hoover had lived to discover that his minions were assisting Kirsten Fritsch, the notorious sixties radical and murderess.''

''Where did you get that name?'' Donovan asked.

''Claudia Hummitz was the name of my landlady when I lived in Baden-Baden during the summer of 1967. When I got out of jail, I figured that if Jerry Rubin could transform himself into a Wall Street whatever-he-was and if Eldridge Cleaver can become a goddamn motivational speaker, then Kirsten Fritsch can transmogrify into the director of the Midtown Merchants Association. Where were *you* in 1967?''

''A man is entitled to a period of time that he doesn't have to account for,'' Donovan said.

''Ooh, a skeleton in the closet. And I'll bet I know what it is, too.''

''No, you don't,'' Donovan said, opening the paper bags

and distributing the Mexican food by way of changing the topic of conversation. A bit later, munching on a chorizo, he told Anna, "I'm sorry about Erik."

She looked down at her plate for a moment, then picked at her burrito. "Me too."

"You've been down one hell of a road," he said.

"A girl who's born in prison has to do whatever she can to survive," Anna said.

"So you became Princess Anna."

"Whatever works," she said. "The fake title got me into certain social circles, one result of which is that I met Erik." She hesitated for a second, then said, "I miss him."

"Did he know your real name?"

"I told him. It changed nothing. He fell in love with me, not my past."

"Erik must have been a remarkable man," Donovan said.

"I assume you know that he took care of me," Anna replied. "I'm actually a very wealthy woman right now."

"Your butler awaits your return."

"Bliley is a good man," Anna said.

"This time don't pretend to be royalty. I suspect he likes you better as you are."

"But I don't know if I could live in Trump Plaza."

"Oh, *I* could," Kirsten interjected. "I would savor the irony with every breath I took."

"Mom, let's go live there," Anna said, reaching across Donovan's lap long enough to touch her mother's hand. "We have nothing to hide from now."

"They'll fire me if they find out who I am," Kirsten said.

"Why should you care?" Donovan asked.

"True.... Why should I care?"

"Let's do it, then," Anna said.

Donovan held up his hand. "Wait a few days," he said. "Why?"

"Let's not forget that someone still may be trying to kill you. We can protect you better here. I asked my associate,

Brian Moskowitz, to join us tonight. Be absolutely honest with him. He'll put a twenty-four-hour guard on your door."

"It seems like a reasonable precaution," Kirsten said.

"And the four of us will sit down and come up with a plan to catch the man or woman who tried to kill you, Anna, and who is trying to kill Paul."

Nodding, Anna said, "Captain Donovan, I'd like to come see your wife in the hospital."

"She'd like that," Donovan replied.

"When is she due?"

"On Christmas Day. The doctor is going to deliver the baby then."

"You can count on us being there," Kirsten said. "But *who* are your suspects? Beyond the authors of the extortion demand."

"They're not even under consideration," Donovan replied. "Neither the Afghan bunch nor the Montana hoodlums. The FBI is chasing its own tail on this one."

"Pity," Kirsten said.

"As of an hour ago, no one had showed to pick up the diamonds. And there were more FBI agents waiting along Northern Boulevard than there were Afghan immigrants. By tomorrow morning I'm sure that even the FBI will realize it's been snookered and call home its dogs."

"In that case," Kirsten said, "who is trying to kill my daughter?"

"Paul can't be ruled out," Donovan replied.

Both women seemed shocked.

"But I consider him a long shot. As you said, the man has been showing a spark of humanity recently. Then there's June Lake. No alibi for any of the killings. A somewhat shaky motive."

"Which is?" Anna asked.

"To get Paul for herself. By scaring the daylights out of him and then giving him nowhere to turn but her."

"It seems somewhat extreme to imagine that a woman

would kill three people to catch a man," Kirsten said. "Even that man."

"I agree," Anna added.

"Unless there's more to it, she's not the killer," Donovan said. "Next on the list is George Halloran."

"The weather buffoon," Kirsten said.

"He's ambitious and stands to gain a lot if Paul loses his job. However, he has an ironclad alibi for the most recent murder. He was having a drink with me."

"Who else?" Kirsten asked.

"Ever heard the name Valery Koslov?" Donovan asked.

Both women shook their heads.

"He's a Russian mobster and thug that the Manhattan DA is looking for."

"How did the Russian mafia get into this?" Anna asked.

"Koslov has a young and beautiful wife," Donovan explained.

"Oh," Kirsten replied, bobbing her head up and down.

"He also owned the murder weapon until quite recently," Donovan said. "However, he has alibis for two of the murders and I doubt he did the third. Now we come to Tom Tuttle."

"Who?" Anna asked.

"The son of the former owners of E & J Tuttle," Donovan said. "He's an army-trained sniper who was gassed during the Gulf War and subsequently snapped. Until recently he's been making a living by reciting poetry on the street while dressed as a Viking."

"Oh, Erik and I saw him," Anna said excitedly. "Erik gave him five dollars, for which he recited a poem. He seemed harmless."

"He's violent and has a huge grudge against the Japanese corporation that bought out his family store," Donovan informed them.

"I also heard about this man," Kirsten added. "I was told… This is sad, actually, or pathetic, depending on your point of view. Did you know that his family donated the Rockefeller Center Christmas tree?''

Donovan nodded.

"Did you know that Tuttle used to play in that tree during his childhood?''

Donovan hadn't known that.

"And that he actually had a tree house in it once? It's sad to think—"

"—that not only did he lose the family store, but he also lost the tree he used to play in as a child," Donovan said. "Which is now on display, dead as a doornail, around the corner from the store. No wonder the poor fool is howling mad." Donovan made a note on a piece of brown paper bag and stuck it in his pocket. "Tuttle has gone up a notch on the suspect list," the captain explained. "I just wish we could find him."

"Is he your last suspect?" Kirsten asked.

"No. There's Yama Mojadidi."

"Who?" both women asked simultaneously.

"The Afghan enigma," Donovan said. "The only one on the list who's definitely going down for *something,* I assure you."

"Why?" Kirsten asked.

"He took a shot at me. Nothing gets my attention faster than being shot at. What did I tell you this morning? Especially since I'm about to become a father."

"Who is this man?" Anna asked.

"An Afghan immigrant who was running a gyro cart in front of F.A.O. Schwarz three weeks ago when Erik was killed. I was talking to the man when the shots were fired. He went for a gun; very jittery. By the time I got through at the crime scene he had disappeared. Curious, I went looking for him. And he shot at me."

"You said he was standing in front of Schwarz?" Kirsten asked. "Did you know that Paul used to walk to and from work passing by that spot?"

Donovan knew. "There's a good chance that Mojadidi was lying in wait for him, hoping to kill him. He was carrying a picture of a young woman, possibly a daughter."

"And Paul was in Afghanistan, covering the war there," Kirsten said. "Of course he seduced the daughter. Ergo the assassination attempt by the outraged father. They take family honor very seriously in Muslim countries."

"My God, you have five or six suspects on your list," Anna said.

"This *is* New York, after all," Donovan said. "And there used to be more names on the list."

"There were?"

"Your mom was on it," he replied.

Kirsten smiled sheepishly, putting down her fork. "Oh, the joys of being a retired murderess and murder suspect," she said. "You know, I think I *will* quit my job and go live in Trump Plaza. Fuck the Midtown Merchants Association and their money."

Donovan smiled and stood so mother and daughter could move together on the couch and hug. *Parenthood,* Donovan thought, *it looks good to me.*

After a minute, Kirsten looked up and asked, "What's next?"

"We wait for Moskowitz to get here from downtown," Donovan said. "Then I call Paul Duke and tell him that the mother of his unborn child wants to talk to him, on Christmas Day, at the Fifth Avenue Medical Center."

TWENTY

"YOU INVITED A SERIAL KILLER TO THE BIRTH OF OUR SON?"

MARCY'S POSITION was typically resolute, with only the slightest trace of hysteria. "I'm glad I'm going to be sedated most of the day," she said. "Because I've having trouble with the idea that you invited a serial killer to the birth of our son."

"I don't know if I'd put it that way," he said, keeping a wary eye on the door while browsing about in the medical records computer.

"What other way is there?" she asked. Marcy was sitting up in bed, brushing her hair, waiting for her doctor to come in and tell her that only an hour remained before she would be led off to be prepared for the delivery. It was ten on Christmas morning. A miniature version, maybe three feet tall, of the Barnes family Christmas tree stood on the end table. It was green plastic—no real evergreens allowed in the neonatal intensive care unit—and had an array of expensive miniature ornaments and was topped off by a crystal Star of David.

"For one thing, I could be wrong," he said.

"You, wrong?" He wasn't sure if her remark was a compliment or sarcasm. "What if Tuttle or Mojadidi did it? I couldn't even find them, let along invite them to drop by today."

"So the Viking who stands in the street and spouts poetry and the Afghan who took a shot at you—"

Donovan glanced at her, then back to the monitor as she gave him a dirty look.

"I heard about that. You didn't think I would hear about that?" Marcy said. "So these two men aren't going to make it to the birth of my son. I'm mortified."

"What does *chlamydia trachomatis* cause?" he asked, seeking to change the subject. "Is it pelvic inflammatory disease?"

"Don't try to ignore me," she said.

"I'm not ignoring you," he replied. "I'm trying to say that, maybe, someone else is the killer I'm looking for and not the people who are coming here today."

"Such as the Mountain Brigade? Whichever one."

"Such as them."

"The FBI folded its surveillance and went home two days ago," Marcy said. "The diamonds are back on Fifth Avenue, where they belong. Once again you were right."

"Let me explain how you came to have so many and colorful visitors," Donovan replied.

"I can hear my mother now."

"Koslov wanted to turn himself in, and it had to be today in Manhattan. So I said he would have to come here. Then, Anna and her mother asked if they could come to see you and the baby. Anna was a victim of this crime. Was I going to say no?"

"Not you," Marcy said.

"Duke and Lake have been here already, so they were naturals. Halloran more or less moves in Paul's shadow. All of a sudden, it turned into a crowd. Add family and guys from the office and it becomes a mob scene. Fortunately, the guys from the office all are cops, so I wouldn't worry too much about being shot or anything."

In fact, the policemen and policewomen—dozens of them, dressed as orderlies, nurses, or physicians—were everywhere, grateful to have shed the Santa's Angels getups, trying to remain unobtrusive but, in fact, giving the floor the look of a busy emergency room on New Year's Eve.

"Oh, that makes me feel reassured," she said. "These are the same guys who couldn't find Tuttle or Mojadidi? What makes you think they'll be able to stop someone from turning violent?"

"The violence, if any, will be directed at Paul Duke," Donovan told her. "And none of this will take place until visiting hours, which start at one this afternoon. Daniel will be several hours old by then, and I'll have plenty of time to pluck the killer from the crowd of also-rans and pack him or her off to the hoosegow."

"Would you stop playing with the computer and finish putting on your scrubs?" she asked.

Like many expectant dads who plan to be in the delivery room, Donovan told Dr. Campagna that he wanted to be a part of every aspect of the delivery. Then he donned yellow scrubs—paper ones that fitted over his regular clothes and rustled when he walked. But he had proven unable to get the paper booties over his sneakers. So he sat at the computer, working the mouse with one hand, holding the slip-on paper booties in the other.

"I'm almost done here," he said.

"Put on your booties."

"They don't fit over the sneakers."

"Then wear them over your socks," she replied.

He nodded in agreement, slipped off his sneakers, and pulled on the yellow paper shoes. "Now are you happy?" he asked.

"Rabbi Weiss came in this morning when you were in the shower," Marcy said.

"After this pregnancy, you know everything there is to know about reproduction," Donovan said. "Can chlamydia cause pelvic inflammatory disease?"

"Yes," she said sharply.

"And what can *that* do to you? Make you infertile? I mean—"

He was interrupted by the blaring of a warning signal. The alarm that was part of Marcy's fetal monitor went off; it was a sharp beeping sound that wasn't really all that loud but, given what it meant, seemed to dwarf the horn on a Mack truck.

"Oh my God!" she shouted, craning her neck to see the screen.

"What is it?" he asked, pressing the off switch on the computer and clambering to his feet, the paper coveralls rustling.

"The baby's heartbeat is dropping!" she said as nurses came running.

"What's that mean?"

"The fetus is under stress," said one nurse as the room filled up with medical people. Donovan went to his wife's side and held her hands as the sounds blared on and more people poured into the room from the hall. One of them was Dr. Campagna, for whom the crowd parted as did the Red Sea for Moses.

"Is he dying? Is he dying?" Marcy asked, frantic, squeezing her husband's hands so hard he could feel the bones crunching together.

The doctor peered at the monitor, looked at the strip of tape pouring out of the instrument, and felt Marcy's cervix. Then he said, "The heart rate is down. I don't know why. Sometimes it happens and you never know the reason. But I'm taking the baby now. Get Mrs. Donovan into the delivery room right away. She needs the epidural immediately."

Within half a minute, Marcy's bed was borne out of the room at the center of a moving cluster of doctors and nurses. As her hands pulled away from her husband's, she gasped, "William!"

"It will be all right," he said, his head spinning.

She was on her way down the hall then, but Campagna

lingered momentarily in the doorway, looking at Donovan standing alone in the room. He said, "I'll need you in fifteen minutes. Be ready."

"Will everything be OK?" Donovan asked.

"I won't know until I get in there."

"What can I do?"

Campagna said, "If you want to go down to the chapel, it's on the first floor." He, too, then disappeared.

Donovan stood in the room alone for a minute, thinking of his wife and unborn child and the awful possibility that his son could draw so near to life only to die. Donovan looked around the empty room, which also was silent, the blaring monitor having disappeared along with his wife, and felt more alone than ever. He sat for a minute on the edge of the reclining chair that had been his bed in recent weeks. Then he got up and, feeling a bit ridiculous but unable to prevent himself, trudged down the hall in the direction of the elevator that led to the chapel.

The small, sedate, and wood-paneled room was scrupulously nondenominational. There was no cross, no Star of David, no Muslim crescent, but rather a backlit stained-glass panel that suggested tranquillity. In it were depicted leaves, flowers, soft and mosslike earth, and sky and clouds. Seven rows of leather-cushioned pews faced what passed for an altar—the stained-glass panel and a kneeling bench and rail that stood in front of it.

Half of the room was under renovation. A new floor was being put in. That area was separated from the rest by the same sort of red velvet rope that banks use to channel customers, and a smallish sign read: Danger, Construction.

Donovan looked around to make sure no one was watching. Then he slipped into the chapel and let the door close behind him. He was alone again, or not alone, believers would say, but at least saw no other persons in the chapel. The scrubs rustling, he walked up the aisle, skirting the area under construction, and after a moment's hesitancy knelt on the bench.

He tried to think of a prayer. The Lord's Prayer should have come back to him from his childhood but didn't. He got as far as "Our Father, who..." and forgot the rest. Donovan had heard Marcy's mother say the Sh'ma, the Jewish prayer that affirmed one's belief in one God. Donovan always thought of the Sh'ma as being the perfect airplane crash prayer, for it could be said in five seconds—after the alarm sounded but before the 747 hit the mountain. But try as he might, Donovan couldn't remember the Jewish prayer, either.

At last he elevated his eyes to the ceiling and thought of what the cardinal had told him. That he would lose his atheism at the moment of his son's birth. *Well,* he thought, *this is the time.* Tears welling in his eyes, Donovan said, "I'm sorry if I did anything wrong. The best I can say for myself is that I tried hard and meant well always. Don't forgive me if you don't feel like it, but spare my wife and child."

Then he stood, the warmth of newfound belief filling his heart, and piously backed away from the altar. In so doing, Donovan backed through the red velvet ropes and into the construction area and stepped down firmly on a rusty nail.

"Shit!" he swore, hopping onto his other foot and off to one side and crashing down into a pew. He picked his foot up and looked at the bloodstain that grew quickly to the size of a quarter on the sole of his right foot.

He pressed two fingers against the wound in an attempt to stop the bleeding, but that didn't help much. So he gave up and, glancing at his watch, saw that his time was up. He got to his feet and limped out of the chapel and back to the elevator, leaving little spots of blood along the scrubbed floor.

"Captain Donovan! What happened?" asked a nurse as he hobbled up to the delivery room.

"God struck me down," Donovan muttered.

"You're bleeding. Let me see your foot."

"I stepped on a nail. The bleeding will stop on its own."

"You'll need a tetanus shot. Here, let me bandage it."

"How's my wife and child?"

"Your wife has had the epidural and is being prepped. The baby's heartbeat has stabilized, but Dr. Campagna still wants to deliver him right now. You have five minutes. Take off your sock."

Donovan did as he was told, standing on one foot and leaning against a supply cabinet as the nurse cleaned the wound and applied a patch of gauze. Then he pulled the sock back on and was given another slip-on bootie.

Marcy was lying on her back with all of her body below her breasts hidden behind a blue curtain. The anesthesiologist stood by her head, alternating glances between his monitors, his patient, and what lay beyond the curtain. Donovan was waved into a folding chair by her head.

"Hi, honey, I'm having a baby," she said, a bit groggily.

"Can you feel anything?" he asked.

"Nothing."

"Daniel's heart rate stabilized. The nurse told me."

"I know. It's wonderful. I'm having a baby. After all those years, I'm having a baby. Hold my hand."

He did as he was told. He also petted her cheek with his other hand, and the two of them looked at one another and at the blue curtain while whatever the doctor was doing on the other side caused her body to lift up and down and rock from side to side, motions she swore later she was never aware of.

Fifteen minutes into the procedure Donovan heard the anesthesiologist say, "You have a baby boy," and break into a grin. Marcy began crying and Donovan asked, "Can I look?"

"No," said the anesthesiologist firmly.

"You're not a doctor yet," Campagna added.

Then came a baby's cry and assorted technical talk, all

of it, Donovan noted with glee, spoken in matter-of-fact tones. Another couple of minutes and Campagna's head came around the curtain. He said, "There's a large fibroid—a benign tumor. That's why the baby didn't drop. I'm going to take it out."

"What difference does this tumor make?" Donovan asked.

"About nine thousand dollars to your insurance company."

"Take it out."

Another ten minutes later, Campagna's hand snaked around the curtain. It held a tangerine-size blob of red. "Would you look at the size of that thing...Doctor," he said.

"Thank you for sharing," Donovan replied, a bit pale.

"Your wife and child are perfect. Here, let me show you." And with that a nurse brought the baby around, a perfect little blend of both Donovan and Marcy, with his chin and forehead but her amazing eyes and dark complexion, swaddled in white cloth.

"'And unto this day a child is born,'" Donovan said. "To a wonderful mother and a not-so-bad father who just stepped on a nail."

Marcy didn't hear him. She was crying nonstop, holding her baby, laughing and crying, the tears soaking her face and neck and baby and the pillow below.

Later, as they were wheeling mother and child off to separate destinations—her to the recovery room, him to the nursery to be checked out more fully—Donovan took Campagna aside. "That fibroid, can it prevent her from having more babies?" he asked.

"No. Absolutely not. Only time can do that now, and more and more, we can negotiate with time."

"Fibroids aren't like pelvic inflammatory disease, are they?" Donovan asked. "*That* can make a woman infertile."

"It certainly can. Untreated PID is a major problem, especially considering the emotional issues attached to sudden infertility. Severe emotional stress is not uncommon. Why do you ask?"

"I have a friend. Well, you know Paul Duke. About ten years ago, he had chlamydia. He gave it to his girlfriend. But she wasn't properly treated and became infertile. She had a nervous breakdown as a result of it, too. Never quite got over the whole thing. I believe she was your patient."

Campagna was silent for a moment. Then he said, "I forgot you're Paul's friend. So they told you about it. Well, I guess that makes it OK for me to talk about it. June took that especially hard. In fact..." Here Campagna lowered his voice. "She had a complete mental collapse and was hospitalized for several months."

"The network portrayed it as being a leave of absence," Donovan remarked.

Campagna sighed. "She always wanted children. What a shame. But, as you can see, she rebounded. She became stronger than ever. Now she can have everything she wants."

Including revenge, Donovan thought. *"Whom the gods would destroy they would first make crazy."*

"Except children," he said.

"Except children," Campagna agreed.

TWENTY-ONE

"YOU DID RIGHT BY MY LITTLE GIRL"

MOTHER AND CHILD rested peacefully in the nursery, she on her gurney and he nestled under her arm. She slept lightly, and so did the baby, while nurses watched and total strangers admired the scene from behind plate-glass windows. Across the nursery from her, a woman of some importance from Kenya bottle-fed one of the quadruplets Campagna had delivered the day before. Her husband, a stout man with very expensive clothes and vaguely regal bearing, exchanged rapid-fire conversation, all totally unintelligible to Donovan, with several younger men, apparently aides.

Other visitors came and went, among them Kirsten Fritsch and Anna Hebel. They had dressed for the occasion, sort of, looking motherly and daughterly all in all, all other guises having been discarded. And following them around, carrying a basket of presents for the newborn, was George Bliley, his employment uninterrupted.

Donovan left the nursery and limped out into the hall, the door sliding shut behind him. A new bandage was on his wound and he had had a tetanus shot, but the foot had swollen enough so that the sneaker was a tight fit and limping remained a necessity.

Moskowitz joined him then, saying, "Mdivani and Koslov are still on the first floor with the lawyers, waiting in the chapel."

"Did you tell them to watch out for nails?"

"Yeah, and you should have heard the reaction I got from that mob of lawyers. Three of them gave me their business cards, and one told me, 'Fifth Avenue Medical Center has an endowment of one hundred million and that's exactly how much we should ask for.'"

"I'll take it under advisement," Donovan replied.

Mosko said, "The assistant DA is in the lobby, along with a handful of his investigators."

"Any assassins among them?" Donovan asked.

"Not one that I can see."

"So the deed is ready to be done. Do I have to be there?"

"It would be nice if you made the introductions," Mosko said.

"OK, here's the deal. You take Kirsten and Anna into that room I showed you, the residents' conference room. Let Bliley wait in Marcy's room with the goodies. When Duke and Lake appear, keep them here by the nursery until I return."

"How am I supposed to do that?" Mosko asked.

"I don't know…. Tell baby stories. Yes, tell lots of baby stories. How wonderful it is to be a parent. What a great mom Marcy will be."

"Rub it in good, huh?"

"You got it. Make her snap."

"She did that when she shot Erik Melmer," Moskowitz replied.

Donovan went downstairs, limping, with the assistance of a functional wooden cane that an orderly had brought up from the basement. He found Koslov and Mdivani sitting in a pew behind a phalanx of lawyers, all of whom were twisted around, the better to see their rich and dangerous client.

Upon seeing the captain enter, Koslov reached into a pocket and withdrew a small gift-wrapped box that he handed over. "This is for your son, with my best wishes for a long and prosperous life," Koslov said.

"Thank you."

"I understand that in a few minutes I will be in the custody of your criminal justice system. My lawyers assure me that it is a good system and that I have an excellent chance of...of beating the rap.''

"I know your lawyers," Donovan said. "They don't lie." Then he thought for a moment, and added, "At least not about your chances of beating the rap. Well, good luck to you. I checked all the things you told me through my friend Georgi here''—Donovan patted Mdivani on the shoulder—"and it seems that you are entirely blameless in the murder investigation that is taking my time lately."

"It is foolish to kill a man over a woman," Koslov said. "There are so many other good reasons."

The chapel door opened and the representative of the DA's office walked in, followed by three of his detectives. Before too long, Koslov was on his way downtown to an arraignment at which it was fully expected he would make bail. Donovan thanked Mdivani and saw him to the door, then hobbled back into the medical staff elevator.

"Task two of the day accomplished," he said to Mosko when again they met.

"Task one being having a baby?"

"That's right," Donovan said, as the two men approached the anchorpersons, who waited by the nursery window. The onlookers formed a respectful halo around the stars, getting neither too close nor too far away. "Hello, Paul. Hello, June."

"That is one beautiful baby, Bill," Duke said. "Congratulations, Dad."

"Thank you," Donovan replied, shaking the man's hand.

"Your wife is more beautiful than before," Lake said, a bit formally, as if she were making a statement to the press.

"Daniel looks just like you," Duke added. "His eyes are your eyes."

"Including the bloodshot part, right?" Donovan replied. "No, he has Mom's eyes and complexion, my chin and forehead."

"And lips," Duke said. He seemed much more into the baby thing than his lady companion, who hadn't mentioned the child but was smiling more and more, the Barbie smile that had made her America's sweetheart. The smile, in fact, seemed painted on, a special effect or the product of really good makeup.

"We're delighted to see you and your lovely wife again," Lake began, "but we wonder about the reason for the invitation."

"I need to straighten some things out regarding the attempt on Paul's life," Donovan replied. "And you can help me."

"You can rely on us," she said crisply.

"To begin with, how did you get here today?" Donovan asked.

"Why, we walked...from my apartment on Central Park South," Lake said.

"Which way did you go?"

"Across Central Park South, past F.A.O. Schwarz, and here," she said.

"Weren't you afraid of being mobbed by fans?"

"You haven't been outdoors much lately, my friend," Duke said. "It's Christmas Day. All the shops are closed. There's no one on the streets."

"And no one followed you?"

"There was one man walking about a block behind us," Duke replied.

Lake gave him a look, and he quickly said, "I didn't want to worry you. Besides, the man looked familiar, so I assumed he was one of the captain's men."

"Did we have anyone tailing these two?" Donovan asked.

"Not on foot," Mosko replied.

"What did the guy look like?"

"Middle-aged, with a beard. But I couldn't really see him."

"When did you first notice him?"

Duke thought for a moment, then said, "After we passed Schwarz, I guess."

"Send somebody out on the street to look around," Donovan told Moskowitz. "You know who we're looking for."

"I do indeed," Mosko replied. He then gave an order to one of the field detectives.

"Paul has found it very liberating to be away from the pressure that this awful situation has put him under," Lake said, taking his arm.

"Have you?" Donovan asked.

Duke bobbed his head up and down. "When the news of my resignation hit the papers, we were mobbed with reporters. They were outside the studio and both our apartment buildings. But after two days they gave up and went home to spend Christmas with their families. It was fun to walk the street for a change. June has convinced me that whoever the madman was that wanted to kill me—probably one of the Mountain Brigade loonies—he has gone away and will never be back." Then Duke laughed, a bit nervously, perhaps, and added, "As long as I stay with her, that is. She says she's my guardian angel."

Donovan said, "Hmf," but doubted anyone heard. So he added, "Yes," and then asked, "Have you see George Halloran?"

"Is he coming here, too?" Duke asked.

"Yep. I'd like to talk to everybody, and the number of those unaccounted-for appears to be dwindling. Are we done here?"

"Done gawking at your beautiful family?" Duke said, looking again at Marcy and the baby. She opened her eyes a crack and, still groggy from the anesthetic, smiled a faint but loving smile at her husband. Then she went back to sleep.

"'Cause if we are, there's someone I'd like you to meet, Paul."

"Who?" Lake asked.

"Two people, actually. Well, three. Walk this way."

With that he led them away from the nursery and around a corner and down the corridor to the residents' conference room. Three detectives stood guard outside the door. One of them, chosen because he looked especially technical and nerdy, held an official-looking black box that was covered with buttons, knobs, and displays.

"Open, please," Donovan said, and with Mosko's help ushered Duke and Lake into the same room with Kirsten Fritsch and Anna Hebbel. The other detectives followed, two of them keeping their hands on their weapons and not being very discreet about it.

The two women sat on the far side of a round conference table, sipping tea and nibbling at a plate of gingerbread cookies baked by the nurses' aides. They seemed in good moods, despite the bulletproof vests hidden beneath their jackets. They chorused, more or less in unison, "Hello, Paul."

Duke's eyes widened to saucerlike proportions. He said, "Anna! My God, it's you! You're all right. I'm…I'm so sorry what happened to your fiancé. Are you? I mean is that…?"

"Our baby?" Anna replied, patting her tummy. "Yes, this is our baby girl."

Donovan watched closely as Duke and Lake changed. As he grew warmer, paternal, more open and misty-eyed, she hardened. The smile disappeared. Her normally full mouth became a thin slit drawn out across her face. And the skin at her temples tightened until Donovan could see the veins throbbing.

"Go to her," Donovan said, urging Duke to walk around the table. He did, and Anna rose, and the couple embraced, tears in their eyes, genuine tears, not Hollywood tears and not TV-studio tears.

At the same time, Lake's spine stiffened and she clutched

at her purse with one hand and at the back of a chair with another. At last, she stared at Fritsch through the cold eyes of madness. "What is *she* doing here?" Lake asked.

Paul broke away from Anna then and looked down at Kirsten, who smiled the same ironic smile she had shown to Donovan and gave a half-wave.

"Claudia?" he asked. "Yes, what are you doing here?"

"She's another one who recently changed careers," Donovan said.

"My real name is Kirsten Fritsch," she said. "And I'm Anna's mother."

Paul looked at Anna, who smiled sheepishly and bobbed her head up and down, then over at Donovan, who shrugged. "I'm sure it happens more often than we think," he said.

Kirsten added, "Now you know why I threw you out that night."

Anna said, "I don't care, Paul, and neither does my mom. I just wanted to see you again, and to—"

It was at that point that Lake screamed, "No! Tell me you didn't sleep with *both of them!*"

Startled, Duke said, "It wasn't intentional."

"You bastard!" she shouted, backing away from the scene, against the wall next to the still-open door.

Then Donovan made a gesture, and the nerdy man with the fancy instrument poked a long and slender probe close to Lake's hand. The black box emitted a riot of peppery noises, causing her to look down at it and then jerk her hands away.

"What are you doing?" she shrieked.

"I'm getting a positive reading, Captain," the man said in a flat voice. "I'm reading depleted uranium here"—he poked the prod at her right hand, and again the noises filled the room—"and here...." He did the same thing with her left, getting the same result.

Donovan commented, "The Kammacher Stedman that you used to kill Erik Melmer, Terry Seybold, and Tony

DeStanzio fires depleted-uranium bullets that leave detectable traces wherever they touch. They last for weeks. We also found such traces in your dressing room."

"What?!"

"The television studio is a quick walk from all three murder sites. The hall past the dressing rooms is open only to the stars. The corridor that leads to the street is often deserted. You have no alibi for any of the murders. You have traces of radiation on your hands. And you have all the motive in the Western Hemisphere for wanting Paul Duke broke and ruined if not, in fact, dead."

"What's that?" asked an astonished Duke.

"Giving her the infection that made her infertile ten years ago, when what she wanted more than anything was to have a baby," Donovan said. "A baby like the one Anna is carrying for you."

"How'd you find out all that?" Duke asked.

"I got her Social Security number off that pay stub you and I talked about. After that, her medical records opened up like a ripe plum."

"That's...not...legal," Lake stammered, her face a mask of fury and her hand fumbling with the catch that opened her purse.

"Hire a lawyer and sue me," Donovan said. "There's a whole flock of 'em in the lobby."

With that Lake tore open her purse and pulled from it a small revolver. As Donovan and two other detectives went for their firearms, Lake fired two shots, missing Duke, who covered Anna with his body, protecting her. Furious and panicky, Lake fled into the hall.

It was still packed with people, most of them police. But she got a few paces down the hall, waving the gun around, her eyes ablaze with fury, Duke and Donovan chasing her, the captain limping with the help of the cane.

She fired two more shots that sent onlookers diving to the floor and behind the assortment of carts and gurneys left at various spots in the hall. Donovan pulled up ten feet from her; Duke was at his side but slightly behind.

"June, wait," Duke said, holding a hand up, as if the gesture would stop her.

"I went through hell for you," she replied, raising the gun and aiming it at him.

"Put that down," Donovan snapped. "I already have problems with my boss. Don't make me shoot America's sweetheart."

What escaped from Lake's mouth could only be described as a wail of anger and frustration, and she closed her eyes and was about to pull the trigger when she felt the cold steel of an automatic weapon at the back of her neck.

"Drop your gun," said a voice, a man's voice; to Donovan, an oddly familiar voice.

The wail turned to mere frustration; after a momentary hesitation, June Lake dropped her gun and immediately was swarmed over by police officers and dragged off. Duke came out from behind Donovan and stared across the circle at the man who had been following him on the way to the hospital that morning, Yama Mojadidi.

"Didi?" he asked, stepping forward, as did Donovan. "Didi, is that you?"

"You know this clown?" Donovan asked, without lowering his own weapon.

"Of course I do. He was my good friend when I was covering the war in Afghanistan. Didi was the leader of a mujahideen group that fought the Russians in the hills near the Great Buddhas of Bamiyan."

Mojadidi lowered his gun, the same automatic that Donovan had seen in his waistband outside F.A.O. Schwarz, and gave it to a detective. Then the Afghan went to Duke and the two friends embraced, crying and hugging. Donovan put away his Smith & Wesson and awaited the explanation.

"I'm sorry I shot at you, Captain," Mojadidi said at last.

"I was going to bring that up."

"But I thought you were an Immigration man who wanted to send me back to Afghanistan."

"That may happen anyway," Donovan replied. "I just became a father, and don't take my own mortality as lightly as I once did."

"Doesn't matter; I am going. I only came here to see Paul...and to thank him."

"For what?"

"My daughter, Melly...."

Donovan rolled his eyes.

"No, it is not what you think," Mojadidi said quickly. "She was only seventeen when I brought Paul home to have dinner with my family. She was a bright girl, very bright, and wanted to go to university. But there was no chance of that, for I am a man of extremely modest means. Paul gave her the money for college...all four years...no strings attached. He is like that, you know, very selfless."

"I told you I spend lots of money on women, but I forgot that one detail," Duke added.

"And you didn't sleep with this one?" Donovan asked.

"On my honor," Duke said. And when that argument cut no ice with the captain, Duke added, "Not even I am crazy enough to sleep with the daughter of a mujahideen guerrilla leader. Didi, how is Melly?"

"Melly is dead," Mojadidi replied flatly.

Donovan said, "Your daughter is the girl in the photograph of the Great Buddhas."

"Yes. She was very beautiful, was she not?"

"Very beautiful," Donovan said.

"What happened?" Duke asked, grasping his friend's hands and holding them.

"She was killed by a stray rocket during a Taliban attack. It happened just last year, after she got her degree and came home. Before she died, she asked me to find you and give you this."

From his pocket he took a gold chain, from the end of

which dangled a gold dog tag with Duke's name on it. He dropped the chain into Duke's palm.

Duke said, "The army gave me this after I raised my fist at that Russian chopper. I gave it to Melly as a memento."

The men embraced again.

"You helped her," Mojadidi said. "You did right by my little girl."

"Are you ready to do right by another little girl?" Donovan asked.

Duke nodded several times, tears running down his cheeks. And a while later Donovan reunited him with Anna and their unborn child.

DONOVAN HELD DANIEL under his arm and played with his tiny hand, which fit neatly between the captain's thumb and forefinger. The infant made mewing sounds and looked up at his daddy, who wondered what he saw. Would this child, coming into the world in his papa's fifty-second year, mirror only the mature, thoughtful Donovan? Or would he carry some genetic resemblance to the old boozer and brawler who had wasted so many hours, months, and years hobnobbing with Broadway lowlifes? "I can't figure out if this kid will grow up to be a college professor or a punk rocker," Donovan said.

"Whatever he does, we'll always love him," Marcy replied, extending her hands to take the child.

Donovan handed her the baby, holding him as carefully as if he were a Ming vase, moving with the child and taking every precaution to avoid dropping the priceless little boy. She brought him to her breast and leaned back, letting out a satisfied sigh.

The family, hers, his, and theirs, had gone. Guys from the office and their wives had come and gone. George Kohler and the rest of the staff of Marcy's Home Cooking over on Broadway had come and gone. So, too, had several of the boys from Donovan's old life, scrubbed for the occasion and squeezed into clean clothes. Every one of the red-and-green Christmas cupcakes baked by Mosko's wife had been eaten, the paper cups littering the floor around a trash basket already stuffed with gift wrappings.

Donovan switched on the television. After surfing around the channels, he stumbled over the ten o'clock *Wolf News* and was startled, but not entirely displeased, to see George Halloran sitting in the anchor's chair. The lead item on the news that Christmas Day was, of course, the arrest of "America's sweetheart," June Lake, for the murder of three people on Fifth Avenue. But typically, Halloran had a personal touch. Tom Tuttle, bad-boy scion of the E & J Tuttle store chain, had been found, on Christmas Day, sitting beneath the tree in which he had played so happily as a child so very long ago. A Rockefeller Center guard found him, whimpering and reciting Keats's "On Melancholy." He was taken to Bellevue for psychiatric evaluation, after which his family was expected to take him in and nurse him back to health.

"Everyone is accounted for," Donovan said, switching to the Weather Channel.

"How is Paul?" Marcy asked. "*Where* is Paul?"

"OK at last, I think. And probably overnighting at Trump Plaza, busily tackling the first night of the rest of his life."

"How are the three of them going to work out the sleeping arrangements?" Marcy asked.

"Kirsten and him are sixties people. They'll think of something."

"So she's out of a job. He's out of a job. And all are filthy rich. There is a story here someplace."

"You bet, and that's the book that Paul intends to write instead of *Tales of a TV Tough Guy*," Donovan said. "The last I heard, he was asking around trying to find the name of Danielle Steel's agent."

"And the Afghan who shot at you? Mojadidi? What will

happen to him? Are you going to charge him with attempted murder for shooting at you?''

"What for? The best I could do is get him deported, and he wants to go home anyway. The man has to fight the Taliban, after all. And I'll support anyone who fights religious fundamentalists.''

To accent his point, he tapped his cane on his bandaged foot.

"I guess that's it for you and organized religion, isn't it?'' Marcy said.

"Actually, you're wrong,'' he told a surprised wife. "I believe in Him now. That He *may* be out there someplace, in the clouds. What happened to me today was His warning. A shot across the bow.''

The baby pulled his head off Marcy's nipple for a moment, long enough to make a mewing sort of sound, then resumed what he was doing.

"God knows that it's a safe bet that the Geiger counter stuff was all made up—''

"Entirely fictitious. But she bought it.''

"And that you figured out how she disguised her voice and phoned in those extortion demands to throw you off.''

"Any good computer can be equipped to alter voices,'' Donovan replied.

Marcy thought for a while, until the baby was finished eating and had fallen fast asleep. "I'm exhausted,'' she said. "I'm as tired as he is.''

"You both have been through a lot.''

"And your day was a cakewalk?''

"I do what I can,'' Donovan replied, a remark that was essentially meaningless but was the best platitude he could emit at that time of night.

"I don't want to let go of him, but you'd better take him back to the nursery,'' Marcy said.

She kissed the baby on both cheeks, both hands, and the

top of his head, which was covered with a layer of fine dark brown hair, before handing him to her husband.

"Daniel Magid Donovan, whose name means 'story-teller,' let's go to bed," Donovan said, struggling to his feet while holding the baby safe in both arms.

"Good night, Daniel," Marcy said.

Unable to use the cane without trusting his son to the safety of just one arm, Donovan hobbled down the hall, wincing at every step, pausing halfway to the nursery to kiss the boy and whisper, "I love you," in his ear. And then he held his son to his heart and limped on.

Michael Jahn's new Bill Donovan mystery is
MURDER IN CENTRAL PARK

LIBATION BY DEATH
DORIAN YEAGER

This book is for Robert Guss, Ruth Prindle,
and Bernard Wittie

ACKNOWLEDGMENTS

McAleer's Pub for allowing my imagination
to run wilder than usual

PROLOGUE

WORK SUCKS.

Aside from money, there is absolutely nothing in the world to recommend employment of any kind. Let's face it, "work" is downright time-consuming. Gainful employment inevitably diverts attention from "fun," and—worst of all—it will bind you intimately with one or more noxious persons with whom you would not voluntarily share a seat on a public bus. There. I've said it, and I'm *glad*.

This is not bitterness. It is the logical conclusion of a steep learning curve. A towering Mount Fuji of experience.

Until a month ago, I had a perfectly normal love/hate relationship with employment and the seeking thereof. Actors are always desperately searching for the four-letter "W" word. Of course, we are looking for acting work, as opposed to the real kind, which, as far as I'm concerned, shows an admirable self-nurturing quality among my fellow thespians. That is the "love" part of the relationship. It is also the delusional part, since *most* people are looking for a job that is short-term, narcissistic, and mainly involves looking better than the audience. Which brings me to the good advice of friends.

When I was offered a bartending job to fend the wolf from the tenement door until I got a real (acting) job, I thought what the hell. Work is work, right? Silly me, or as Shannon, McAleer's manager, commented, "You'll wish you were dead." Silly her. I took the job because I was already wishing I were dead. Unemployment will do that to you.

I had only been out of work for one day, but I know where that trip leads. Two weeks before, my last show-business gig sounded perfect. All right, it sounded perfect for an immature thirty-ninish woman with no actual skills aside from the ability to weep on cue and sing on key. Granted, the pay was lousy, the out-of-town housing was lousy, and the technical director had had a very bad time for himself in Vietnam and was taking it out on anyone who couldn't out-booby-trap him. Really, aside from the fact that someone was trying to bump off the entire cast, I have had much, much worse theater experiences. Trust me.

I should have finished the summer in East Port Nowhere, Maine, taken the new musical on to Broadway, become a filthy rich celebrity, and married my handsome, famous co-star with whom I was accidentally having an affair. That was certainly a plan. It was a *wonderful* delusion. But the theater closed, the musical never happened, and my romantic afterglow lasted until my summer lover's plane took off from Portland International Jetport. (Thank you, Canada, for being near enough to make such grandiose titles possible.)

I'm malleable. Everyone says so. I was miserable, but I knew that one gets over love. Live and learn, yeah, yeah. There is an old theater expression—"Get over it." I just didn't know that slinging highballs—unlike passion—is, apparently, forever.

But, hey, I was a little drained. So was my bank account. I thought it would be good for me to be around normal people (mistake #4,971 in the Vic Bowering logbook). I am woman enough to admit I was liking the idea of regular hours and income. All that "Life upon the Wicked Stage" crap is nice to dream about, but real life is more than a sixteen-week run, and health insurance ain't bad, either. I'd had more applause than most people get in a whole lifetime; I'd had my fling with a television star; if I'd been home a few years earlier tending my marriage instead of on the road, maybe I wouldn't have an almost-ex-husband now. What more could I learn from show business now that I have mastered the art of applying false eyelashes in a moving car? Despite what the men in my life say, I do know when to come in out of the rain.

I *can* walk and chew gum at the same time.

There is no doubt in my mind that this thirty-ninish dog can learn new tricks.

After all, bartending is not brain surgery; world peace is not dependent on my ability to make a perfect frozen daiquiri; and every shift comes with a free meal.

It wasn't as if I were having a career or a life or anything. What could possibly go wrong a block from home?

ONE

HELLO August in Metropolis. The television I had left on the night before updated my subconscious on New York City's terrorism season as I slept.

There was a rogue Palestinian shooting up the observation deck of the Empire State Building, Sikh separatist cab drivers' unionization plans, rioting over Zionist tunnel-building projects, militia groups uncovered in Brooklyn, Irish nationalists marching on the United Nations. It was enough to give a person a sleep disorder.

Or very bad dreams.

Copious pigeon droppings had clogged the exterior vent of the bedroom air conditioner while I was away, making it wheeze like a chain smoker lugging a stubborn Rottweiler uphill.

It was a beautiful dawn by Manhattan standards, the time-release heat oozing from the greasy hot-topped alleys and streets and rising through the misshapen window frame of my bedroom to free-fall like a cow flop directly back onto my platform bed. The travel alarm bleeped annoyingly over the cooing of the flying rats pooping prodigiously from the window above mine. Slasher, my cat companion of nineteen years, snored from beneath the sodden sheets—Krazy-Glueing cat hair from my sweaty knees to ankles.

The alarm drilled. Slasher jumped into startled consciousness, used his lethal back claws to drive off into the top sheets and scramble his escape up my stomach, and bounded from the pillow to the nightstand to the top of the pathetic excuse for an air conditioner. His coordination not being what it once was, he fell off twice before getting a ringside seat for cat cable TV—all pigeons, all the time.

The shell-pink bedroom smelled of bird doo. My nose itched from the Slasher fur sucked up my sinuses with every breath off the pillowcase. The cat made a valiant attempt to beam himself directly through the window glass for a surprise Tweety attack, lost his footing, and sprayed paperback books, which had been precariously balanced on the high windowsill, across my sweaty, furry face. I believe I sighed, heavily. Or something.

Reconciled to the richness of big-city life, I hit the alarm and tried to remember why I would want to be waking up to experience such a plethora of sensory delights. Intuitive Slasher picked up on the first signs of intelligent life and hurled himself off the air conditioner and back to within an inch of my cheek on the bed, yowling as though he hadn't eaten since the Pleistocene era. I kept having the eerie feeling I was supposed to be out of town. Of course, under the circumstances, who wouldn't?

The coffee machine in the kitchen seemed as far away as Kuwait. Slasher's feet ground small, irritating boreholes up and down my chest until I rolled over. Always open to change, he then paced furiously back and forth from my butt to scrunched shoulders, pausing only to nudge his cold, wet, pink nose into the nape of my neck.

I surrendered.

"Arghhhhhhh."

"Mewrlllllllllllllllll."

"Listen, cat, if I didn't have to keep a roof over your head, I wouldn't even be up."

"Mewrllll."

Slasher did not take any prisoners. I knew he would not leave me alone until I fed him. Pretty much just like a man. I swung my feet over the side of the bed and landed in the middle of my unpacked luggage. The pressure from my foot exploded a previously innocuous tube of toothpaste through my toes and up the side of the bed. My father's credo shot through my head like a migraine.

"Nothing good can come of a day that starts with getting up in the morning."

The cerebral synapses were firing, but I still couldn't remember why I was up. Slasher bleated as though he were about to have a coronary.

"All right, all right," I griped, walking toward the kitchen, right foot, left heel, right foot. I balanced groggily to open a can of cat food and load up my caffeine machine. The coffeemaker blurped and spit as I paper-toweled the green paste off my foot. A car alarm screamed from Eightieth Street. I reached for the aspirin and promised myself I would stop drinking alcohol forever. The alarm clock went off again in the bedroom. Overall, it was turning out to be a really crappy welcome home.

As Slasher smacked away at his dish, I quieted the snooze feature on the clock and grabbed my cigarettes off the bedroom floor, promising myself I would quit smoking tomorrow after I got used to not drinking. The match spit a burning hunk of sulfur onto a balled-up sock near the closet, but I crushed it with the matchbook cover without completely obliterating the note I'd made to myself on the interior of the green cardboard: 6:30—see Dave.

No date. No a.m. or p.m. Slasher ambled back to the bed for his post-breakfast nap. The cigarette tasted as though I was smoking dust bunnies, and then it hit me.

I don't know about you, but I loathe moments of perfect clarity. That was the other bad taste in my mouth.

Six-thirty was (gad!) a.m. Dave was the "day man" at McAleer's Pub. I had an appointment with him because (I begged my memory to betray me), in a fit of financial desperation, the night before I had told Kerry McAleer I would be his new swing bartender. And it was already—I checked to make sure—6:20 a.m. I knew—in that woman way—that I looked like the underside of a felled tree. Against my better judgment, I took a look in the mirror. Right again.

The good news was that the bar was only a block away.

Of course easy access was also the bad news, or I wouldn't have been throwing on whatever was at the top of my unpacked bag to go to (pardon my use of the word) work.

As my dear old grandmother used to say, "A little hard work never killed anyone."

How little grandmothers know these days.

No surprise to those of you who know me so well, I arrived at McAleer's wearing black spandex and an oversize black T-shirt. I didn't fuss over my makeup, figuring I'd just lower the lights the minute I got behind the bar, making myself and everyone else just a little bit better-looking. My mistake.

Early-morning sunlight streamed through the picture window facing onto lovely Amsterdam Avenue, illuminating a space I had only seen in comfortable overcrowding and darkness. The jukebox was taking a well-deserved rest, and the large, tin-ceilinged room hummed with low-decibel street noises: bald cab tires, metropolitan sparrows, schoolchildren dissing one another. Two elderly men sat at the near corner of the oak bar ignoring each other. The man who was awake read *The New York Times* and sipped on a glass mug half-full of creamy coffee. Neither paid me a bit of attention. The bartender, Dave, was nowhere to be seen.

"Excuse me," I muttered, sotto voce. "Excuse me," I repeated, louder. No dummy I, I walked over to the reading gentleman and laid my hand on his shoulder. "Excuse me." He finished the paragraph he was reading and carefully folded the paper before taking another sip of coffee and answering me.

"Yes, me dear, what can I do for you?" His sweet face crinkled in that peculiarly Irish fashion, pale blue eyes interested but not overly so.

"Are you Dave?" He certainly looked like what one would expect of a day bartender at McAleer's Pub.

He jabbed the sleeping man with his elbow. "You hear that, Bob? Am I Dave? Well, me darlin', I sure was—about fifty years ago.'' He gave me a most charming tilted grin and an experienced once-over. "I must say, the boyo's taste has improved. Can I get you a cup of coffee?''

There I was, hungover at six-thirty in the morning having a stream of consciousness conversation with a leprechaun. I rallied. After all, I was about to become the master of that particular ship, and it wouldn't be good to look too girly-girl and wimpy.

"I'm supposed to speak with Dave. I'm the new swing bartender here, and he's supposed to show me the setup.'' There. That was strong, controlled, and non-gender specific.

The old man laughed until he had to calm down the resultant coughing fit with another shot of coffee. The sleeping man roused and reached for a bottle of beer sitting in a puddle of condensation on the bar. He took a swig and settled comfortably back on his stool for a pleasant "Harrumphh.'' His eyes closed, and I heard a snuffle enter to what would become a low, buzzing snore.

"You're a funny one, you are,'' the coffee-drinking man said. "Let me buy you a drink.''

"No, thank you.'' I looked back toward the kitchen for signs of the missing bartender. It was not with any pleasure that I realized I might have to make an assault on the men's room at the far back to find Dave. Frankly, the ladies' room experience had always been enough for my delicate constitution. More low laughter from the old man. Why are all disagreeable situations more complicated than you think they'll be? I shifted from leg to leg.

"Never seen a woman behind the stick at McAleer's, darlin'. This is an Irish bar.''

"Stick?''

"The pull thing for draught beer, darlin'.''

"Yes, well,'' I responded cleverly. "Dave?'' I called hopelessly, feeling my hands start to flutter a little stupidly. What a really dumb situation. I could have stayed in bed and gotten better rejection. A light shone from behind the swinging doors to the kitchen at the rear of the bar, so I smiled benignly and marched myself back. The right door swung open easily, and I stuck my head in for a quick look. Nothing. "Dave? Dave?" I tilted back out and directed my inquiry to the battered paneled door of the men's room. *"DAVE?"*

By that time I was nearly fully awake (not a good thing for me) and walking a fine line with righteous indignation—which is a luxury no one who works in a bar can afford. Obviously, I had to take action or just go home. Obviously, I had to get hold of someone who could tell me how to do that. Margaret Thatcher was unavailable, so it would have to be Shannon, the bar manager. Unfortunately, she frightened me.

I marched deliberately behind the bar, hoping I wouldn't be mistaken for a common pilferer, and started searching for a staff contact sheet. Shannon would tell me to give up and go back to bed. She had an answer for everything—even things that did not pose a question. She was better than Iron Maggie. She was certainly more officious. Absolutely more warlike. Without much digging around, I found a red fake leather ledger propped between the cash register and a dusty bottle of Black Bush. Like restaurant ledgers everywhere, the staff was listed by first name only in some order unknown to the alphabet. I dialed her number from the phone behind the bar. On the fourth ring she picked up.

"I sincerely hope you have insurance, because I believe you are walking dead," her low voice reasoned in its British Broadcasting Corporation accent. I considered hanging up and forgetting the whole mess, but then figured she'd find some way to hunt me down like the spineless dog I was, anyway.

"Shannon, I'm sorry. Really, really sorry, but I'm here at the bar, and I can't find Dave. I can't find anyone and I'm supposed to start this morning and..."

"Victoria?" Shannon cleared her throat. "Don't blubber. My God, it's only a pub. And," she moaned deep in her throat, "it's only past seven in the morning."

The sleeping man awakened again, pushed his bottle forward, and ordered, "Budweiser!"

There was the sound of muffled movement at the other end of the line, and Shannon asked, "Good Lord, is Sleeping Bobby there already? Never mind. Victoria, just move to the center of the bar and look castrating. I'll be downstairs in five minutes."

"Oh, thank you, Shannon, I really apprecia—"

"Shut up now and find the baseball bat behind the bar. It should be leaning against the ice machine."

"Nobody looks dangerous here, Shanno—"

"Because when I find that sot, Dave, I'm going to give him a whack like he hasn't seen since he met his mum." She hung up.

"Budweiser."

I looked around nonchalantly for the beer cooler and found two: one at either end of the bar. I dug into the icy water nearest me and located a Budweiser for "Sleeping Bobby," but was unable to locate an opener. The day was off to a grand start. As I fumbled around, I ran, literally, into the awake old man pouring himself a fresh mug of coffee.

"It's twist-off, dearie," he coached, and ambled back to his paper. I think I had enough pride left to blush as I twisted. "Kerry, the man, will be in soon, anyway, to do the bankin' and whatever else it is that he thinks demands his undivided attention. That'll be a test for ya'. Of course, I gotta commend you, waking the she-devil herself." He nodded toward the phone. "Aye, you'll be payin' for that, ya' will."

The story of my life. I slumped against the worn wooden rail and tried to remember how to make a martini, just in case anyone asked for one. Briefly, I considered running an experimental batch, swilling it, and disappearing into Dave-land, wherever that was. Not very professional, but, okay, I was reaching for the Bombay gin at the same time I considered.

"DAAAAAVE, you damned fool!" Shannon screamed from the door, pulling off a gorgeous, beaded, ivory-cashmere cardigan. She was wearing pale yellow Lycra bike shorts and matching midi top. The beading on her socks under the Nikes matched the discarded sweater. Backlit from the window, her long red corkscrew curls looked like fire. "Sean?" she asked the reading man, "have you seen Dave this morning?"

"Nope," he answered. "Not hide nor hair. The door was open when I got here. Bobby's got his beer, though. And judgin' by the sweat off the bottle, I'd say he was around about twenty minutes ago."

I'll admit it. That kind of mixology forensics impressed the hell out of me.

"DAAAVE!" Shannon launched herself to the men's room and flung open the door. That impressed me, too. I guess I'm not quite the icon of feminism I've prided myself on being. I heard the stall door slam against the wall. Shannon reappeared, muttering, "Damned sot."

"Does he do this often?" I asked.

"Often enough to get his ass fired," Shannon said. "Well, let's get to it, then, and don't say I didn't warn you."

"You warned me."

"Ah," Sean breathed, "so long as you were warned, then." He carefully folded over the paper and started on another section. Shannon was already behind the bar. "You'll be wishin' you'd listened, I warrant."

"I can do this," I defended myself.

"I've no doubt of that, darlin'. I was just wonderin' why you'd want to make yourself all hard and suspicious with life, that's all. I'd truly hate to see that."

Shannon peered into a khaki metal box and threw it back

onto the counter. The clanging roused Sleeping Bobby for a moment but did not bring him around to full consciousness. The loud ping of the register opening had no effect at all.

"Well, he didn't rabbit with the bank." Shannon quickly inventoried the cash in the drawer. "It's all here, except for Bobby's beer." She lifted a five-dollar bill from beneath Bobby's arm, rang the price of a Budweiser, and slid the change back under his flaccid hand. "Price list is"—she dug around under the ledger—"uh, here. If they're a pain in the ass, you can charge more." She slammed the aluminum cover of the beer cooler back hard enough to shake Bobby's beer bottle, and slammed it closed. "Day bartender stocks the liquor and the beer, loads the ice, has custody of the remote control, sets up the waitress for food at night—gets cutlery from the kitchen—cuts the fruit for garnish, loads up bevnaps, straws, and swizzle sticks, marries the orphans—"

"Excuse me?"

"If there's a drizzle in a bottle, just pour it into a new one. Waste not, want not."

"Right." It seemed to me there was a bit more to this bartending than I had thought. "Anything else?"

"Baby-sit, listen, and give therapy. You like crossword puzzles?"

"Hate them." I followed Shannon meekly to an ominously hidden door behind the dartboard near the forbidden men's room. She opened the door and started down the creaky wooden stairs into the gloom of the basement.

"Then you are going to be bored, quite out of your mind. Make a list of the empty liquor bottles upstairs and pull them from the shelves down here. Make sure you mark what you take on the inventory sheet, or Kerry will accuse you of either stealing or drinking."

"I quit drinking."

"When?" Since Shannon is exactly as overtall as I, her astonishment shone directly into my eyes.

"This morning."

She marched to the heavy oak walk-in door. "I give you four hours." In two swift moves there was a dull click and a blackboard screech. She pulled with a small grunt. "Beer is in here, but you have to ice it again upstairs. Replace the chilled cases with the ones in the corner." The door squealed as it opened. The bare bulb in the center of the refrigerator was already lit, the chain hanging steady.

There was more than enough light to clearly see the body slumped unceremoniously on the floor, propped against a frosty wall of Miller Lite.

"Aw, Dave, you sorry sack of shit." Shannon bent over and smacked the lifeless form up the side of his shaved head. I would have protested, but Shannon has quite an arm on her. "Dave!" She stood upright and gave him an emphatic kick to the thigh. I could not see any breathing happening from the battered Dave.

"Shannon," I said, and wiggled in closer in the small space, "I don't think he's breathing." There. I had done my intervention of the day. Shannon gave him another crosstrainer to the side, using the swing of her upper body for emphasis. The momentum was sufficient to crook the bartender's knee upward and reveal the hypodermic syringe hidden beneath his cold leg.

"Mother Mary," Shannon said, falling to one knee and placing her beautifully manicured fingertips to the prone man's throat. "Call 9-1-1." She shoved me toward the opening. I could see Shannon's breath in the chill, but not Dave's. "Get on with it," she demanded, pushing me outside to the cold and into the gloomy basement.

As I bounded the stairs two at a time, I could hear Shannon swearing at Dave. "Snorting, okay, smoking, okay, but *shooting?* Aw, Dave, you damned fool."

Sean met me at the top of the stairs, getting himself yet

another cup of coffee. "EMS will be here directly," he said, pouring a shot of Baileys Irish Cream into his mug. Before I could thank him for making the call or chastise him for helping himself to the bar, he pulled a five-dollar bill from his pocket, rang the register, and pushed the money into its slot. The one dollar in change he pressed into my limp hand.

"Thank you," I said reflexively. I can't say it was the easiest dollar I've ever earned, but it was close. And I decided in that instant that maybe a dollar was enough for this day.

I dragged myself back to the basement stairs to help Shannon however I could, and then render my heartfelt resignation.

You see, I believe that God gives us little clues when we're supposed to cave in, take our dollar, and find a new degrading job. I don't want to say that Dave's carcass in the walk-in was the voice of God speaking to me, but I know when to take a hint.

McAleer's just wasn't feeling as homey to me as it had the night before. Of course, I was sober now and had all of one dollar in my fanny pack. I hoped I wouldn't have to resort to calling my almost-ex-husband to mooch lunch.

The gods chose to save me from myself.

Three emergency services personnel crashed through the doors, shouting. The two women were carrying equipment, the chunky Hispanic man held out his hand. I decided right then and there that he'd have to wrestle me to the ground for my tip.

"Vicki, right?" I shook his hand without thinking, but I guess I looked dumb as a bucket of hair, because the man continued. "Rico. Aw, c'mon, you remember." I did not. For some reason I never do. "That old guy, your neighbor croaked last fall and you were wearing that really short, pink nightie thing when we came to get him?"

"Jeez, Rico," the taller of the female paramedics groaned and pushed by the man to me, "where is the cardiac?"

"Downstairs." I pointed. The women bustled past and down the stairs. I heard Shannon call to them. Rico, apparently, had all the time in the world.

"So," he said, "maybe we should stop meeting like this, huh?"

"I'll drink to that." It was a little early for a martini, maybe, but one of those coffees with a little Baileys probably wouldn't make me barf.

"So why don't we get together for dinner sometime, huh? Whaddya think?"

"RICO!" someone screamed from belowdecks. It caught his attention briefly. "We got a pulse here, Rico, you rat bastard!" Contact was fully made.

"I'll give you a call, okay?" I nodded, incredulous. "You work here?" I nodded again with more emphasis, darned sure McAleer's would never see me in the daylight again. "Got some matches with the phone number?" I handed him a pack from an ashtray on the bar. What the hell. I was history.

Rico made it to the basement door just as the two women reached the top of the stairs, carrying poor Dave on a stretcher. Just as they rounded the corner into the main room, the black paramedic yelled out: "CODE. Cardiac arrest." The tall woman pounded Dave's chest, making an unnaturally resonant whomping sound. "RICO!"

To give him credit, Rico raced ahead to open the exit door and unlock the ambulance. Through the window I could see the shorter woman rip open Dave's clothing before they loaded him into the back of the vehicle. Morosely drawn, I walked outside, as though there were anything I could do to help. I couldn't.

"Shit," the female paramedic said. Three packs of matches flew out of the back of the ambulance. Dazed, I picked them up and waited for something, anything to do besides policing the sidewalk. "The shit people shove down their pants."

I looked down at the matches with new appreciation, and dropped them into a nearby waste can, even though all three books were full. If I were desperate for Blarney Rose matches, I supposed I could get some that hadn't been sitting next to a junkie's ass.

"See ya'," Rico called out the window as he tore away from the curb, leaving me feeling perfectly useless on the sidewalk.

No reflection on Rico, but I hoped we wouldn't meet again. Twice was quite enough.

"Cardiac?" I asked Sean when I reentered the bar. "How did you know?"

"I didn't, dearie. I figured old Davey had just had himself a wee bit too much pleasure again, but our friends the medics won't always come so fast to a bar unless you tell 'em it's a heart attack." Sean smiled. "You'll learn the ropes soon enough, if you decide to tough it out."

I'm not absolutely sure, but I think I just stood there with my mouth open for a moment or two.

Shannon grabbed me by the arm and swung me onto a barstool before getting behind the bar itself. She flipped two shot glasses onto coasters, and poured shots of Jameson's. Lifting hers, she threw the Irish whiskey down her throat and poured another. She clinked her glass against mine and nodded for me to upend the drink.

"To Dave, the bag of shit."

Pledges are made to be broken, especially when they are made to oneself. I drank to that.

"Are you all right?" I asked. I didn't want to sound melodramatic, but one of her coworkers had just been carried away in critical condition. I assumed that Shannon would have some kind of reaction.

"Of course I'm all right. I'm not the one shooting up in the basement, am I?" She paused for a moment. "I always rather wondered what Dave did downstairs so much of the time."

"Pretty hard to tend bar from down there."

"Pretty easy to smoke, though. I don't know. It was a joke, his disappearing all the time. It doesn't seem all that funny right now."

"He had to go to the basement to smoke?"

"Not cigarettes, Victoria. That was about the only vice Dave *didn't* have."

"Oh. That explains the matches in his shorts, then."

Shannon looked at me the way I obviously deserved.

"I can't think of a thing that would explain matches in a man's skivvies," she said.

Neither could I, but then, I wasn't a junkie, so I filed the information where it belonged—in my short-term memory bank.

"Now," Shannon continued, "bring up the beer."

I stood up, so as to be in a forceful position to render my reluctant resignation and express my sincere thanks for all Shannon's help.

A dozen workmen walked in the door calling for Dave at the top of their lungs.

"Never mind," Shannon said. "This once I'll have Benny, the cook, bring up the stock. You've already got your hands full." The men swarmed around us like wasps at a soda can.

"Where's Davey?" the man with the leather tool belt asked.

"He's off today," Shannon told him with a straight face. "Meet Vic. She'll be filling in for Dave for the duration."

The man offered his hand. "I'm Terrence. Good to meet you." His voice was heavily accented, and melodically deep. "We'll be missing Dave, surely, but it'll be lovely having something prettier to look at at the end of a hard shift, won't it, boys?"

Shannon collected extra ashtrays and placed them around a table for six. She addressed me without bothering to lower her voice.

"These nail whackers are right off the boat, so you just take a buck or two off the pile for your gratuity every round, otherwise you won't see a nickel." The gang laughed and started to shout orders for shots and beers before I was quite ready to absorb them.

"I..." turned to grab a paper and pencil, and stuttered directly into the face of the man I had left behind to go on the road two weeks ago, Dan Duchinski, sergeant, NYPD. He looked at his watch and waved his thick hand in front of his nose.

"Jameson's? At seven-thirty in the morning?"

"Dan?"

"You remembered after all this time." He pulled a stool away from the bar and sat. "I'm touched. When did you get back in town?"

When the going gets tough, it only gets tougher. Having been faced thus far with unemployment, broken dreams, and a myocardial infarction, I could add to it the worst of all: guilt.

"Only last night. I flew back standby."

"Ah." That was it. *Ah.*

Dan knew I had fallen off the old celibacy bandwagon with Nick Jacobs. He didn't tell me he knew, but I knew he knew, and he knew I knew. I didn't call him the night before because I was waiting for my incredible powers of rationalization to kick in before I saw him face-to-face. I knew he'd never ask about Nick, and if I could only have the time to make myself believe my own litany of excuses, I could keep from spilling my guts. Don't ask, don't tell. Bill Clinton would have been so proud.

"Dan," I started, flabbergasted by his appearance in McAleer's at 7:30 a.m., before I was ready to forgive myself. How did he *know?*

"Sit down, Vic. I'll buy you a coffee, and you can tel'

me all about what you did on your summer vacation.'' He lit a cheroot. ''You haven't been out all night, have you?''

''No!'' I sounded injured.

Guilty people always do.

TWO

CHAIRS SLAMMED. The jukebox blasted Celtic step-dance music. Dan's eyes were glacine acceptance. I had a headache, free-floating anxiety, and a tiny case of temporary amnesia. The Irish carpenters were shouting for drinks, and I wouldn't have minded another shot myself. Then it hit me.

I was the bartender, sort of.

I was saved, temporarily.

With relief, I rose from my stool and walked (with perfect, guilty posture) to take my position behind the bar. Sean glanced up briefly and winked at me as he reached under the bar, took possession of the television's remote control, and turned on the morning news. My hands flashed as I drew draughts and filled shot glasses.

"Where exactly *is* our Davey?" one of the customers asked.

"Someplace warm, I'm betting," Terrence postulated with a laugh. "My guess is that it'll be some time before we see his smilin' face again."

I wondered what the etiquette was for announcing the removal—literally—of a member of the staff.

"I don't know," I mumbled, clearing the first round.

"What a pity," the leader-apparent crooned to the hearty agreement of all. "But you're a damned sight easier on the eyes." "Hear-hears" were heard all round. Dan squirmed on his seat. "To a true daughter of Eire!" Terrence toasted. I attempted a saucy skip to my step. "And to poor sad Davey, the runaway scoundrel!" The reference somewhat dampened my enthusiastic performance.

Emotion well spent, the carpenters quieted and got down to trading stories after their night shift. As they regaled one

another, they emptied their pockets of work residue and settled in.

Dan chewed on his cigar and waited for the punch line
to my uncanny impersonation of a bartender. Sean doubled
over the top of the bar once more and hit a red button above
the far beer cooler. The raucous jukebox went dead. The
carpenters yelled at the sudden lull. Sean adjusted the television volume to deafening.

"Aw, shut up ya," the old man bellowed. Sleeping
Bobby let out a snort. "Yer fellas probably just got themselves blown to perdition, ya fools, ya." The sixty-inch television screen was afire. Screams and sobbing bounced from
the speakers off the brick walls, and the group of men fell
silent as the lettered location strip at the bottom of the screen
read *Bronx*.

"What are you doing back there, Vic?" Dan asked me.

"What does it look like I'm doing?" Another trick of the
guilty: always answer a question with a question. I hadn't
been dating a cop for a year without learning anything.

"Don't answer a question with a question, Vic. It makes
you look guilty. Now get out from behind there before the
bartender shows up and throws that cute butt of yours out
of here entirely." Sean shushed Dan. Dan lowered his voice.
"Though I think you've had enough already."

"I am NOT drunk! And what are *you* doing here?"

"Hush, you two," Sean ordered, and turned the volume
up another notch. A finely hewn blond woman who was
born about the time I graduated from high school spoke into
a microphone.

"—and flattened this section near Riverdale. The fire department is cooperating with the FBI in the investigation.
The cause of this explosion is unknown, but the presence
of the FBI indicates…"

One of the men in the group at the back of the bar let
out a groan and ran outside, flagging a car-service limo double-parked in front of the Korean greengrocery next door.

The smallest man in the gang threw a twenty-dollar bill on the bar and raced out to join his friend. The others made hasty change from the twenty, leaving ninety cents.

I left the bar and went to their table.

"Is something wrong?" I asked, though it was obvious that something was.

"That," the ruddy man answered, "is our neighborhood. We'll have to be leavin' now." He reached in his pocket and crushed a folded wad of paper into my hand. "Pray for your folks, darlin'."

Another worker hastily located a quarter in the coins on the table and took it to the pay phone by the kitchen. The rest of my short-lived clientele finished their drinks and hustled to the exit just as a very handsome, gray-haired man entered.

His eyes sparkled with good nature and curiosity at the mass exodus. If he hadn't been built so much like Duchinski from the neck down, I might have found him attractive. All right, *more* attractive.

"Well, I still know how to clear a room," he said. He slapped Sean on the back and took the stool between the old man and Duchinski. "I'll have a coffee. Black."

"She's not the bartender," Dan said.

"Am too," I came back smartly.

"And she's not even Irish," he added.

"She has to be, or she wouldn't be here," the man disagreed. "You got Sweet'n Low?" he asked me.

"I don't know." But I looked around, just in case.

"George, this is Victoria Bowering. Vic, this is George." Dan blew smoke in my direction. My agitated, empty stomach churned. "Now get your ass out from behind that bar before you get in trouble.

Get into? This isn't trouble, wise-ass? At least I found the Sweet'n Low for my new best friend, George.

"This is Vic?" George reached over the bar and shook my hand. It was immature of me, but I cast a superior look at Dan. *That* would teach him for making me feel guilty for cheating on him. Accidentally. *Days* ago. After I was driven to it because he wouldn't sleep with me just because my divorce hadn't come through. Okay, hadn't actually been filed, but *still.* "Wow." George grinned hugely and elbowed Duchinski.

I hoped it hurt.

"Now get out from back there, Vic," Dan said one more time, and rubbed his arm where George had made contact.

"Her shift isn't over until six, Dan." Kerry McAleer stood in the doorway, glowering. Tall, well built, like a linebacker buffed on steroids. With a personality that makes a girl forget all that good stuff within seconds. A beautiful black man with a beatific smile and a gold earring stood next to him.

"Beau, get her a McAleer's shirt." Kerry's face was red, and it wasn't from the sun. "People need to know where they are. They look at the bartender, they need to see McAleer's right across the boobs."

"In case," George drawled, "they miss the six-foot neon sign in the window." My hero.

"Nice girls don't tend bar," Sean opined.

"Shut up, Dad," Kerry shot back. "Business is off. We're desperate."

Desperate?

"Shut up, Kerry," George threatened.

"You shut up, Georgie," Kerry said. "Where the hell are you going, Beau?"

"To get Vic a shirt from your office." The black man smiled at me.

"How do you know they're in my office?" Kerry barked.

"Never mind." He dug in his pants pocket irritably. "Here, you need a key."

Beau continued, unflustered, toward the back stairs. "Got one," he said over his shoulder, and disappeared.

"How does he have a key?" Kerry blustered, redder still.

Just about the next-to-last thing I needed that morning was to have Kerry throw an embolism. That would mean dinner with Rico, for sure.

"He's the porter, you asshole," George answered.

"*I'm an asshole?*" Kerry shouted. "*You're* the asshole. You've always been an asshole, asshole. And what are you doing in town anyway?"

Sean stood slowly. "Now you boys shut up, or I'll box your ears. And I can still do it."

Ah-ha.

"Okay, Pop," the men answered in unison.

I had entered the central hive.

"So, Vic really is the bartender here," Dan said, not a question.

George nodded. "Yep, I dropped by last night and Kerry told me he'd hired a babe."

"Not for long," Kerry answered, "if she doesn't bus this god-awful mess in the next minute. Looks like a bomb hit, for chrissakes. Have to do everything myself around here, by God."

"It is a sin to take the Lord's name in vain, Kerry," Sean advised. "But perhaps you're just hungry, is that it?"

"George," said Dan, "let's get out of here and let everyone"—he definitely looked at me—"get some work done." I was not being paranoid. Paranoia is when loved ones *aren't* out to get you. He leaned across the bar, ostensibly to snuff his cigar. As he exhaled he mouthed the word, "quit."

"We can take my car," George agreed.

"Out of the neighborhood, George," said Kerry. "Looks bad subsidizing the competition."

George threw a twenty on the bar and held up his hand when I went to make change. Cool. "Kerry, what you'll never understand is that McAleer's *has* no competition. Right, Pop?"

"Right you are, me boyo." Sean accepted a kiss on the cheek from George and said, "Can we talk a moment?"

Duchinski grabbed my hand off the polished surface of the bar while George was occupied, and reiterated, "I'd swear you do these things on purpose, if I didn't know better. You know this isn't a job for you. You'll get a show and end up quitting anyway. Do it today and give the McAleers a chance to replace you with someone suitable. Play fair, Vic. George and I go way back."

I could hardly believe my ears. Who was Dan Duchinski to tell me what to do? And what was that "play fair" remark all about, anyway? I may not be Irish, but I can be suitable. Let George tell Dan about dead Dave. I would be damned if I would.

I pointedly turned my back and did not wave good-bye. The hell with him and the big old gun he walked in with.

"Damned ulcer," Kerry muttered, clutching his midsection. "Yeah, I guess I am a little hungry. Makes me cranky."

Cranky? Understatement was not something I would have previously attributed the younger McAleer son. Since I was afraid I might actually say so, I busied myself clearing the dirty glasses, emptying ashtrays, and wishing I had made the choice of starving to death rather than take this stupid job.

I pocketed the sundry matchbooks discarded by the carpenters that still had lights left in them and sixty-five cents in change before the one on the phone decided he wanted another three minutes with Ma Bell.

The paper folded in my hand was getting mushy. I sneaked a look to see what denomination of bill I'd been passed.

After unfolding the plain manila paper, I found a tiny plastic bag. No wonder my hands were sweating. I had been tipped with a baggie of cocaine.

Terrific. One day on the job and I was already involved

in illicit drug trafficking. I tucked the contraband in my bra and wiped my hands on a paper napkin.

Sean walked past the bar and toward the kitchen. "A couple of eggs and bangers will set you right, son."

"Thanks, Pop."

"My beer's warm," Sleeping Bobby complained. His stool scraped like chalk on a blackboard as he pushed back from the bar. "Gonna water the flowers," he announced unnecessarily, as the men's room door slammed behind him.

Alone at last. Finally, I had the chance to flush the evidence and quit while I was ahead. Unlike Dave, I don't like to experiment with anything that I will probably like, and never be able to afford.

I was twenty-one dollars and sixty-five cents to the good. The last thing I needed was a petty drug conviction to interfere with an honest unemployment claim.

"What's the matter with you?" Kerry asked. "Broads. Can't even keep a cold beer up on the bar. Listen, babe, I gotta do inventory. See if you can get out of your own way, and keep the customers happy, okay?" Beau reentered the bar and threw me a charming size-kazillion McAleer's T-shirt. "Why don't you start with putting on that shirt, and wetting it down?" Kerry laughed all the way to the basement at his own wit.

I don't know if it was the early hour, the hangover, the shot of Irish whiskey, the bombing in the Bronx, the unconscious bartender in the beer cooler, or just plain spite at advice from Dan, but I was not about to give Kerry McAleer the satisfaction of quitting on my first day. Or, as Scarlett O'Hara said: "Tomorrow's another day!" When I quit, I want the boss to be *sorry*.

I could be the soul of efficiency for one lousy shift. At the rate I was raking in the big bucks, I would be quitting with grocery money for two weeks. So, I tried. I even delivered Kerry's breakfast to him in his office, but God was still punishing me, and he brought it back upstairs to eat. Then God gave me a break.

"Blauwwwww."

Kerry threw up all over the bar.

Sure it was my job to clean it up, but it was worth it. I went as far as to lay a cool wet rag on the back of his neck and offer the poor retching brute a roll of antacids I had rattling around the bottom of my purse.

"Better watch that ulcer, Kerry," Sean advised.

Kerry rushed through the door, nearly knocking over Shannon. She had changed into an ode-to-country-western ensemble of fringed, faded denim—short enough for a fast dart to one side and out of Kerry's way.

I dashed from behind the bar to make sure that Kerry had really left. I couldn't see him from the window, so I was about to open the door to peek around the corner, down Amsterdam. At the small, square, door window, I stopped cold.

Staring back in at me was Buck Sawicki, the lunatic tech director from the theater I'd just left in Maine. At six-foot-two, he loomed. Sweat speckled his forehead and caught in the two-day growth of beard. I jerked back and smashed my spine into the doorknob of the interior door. When the tears of pain cleared my eyes, he was gone. I gathered the courage to open the exterior door, but there was no sign of Buck—though I did catch sight of Kerry pulling away from the curb in his new red Porsche.

It was definitely a surreal sort of day. Buck Sawicki could not possibly be in New York City, and I knew it.

First of all, he was on probation in Maine for assault and possession of illegal weapons, and he wasn't allowed to leave the state. Secondly, why would he *want* to leave Maine in August and come to New York City? He was crazy, but not *that* crazy. I shook out my hair and stretched. It must have been someone who just looked like Sawicki.

Shaved head, sinewy muscles, marine tattoo, smoldering

black eyes, and gash of a mouth. Sure. A dime a dozen. After all, this is New York. And I was a little stressed out.

And a lot creeped out.

I squeezed my eyes shut and took a deep breath. I opened them to the good news that Shannon had already cleaned up the remainder of Kerry's breakfast from the bar and had poured herself a cup of coffee.

"Are you all right?" she asked. "You look absolutely shattered."

It was all too stupid for me to get into. "Yeah," I answered, "I'm okay." I chewed on an ice cube to try and lower my temperature. "What are you doing back here? Don't tell me you couldn't get back to sleep."

"Well, I couldn't," she said, taking a sip of coffee.

"Can I get you something to eat?"

"No, thank you. I couldn't swallow."

"For heaven's sake, Shannon, I've never seen any day so bad you couldn't choke down some mashed potato."

"I got another phone call."

"And?"

"It was the hospital." My knees weakened. "Dave's dead."

"Just like that," I muttered.

"Not quite. The attending physician thinks Dave had some help." Shannon pushed her coffee to the rail. "So much for any of us leaving town."

THREE

"CAN'T SAY Dave hasn't been trying hard enough to kill himself anymore," Sean observed.

Shannon nodded in agreement. "I take back everything I ever said about his being a failure."

Sean chuckled softly to himself and reimmersed himself in the morning paper. I waited a long moment for—I don't know—an expression of horror; grief; bewilderment, perhaps. The silence was numbing.

In awe of New York adaptability, I asked, "What makes you so sure it was suicide? According to the attending physician, there's a question about the bruising. For all we know, we're talking about murder."

"Oh, I'm sure it wasn't murder *or* suicide," Shannon answered. "The thing you don't know about Dave is that the damned fool could screw up a nocturnal emission." She looked to me for a laugh. I didn't have one in me.

"Don't you care?" I asked.

Sean looked up briefly from the page he was reading and then dipped back behind it.

"I can't afford to care, Victoria," Shannon said. "Neither can you. If the police investigate this, they'll show up here to get our statements. In the meantime, since I'm up anyway, I'm going to bop around the neighborhood and run some errands."

"Bop," I grunted to myself. Shannon observed me rather like a scientist discovering an errant E coli bacterium on his burger.

"Victoria," Shannon said, "you are a novice around here. And by here, I mean New York City and this bar. I will explain myself once because I think you are genuinely upset by Dave's passing—even though I cannot for the life of me figure out why.'' She pushed her chair into the bar. The scraped and battered legs screeched across the pitted floor.

''Big city bartenders end up one or more of three ways: disgusted, disinterested, or drunk.'' She allowed me a short pause in which to consider. ''The healthy choice is always apathy. There is nothing that happens here that you can fix. You'll only end up killing yourself if you even try. Got it?''

''I think so.'' I didn't think so.

''So can I get you anything from outside?''

I shook my head ''no.''

A frontal lobotomy would do the trick, I thought. Prozac cappuccino, perhaps. Or an apartment in a doorman building might go a long way to dulling reality.

Sean spoke as the door closed behind my mentor. ''She's right, dearie. It's best not to dwell on the past.''

''Even if it turns out to be murder?''

''Especially if it's murder,'' he advised. ''Especially then.''

I grudgingly admitted to myself that they couldn't both be totally wrong. My stomach was in knots and would remain so until I got myself under mental control.

Given the vast amounts of time I have spent in the beautiful State of Denial—come on down, the weather's fine!— I set to the task at hand. First I polished the already clean glasses and memorized the price list, which only made me realize that I was erasing the final fingerprints of the late Dave, which made me feel insensitive. I tried to remember old show tunes, and failed, which reminded me of why I was trying and right back to the body in the walk-in. In desperation, I plunked myself down in a fantasy rehash of my last lover. Guilt usually washes everything peripheral from my mind.

Just in the middle of a Cinemascope shot of gentle fingers sweeping softly from my jawline to clavicles, the daydream did a quick cut to Buck Sawicki's hard hands tearing a defective set platform into kindling. Pan to: Dave's broken body lolling against the frigid cases of beer.

My mental meanderings kept me going in circles. And, as though I didn't have enough to ignore, my traitorous brain kept throwing Sawicki into the mess.

Reasoning with my overactive imagination did no good. Even though I knew Buck could not possibly be in town, I found myself checking over my shoulder at the huge plate-glass window which was aimed like a laser gunsight at my back. The afternoon ticked by.

Sean busied himself with plans for Dave's Irish wake, though to this day, I don't know whether or not Dave was Irish. He didn't *look* Irish when I saw him lying on the damp concrete of the walk-in. He just looked dead. I couldn't help it; I hoped that, had it been me, *someone* would have cared. Or cried. Or *something*.

Shannon flitted around the neighborhood, stopping in periodically to bring me a new newspaper. I hadn't read the trade paper, *Backstage,* for over a month. It was as boring and ominous as the quiet bar, but I highlighted an ad for an audition for an off-Broadway show that night in the Clinton district of the city.

Clinton is the politically correct, late-twentieth-century aphorism for Hell's Kitchen, covering the area of Manhattan from about Thirty-fourth Street to Fifty-sixth and Broadway west.

I mentioned to Shannon that, given the day so far, I thought the hell part was a sign. She gave me a profoundly jaded look.

"Oh, don't go all poofy and Druidic here, Victoria. We're both redheads. We wouldn't follow a sign if it read 'Free jewelry.' Besides, when things are going really badly, the only civilized way to cope is to go straight home, have a nice cup of tea and a shot of Scotch, and don't answer the phone.''

"Thanks, Mum, but I think I'll go downtown." I counted my tips for the day.

It didn't take long. Thirty-two dollars and eleven cents. Shannon read the circled ad over my shoulder.

"Uh-huh. A lovely jaunt through Times Square after dark ought to bring your perspective right back. Gad, but you're either a masochist"—she tossed a twenty-dollar bill onto the paper—"or a French tourist. You can pay me back tomorrow. You don't even have enough for cab fare both directions."

"I'm a subway kind of woman," I said, handing back the money. "Three bucks, round trip, and free sleazy entertainment everywhere you look." Maybe I am part French.

"Don't," she advised.

"Go?"

"Or look."

SLASHER IGNORED my ripping apart of the living room to find a résumé picture that still looked like me. I threw on a short white shift and cinched the whole look with a wide elastic belt. The white heels looked good but felt as though they belonged to a much smaller woman who hadn't been standing on her feet all day. The price of beauty was getting higher as I got older. I felt peculiar in my outfit, my skin, and my own apartment.

Shannon had given me the creeps, so I left the lights on for the cat. Or maybe I did it for me. I don't like to over-analyze.

This is a good character trait for anyone taking the subway in New York during the summer. It would drive a person crazy just trying to figure out "What is that odor?" Not to mention "Is that really a woman?" and the ever-popular "Why are those guys admiring my purse?" If it weren't audition protocol, I never would have drawn attention to myself on public transportation by wearing a skirt and adult shoes.

On the brighter side of being a public spectacle, the pumps made me at least six inches taller than anyone else on the crowded train, so what little air was left was mine. And no matter how little sense it made, I had a good vantage point from which to scour the crowd for men who looked like Buck Sawicki.

I did not allow myself to think for a minute that Shannon was right. I *am* a masochist.

After signing in for an audition slot, I waited in the crummy unventilated rehearsal hall for two and a half hours before getting my three minutes, sixteen bars, and let's see if you can move. I could, and it was over only sixteen and a half hours after the alarm woke me.

Hard work never killed anyone my butt.

"You going uptown?" asked the muscular blonde who auditioned just before me. I thought about denying it since I hate straphanging next to anyone who works out—triceps insecurity, I guess. But the idea of company on the IRT seemed comforting. Especially the companionship of a woman with biceps of steel and a little tattoo circlet of barbed wire.

"The Number One to Seventy-ninth street."

"Thought so. I heard you're tending bar at McAleer's." She picked up her duffel bag and water bottle. "Oh, I'm Kristin, by the way."

"I'm Vic," and my feet were killing me.

"I know. You're the one who looks like Shannon."

"You think so?" Not that I minded. I just never thought that I looked like anybody. If I did, I wouldn't keep getting blamed for the things I do.

"Everyone thinks so." We lowered ourselves into the uptown hole at Forty-second Street. It was like being in an overly warm swimming pool. I could feel the clammy heat creep up my legs and wash up and over my face as we descended. "How was your first day behind the stick?"

"How did you know it was my first day?" I dropped my

token in the high-tech bucket and waited for the obnoxious green digital "go" to flash. Who said I can't take direction? Kristin had a MetroCard and swiped it efficiently through its designated crevice. I hate technology, so I'll be clinging to tokens until Big Brother forces me to stop.

"Everyone in the business knows." She swept her hair up in one hand, rolled the tail, and secured it into a neat chignon with a chopstick from her duffel bag. "It's Bar Wars."

"What?" I shouted over the scream of the uptown express. The ensuing wind blew a curly red whippet of hair from the back of my head directly into my mouth.

"The bar wars on the Upper West Side. I tend bar at the Opossum, three blocks down from Mac's. Your day guy, Dave, used to come visit me all the time. Three, four times a week for two years now. Kamikazes three for ten bucks. I'm gonna miss old Dave."

"You heard, then."

"It's a small community, as you'll soon see. It's really strange that nobody knew how bad Dave's problem was. I'll be damned if I can figure out how he did the day shift with that kind of habit. Hell, I don't know how he paid for it without working a little something on the side."

"Depressing."

"Very. So, let's not worry our pretty little heads over it. How about dropping by the Opossum with me for an uplifting nightcap? Ladies drink free ten to close every night. Whaddya say?"

"I say, what makes you think I'm a lady?"

"Just pretend you're Queen Shannon. With the height and that hair, no one will doubt it in the dark." Kristin obviously knew everything about my new life before I did.

"Kris, did Dave deal?"

"Drugs? Hell no. He was a cokehead without any aspirations at all. If he was dealing, he would have been a better tipper. The day shift pays garbage, as you know."

"I was hoping it was an off day." I held my exploding hair from my face. "Although a guy tipped me in coke today."

"Yeah?" Her eyes lit up.

"Sorry. I flushed it." Kristin looked a little incredulous. "If the guy's a regular, I better let him know that the gesture is wasted on me, huh?"

"Send him to me," Kristin laughed. "But you'll do better if you just let them believe whatever they want. Tell them what they want to hear. Think of it as an acting exercise."

The Number One/Nine train took its own sweet time pulling in to the platform, crawling along as though it was as hot and uncomfortable as the rest of us. The extra half hour it took us to reach Seventy-ninth Street provided me with all sorts of random information I should not have cared about, but did.

I was vaguely aware of the proliferation of bars in my old neighborhood for the past couple of years. Because I am a creature of habit, I never paid much attention to the specials they all ran to coax Columbia students and other ne'er-do-wells into getting sauced regularly.

The Opossum gave away drinks to women, the Black Hole *paid* women a nickel for every drink they ordered, Bunnie's threw in Buffalo wings with every pitcher of beer, and the Pike provided Jell-O shots with every third round. McAleer's specialty was really cool bartenders and the fact that it was less than a block from my door. The bar owners were at war, all right. There were no fewer than three joints per block in what was once a very sedate, residential enclave.

"BACK OFF, SCUMBAG!" Kristin yelled past my ear, over the clatter of the train. She was shooting the finger to the rear door. Being a Manhattan resident for over ten years, I turned to see who was the object of Kristin's affection without being especially startled by her outburst. The conductor chose that moment to open his cubbyhole at the express side of the train and walk to his local cubby, obscuring my view.

"What happened?" I asked, expecting a tirade about the usual sort of groping incident.

"Oh, some scumbag dishing your legs. Made me nervous. Didn't even look away when I caught him, the scumbag. What a creep. I'll tell you, it's about time they stopped putting these mental cases back on the street without supervision."

"Mental case?" The car shook as though it was about to derail, but I knew it was just the final turn into the Seventy-ninth Street station.

"Looked like frickin' Rambo."

The hair that wasn't plastered to my neck stood on end. The only psycho I knew who looked like Rambo was Buck Sawicki.

Lack of sleep had obviously started to make me hallucinate. I could accept that. I just couldn't accept that my sleep deprivation was causing Kristin's hallucinations. That would be a stretch, even for me. Under normal circumstances, I would have called Duchinski for a little comfort and plain talk, but not much of my ignominious return to the big city was normal this time.

And Duchinski and Sawicki had a history of some sort. Dan warned me to keep my distance from the ex-marine way back in Maine on the basis of that perp versus perp-ee history. I did. I was good.

Well, I was good about *that*.

My guilty conscience had become nonspecific radiating pain, or so I lectured myself. I know how I can get.

"Vic, whaddya say? We'll call it a going-away party for good old Dave."

"What?"

"Dave. We'll have a drink on Dave. Say, you're really bummed over this, aren't you?"

Rather than look like I just fell off the bar banana boat,

I evaded. "I never even met him. It must be much worse for you."

"Hell, no. I mean, it's not like I really knew him or anything."

Hmmm. Three or four times a week for over two years. Idiot math total is 236 visits from old Dave, and Kristin never really knew him.

Speaking as a person who has a close, personal relationship with anyone to whom I speak more than two sentences, including the rats in the walls of my apartment, I was very impressed with Kristin's *sange froid*. I could have used a little transfusion.

I passed on the free drink at the Opossum and, like a lemming, headed directly back to the comfort of home. Not my apartment, to McAleer's.

Amsterdam Avenue was not deserted—it never is—but it was Tuesday-night-quiet as I turned off Seventy-ninth Street and headed north. From even a block and a half away, I could see that a line had formed at McAleer's kelly green door. Good for them, I thought. Maybe a brisk business would sweeten Kerry's disposition a bit.

As I crossed Eightieth Street, my hopes dimmed. The crimson velvet rope was not positioned down the sidewalk, and the milling crowd was not composed of thirsty students, but a mixed bag of homeless men. Black, white, Hispanic, young, old, middle-aged, drunk, stoned and/or psychotic. Contemporary primordial ooze waiting for the lightning strike that would signal chemical change. I can't wait to see what evolution does with it.

But as familiar as the scene was, there was still something askew. New York's apparent chaos follows some pretty uncontested rules.

There is not a "kiddie bar" in NYC that doesn't have a beggar posted by the front door. One apiece. Each territory is staked out and presided over on the basis of seniority. If there are two panhandlers, it is by mutual consent.

McAleer's assigned beggar was a chap named Picture Frame, whose theatrical bit was to cajole the patrons with his face stuck in the opening of—you guessed it—a picture frame. He was a friendly face and a familiar neighbor, and nowhere to be seen in the milling crowd.

The only time I was used to seeing so many of New York's disenfranchised together as a mass was at the tri-weekly All Angels Episcopal soup kitchen lineup. I was pretty doggoned sure Kerry wasn't giving anything away, so the assembly confused me a bit. Still, I wasn't afraid of them.

The bars being as much a part of the men's economic security as they now were mine, I didn't worry about my personal safety and just plunged through the flailing arms and into the dark bar.

Kerry jumped over the oak strip as I elbowed my way to the rail. He pushed Frankie, the 280-pound all-American bouncer ahead of him toward the exit, yelling to beat the band.

"Whaddya think this is? A SOUP KITCHEN? Break that up, Frankie." No fool, Frankie stood at the door and surveyed the situation. Kerry turned his back confidently for a swagger back to the register when an explosive slam shook the walls. The clientele pushed away from the plate-glass window like a giant organism.

A wire-mesh garbage can ricocheted off the window, making the neon advertisements flicker. The "Guinness is good for you" sign gave up the ghost with a decided crack. Vegetables commandeered from the Korean grocery next door started smashing in through the doorway, catching Frankie a good one in the middle of his chest. Roaring, he plunged into the riot.

The bartender, Timmy, dialed the number for the Twentieth Precinct as Kerry reached behind the bar, palmed something, and dashed across the deserted floor to the mélée outside. He grabbed my cigarette and a pack of matches as he raced past. Odd, for a man who didn't smoke, but, then, what better time to start?

The patrons compressed against the back wall. Kerry stood just inside the door and sucked madly at my cigarette, until the glowing end illuminated his face devilishly. He leaned forward briefly, took a step back, and pitched into the mass of men outside.

The mega-firecracker exploded as the blue-and-white patrol car pulled up at the curb.

"Sons a' bitches," Kerry swore, smashing my cigarette under his foot on the marble chip floor. "You"—he pointed at me—"no freebies for the help and"—he threw my matches back at me, the logo side of the Blarney Rose up—"stay out of the competition."

It did not seem the time to protest my innocence. Shannon appeared out of nowhere carrying four pitchers of Bass, two per fist, positively unimpressed with the circus leaving town.

"What can I get you, Vic?" she asked.

"Nothing." Suddenly, I wasn't a bit thirsty. And the thought of being at all impaired for the short walk home seemed improvident, to say the least. "I better get to bed. Six-thirty comes pretty early."

"Walk you home?" asked a very handsome, mustached man at the bar. He had not moved during the altercation, simply observing. His well-developed arms meant he walked one of two sides of the criminal justice system.

"Vic," Shannon introduced, "this is Silva. He's a cop." It was reassuring to know that all my powers of intuition had not failed me.

Silva offered his hand. "Nice to meet you, Vic. Can I buy you a drink?"

I shook his hand. "No, thank you."

I reconsidered. "Yes, thank you. I'll have a Guinness." Silva had one of those wide open faces you like to see in a city cop. Handsome enough, on the tall side for an Hispanic. "I guess you're off duty, huh?"

"Never off duty in this neighborhood, but the guys look like they have everything under control. Otherwise they'd have grabbed me."

"So you work this precinct?" The Guinness was a little colder than I generally like, but it hit the spot.

"Yeah. The Twentieth is mine. Speaking of which, I heard you had some day, yourself. Your first?"

"I really stopped drinking so—"

"No, I meant your first body."

"Oh. Uh, actually, no." He seemed disappointed, so I added, "First one here, though."

"Yeah," he said and ordered another Bud, "they're rare here."

I sensed that we had hit a communication impasse.

"So, will you be investigating or will they bring in homicide detectives?" I asked.

"For what?"

"Are we talking about the same hell of a day? The dead bartender in the basement?"

"Yeah, we're talking the same thing. No, no detectives. Overdoses aren't sexy enough for those guys. You don't have to worry about a thing."

Why do men always say that to me?

"Well, I heard there was some suspicious bruising on the body."

"Yeah? No kidding. Well, I didn't see anything like that." He turned his chair to face me. "So, you single or what?"

"What?" The music wasn't really loud enough for me to feign total deafness at a distance of one foot, but it was the best I could do under the circumstances. I screamed into his face. "Sorry. Thanks for the drink, but I have an early morning."

Before he could argue with my personal sleep deprivation, I slapped him on the arm and exited with, "Drop in and see me!"

The police had dispersed the crowd outside. If I left immediately, I'd be within their sight all the way home.

Unfortunately, my timing was way off, and the patrol car was gone before I had even crossed the street. I picked up my pace. The narrow heels of my pumps caught in the cement grout of the sidewalk about every third square. I ran a one-woman debate through my mind as I strode.

Turning around to cover my back would be a show of weakness, and it just might precipitate action from the guy behind me.

I sped up, eyes forward, listening for the stranger's next move.

He sped up. My right heel jammed deep into a crack in the pavement. An A.A. Milne poem from my childhood flashed into my mind: "Whenever I walk down a London street."

I pulled off the offending shoe, which hurt like hell anyway, and positioned it, spike up to use as a weapon.

My pride now entirely evaporated, I sprinted up the six stairs to the front door of my building and turned to confront my stalker. My pulse pounded in my ears, but by then I was so annoyed at being frightened, I looked forward to beating the crap out of someone.

Just let me at him.

But he wasn't behind me. It took a long minute in the dull glow of the streetlamp to locate him. The Yuppie scum was sighing in relief as he urinated down the stairwell of the adjacent building. Disgusted with myself (and him), I unlocked the exterior door and limped to my apartment.

Slasher yowled a "Welcome home, I'm hungry" before the door was open more than two inches. The apartment appeared unnaturally bright to me after the darkness outside. The six-foot window in the living room radiated blackness from the back alley. It was disconcerting. Then I remembered that I had left the lights on when I went home that afternoon to pick up stuff for my audition. I chastised myself for being so high-strung.

Then I wondered why I would have turned the lights on in the first place. When I left for work that morning it was full daylight. Why would I waste electricity like that?

Then I remembered I didn't.

Someone had turned on the lights after the apartment darkened in the late afternoon. But who? The only person with keys was the super, Carlotta. I could hear the dripping faucet in the kitchen from where I stood in the living room. If Carlotta had come in, she had not fixed anything. My television still stared blankly at me from the antique sideboard at the wall to my left, and it was about all there was in the apartment to steal. I crossed burglary off my mental list.

Ultimately, I reassured myself that I was just losing my mind.

FOUR

I DID NOT SLEEP WELL. Twice I got out of bed to check that the windows were locked and the dead bolt thrown. The fact that Slasher peacefully snored his way throughout the night only annoyed me further. The more lights I turned on to reassure myself, the deeper the cat buried himself under the eyelet sheets. I fervently hoped that in my next life I would return to earth as a mangy alley cat instead of its legal guardian.

For the first time ever, the bleeping of the alarm was a relief. Never large, my apartment had become claustrophobic. And though I generally adore time alone with myself, that morning I yearned for human companionship. To my horror, I was actually looking forward to going to work.

A quick shower got rid of the essence of stale cigarettes and spilled beer. The McAleer's shirt I'd worn the day before was soaking in the sink, so I chose gray bike shorts and the tightest pearl gray jersey in my drawer. It was shallow of me, but I knew Kerry wouldn't even notice the absence of his logo as long as I maintained perfect posture. I changed the message on my answering machine leaving the number of McAleer's, on the off chance that David Merrick needed to make me a star immediately, and closed the door behind me.

Except for office-attired Yuppies heading in the direction of the subway on Broadway, the street was empty of real people. As far as I could tell, the bums were still asleep, and the rest of working Manhattan was pointed west to my east. Sort of a variation on the story of my life.

As I reached for the heavy outside door of McAleer's I

could already spot Sean reading his paper on the stool next to Sleeping Bobby. My little world was firmly on its axis.

Bright sun shone through the window and painted a geometric splash across the black-and-white marble floor. All evidence of the previous night's disturbance had been bleached squeaky clean by Beau, while I'd tossed and stewed a block away. The still air inside smelled of fresh-brewed coffee, and I smiled without thinking about larger issues of life and death. One day on the job, and I was home. I welcomed my rediscovered shallowness.

"Morning, darlin'," Sean said, not looking up from his *New York Times*. He was still on the front section. "I made up a pull sheet for you. Better start stocking before Mr. Miserable tells you to."

"Kerry's here already?"

"Wanted to catch you bein' late, I guess. He's in his office downstairs crunchin' numbers and trying to track down a case of beer that's gone missing."

I checked my Mickey Mouse watch to assure myself I was early.

"You're late," Kerry shouted from the basement door. "I'll dock your pay this time, but one more time and you're outta here. Now make your pull sheet, restock, and I'll give you today's bank." Without waiting for my denial of tardiness, he disappeared back into the flickering fluorescence of the cellar. And the clammy chill of the walk-in.

"Sean," I asked, "has anyone told Kerry about what happened to Dave?" He handed me the pull sheet, and I smiled a genuine thank-you. "He hasn't mentioned it at all, but he seems upset." In the presence of humanity and a bright new day, I was in a mood to offer all comers a bit of bartenderly understanding.

"Aw, the nip is always upset about something. Today, it's a case of beer, tomorrow it'll be something else. He spends every wakin' hour hunting down some kind of conspiracy or another, and he doesn't have the nose for it."

"So he does know that Dave died downstairs."

"Oh, sure," Sean answered blandly.

I did a masterful job of not commenting on Kerry's lack of interest in the subject of dead employees.

The stairs to the walk-in were steeper than I remembered. Far to the right of the basement I could see a sliver of light from what had to be Kerry's office. I had not noticed the day before how low the tangle of pipes and wires hung from the ceiling, or how spotless the storage area was kept. Non-perishable supplies were arranged on shining aluminum racks in perfect military precision. I threw the heavy brass bolt on the oak walk-in door up and forced it to the right. Either it needed oiling badly, or I just wasn't as strong as Shannon. Yesterday, on the other hand, we had Dave inside, so the bolt would not have been thrown.

Still, it seemed to me that I remembered Shannon flipping and sliding. Of course, a lot happened the day before and I was trying to learn as I went, and...

That's the trouble with losing your mind: memory loss.

"IS THAT BEER LOADED?" Kerry screamed from beyond the wall. "MAKE SURE YOU RESTOCK AFTER YOU BRING UP THE COLD, AND I'LL BE CHECKING TO MAKE SURE THEY'RE ALL ACCOUNTED FOR."

"What's missing?" I shouted back. I reveled in my guiltlessness. After all, this was the first day I had attempted to stock the bar.

"LIKE YOU DON'T KNOW," Kerry screamed back. "PABST. A CASE OF PABST, FROM YOUR SHIFT!"

Damned fool, I thought. I'd remind Sean that this was my first load-in. I checked the handwritten liquor list. Sean recommended five cases for upstairs: two Budweiser, two Coors Light, and a Miller. I took a deep breath, trying not to wonder what might be lying on the cement floor this morning. The adrenaline rush pumped and, when I threw the door open, it slammed against the wall as aggressively as though I had done it on purpose. To my surprise, Kerry did not jump me over the thundering whack, so I counted my blessings with every trip up the wooden stairs.

As I loaded the beer into the ice, I set a Budweiser in front of Sleeping Bobby and made idle conversation with Sean. I thought it was a bartender kind of thing to do. No call for Pabst. I will admit, I have never heard anyone order a Pabst. Sweat ran down my face and chest.

"Where's the air conditioner switch, Sean?"

"Kerry will turn it on when you get some real customers, or when he's damned ready. Whichever is last."

"Aren't you hot?" I asked, running an ice cube over my throat.

"I'm not hauling beer," he answered amiably. "I already married the bottles for you," he added. "Have a cup of coffee before you reload the walk-in. Don't want you catchin' yer death." He grimaced at the irony of death in the walk-in. "Sorry, Dave," he apologized skyward. I cringed and changed the subject even though I thought it was about time that someone talked about it.

The lack of interest was interesting, indeed.

"So, you have two sons, Sean." The coffee was excellent, even black, the way I like it. I would have to learn how to make it myself sometime that morning.

"That I do, darlin'. There's Kerry, and then the real barman in the family, George. Small family by Irish standards."

What was Duchinski doing meeting with a bar owner first thing on a Tuesday morning? In *my* bar? I didn't believe in coincidence any more than Dan did. "Where is George's bar?" I asked innocently.

Sean laughed. "Wherever he sits, darlin'." I know I looked slow. "There's only three careers for the Irish here. Barman, fireman, or cop. We McAleers don't take to ladders much, and George being the oldest got his choice of the remaining two. He's a cop, God bless him, but he has the personality for the bar, he does."

"I can see that. Did Kerry want to be a cop, too? Is that why they don't seem to get along?"

"Oh, no. Kerry wanted this life, all right, but he always resented the fact that he just doesn't have the touch. I guess that's why he's always so grumpy. He works so hard, and it all just gets harder instead of easier. George is the bar man, but it's Kerry behind the bar. If Georgie wasn't posted in Washington, I think seeing him so comfortable around here would drive Kerry right over the edge. Life's funny, it is."

A laugh riot.

Duchinski was huddling with another cop, then. For no reason at all, that did not settle the matter for me. Why in this bar? Why so early? Dan had never mentioned George, so they weren't old buddies that I knew of. And how could they be coworkers from three hundred miles away?

"I'd better restock the walk-in before we get some customers in here." My forehead was crinkling, and I thought some heavy lifting would distract me. I made a mental note to try to be more sympathetic to Kerry.

"Good idea, dearie." Sean folded the front section of the paper and stood. "And while you do that, I'll just turn on the air conditioner."

Rather than end up another frozen bartendercicle, I propped the door open as I loaded warm beer to replace what I'd brought upstairs. When I was through, I called to Kerry in his office. He did not answer. I called again.

I don't want you to think that I was overreacting, but the last time someone was in that space and did not answer, he turned up dead. The silence made me ill. I slammed the heavy door as loudly as I could and waited to be yelled at. Nothing. I called again. More nothing. I filled a clean garbage can with ice to carry upstairs, and peeked around the corner toward Kerry's office. The slice of light still cut across the cement floor, but there was no sound. I parked the ice by the steps and approached the illumination.

"Kerry?" I fingered the ajar door. "Kerry? The bar's all stocked. Kerry?" With just my forefinger, I tapped the door open six inches and peeped inside.

The room was nine feet by eleven. The walls were paneled with a cheap walnut that had either been salvaged from or rejected for the bar upstairs. A worn blue velvet sofa hugged the wall to the left. The pillow at one end told me that it doubled as a bed when necessary. A brown metal desk and chair sat catty-corner, backed with nine tall, beige filing cabinets. A small television sat atop the one nearest the foot of the sofa. Kerry was not in his office, and he was far too big to have vanished into thin air. Not that I *cared*.

Not that it made any sense at all.

Not that I was getting that creepy feeling, all over again. But I was.

My arms and the small of my back had begun to ache with the unnatural effort of doing "man's work." The logistics of hefting an ice-laden garbage can up eleven (yes, I counted) steps were daunting, and in order to lift the damned thing at all, I had to cradle it like an obese infant up in front of my face, obscuring my view of my feet and the treads. Every leaden heave up to the bar felt as though I would misstep and fall backward to be found later in a shepherd's pie of ice and splattered brains. Poking forward with my foot, I finally steadied myself at the top of the landing, when the plastic ice bin was ripped from my hands. The weight correction almost flung me backward and down, but as I teetered, a strong hand grasped my flailing arm.

It was Barry Laskin, my almost-ex-husband. Early as it was, he was wearing his lawyer uniform: summerweight, light blue suit, crisp white shirt, and Daffy Duck silk tie.

"Nice tie," I said. "New?"

"A gift," he grunted, walking the ice to the bar.

Like I couldn't recognize a gift tie when it was staring me in the mouth. New girlfriend?

"Your mother?" I asked, hauling the ice to the beer

cooler nearest. We both knew that Estelle Laskin had never had a puckish impulse in her life.

"What are you doing?" The sure sign of guilt—answer a question with a question. He looked good. Dark as a storm cloud, tall and wiry. A little balder than the week before, but it served him right for leaving me. Unmussed, even in the heat. As we all know, that is a side benefit of a Juris Doctor: the sweat glands seal up permanently. I myself was sweating bullets, but hoped it could pass for a "glow."

"Look at you, sweating, like a common…"

"Bar wench?" I asked, and dumped my bucket. "Can I get you a drink, sir, or is this just a drive-by?" Barry checked his Rolex.

"I'll have a cup of coffee. Touch of milk, half a teaspoon of sugar—unless you have honey." He planted his briefcase firmly between his feet against the footer of the bar. I slapped a quart of milk and handful of sugar packets next to his mug. He took a deep breath and regrouped. "Is this about alimony?"

"I didn't ask you for any, so the joke's on me." I pointed to his mug. "That'll be three big ones, please."

"Three dollars for a cup of coffee?" He pulled his designer wallet from the inside of his designer jacket. The bills were arranged in ascending order. He pulled out four singles.

"Free refills and gratuity included," I answered, ringing a dollar-fifty on the register and pocketing the change. "*Thank* you, sir."

"You are impossible." *He noticed.* "Are you crazy?" *Why do people keep asking me that?* Barry leaned forward intimately, and gave me the hundred-watt sincerity face. "Vic," he fairly whispered, "if you're having money problems, we can work something out. You shouldn't have to do"—he looked around as though the walls would provide him with the perfect word—"this." As always, I found myself mellowing. I waited for elaboration. My feet already hurt, and it wasn't yet eight o'clock. "I could use a gofer."

Ah-ha, the payoff.

"I've *been* your gofer, Barry, and the benefits sucked. Now, don't you have to be serving papers or litigating or something? I have menial labor to perform until six." From the corner of my eye, I spotted two truly frightening men enter the door. One was bigger than the other, both wore dark glasses and black Henley shirts stretched tightly across their massive chests. I could tell from Barry's expression that he was unused to being in a room with such men—without benefit of ankle restraints and armed guards. Obviously, I was in danger. That would show him. "Hi, guys!"

As expected, the men grunted. They walked directly to the sleeping jukebox. I believe one of Barry's sweat glands burst open. The less massive of the two pulled a long screwdriver from his back jeans pocket, as the more titanic took a position at the door. Another of Barry's previously shutdown glands popped. I could hear Sean whistling from the kitchen. *Finnegans Wake,* if I wasn't mistaken. Sleeping Bobby, too, had deserted his post for, perhaps, the first time ever. The front piece of the jukebox fell to the floor with a clatter.

The infamous Victoria Bowering karma had struck again.

"Hey," I protested smartly. I looked to my ex, the wordmeister, for something more appropriate to the situation. He was gazing intently at the phone behind the bar. "Hey," I repeated, coming around from behind the bar as quarters and dollar bills tumbled from the jukebox into a grimy canvas bag. Barry sprang to action, hiding his briefcase behind the bar. He slipped the phone from the receiver and hunched behind the oak barricade.

"Inna minute," Mighty Joe Young cautioned me with a wave of his hand. He sat at the nearest table and pulled a card-sized calculator from his tight jeans. "Gimme a Coke, willya?" Kong, by the exit, continued to monitor the street.

"No ice." I could hear a flurry of telephone buttons being depressed from behind me. I edged toward the kitchen, back to the men's room.

"What are you doing?" I asked.

I thought the question was suitably insipid and nonthreatening. I sidled close enough to the swinging kitchen doors to open one a few inches and slide my arm through for a little frantic gesticulating to Sean. Very subtle. The man with the screwdriver continued to count. The man at the door continued to watch. From what I could gather, Barry continued to dial. My new buddy decided to answer me.

"What does it *look* like I'm doing?"

Okay, it was the old question-with-a-question ruse. I remembered the baseball bat secreted about fifty-eight thousand miles away somewhere beyond Barry, and did what I had to do.

"SEAN!" I screamed.

The monolith with the canvas bag grasped my wrist.

"You're new, aren't you?" he asked, I thought somewhat unnecessarily. "Never mind the Coke. I'll just take two-hundred-forty bucks out of the register for the balance." He got up, the bag crumpled in his left hand.

"I don't think so." I wish my brain synapses fired as quickly as the ones that jerk my knee. I stood my ground. For one thing, I knew there wasn't $240 *in* the register, and for another, I was pissed. I can bend with the wind, but this was a monsoon spitting all over me.

"Ah," Sean said from the kitchen doors, wiping his hands on a vividly white dish rag. "Some breakfast, boys?" he asked. The thug with the bag walked toward the frail old man. I made a balletic leap over the bar to grab the baseball bat. My sneaker lace caught on the Pilsner Urquel tap, landing me facefirst onto my almost-ex-husband. As I scrambled for my weapon and to my feet, I saw Sean taking a slip of paper from our erstwhile thief. It seemed a little late for a stick-up note, to me.

Sean pulled a pair of magnifying glasses from the pocket of his plaid, short-sleeved shirt and pushed them onto his nose. I stepped carefully over Barry, who was still mashing telephone buttons. He reached to pull me back, but missed by about a mile.

The watchdog's eyes were still glued to Amsterdam Avenue as I sneaked forward. Every step sent a shudder of common sense up my spine. When I arrived at my target, I would have to swing as hard and as fast as Mickey Mantle.

Sean caught my torturous progress out of the corner of his eye. I prayed for him to be circumspect.

"Vic, darlin'!" he waved me to him. *What?* It was a small bat, but I still had a hell of a time hiding it behind my back. "Meet the boys, Eamon and Matt. They service our jukebox, here, don'tcha boys?" Eamon, to his side, nodded, casting me a very suspicious glance. Matt continued to stare down the street. Barry stood and hung up the phone, a gash of mildew across one powder blue jacket sleeve. I felt as though I were a balloon deflating in the breeze.

"Oh." I backed up. "Oh. Did you give them the balance?"

"What balance?" Sean furrowed his brow and turned to face Eamon.

"Two-hundred and forty dollars," I answered, sliding the baseball bat back behind the bar. Sean whacked the big man a hard one up the back of his head with the dishrag.

"Ah, ya' punks, ya' go piss up a rope, don'tcha?" He shoved Eamon in the small of the back and shouted behind, all the way to the front door. "Big Tommy'll be hearin' of this, he will. Now getcha both to hell, with ya'."

"The police are on their way," Barry reassured me. I had forgotten he was there. I wonder why.

"Thanks, Barry." I blotted sweat from my face with the upper side of my forearm. "I don't think we need them anymore."

"I think you do. You know what you've gotten yourself

involved in here?'' He didn't wait for me to lie. ''This is obviously a 'Westies' bar. Those hoodlums were here to extort money from you under the pretense of servicing a music contract.''

''Just call me Moll,'' I dismissed him, and waved to Silva as he walked past the picture window. He was in uniform, unlike the night before.

''What's up?'' Silva asked from the doorway. ''The dispatcher says you've got a robbery in progress.'' He sat at the bar and looked around. ''Did I miss it?''

Barry picked up his briefcase and moved it down the bar to Silva. ''I believe, Officer, that it was a mob shakedown. I was mistaken when I reported a robbery.''

''Fancy that,'' Silva commented. ''Vic, can I have an ice water? It's hotter than hell out there. So''—Silva turned his attention back to Barry—''did they put any new tunes on the juke?''

''You know about this?''

''I know what civilians *think* about this. You think the Westies are strong-arming McAleer's, right?'' He waited for Barry's nod in that patient police way. ''Right. Well, sir, there's really no such thing as the Westies Gang anymore. Now''—he held his glass up for a refill—''twenty years ago, you might have been correct, but not these days. The Italians pretty much whacked them out of the business, except for some garbage routes here and there. *They* may think they're still a gang, but they're the only ones who do.''

''Pardon me, Officer''—Barry checked out the silver NYPD shield—''Silva, but I *heard* the men attempt to extort two-hundred and forty dollars from the bartender here.''

''Yeah, well, they were just freelancing. I imagine Sean set them straight, didn't he?''

''Yes,'' I answered.

''Yes,'' Barry echoed. I heard the toilet flush in the men's room. Sleeping Bobby wandered past us and back to his regular stool. Sean carried a plate of bacon and eggs from the kitchen to the basement stairs.

"Sean," Silva called, "you want me to write a complaint for you?"

"Oh, fer God's sake, Silva, ya' dumb PR, no." He took his breakfast downstairs.

"Vic, you want to file a complaint?"

My biggest complaint at that moment was not being informed of what to expect on this new job. "No." Barry shook his head in disgust.

"No wonder this city is falling to pieces." He picked up his briefcase and stood to face me. "Citizens have a responsibility to the justice system to lodge complaints against lawbreakers. If you won't help yourself, Victoria, you can't expect everyone else to protect you."

Shannon spotted the expensive suit the moment she rounded the corner from the basement. She picked up the ringing phone on her way to entrance the men. As she spoke into the phone, she made eye contact with Barry. He casually sat back down. Disgusted, I walked over to take the phone from Shannon, but she hung up as I reached for the receiver.

"It was for you," she informed me. She mimicked a Brooklyn accent, and droned, "You have been cast in the show *Sylvia and Reynaldo's Dinner Party*. Rehearsals begin tomorrow night at seven o'clock, same place as the auditions. Please bring your union card and extra head shots. Break a leg."

"Really?"

"Victoria, how could I possibly make that up?" She fluttered her eyelashes in Barry's direction. "Aren't you going to introduce me to your friend?"

"Sure. Shannon, I'd like you to meet my ex-husband, Barry Laskin."

"The husband who took your microwave?" Shannon frowned.

"I've got to go, Vic." Barry collected his briefcase one last time and headed for the door. "Congratulations on your new show and quitting this job. I'll call you later in the week."

"Did you quit?" Shannon asked from the stool next to Silva. She sipped his ice water.

"No, and I can't afford to for a while anyway."

"You're nuts," Silva offered. Shannon nodded her agreement.

"Working days and rehearsing nights will kill you," she said.

"It'll be all right. Once I get used to the routine around here, I'll be able to do the job in my sleep. Speaking of which"—which I wasn't—"how did you sneak by me and the Guido brothers to get into the basement?"

"Celtic magic," she grinned, "and the stairway door from the apartment building next door."

"So that's what happened to Kerry?"

"Whatever happened to Kerry is strictly between him and his God," Shannon answered. "But, yes, Kerry often sneaks his nasty bottom out through the back stairs so that the workers will think he's keeping an eye on them. Of course, it only works until they find out the trick, which usually only takes a day or two."

"I've looked around the basement and I never saw an extra door."

"Well, you're not supposed to, Victoria. The next time you're downstairs, you'll notice one wall to the right in Kerry's office with no shelving. The panel slides back. According to Sean, all the old family bars have a back stair, left over from Prohibition days."

"Makes sense to me."

"It'll make even more sense when the day comes that you've got two or three men you're dating, waiting for your shift to end. Or your bar groupies start to get confident enough to want to find out where you live."

"I don't have any bar groupies," I said.

"Sure you do," Shannon answered. "You just don't know who they are, yet." She glanced over to the entrance with a seriously knowing look. One of the carpenters who had visited on my first day was back. It was Terrence.

Shannon winked annoyingly, and left me alone to do my job.

"Terrence," I greeted him. He sat at the end of the bar, farthest away from the door, near the coffee machine. None of his buddies were with him, and, as he did not park at a table, I assumed were not expected to join him later. "What can I get you?"

"Just coffee today," he answered, lighting a cigarette and pulling a green melamine ashtray off the rail. "It's been a hellish two days, I don't mind sayin'."

"Are your friends' families all right?" I asked, remembering their hasty departure. I chided myself for not thinking of it sooner, or of him. "And yours?"

"None of the immediate family were hurt," Terrence answered quietly. He seemed just a husk of the man I had met two days earlier. He stared into his coffee and drew on his cigarette. He seemed to need something more from me.

"Do they know the cause?" I asked, wishing for some customers to drift in and pull me away from the brooding workman.

"Gas leak," he explained in a waft of smoke. He looked up into my face. "They say," he finished. I could see that he wanted some additional interaction. This bartending thing is a lot more than just drawing a beer or two and wiping up spills.

"They?" was all I could muster.

He searched my face for more of a reaction. I didn't have one, so I relied on my theater background and made one up. I chose *dawning realization*. When Terrence seemed gratified, I followed it up with *companionable empathy*. He nodded, apparently satisfied with my performance.

It has been my experience that faking an appropriate response is not nearly as dangerous as an amateur might believe. Usually, it lulls the person who wants the response into giving me enough information to ultimately provide a real expression of understanding.

That, naturally, is on a *good* day.

I dug around under the bar, searching for an abandoned crossword puzzle or newspaper in which to immerse myself. When that option failed, I tried to find something that needed doing, but my New England work ethic had screwed me up again. Everything was done, and Terrence wasn't spewing out additional information.

I was afraid I was caught in my own inventiveness, that time. It served me right.

"Department of Health," announced the rumpled man in the doorway. "We've had notification of numerous violations and we have to do a complete inspection of the premises."

Punishment comes in so many ways.

FIVE

DUCHINSKI SEEMED not the slightest bit surprised to get my call. I believe he would say that his unflappability is a major part of his charm. He would be wrong. His charm at that moment would be his ability to navigate the ins and outs of the New York Metropolitan Justice System. He felt strongly that the Health Department would not be sending me up the river, even if Dan requested it right again.

The health inspector did his darnedest, but there was not a violation to be had at McAleer's that morning. Without too much sweet talk, Sean elicited the name of the stool pigeon who reported us to the Department of Health. I did not recognize the name, but Sean certainly did. It was the owner of the Opossum.

"Bar Wars strikes again."

Sean sent the inspector off on his merry way with a little inside information on the sorry state of the distance between kitchen and fire egress at the Opossum.

"All in a day's work," Sean commented before going to the office for an afternoon nap.

Fine for him to say. In exchange for Duchinski's looking into our problem, I had agreed to have dinner with him that night. I was going to have to rationalize my brains out all afternoon to be able to face him in shameless innocence. Fortunately—or unfortunately, as the case might be—business was so slow I could give self-delusion my full attention.

We met at the bar of Miss Elle's Homesick Bar and Grill on Seventy-ninth Street, near Broadway. Maurice paced behind the bar like a caged animal, squeezing grapefruits in his bare hands and shaking the bejeezus out of margaritas in the pursuit of a transcendent drinking experience. The Yuppies loved it. The locals chatted over their vodkas on the rocks and tried to stay out of the line of spillovers.

Dan had planted himself with his back to the mirror in the corner nearest the door, a chilled martini on the napkin in front of him. As I settled onto the rattan chair next to Dan, Maurice dropped a Dickel's bourbon straight up in a brandy snifter into place. He snapped his hand back with a flourish and sped off before I had the chance to tell him that I had quit drinking.

Oh, well.

The bar was filling up rapidly with stragglers on their way home via the alcohol turnpike. I fished in my fanny pack for my cigarettes. Dan handed me a cheroot. Oh, well. It was as fine a way to stall for time as any. The second I put cigar to lips, Maurice appeared with Zippo aflame. I thanked him. He disappeared again behind a massive bowl of fresh fruit.

Animated conversation bled over the whir of the overworked blender. Cool air poured from the air-conditioning duct. The light blinked furiously on the smoke eater in the center ceiling of the narrow room.

Oh, well.

"Hi, Dan." Someone had to break the ice. "Sorry I bothered you about that health inspector. It was nothing."

"I know. Are you hungry?"

Dan knows that I am *always* hungry. That's the greater part of my charm. "Are you?" A question. Damn. Someday I am going to learn to spare myself and everyone else a lot of trouble and just confess my guts up at the start. *Okay, Dan, I had this affair thing while I was out of town, but it didn't mean anything, and now I'm back.* Sure. And someday my prince will come, too.

"Always. Let's take our drinks upstairs and order some dinner." Dan threw a twenty on the bar to cover the tab and tip and lifted his glass to Maurice, who waved us off.

We climbed the steps of the converted town house to the smoking area and settled into the banquette facing a rolltop desk where Elle, herself, was doing some paperwork.

The room was cool celadon green, ivory, and soft pinks. Small glass candle lamps lit the center of each lace cloth, and Martha Stewart floral arrangements lounged on windowsills and side tables. Our table was so quiet, I thought I could hear the smoke curling from our cigars as we perused the hand-lettered menus.

"Aren't you going to ask me how I'm doing at work?" I asked from behind the safety of the lavender menu.

"Do I need to?"

"Don't you?

"No."

"I had some excitement the first day."

"So I heard."

"Dan, are we talking about the same thing?" When we get into these "I'm not really speaking to you, despite what you hear" conversations, I sometimes lose my place.

"I'm a homicide detective, Vic."

Ah. "So you got the report?"

"No. George told me." Dan looked around the dining room for a waitress to intervene.

"So what do you think?"

"I think he's not your type. Where's our waitress?"

"Dan! I meant about the murder."

Dan turned in his seat as though there might be a waitress hiding under some other table. It was not to be. "Vic, if it had been a murder, I would have seen a report. Besides, I would think that you have bigger and better things to worry about than some lowlife pothead. The man was scum, and stupid scum to boot. Don't go turning this into some melodrama. You're not on stage now, Vic." He must have realized that he'd raised his voice because he looked at me sheepishly. "Can we let it go for now?"

Under normal circumstances, I would have been furious

with him for speaking to me that way, but, unfortunately, I owed him one. And I didn't want to talk about *that*.

"Sure."

"So, what else is new?"

"You'll never guess who I thought I saw yesterday," I ventured. I supposed he couldn't guess, since he didn't respond. "Buck Sawicki. Can you believe it?"

"Want to eat outside?" Dan asked, snuffed his cigar, and left me at the table. Miss Elle turned around at her desk and smiled at me. Dan held her chair as she rose. "C'mon, Vic, it's a beautiful night." We followed Elle into the dining room beyond ours and waited as she opened the French doors onto a tiny balcony.

The white table and resin chairs were barely large enough for an intimate dinner for two, let alone an estrangement reunion. Elle brushed off the seats and placed our menus on the table before lighting the candles and closing the French doors behind her.

"Dan, it's eighty thousand degrees out here."

"You think so?"

"And it looks like rain."

"Is that what the weatherman said?"

"Dan, stop answering me with a question. I told you I saw Buck Sawicki yesterday, and you didn't answer me."

"It wasn't a question. And you said you *thought* you saw Sawicki. How about a bottle of that Buzet you like?"

"And?" I waited him out.

"And we can have another bottle if we finish the first one. What do you want from me, Vic? I'm not made of stone, here. You leave town and *(lethal pause)* don't even call when you get back. Then you take a dangerous job without consulting anyone, and now you're seeing things."

"Now you sound like Barry."

"So you called *him?*" The waitress appeared and took the wine order. "Never mind. Anyway, a lot of men look

like Sawicki. Hell, Maurice the bartender here looks like
Sawicki.''

That was actually, frighteningly, true. But Maurice was
not Buck. The more Dan denied it, the more certain I was
that Sawicki was in New York. And in this neighborhood.

Since linear conversation wasn't working, I decided to
take a lateral approach.

''You never did tell me how you met Buck.'' The waitress poured our wine, and took our orders for two prime rib
dinners, rare. ''Did you arrest him?'' Dan tore off a piece
of warm pumpernickel and buttered it. I waited patiently.
Another cop strategy. Don't talk, and it will force the other
to fill the dead air. He chewed. I waited.

''We served together in East Asia.'' He took another
mouthful.

''Vietnam?''

''Thailand. It was a long time ago.''

''Military police?'' I looked earnestly over the rim of my
wineglass.

''We were kids.'' I continued to gaze, enthralled. ''We
were infantry grunts, that's all. Vic, I don't like to talk about
those days, okay?''

As a woman of ''a certain age,'' I have learned that there
are two kinds of Vietnam-era veterans. Those who talk
about it endlessly, and those who never talk about it at all.
Dan was the latter. He was very consistent on the point, and
I couldn't bring myself to press that button. I suppose I
knew that it couldn't ever be unpressed.

''I know.'' He sensed my retreat and settled back into his
chair, surveying the view from the second floor down Seventy-ninth Street toward Central Park. ''I missed you.''

He looked at me across the sputtering candles and smiled
a very tired smile. I examined my gold bracelet.

Dinner arrived with a second bottle of wine, compliments
of Maurice and Miss Elle. By unspoken mutual consent,
Dan and I settled back into each other's company. I under-

stood that Vietnam was not the only thing of which Dan Duchinski did not want to speak, that night or ever. By cognac and banana layer cake, my date was relaxed in the knowledge that I was going to leave him alone regarding my imaginary stalker. I am not, however, noble beyond human bounds. I still had a question about Dan's meeting with George McAleer. This time I approached horizontally and on the curve.

"So Sean McAleer's son is FBI." I lit Dan's cigar, and a cigarette for myself. "The old man is so proud. You should have heard him go on."

"He said FBI?" Dan rolled the dead end of the cigar in his cognac.

"I don't know, I think so. FBI, DEA, initials. You know, Washington, D.C., too many letters, not enough time."

"ATF." Duchinski looked into my eyes and took breath. He rattled, "INS, IRS, EEOC, they're all Feds to me."

Settle down, Sergeant. I didn't catch a thing.

"You say po-ta-to, and I say po-taw-to," I sang. Smooth, huh?

Dan's pants broke into their own "Anvil Chorus." Actually, it was his beeper.

The waitress arrived with the check as though she were wired directly to headquarters. Dan handed her four twenties, and pulled out my chair for me. "I have to call in, babe."

"There's a phone behind the ficus benjamina in the bar," I said, following him through the two dining rooms and down the stairs.

I stood outside in what passes for air on any bus route in New York City, while he used the phone just inside the door.

"Can you get home alone?" he asked after hanging up.

He was already backing away to the right, in the direction of Amsterdam Avenue. I could see his red Toyota parked on the corner of Broadway, to my left.

"It's only a block. I'm fine."

He kissed me and without a backward glance tore down the sidewalk away from me. I tore after him. I reasoned that if he didn't need his car, whatever the problem was, it was nearby.

I slowed down as we turned the corner at Amsterdam uptown. The coins in my fanny pack made me sound like a jogging tour of Swiss bell-ringers, and I didn't want to attract Dan's attention. Besides, the blipping blue lights highlighting McAleer's door revealed our destination without my having to break any minute-mile records.

At a distance of two hundred yards, I could clearly make out Shannon standing on the sidewalk, baseball bat poised over a limp body on the pavement. Her wild hair strobed red/blue/red/blue by the police-car lights. Dan had already disappeared into the bar.

A police van pulled up at the curb at the corner of Eightieth Street as the uniforms started to lead a banged-up bunch of men in shorts out of McAleer's and into custody.

The man at Shannon's feet muttered. He was not nearly as dead as he had initially appeared.

"Silva!" she yelled inside. "Come get this mess off my shoe." Silva stood at the door, holding a bottle of beer.

"I'm off duty." Shannon gave him her world-famous, patented, would-wither-the-Ayatollah glance. He caved in. "All right. Jeez." He handed me his beer, pulled the supine man to his feet, curling the wrist up behind the back with a clean sweep, and pushed him to the van.

"What happened?" I asked, watching a line of young athletes pile out of the bar, herded by the boys in blue.

"We are having a perfectly lovely wake for Dave," she took the beer from my hand and took a deep swig, "when this touring side scum comes in and starts breaking up the place." She rolled the cool bottle over her chest.

"A wandering rugby team just fell in off the street and started a riot at Dave's wake?" Through the window I spotted Dan coming at us, taking notes as a uniform talked. I pulled Shannon around to the door and scrunched down behind her.

Dan glanced up briefly, seemed startled and then passive at the sight of Shannon and her baseball bat. Maybe we look more alike than I had credited. The important thing was that he didn't see me.

Kerry followed the last of the police to the sidewalk. His cheek was badly scraped, and the start of a doozy of a shiner was erupting at his left eye. He noticed Shannon and ordered, "Table five needs another round and burgers." Shannon shrugged and went back to work. Then Kerry spotted me leaning against the window. "And you. Don't let me hear that you're drinking anyplace else in the neighborhood besides here again, or you're fired. Understand?"

I stood for some time wondering how Kerry could have known I was at Miss Elle's. It wasn't as though someone had plastered me with a promotional bumper sticker while I was parked. Neurotically, I checked my rump, since the idea had even fleetingly occurred to me.

"Nice," said Silva, also checking my rump. "Where's my beer?"

"Shannon took it." I pointed into the window, as though he needed to know where to find Shannon. Timmy, the bartender, chose that moment to turn up the lights in order to right the room, illuminating the bar all the way to the kitchen. I grabbed Silva's arm. Leaning against the paneled column at the rear of the room, staring back at me through the window, was Buck Sawicki. "That man," I whispered, "back by the dartboard, leaning against the wall."

"Yeah," Silva squinted into the glass.

"Can you go card him?"

"Everyone is carded when they go in, Vic, you know that." I pushed him to the door.

"Please," I begged. "Get the name of the man with the

buzz cut and the marine tattoo.'' I shoved again. ''I think he's following me. I'll wait in the store next door. Please!''

''Okay, sweetie, you go next door. I'll check it out.''

I didn't need more promise than that and scurried past the tattletale window into the Kmart-bright greengrocer's. Under the hostile scrutiny of the Korean shopkeepers, I bought a pack of cigarettes I didn't need, and waited. Then I bought a pack of Pepperidge Farm cookies I didn't want, and waited some more. Then I stood outside and fingered the flowers set in buckets on the sidewalk until I felt compelled to buy another pack of cigarettes I didn't need. Silva finally showed himself.

''There was nobody like that in there, babe.''

''I saw him.''

''It was pretty dark, Vic. I looked real good. No buzz cut or marine tattoos. If he'd left, you would have seen him go out.''

''Did you ask Shannon?''

''How many hours you been working?''

Another lost cause. I don't need to be kicked in the head twice. I *was* a little behind on my sleep, and I *did* have more wine at dinner than people who have quit drinking usually do.

''Will you walk me home, Silva? I'm a little edgy.''

''You bet,'' he answered.

You Bet Your Life, I thought. Groucho Marx. Ducks with cigars. Maybe it would be funnier after a good night's sleep.

Maybe not.

SIX

I COULD HEAR the screaming from across the street.

Kerry stood in the middle of McAleer's, supervising, as Beau swabbed the deck, apparently oblivious to the verbiage. The smell of ammonia was overpowering from the moment I opened the outer door. The stool which normally propped up Sleeping Bobby was empty, as was Sean's usual seat. It was like finding myself unarmed in a rabid badger den.

"SHUT THE DAMNED DOOR!" I didn't realize I was holding it open. It seemed like a rational thing to do to me. Of course, I'm not Kerry McAleer. The phone rang, the red light at the top of the casing flashed enthusiastically. "AND GET THE DAMNED PHONE!" I slid cautiously across the wet floor in my best Ice Capades routine and grabbed the wall phone.

It was Duchinski asking if I'd gotten home all right. He was still trying to get to the bottom of last night's incident.

"I saw Buck Sawicki, Dan."

"I thought we covered that over dinner."

"He was at McAleer's. I saw him through the window while the police were taking the rugby team away."

"I told you to go home."

"What about Sawicki?"

"Wouldn't *I* have seen him, Vic?"

"Did you?"

"Did I say I did?"

"NO PERSONAL CALLS, VIC!" Kerry punched the disconnect and hung the receiver up for me. It didn't really matter. Dan and I were trapped on the question-for-a-question merry-go-round, anyway.

I welcomed the chance to stock the bar for the night man and get out of Kerry's line of fire. As I began the seemingly endless trips up and down the basement stairs, my eyes were drawn each time I passed it to the spot where I had thought I'd seen Buck Sawicki the night before.

I don't know what I hoped to see: a chalk outline of his body, perhaps.

When the bar was ready for customers, Sean entered and threw down a kick rod to hold the door open.

"Whew! Smells like a forsaken flounder in this place. Beau"—Sean handed the man a few dollars—"run next door and pick up some Pine-Sol or something, will you? It's a good thing the health department didn't pick today for a look-see."

"There's nothing wrong with ammonia, Pop. We save a lot of money by cutting out the frills." Kerry pulled the dollar bills from Beau's hand and stuffed them back into his father's pocket. Sean retrieved the money, smoothed out the wrinkles and gave them back to Beau, with a pat on the back to get him moving.

"Ammonia stinks, my son, that's what wrong. This business is filthy enough without having to hold your nose for the mop-up. And you oughta know, when another man's paying, to shut yer yap."

"I give up. Have it your way, old man." Kerry flicked on a tremendous floor fan. The oscillating whoosh, whoosh was pleasant to hear and feel. The air was not only pungent, but mushy with humidity. The morning was dark as dusk. Kerry picked up his satchel, and I had high hopes of his disappearing downstairs, outside, or into the ozone. Instead, he pulled three wadded-up balls of fabric and threw them on the bar. "Put one of these on," he said to me. "I had them special ordered from those Hooters guys."

I held one of the cutoff T-shirts to my chest. It was Day-Glo pink with black letters stretching across the center. The neckline was cut to within four inches of the hem, which rose three inches from my waist. The size tag read "Small." My bones alone are a "Medium."

Sean toddled by. "How about some breakfast?" he asked.

"I don't think I'll ever be able to eat again," I answered, eyeballing my new uniform.

"Don't you have anything better to do, Pop?" Kerry poked around the bag. "Damn. They forgot the shorts." *Shorts?* "Vic, put on a shirt; I'll go back and get the matching shorts. That ought to get us a better ring this afternoon, especially without you giving away the store," he added meaningfully. He pulled the door tight behind him on the way out.

I asked Sean, "Does that have anything to do with the missing Pabst?"

"What do you think, dearie?" he asked in return.

"I don't know. I don't drink beer. I wouldn't even know how to walk out of here with a case of it."

He examined me, openly. "Ah, maybe you wouldn't." I frowned in frustration. "You see, the beer probably wasn't carted off. Bartenders have been known to plant extra stock upstairs, give it to customers, and pocket the money. It's an old trick. That's why we keep such close track of the inventory."

I hated myself, but still I said, "But Benny brought up the liquor my first day."

"So I reminded Kerry, but Benny didn't write down his pull sheet, so we'll never be sure. Never mind, darlin'. You just be extra careful. Extra careful."

All I can say is, it's a good thing I don't have any dignity left to offend.

I went to the ladies' room to change as Kerry thundered up his Porsche. I tried on the pink, the white, and the chartreuse. They all looked like a Maaco paint job on a thirty-ninish-year-old car. I settled on the white, since it was, at the very least, a classic color to match the model.

BOOOOMM.

I slammed out of the rest room, and had to admit, the air felt good on my bare midriff. From the back of the bar I could not see out the front window.

Billows of smoke played against the glass and wafted heavily down the sidewalk. Kerry's Porsche looked as though someone had painted the windows white. Kerry, too.

I ran to the door, with Sean shuffling behind. The Koreans from next door were yelling to beat the band in several languages. When I opened the exterior door, I knew why.

Kerry's sexy transportation had been rigged with a good old-fashioned stink bomb. Kerry himself rose from the mist like the Swamp Thing.

The Bar Wars had stooped to chemical warfare. Sean pulled the door closed and bolted it before his son reached the handle.

"Oh, no ya' don't," Sean shouted to Kerry through the small square window. Sean turned to me. "Go bring me four cans of tomato juice, darlin'."

Kerry pounded on the door and shouted four-letter words at the top of his lungs. I cradled the industrial-sized cans of juice in my arms.

"If you come in here," Sean screamed through the glass, "we'll never get the stink out. I'm going to crack the door and Vic will toss you some tomato juice." I nodded my readiness. "Then you go straight to the fire station on Seventy-seventh, douse yourself with the juice, and get them to hose you down."

The entire three-block-wide area must have heard Kerry's "Noooooooo." Sean pulled the door, and I threw the cans into the street. Sean bolted the door tight.

"Now you go on, boy, and I'll call the station." He turned and waved to the back wall. I followed because I just didn't have the energy to lead. Ever the company man, Sean used his own quarter to call the fire station on the pay phone at the back wall. By the time he took his usual place at the bar, the smoke had cleared.

The Koreans were hosing down the produce in much the same way Kerry himself was probably being watered by the firemen a few blocks away.

"My God," I muttered.

"God has very little to do with stink bombs, dearie," Sean commented from behind his paper. "He doesn't have time for childish pranks."

"Some prank."

"Childish."

"Juvenile, and dangerous."

"Just a stink bomb, darlin'."

"I'll bet it was planted by the owner of the Opossum."

"That would be the smart money. Now let me read my paper in peace."

Which I did for the rest of the morning and most of the afternoon. Kerry did not return, but Sean wandered outside and fed quarters into the meter at the Porsche every fifteen minutes, like clockwork.

Terrence and one of his carpenter friends arrived at ten past three. Once again, rather than take a table, they sat at the far end of the bar. I took heart in the fact that Terrence looked much less frazzled than he had the day before. Perhaps my little acting exercise wouldn't need to be exposed, after all.

"Two pints, here," Terrence called. I started the slow pour at the Guinness tap, rolling the dark brew down the sides of two pint glasses and setting them to stand before topping them off. "And some matches." I sailed two match-books across the polished bar surface to the men.

"Anything to eat, boys?" I asked when I delivered the pints. Terrence dug around in his pants pockets, and I re-membered that I ought to let him know that, as touching as the generosity of his cocaine tip on my first day, I'm just not that kind of girl.

And jail does not become me.

He counted the loose bills in his hand. "No, thanks, dar-lin'. Dennis and me are just passing through." He tossed a bill onto the rail to pay for the two pints. I rang the total and gave him back his change, all the while trying to for-mulate a smooth way to broach the subject of recreational pharmaceuticals and my non-use of such.

"Didja enjoy yourself Tuesday night?" he asked, as though reading the shallow half of my mind. "When we heard what happened to poor old Davey, I was thinkin' you might be needin' a little pick-me-up."

"Actually," I began with all the good intentions of the world, and then stopped. "How did you hear about Dave?"

You see, news does not travel in New York by conven-tional methods. In America, citizens discover who has passed away and how by reading the newspaper or by lis-tening to the radio. In Manhattan, we have *The New York Times* and Imus—neither of whom have the time or incli-nation to report any incident except that of profound na-tional or lurid interest.

If the building next door to mine burns to the ground, I have no way of finding out why unless the body count is over three, and then it will be buried on page 977. If my upstairs neighbor is hacked to death with a machete, there will be no publicity unless the body is then thrown onto the subway tracks *and* causes rush-hour transit delays.

Too much violence, too little ink.

"Patrick, the day man at the Blarney Rose, told us." Terrence held up his glass for another pint. "He was at the wake, don'tcha know."

"Ah." I poured another Guinness. Slowly, so as to or-ganize my thoughts and apologies at not being a drug abuser. "About that—" I started before being interrupted.

"Davey was a true friend," Terrence intoned.

Dennis nodded agreement. "I'm glad he didn't have to

live to hear of the trouble up north. Sure, it would have killed him.''

I took a flyer and assumed Dennis meant the explosion in the Bronx as opposed to Northern Ireland. Nothing ventured, no tip gained.

"Sad," I pronounced, wondering whether I should have gone for "tragic." I decided that would have been overkill. In theater, we like to say, Less is more.

Someday, if I ever learn, I will apply that good advice in my real life.

Customers trickled in and out. Wardrobe à la Frederick of Hollywood be damned, more than usual stayed too long and drank too much. Not one of the malingerers a documented "leg man." I stayed away from Terrence and Dennis as much as possible; carrying on a conversation made up entirely of subtext was exhausting. If I do say so myself, I was brilliant, though, and the men finally left looking as though I were the most sympathetic listener they had ever encountered. I pocketed my two-dollar tip and a box of good matches, and began to think I might have a future in the business.

But then two of our most popular draught beers ran out, and there were no backup kegs downstairs and I was getting a cramp from having to suck in my stomach nonstop. Were it not for my first rehearsal that night for a new show, I would have been totally demoralized.

"C.O.D.," the deliveryman shouted over the slamming door and the scream of the hand-truck wheels.

"I sign," I said, laying aside the *Old Mr. Boston's Deluxe Official Bartender's Guide,* copyright 1972. I'll tell you, the next time someone wants a sidecar, I'll be ready for them.

"C.O.D. means cash, honey," the deliveryman explained. "Nice shirt, by the way."

"Thanks. How much?" I did a quick calculation of the drawer total. About $220.

"Five hundred sixty-four and change. Man," he looked at his yellow sheet, "you guys are out of *everything*."

"Sean!" He slowly folded the *Times* and looked at me. "I need money for a delivery. Five hundred dollars."

"Call Shannon."

"She'll kill me."

"Well, darlin', life is all about risk, isn't it? You should have listened when you were warned." If I didn't like the old man so much, I would have sworn he was enjoying himself at my expense. "Shannon's the only one with access to the safe. You can wake her up, or get fired by Kerry." He shrugged. "Or you could quit and let me worry about this afternoon."

I dialed. I could afford to die; I couldn't afford to live without a job. Within ten minutes, the beer was stashed away in the cellar, the deliveryman paid, and Shannon was white with shock at my new bartending attire.

"Kerry is bringing me the matching shorts," I admitted.

Shannon buoyed me with her support. "It's appalling. I thought you had more pride than that, Victoria."

"I did," I protested, "until right before my tragic fall." I hate explaining, but I hate being thought of as a strumpet, even more. "You see, getting that show was the worst thing that could have happened right now. The rehearsal period is under a workshop contract—no money—and I need to work to pay my expenses for the next couple of weeks until we open. And, while I'm rehearsing, I won't be able to take the time to find another job. So."

"Truly Draconian," Shannon agreed. She twirled me around. "You know, the outfit might not be so bad in another color. Pink, perhaps." I pulled the fuchsia sample from my fanny pack. "Oh, dear. You must be desperate." I tried to look brave. "For God's sake, go home. Take a nap. Slather yourself with some self-tanning cream."

"I have to go to rehearsal."

"Suit yourself, but I would seriously consider the bronzer, if I were you."

THERE IS a special place in hell for the civil servant who designed the direction signs in the Times Square/Port Authority subway station.

I envision hell itself looking exactly like the Times Square/Port Authority subway station, only not quite so damned hot. Every time I find myself lost in the maze of tunnels and stairs—which is every time I get off the subway at Forty-second Street—I calm myself by imagining that same nameless bureaucrat circling for all eternity, searching hopelessly for a sign that reads "Exit" and really directs to one.

All right, so I finally found my way out onto the street at Forty-fourth and Eighth Avenue, a mere long block east and a short one south of where I was supposed to be. I sprinted through the pretheater crowds, past the gay porno houses and designer-watch vendors, and made it to the rehearsal only ten minutes late. That, naturally, made me the first to arrive.

I will obviously never learn that being punctual for any of the arts in New York is a dead giveaway for low self-esteem.

Rather than be pegged for a loser at the first rehearsal, I asserted myself by smoking a cigarette and flicking the ashes on the floor while I waited. Forty-five minutes later, the complete cast and crew were assembled.

The director, NYU Theater Department, Class of Yesterday, welcomed all twenty-two of us. If he had ordered a beer at my bar, I would have asked for a driver's license, and then wouldn't have dared serve him. Kristin, from the Opossum Bar, was cast, too. I heard her groan under her breath. I didn't groan, because I am a *professional* actor.

My eyes telegraphed my inner groan.

There was no script. Herr Direktor felt it would be more

"revelatory" if we, the actors, "played" with the basic concept and "developed" our characters before committing to "formulamatic interpretation" of the playwright's artistry. Yes, I had dived headfirst, without looking, into a National Endowment for the Arts project pool. NEA. More initials and no script.

The good news about working this kind of project is that rehearsals take either twenty minutes or eleven hours. Ours was the former. It *felt* like eleven hours, but we were sprung by nine-thirty. I would have quit on the spot, but Duchinski's words were still ringing in my ears: *Play fair.* Besides, if I quit the show, I wouldn't have any kind of real life at all.

Kristin gathered two of the more presentable of the cast and took my arm. "We're going for a beer, wanna come?"

I was too disheartened to mention that I had quit drinking, and so I followed like the sheep I had become.

Two blocks away was the local Irish joint, Blarney Rubble.

Cute.

It was decorated almost exactly like McAleer's except smaller, darker, dirtier, and cheaper. I liked it. There was not a theatergoer or tourist in the crowd. It looked like a stagehand and techie convention. Commercial sanitation workers slugged shots in preparation for a long night of hefting garbage. Kristin bought the first pitcher of Guinness. I tipped and carried the glasses to the red leather booth.

"So, what do you think?" I asked Kristin and her two friends. "Is it too early to contact our union rep?"

Kristin poured. "I have only two words to say about this show." She raised her glass in a salute. "Pro-zac." Glasses clinked all around.

After the second pitcher, I excused myself on the lame excuse that I had accumulated no more than ten hours sleep in the last three days and was beginning to "see things." I was advised that, should I "see" a script, I was to make copies for everyone.

On the way east to the IRT subway line, I realized that I was exactly halfway between the Forty-second Street and Fiftieth Street stations. Weary of adventure, I turned north on Eighth Avenue for the less exotic Fiftieth Street stop. The sidewalks were crowded, but without company I felt oddly alone. These moments of perceived isolation wash over all New Yorkers, and we all have our ways of dealing with it. My particular favorite role-playing diversion is "Undercover Decoy."

Undercover Decoy is for those times that my spine tingles and I start to lecture myself about free-floating paranoia. The healthy aspect of U.D. is the body language: head high, walk brisk, relaxed demeanor, eyes alert. It scares the hell out of muggers-in-training, and radiates a little confidence to the player as well. The only thing I *don't* like about the game is not being allowed to look behind me.

I realize that it's my game and my rules, but I am very conventional when it comes to pretend discipline. My character shoes ate up the distance from Forty-seventh to Fiftieth, past the tawdry Holiday Inn and the deserted school tarmac with its razor-wire enclosure. Buses flew by designated stops without slowing down, and I remembered why I never walked this trail at night: I was the only unaccompanied woman for as far as the eye could see.

There was a good reason for that. There aren't very many women dumb enough to try it. The area had enough kinetic hostility to make Stephen King's skin crawl.

I took a hard right on Fiftieth and crossed to the north side in the middle of the street. Undercover Decoy—woman did not deign to acknowledge the torrent of French profanity from the offended cabbie in front of whom I stepped. I did not turn around. It was a matter of honor. But I picked up my pace and speed-walked to the better lighting of Broadway, listening for sounds of pursuit. I was not enjoying the exercise.

At the first landing down the vast granite staircase, I silently pronounced myself the winner and jerked to a full stop. The small Asian businessman trying to squeeze past me nearly toppled to his death. I leaned against the polished stone and had myself a breather. Either I needed to get some sleep or I was going to have to seriously reconsider my cab boycott. The old nerves were shot.

By getting on the last car, I found a vacant seat. I should have known better than to congratulate myself on my good luck.

We crawled to the Fifty-ninth Street/Columbus Circle stop, where the approximate population of Sierra Leone boarded my car. At Sixty-sixth Street/Lincoln Center, every little old lady out of the home elbowed her way on. Masochist that I am, I stood to give up my seat, which was immediately filled by a Juvenile Detention wanna-be. Two passengers got off at Seventy-second Street, until the loudspeaker announced that express service was not operating and the entire platform slammed in. I was beginning to wonder how many would have to die so that I could exit at the next station, when the conductor announced that "Due to a police action, there is no service at the Seventy-ninth Street station. All passengers for Seventy-ninth Street should detrain at Eighty-sixth Street."

It's a good thing that feet cannot scream.

Mine wouldn't have been heard over the crowd, anyway. Getting up the stairs to get out from underground was like standing in an unemployment line, only slower. When I finally reached oxygenated air, I saw the problem. The Upper West Side was being held hostage by what is referred to as a pub crawl.

Listen closely, parents. A pub crawl is a formal rotating party of between fifty and a million marginally legal drinkers who descend on bar after bar. This one was a dinosaur.

Young bodies clogged the streets like cholesterol in a narrowed artery. My neighborhood looked like the bus and truck tour of *Leaving Las Vegas*.

Young men relieved themselves on anything vertical. Young ladies puked delicately down their Jennifer Aniston shirts. Frat brothers shoved one another in front of speeding traffic, and I had six blocks to bully my way through. All that saved me were my long legs and sour disposition.

I unlocked the door to my building and was closing it behind me when I heard shrill screams and shattering glass. Since the noise was behind me and the flying beer bottle missed, I just kept walking down the hall.

It's not that New Yorkers don't care. We just have limited energy.

I took the phone off the hook and took an exquisitely long bath—with bubbles. The next morning at the bar was someone else's problem. I had the whole day off until the next rehearsal, and I was going to spend it productively.

For Slasher and me, that would be asleep.

I set the alarm for five p.m. and dozed off somewhere in the middle of late-night *NYPD Blue* on A&E.

Visions of initials danced through my head, closely trailed by Buck Sawicki, cloaked in camouflage fatigues and whacking his way through the humid, concrete jungle.

Dead Dave floated behind.

SEVEN

ALL THE STREETLAMPS had been shot out, and the only light that wept onto the streets was from the sporadically lit upper apartment windows.

My high heels wobbled and snagged on discarded newspapers and, in the darkness, I fell, hands outward. But where there should have been concrete there was nothing, and I tumbled over and over into the cavernous hole of the Fiftieth Street entrance to the subway. And just when I thought I would splatter on the electrified rails, Margaret Thatcher screamed my name.

"Victoria! Victoria, I know you're in there, and I'm not leaving until you answer me." Bang. Bang. Bang. "Your job is at stake, here, Victoria!" BANG. BANG. A million pigeons launched skyward in panic, careening and trilling.

Slasher fell off the air conditioner. I opened an eye to see if he had broken a hip. He shook his head until his ears made flapping sounds, and he jumped back on the bed for some rest.

"Victoria!" BANG, BANG, BANG, BANG. The wall behind my pillow vibrated with the abuse to the door two rooms away. I squinted at the digital face of the alarm and tried to force myself into wakefulness.

If I was going to entertain Margaret Thatcher, I ought to be alert.

"Victoria, if you don't answer this door, I am going to rip off your face. I promise you nothing but pain—" *Oh.* "—and despair for as—" I was mistaken. "—long as you can remain upright and—" I unlatched the lock. "—able to chew real—" I opened the door. "—food."

"What time is it?" I asked. Coffee. I needed coffee.

"I don't know," Shannon answered. "Friday. After-noon." She followed me into the kitchen. "My, this apartment is dark. It would drive me completely bonkers to have to live without direct sunlight." Slasher wandered out to us to inspect the company and, while he was at it, his food dish. "What an adorable cat!"

"He's yours. Just let me get back to sleep."

"Were you sleeping? It's after noon."

I pushed my coffee cup under the hot drizzle from the machine, unable to wait for a full pot. "Why are you here, Shannon?" She found the overhead light switch and flipped it on.

"Egad. You look like forty miles of rough road."

"Why are you here, Shannon?" I repeated, replacing my mug with the coffee carafe.

"May I have a cup?" she asked.

"Yes. Why are you here, Shannon?"

"Thank you. Frankie's in the hospital."

I took three long draws on my coffee. "How terrible. Couldn't I lose sleep over this tomorrow night when I'm more rested?"

"Whenever you like. It's just that the bar back is going to have to work the door in Frankie's place, so you're going to have to pick up the bar back's shift, ten to close."

"Tonight? I can't. I have rehearsal downtown from six to ten." I poured her coffee. She got her own milk from the refrigerator. "What's a bar back?"

"Like Prince Harry to Prince William. A spare to do the mindless chores. Heavy lifting, you know, picking up the slack. I'll cover until you get back uptown, but you'll have to take a cab."

"I don't take cabs. Isn't there anyone else who can fill in?"

"No one who speaks English." Shannon rinsed out her cup. "See you at ten."

I just could not get a break. "Ish," I called to Shannon's back as she exited my building. "Ten-*ish*."

Rehearsal was a joke, albeit not a funny one. Our fearless director led us all in theater games for nearly four hours. That is about three and three-quarter hours more than I have ever spent getting in touch with my inner child. If God wanted people to regress willy-nilly, He would never have invented adulthood. I left my companion sufferers at the Blarney Rubble and flagged a cab going east on Forty-sixth. When I arrived at McAleer's, there wasn't a drop of blood left in my white knuckles.

Timmy, the regular night bartender and bouncer *du jour*, was checking IDs at the door, assembly-line fashion. His beautiful Turkish girlfriend, Nouris, sat beside him on a straight-backed chair, thinking serene thoughts. Timmy was shouting jokes to the crowd and being generally entertaining, mostly because that's just who he is. Personally, I lose my sense of humor in direct proportion to population density.

And I have seen anthills less crowded than McAleer's that night. I tried to squeeze my way through the logjam at the door. Timmy threw ice cubes from his drink at the patrons until they moved aside for me to enter. Not that I wanted to. Inside was such madness that even Benny, the cook, was helping to bus tables.

I bent double to crouch under the waitress station at the far end of the bar, the polished surface a choppy sea of dirty glasses, overflowing ashtrays, and slopped drinks. I started washing glasses. And washing glasses. And washing more glasses. And getting ice up from the basement, and cutting fruit, and collecting dirty glasses. Then I started washing the new dirty glasses. Don't tell anyone, but I was beginning to enjoy the mindlessness of the job.

The odd second I had to think about it, I weighed the possibility that one of the reasons I make myself so crazy is that I have so much idle time to worry about going crazy.

"PHWEEEEEEET." Every youthful head in the room came to attention. "PHWEEET. PHWEEET." Chairs scraped back from tables, barstools were pushed to the side or over. The crowd shifted like a giant worm, undulating to the door. Flashes of light reflected off the bottoms of up-ended pints. And then they were gone.

Poof. My ears were ringing. There was a low fog of cigarette smoke hanging in the air. Timmy danced Nouris back into the bar and sat by the door.

"RAID!" he impishly yelled into the air.

Shannon pulled the plug on the jukebox and started to bus the war-torn tables.

"What happened?" I asked.

"The pub crawl has bolted," Shannon answered. "If I'm not mistaken, three whistle blows means they're on their way to Bunnie's, God save them."

"ELVIS HAS LEFT THE BUILDING!" Timmy announced.

Sleeping Bobby walked in as though he had been notified by the tour guide, and sat at his assigned spot. Jack, the head bartender, swabbed the bar and put up a Budweiser. Timmy and Nouris waltzed in the silence.

"Is that it, then? Can I go home?" I asked.

"Nope. Shift goes to four." Jack handed me six sticky pitchers, which I dropped into the wash water. "The regulars will start dripping in now." And they did.

One by one and two by two familiar daytime faces took their usual spots at the bar, but the rush was definitely over. By 2:00 a.m. I had nothing left to do except smoke cigarettes and wish I had a script to study.

Shannon was doing payroll in the office and Nouris still had not learned English, so I sat and watched stray pedestrians pass by the window.

When I started to imagine lurking shadows on the corner of Eightieth Street, I drew myself a short beer and splashed my face with water. Sure enough, when I looked again, the lurker was no more—moved on to harass a more fertile imagination than mine, no doubt. Street traffic became slower. The only storefronts lit were the bars and the Korean groceries.

My apartment seemed to get farther and farther away.

At 3:00 a.m., Silva came in for a post-shift beer, and Sleeping Bobby awoke long enough to toss a dollar onto the rail and leave for a good night's sleep somewhere else. Shannon came up from the office and made herself a vodka martini. She pushed my cigarettes and matches over to make room for her drink.

"The Blarney Rubble?" she asked, turning over the matchbook. "What were you doing in that dump?"

"If you hadn't been in there yourself, you wouldn't know it's a dump." I looked at the matchbook, myself. I didn't remember picking them up, but matches are like viruses. You just get them, somehow.

Shannon sat at the bar. "Did your friend come back in?"

"I didn't see a friend all night," I answered. "All my friends are out of town for the summer."

"Well, this one isn't. He seemed like an out-of-towner, though, if that helps."

Even with the air-conditioning on low, I felt a chill.

"Did he leave a name?"

"No. He was very attractive, though. Lots of rough edges. I like that." Shannon smiled into her martini. "Rather reminded me of Clint Eastwood."

My mouth went dry.

"In which movie?"

She drained her glass and grinned. "All of them."

I decided to find Silva and ask him to walk me home again. I didn't care that he would think I was a wuss. I was comfortable with being a wuss. Hell, I could learn to be proud to be a wuss.

Scratch that plan. Silva was gone, and I would have to walk my own wussy butt home at 4:00 a.m. As I gazed into

the recesses of West Eightieth, my view was obscured by
the haphazard parking of some dweeb in a Jersey rental car.

"Cheese it!" Timmy called. "The folks are home!"

"At last," Shannon said, pulling a bank bag out from
behind the bar. Kerry slammed the door of his rental and
walked in.

"Hold your horses, Shannon," he ordered. "It's not clos-
ing time yet. McAleer's doesn't close until the last gasp."
He turned and stuck his head out the door, looking south.
"Is Beau here yet?" We all shook our heads. "Well, shit."
Kerry double-timed his way through the room, shouting to
Timmy, "Hold that door."

The alternating doors to the kitchen waved at one another
as Kerry flew through and back, dragging three enormous
black trash bags. They were heavy enough that Kerry was
huffing and puffing them out the door. I saw him crane his
neck left once again and dart with his baggage across the
street.

He dropped his load at the curb in front of the small
Italian takeout restaurant we faced, and then squirreled himself away in the same dark corner I thought had hidden my
mystery man earlier. The black plastic stood in stark contrast
to the resident restaurant's brown bags.

A low growl grew in intensity as it approached from the
south. I could see high-set headlights as a monstrous yellow
garbage truck wheezed to a stop across the street. Two
heavily muscled workers in navy coveralls jumped from the
back of the machine and carefully plucked the brown bags
from the black and threw them into the carnivorous grinders
at the back of the garbage truck. The men grabbed hold of
the side rails, and the Mack pulled slowly away.

Kerry paused for a moment at the edge of the light from
Amsterdam, and then launched himself into the trash bags
left behind. Crouched low, he grasped the twist-tied ends
and heaved the bags athletically into the truck's maw. His
burden disposed of, he bent low for a deep cleansing breath.

Powerful gears ground metal on metal. The truck bumped into reverse. Kerry bounced backward, his body making an amplified "whoomp" sound as he careened through the air.

"Jesus, Mary, and Joseph!" Timmy swore, flinging Nouris to the side and throwing himself outside the door. The truck rolled forward, just missing the hapless Kerry. Shannon dashed to the phone and punched 9-1-1.

I watched from the window as two homeless men stood over Kerry's motionless body, his cheek pressed against a discarded pint of Four Roses in the oily gutter puddle.

Timmy dabbed blood from Kerry's mouth and cursed the truck's rapidly disappearing taillights.

EIGHT

LOW SOBS and fierce ranting played on as background noise. Women rung their hands as men paced and snarled. White-jacketed professionals wandered through the chaos as though self-medicated themselves: blind, deaf, busy. I was reminded of the street scenes in the movie *Soylent Green,* except this was inside the emergency room of St. Simeon Hospital.

Timmy and Shannon argued with the paramedics to take Kerry to any other hospital until the moment the ambulance pulled away, but St. Simeon's is the designated trauma center for the Upper West Side, and no one could argue that Kerry was not traumatized by his run-in with the garbage truck.

I was not aware of what a trauma center in New York means, so I (masochistically) talked my way into a ride for the trip north.

Kerry was wheeled directly into a corner of the corridor, barely delineated from the other examination areas by a heavy fabric curtain. Other patients slept or cried and grew older on pillowless gurneys parked end to end along the walkways.

Police were everywhere. Uniforms and plainclothes paraded in and around the writhing injured and frantic relatives. I watched two patients get treated for superficial gunshot wounds, still wearing handcuffs, seated on plastic contour chairs set in the hall. Meanwhile, junkies were wrestled to the littered floor, veins protruding, their banshee screams drilling the din. I sat cross-legged on the yellow tiles for two hours, unable to get the attention of a doctor or nurse. For all I knew, Kerry McAleer was dead.

Duchinski located me in bedlam within half an hour of my call to him. Both my knees cracked loudly as he helped me to my feet.

"Kerry's all right," Dan assured me. He flicked a plastic straw off my bottom. "Let's get you home."

I didn't ask him how he got a progress report so easily. I'd seen the gold shield in action before.

"How is he?" I asked.

"Banged up pretty good, but he'll live." He opened the door of his red Toyota for me to get in. "Broken leg, no internal injuries. Lucky guy."

"I wouldn't put it that way."

"Buckle up," Dan instructed, before he put the car in gear.

The streets were speckled with early-morning sunlight. The traffic on Broadway headed south was light. On every block, Asian men were washing the sidewalks in front of vegetable displays and setting out bushel buckets of brightly colored fresh flowers.

Joggers loped easily east, toward Central Park. Dog walkers congregated to chat, and black nannies pushed white babies in state-of-the-art strollers.

My Rumanian super, Carlotta, was sitting on the stoop directly facing a vacant curb space, as though guarding the empty parking space just for us. She waved Dan into the slot although he didn't need any civilian assistance, and looked at me out of the side of her eyes.

"Chu haf guten?" she asked.

"Yes, I had a really good one," I answered. I had no idea how I could explain what had happened in that spurious fifth-world language she spoke—a combination of English, Rumanian, Spanish, Yiddish, and Anglo Saxon. Not necessarily in that order.

Dan applied The Club to his steering wheel, engaged the Chapman Lock, turned on the alarm, and made sure both doors were secure before joining me on the stairs. From where she sat on the cement steps as we passed, Carlotta patted the gun Dan carried strapped to his ankle. She likes the world properly spinning on its crooked axis.

"Gut," she commented. "Chu seeta min wus feryu lasni?" she called after us, as we walked down the hall. She had left the exterior door hooked open as she often did so that she didn't have to buzz in the dozens of deliveries and workmen that rang every day. That was undoubtedly how Shannon had trapped me like a rat earlier.

"Uh-huh," I answered in the affirmative.

"What did she say?" Dan asked when we were inside the apartment.

His resonant voice roused Slasher from whatever nap he happened to be enjoying. The cat ran into the living room with a green foam ball popping out of his mouth, and hopped exuberantly around Dan's feet.

"I don't know," I answered, plucking the wet ball from Slasher's mouth and tossing it into the bedroom. The cat tore through the living room as though shot from a cannon. "I can't translate *everything* Carlotta says."

"Well," Dan said, "that's a relief. I was beginning to think you're a witch. GOOD boy!" Dan plucked the ball from his feet where Slasher had dropped it, and pitched it back into the bedroom.

"How about some breakfast?" I offered. Slasher scrambled over my sneakers to get back into position with his play-pal. Dan launched the ball. "I think I have food somewhere in the refrigerator."

I'll admit it, I didn't want to be alone just yet, and was even willing to cook to have a human in the house for a little while longer.

"I have to get to work. It must be nearly eight." Slasher dropped the ball on the coffee table to make sure Dan didn't miss it.

"Oh, damn." I looked at my watch. "I have the day off,

but I still have a rehearsal tonight.'' Slasher patted the ball impatiently. It rolled to the Oriental carpet.

"I thought you quit," Dan scowled.

"I can't afford to quit."

Dan swept the cat up in his thick arm and flipped him on his back. As he reasoned with me, he gently scratched Slasher's chin.

"Vic, bartending is a nasty business. You have to deal with a lot of different people, in a lot of different states of inebriation. You are responsible for the cash register and the safety of your customers."

"I know that."

He tried reasoning with me. You'd think he'd know better.

"You are wide-open for prosecution if you overserve someone." He was losing patience with me, which was okay, because he was lecturing me, and that always makes me testy. "Not to mention that any crackhead in New York can just walk in and blow you seven ways to Sunday for whatever he can steal."

Actually, I hadn't thought about that. It was a tough argument to deflect, even with a baseball bat. So I skirted it.

"Okay."

"Vic, you're doing it again."

"What?"

"Faking it. You're pretending you know what you're doing so you're unable to see that you're in the middle of an unnatural situation at that bar. In one week, you've got a dead guy, a riot, an incendiary device, and a hit and run. This is not *normal,* Vic. This is not a place for a nice girl to be hanging out."

"I am not hanging out; I'm working. And a stink bomb is not an incendiary device."

"Technically, it is." Dan heaved a monumental sigh. "What difference does it make? You're in the middle of friggin' Irish hell there."

"And what would you know about Irish hell, Duchinski?"

"I am Betty Ryan's darlin' baby boy, if you must know."

"You're kidding." The things you find out when you least expect it. "Well, then I ought to be damned safe."

"Damn it!" Slasher opened an eye and gave Dan a suspicious look. At least the cat could make him settle down. He lowered his voice. "Damn it. It wouldn't hurt to look around for something else, would it?"

"I'll look around," I promised.

He snorted. "Whenever you look around, you just end up in more trouble." *Ouch.* "Give your notice, and I'll see if I can't come up with a lead on a temp job for you. There are a lot of jobs you can do, Vic."

I didn't argue. Why should we both have to face the ugly truth of how impeccably underqualified I am?

"Okay," he said, and handed me the cat, who was already dozing off. "I'm on a really murderous schedule for the next couple of weeks. As a matter of fact, I'll probably be out of town entirely, off and on. You keep your nose clean, and I'll call as soon as things start sorting out."

"Okay."

"Really, Vic. I've got my hands full. I don't want to have to be worrying about you, too."

"Really, Dan, okay."

He kissed Slasher on the head, and then me on the head. I was feeling somewhat patronized, and sloppy seconds after a cat, to boot.

Without eating, I crawled under the covers fully intending to do precisely as I pleased. Or at least what I had to do.

Starting with some shut-eye. I ignored Slasher dropping his ball over and over onto my head on the pillow. I was asleep by the fifth plunk.

"MERLLLLLLLLLLLLLLLLLLLLLLLLLLLL."

Slasher had his face pushed into mine. His whiskers tickled like the very devil. I pushed him away saying something hostile when I heard the dulcet tones of my answering machine picking up.

"BELEEEEEP. Vic, this is Barry. I just wanted to let you know—"

"Hi, Barry. I'm here." I squinted at the alarm clock— 9:00 a.m. on the dot. No wonder there were irreconcilable differences.

"Hi, Vic. I just wanted to let you know that I consulted with a few other attorneys who specialize in organized crime and they have assured me that McAleer's is not a Westies bar."

"I knew that."

"You did not, Vic."

"All right. I did not when those guys showed up the other day for the jukebox, but I certainly did know when you woke me up from the first dreamless sleep I've had since, uh, since—"

"That does not, however, negate the potential dangers of this new career of yours. Do you have any idea how many bartenders are sued for damages brought by patrons every month in the city of New York?"

"Thrill me, Barry."

"A lot. A very large number of litigations."

"Huge numbers."

"MERLLLLLLLLL."

"Yes. Is that Slasher?"

"No. It's Sean Connery."

"He sounds hungry. Haven't you given him his breakfast, yet?"

"Mr. Connery is taking me out for breakfast. Listen, Barry, I'd love to chat, but if I don't get some shut-eye before rehearsal tonight, I am going to die. So, good-bye."

"You got a show? Well, congratulations, Vic. I knew you would. Well, this is very good news. Why don't I take you to lunch tomorrow, and you can tell me all about it."

"I work tomorrow, Barry. Drop by, I'll buy you a beer and tell you all about it."

"You didn't quit? Vic, are you doing this to punish me? It just doesn't look good for my wife to—"

I hung up, buried the receiver in a drawer so I wouldn't hear the noxious bleep, bleep, bleep of the off-the-hook warning, and went back to sleep.

I should have stayed in bed until the next day.

Rehearsal consisted of the stage manager informing us that the director was in vital meetings with the invisible playwright and that the show would open in six weeks instead of the eight that had been planned. I spent forty minutes on the subway to be sent home without so much as a script.

I was beginning to feel the stirrings of an attack of artistic temperament. Rather than submit, Kristin and I stormed to the Blarney Rubble to drown our sorrows.

For an early Monday evening, the joint was jumping. We found a cramped space at the bar in the midst of a veritable sea of men.

Discussions were loud, conducted over the noise of the wall-mounted television tuned to CNN, which was featuring an in-depth report on the explosion that took place in the Bronx on my first day at McAleer's.

I am ashamed to admit that I hadn't given the disaster a second thought other than to give Terrence his money's worth of listening. Five adults and three children had been seriously hurt, one man critically. The noise level diminished somewhat in the crowded bar, making the angry debate at the table behind us more intrusive.

I tried to focus on the television report so that I could more intelligently humor my own customers later, but my brain was somewhere on vacation in Puerta Vallarta while my body zoned out on CNN. I let Kristin order our drinks from the harried barman.

She wasn't having any success. We were the only two

women in the dive, and we couldn't even pay to get arrested. I stepped away from the bar to allow her a full frontal assault, and to enjoy some recreational eavesdropping.

Of course, to eavesdrop successfully, it helps to be small and unobtrusive—the tall and intrusive (that would be me) tend to get sucked into the middle of drunken blustering.

"Didja lose someone in the blast, colleen?" one of the men at the table asked in a barely discernible brogue. Translation: Colleen in an Irish bar may be roughly translated from the New Yorkese, Yo! Red! The man was talking to me. I knew better, but I turned my good ear slightly in his direction.

I will never learn that being addressed does not automatically confer the responsibility of answering.

"No. Did you?" I continued to watch the television report. I *had* learned not to make eye contact.

"Me father." That caught my attention. "Me father was murdered."

"Murdered? I don't understand." Kristin tugged on the strap of my fanny pack. The man was nudged by one of his companions and told to shut up. But the dam was opened.

"This is not the free country we're told it is, colleen." He shook off his friend's restraining hand. "The Orangemen are here. They're everywhere."

Kristin gave my strap a good yank.

"We're outta here." She pulled me through the crowd and out onto the sidewalk. "Damned IRA wanna-bes. A woman can't get a drink to save her soul when the bunch of them start wallowing in their precious conspiracy theories. Let's go to the Opossum. No one there has anything on their minds."

In the relative quiet of the subway, I asked for clarification. The man in the bar may have been drunk out of his mind, but he'd lost his father. Kristin's sympathy, however, was played out. Or never existed, as it did not for poor old Dave.

"I heard it all the other night," she said. "People get killed in an accident, and it has to be murder. Stuff doesn't just happen, it has to happen for a reason. Blah, blah, blah. Men just love their plots."

"Where were the women?"

"Women scheme, men plot. It's all so borrrring." She dragged out the word. "This is America, for chrissakes, why can't they leave their stupid war in Ireland where everyone pretends to understand it? Paddy there is convinced the American government is out blowing up stockpiles of Sinn Fein armaments in the Bronx, for chrissakes. Like the CIA and the FBI don't have anything better to do with their time." She shook her head irritably.

A synapse fired in my weary brain.

"ATF."

"All right, Waco, yeah. I've had a bellyful of that, too. This"—she gestured widely as we pulled into the Seventy-ninth Street station—"ain't Texas. And it ain't Belfast, either."

We wove ourselves seamlessly into the heavy pedestrian traffic heading from the subway to Amsterdam, and then south to the Opossum.

The bouncer at the door was a fine example of his species. Six-foot-six, if he was an inch, wearing a Penn State football T-shirt, with three pretty, young women hanging on his every monosyllabic word. He recognized Kristin and bullied a way through the entrance for us.

The air-conditioning was cranked up to the same level as the music being blasted from the deejay's eighty-million-dollar audio system.

Kristin handed me my free drink, which, unless I miss my guess—and in the dark I might well have—was a Woo-woo. Kristin raised her glass and swallowed the chilled shot in one gulp.

Rather than match her, I decided to wait for the chemical analysis. It was exhausting for this old thirty-ninish lady even to try to follow Kris through the packed house. I risked getting a serious vocal node and screamed into her ear.

"I'm gonna go home and sleep!"

"WHAT?"

I mimed an escape and nap. Kristin nodded, then pulled a young, skinny man out of the crowd and into my face. She put her mouth directly to my ear and shouted.

"Vic, this is Ira, the owner! He wanted to meet you!"

I looked down at Ira. He was at least three inches shorter than I. He wore an "Opossum Bar—Hangin'" logo T-shirt. We shook hands. *This* was the bane of McAleer's? Kerry could have squashed Ira like a bug.

Of course, that wouldn't be an intricate plot. I think I was beginning to understand the ground rules. They didn't make any *sense,* but I knew there were rules.

It was way past time to go home.

I looked apologetic and suitably pleased to meet the infamous Ira the Terrible, then pushed and wriggled my way out the door. I sidestepped Marky, the Opossum Bar beggar, and headed north.

At the deserted playground, a movement in the darkness caught my eye. I was trapped again in the big-city conundrum: for safety's sake, look; or for safety's sake, don't look. Personally, I'd rather know what specific bear is lurking around a corner all ready to eat silly me.

Two men drew back farther into the shadows of a jungle gym, without comment. Danger averted, I crossed the avenue before I reached the Walk signal, periodically looking behind me. No one had exited the playground, but I couldn't shake the feeling of being followed. I even ridiculed myself, singsonging, "CIA, FBI, am I scared, no not I."

Fellow pedestrians started giving me a wide berth, proving that there is an upside to mental instability. I don't care what your crazy aunt Edith told you.

As I closed my apartment door behind me, I twitched off an earthquake shudder.

"Whew, Slasher. Someone just walked over my grave."

Slasher dropped a pink foam ball at my feet. I was not in the mood, so I picked it up and dropped it back into the drawer where I kept the cat's toys.

"Where are you finding those damned balls?" I asked.

"MEWRLLLLLLL."

Not that Slasher could answer me, but I was once again asking the wrong question.

NINE

SLASHER could not sleep. And when Slasher cannot sleep, no one is allowed to sleep.

He paced up and down the bed, taking shortcuts across my face. I heard the thud of his paws hit the floor and felt the whump as he jumped back to the bed. He chewed his food noisily, and scratched furiously in his litter box. His energetic pawing at the drawer that held his precious balls was intense and profoundly annoying.

When you think your cat is out to get you, it might be a good idea to consider the possibility that you're getting a wee bit paranoid.

My close friends were all out of town and, even though I was out in society more than usual, I hadn't had a real conversation since my return to the city. The alarm clock read 2:11 a.m., and I was lonely.

And the city never sleeps. I pulled what passed for an outfit out of the still-packed luggage on the bedroom floor, fluffed my hair, and ventured back out into the night.

Shannon was posted at the door of the bar, an attractive younger man Velcroed to her side. The crowd inside had thinned to manageable proportions.

"What are you doing?" I asked her.

"Frankie didn't show, and you didn't answer your phone or door, so I got stuck. Your super, what's-her-name, said she hadn't seen you." She paused. "I think. Anyway, you weren't home."

There is a psychological term known as "the ah-ha phenomenon." It is a conscious state wherein a person suddenly enjoys the light dawning.

I had one of those.

"Did Carlotta let you into my apartment to see if I was hiding from you?" I asked.

"No," Shannon answered. The young man gazed worshipfully at her. If I had any sensitivity at all, I would have given them their dubious privacy. "Would she have let me in if I'd asked?"

"Probably. She is under the impression that you're my sister." The difference in our accents was, at best, a moot point to Carlotta, who did not realize that she, herself, was somewhat English-challenged.

"Cool," Shannon purred, her attention focused on her new swain. Figuring I wouldn't be missed, I went inside and sat at the end of the bar nearest the door. The clean-cut gent to my right signaled to Timmy, who was telling a joke at the other end.

"May I buy you a drink?" he asked. I surveyed the situation. He was tall enough to waltz with. Okay. Boyish smile, very sincere. *Suspicious to me but, hey, I'm paranoid.* Nice suit slightly mussed, iridescent white shirt and conservative tie. *So he wasn't a Perma-Prest lawyer.* Nearly a decade younger than I. *It was dark; maybe he wouldn't notice.* Very good-looking, really. *I'm entitled.* FBI lapel pin. *Ah-ha!*

Rationality ultimately surfaced in my weary brain. So the man was a Fed. There wasn't an Irish bar in the city that wasn't up to its kegs in law enforcement.

"Thank you." I offered my hand. "I'm Vic."

"Quill. Quillen Foster."

Timmy slid impressively to us carrying a bourbon on the rocks for me. He flipped a coaster onto the bar.

"On the gentleman, Vic. Cheers, and don't fall for the handcuff trick." Timmy stirred my drink with his index finger and flicked the residue into my face before dashing off to amuse the hell out of his other customers. I took a sip.

"Cheers," I said. "Do you ever get the feeling that people are watching you?"

"That's my job," Quillen teased.

"I noticed." I glanced down at his lapel.

"I noticed you noticing. That's *also* a part of my job. Though," he leaned closer, "I would think you'd be used to men watching your every move."

Two could play this game. "Do I look suspicious to you, Agent Foster?"

"Very."

"Ah, that's my problem, then. I *look* suspicious. I *look* Irish. I *look* like a woman who is constantly getting herself in trouble." I stopped and took another sip of my drink. I was coming dangerously close to whining, and I knew it. "Well, I just might surprise everyone someday."

"That's not what they told us at the Academy." Quillen sat back to watch my reaction. I was too stubborn to give him what he wanted, so he went on. "If it looks like a quack, and spouts like a quack, it's usually a quack." He tapped his neatly shorn temple. "Trust your instincts."

"I wouldn't dare," I countered. "I have way too many of them for my own good."

"That's what I was hoping to hear." He was so obvious that it was almost charming. "You want to get out of here?" Oops. I sat back and lit a cigarette, blowing the smoke in the direction of the man who was blowing his own kind of smoke. He picked up on the mistake and regrouped. "Sorry. I meant someplace quieter." I crooked my eyebrow. "Sorry. You got me. Can we start again, or should I just go away?"

I considered my conversational options. "Stay. Sweet-talk me about keeping America safe from the Red Menace."

"Which red menace? Shannon or you?" Quillen waved to Timmy for another round. "You'll have to forgive me. I'm just getting to know this territory. I usually unwind in my own neighborhood. Upper East Side," he explained.

"So what brings you to the Hudson River side? An investigation or a sense of adventure?"

"I really can't talk about it."

Ah-ha.

"Oh." I ran my fingers up through the back of my hair and shook it out. Quillen Foster might take some work. "I understand. National security, right?"

"Well, I wouldn't go that far, but we're in the middle of digging around, and I wouldn't want to compromise the investigation. Did you say you were Irish?"

"No, Quill, I said that I *look* Irish. I suppose that's part of the reason that I was hired here. Don't tell anyone, but I'm probably the only redhead in America without a drop of Irish blood."

"You work here?"

"Uh-huh." I nodded. "Afternoon bartender."

"How long?"

"A couple of days." A little ping of uneasiness settled into my mind. Even if I were the hottest ticket on the East Coast, no man should have shown such intense interest in my stopgap job, but Quillen Foster was. Frankly, he was disappointingly transparent up to that point.

"So you replaced that bartender who died. I heard something about that. What was his name? Dave, wasn't it?"

"Uh-huh." Hmmmm. "I was here when his body was discovered." I stuck my toe in the water and punted. "Heart attack."

"Really?"

"Uh-huh."

"Really. *I* heard something about an overdose."

I met his eyes for a deep look. He softened his expression, but did not flinch.

I've been a woman for too many years to fall for the old innocent question routine.

"Oh, that's right. I forgot." *Forgot?* Just as I felt I was getting somewhere, I had to go and shoot myself in the foot with a completely inane comment like that. "You see," I backpedaled, "the paramedics had resuscitated Dave, and on the way to the ambulance he had his heart attack. So I guess you could say it's just semantics.''

''Hmmm.'' He looked at his wristwatch. ''Damn. I didn't realize it was that late.'' *Damn, I blew it.* ''But it was great meeting you, Vic. Do you think it would be possible for the two of us to have dinner some time? Somewhere with tablecloths?''

''That would be lovely,'' I answered, handing him a McAleer's matchbook. ''Give me a call here during the day.''

''You bet. I look forward to seeing you, then.''

''Me, too.''

Timmy dumped a handful of ice in my nearly warm bourbon, and cleared Quill's beer glass. I mixed the drink with my finger, thinking. Trusting my instincts, which were jumping up and down and doing a tap dance.

That particular FBI agent was not in McAleer's accidentally. Everyone at the bar avoided talking about the late Dave almost religiously, but somehow Quillen still had an awful lot of information about the circumstances surrounding Dave's death. I couldn't remember if the FBI was responsible for stopping drug smuggling, but I didn't think so. I seemed to remember that it was a different set of initials. D something. Drug something.

Damn, I wished I could call Duchinski with a clear conscience. But I couldn't.

There was a sort of relief in the thought that all the bizarre business of the past few days might point directly back to a man I had never met in life: Dave, the cokehead.

I wasn't paranoid, I was just misunderstood.

A huge weight had been lifted from my shoulders, just in time to get a few long-overdue hours of untormented sleep. I dropped my cigarette into the remains of the bourbon and ran to make the Walk signal to cross the street.

I really enjoy petty intrigue when it has nothing to do

with me, personally. That's the trouble with relief: it makes you let down your guard.

The streetlamp in the middle of my block was dark, but there were several stragglers making their way in my direction on the opposite sidewalk.

Four in the morning is a strangely reassuring time to be walking the neighborhood. The bars are just closing and dumping witnesses in twos and threes along every route. Their voices carried from every direction on the soft night wind.

As I approached, I could just make out two men ahead of me. They were stopped directly in front of my building. I slowed down to wait for them either to enter or move along. When they didn't budge, I feigned going into the building next door to my own.

If I had to wait them out, I wanted to do it out of sight. As with most precautions, it was inconvenient as hell.

Just as I reached for the lobby door, I caught a swift movement out of the corner of my eye. I jerked to my left to see the larger of the men violently grab the smaller by the throat and slam him against the wrought-iron fencing that ran the length of several buildings.

There was nowhere to go. The restaurants and bars were all sealed tight, and the nearest pay phone was lit like an evangelist's podium at the end of the street. I had cornered myself.

The little man clawed at his attacker and gurgled low in his collapsing throat. No lights flicked on in the surrounding apartments. No early-morning wanderers turned the corner onto my block. There was only one course of action for me to take if I wanted to live on to testify another day. I ran into the middle of Eightieth Street.

"FIRE!"

The assailant dropped his victim, who scrabbled away

like a frightened crab, and stared directly into my eyes, warning me back.

I stood frozen in the half-light.

The assailant was Buck Sawicki.

TEN

LIGHTS SNAPPED ON in apartment windows like falling dominoes—click, click, click, click.

Sawicki was backlit from the window behind him. I could clearly make out the outline of his shaved skull. The muscle in his jaw ground rhythmically as he stared back at me. I stood stock still. The cars along the curb were parked fender to tailpipe. To get to me, Buck would have to leap the width of a Buick or race around from where the fire hydrants hunkered free of parked cars.

Heads poked out from windows on both sides of the street. Buck Sawicki squared his shoulders and calmly walked away. Neighbors shouted to one another until they were convinced there was no fire on West Eightieth Street. I couldn't make out a word over the sound of my pounding heart and chattering teeth.

New York, New York, one hell of a town.

I hoisted my butt on the hood of the 1982 Chevy parked by the honey locust tree planted directly in front of my stoop. I felt the body metal give beneath me as I swung my legs over to the sidewalk and down. My trick knee buckled at first, then took my weight. I dragged myself up the cement stairs and into the tenement.

Carlotta had forgotten to close the security door again. The fluorescent halo light in the hall flickered, dangerously near death, but my eyes were already adjusted to the darkness, and, with a minimum of shaking, I got my key into the Medico Lock on the chocolate brown apartment door.

I turned on the living-room ceiling fan and light before entering. Slasher snored contentedly from where he lay sprawled on the sofa. He cradled one of his beloved foam balls between his front paws. Within a foot of the door, I groped around to my left and threw on the dining-room overhead. Only then did I close and double-lock my escape door behind me.

A creeping inspection of the kitchen, bathroom, and bedroom revealed no serial killers, but I left every lamp lit nonetheless. Slasher did not so much as open an eye. Superstitiously, I put my hand to his chest to check for respiration.

He was fine, unlike his owner.

The light on my answering machine blipped, oblivious to the world. Four messages. I lit a cigarette and punched the "play" button.

"BLEEP."

"Vic, this is Barry. I talked with a friend of mine who could use some domestic help, part-time. You know, some light housekeeping, running errands, laundry, that kind of stuff. I thought you'd be perfect. Call back, and I'll give you her name."

"BLEEP."

Oh, sure. Let her pick out your ties by herself, asshole.

"BLEEP.   Hmmmmmmmmmmmmmmmmmmmmmmmmm. BLEEP."

One hang-up.

"BLEEP. Vic, this is Dan, calling about"—a pause— "2:30 a.m.,"—another pause—"and I just thought I'd let you know that I called Buck Sawicki's probation officer in Portland, and she assured me that she saw Buck just this morning. So"—yet another pause—"you can stop thinking that he's following you or, uh, whatever it is that you're thinking.

"And," his voice rushed on, "there is a temporary file-clerk position open at the two-five precinct. Call the desk sergeant, Dick, for particulars because I'm going to be, uh, out of town for a few days. Call Dick, okay? I'll check back with you as soon as I can. Bye."

"BLEEP."

Liar, liar, pants on fire. "Bad timing, Duchinski," I said *aloud.*

"BLEEP.   Hmmmmmmmmmmmmmmmmmmmmmmmm. BLEEP."

Hang-up number two.

Before curling myself up on the sofa next to the cat to mull over the bizarre events of the evening, I gently pulled the yellow foam ball from beneath Slasher's chin. If the toys weren't sealed back in their plastic wrapping, they turned to powder within a few days. As quietly as I could, I pulled open the toy drawer in the sideboard beneath the television set.

Slasher flew from the couch, stood on his hind legs, and patted around for another ball at the bottom of the drawer.

"No, Slasher," I said, plopping his front paws back on the carpet and sliding the drawer back. His paws were fishing around again before it was completely closed. "No!" I repeated. "Do you know what time it is?" I asked, as if he would answer, and lifted him away again. As I turned away, he wrapped his front paws around the drawer knob and looked at me pathetically.

That cat is indefatigable. I watched him pull and paw for several minutes. He did not have the leverage to actually disengage the wood from the front piece, but he gave it a good college try.

"Sorry, you old fart," I told him. "You're just not man enough for," *ah-ha,* "the job." I pulled the small drawer completely out of its slot and placed it on the carpet. Slasher stuck his face in the miscellany, and came out with his pink prize, smacked it across the room, and chased after it.

Carefully, I turned the drawer upside down. Catnip mice, foam balls, and widgets scattered the floor.

It's amazing what can grow indoors when one doesn't dust properly. My apartment had cultivated electronics.

The device affixed to the drawer bottom was no more

than an inch-and-a-half square and a quarter-inch thick. Tiny wires looped from one side, but there was no connection to any external power source.

Visions of letter bombs danced in my head.

But that was illogical. First, mad bombers had better targets than unemployed actors. Second, this unit was, at best, a detonation device, and it wasn't attached to any explosive unit. Third, obviously I was not supposed to find the thing or handle it, so—fourth, it must be some kind of surveillance toy.

I slid the drawer carefully back into place, automatically dropping Slasher's balls back where they belonged.

Slasher had been reclaiming his balls every time someone came into the apartment to set or check on his equipment. My eyes flew to the Medico Lock above the standard issue on my front door. Knees cracking again, I dug out the old dead bolt from when Barry and I were married and set to reinstalling it.

Every woman in New York City knows how to change a lock.

Or should, given the betrayal rate of New York City men.

ELEVEN

OKAY. "They" were out to get me. Whoever they were, they had been in my home and, probably, in my bar. Dan was right. There was nothing normal about what was happening, and I was sick of it happening exclusively on my turf.

If anything happened to me, let it be in "their" walk-in.

Sawicki was the loose cannon. That would make me the fodder.

Welcome back to New York, Vic, the home of "trust no one."

Yeah, but I still *care,* dammit.

I stewed. Just when I thought I was almost out of options, I found yet another way to endanger my miserable life.

It had been a while since I had gussied myself up and gone hunting the enemy, so the sporting equipment in my crammed closet looked entirely foreign to me.

Several times I wondered what kind of malicious alien life-form had invaded my body and purchased items such as three-inch, red, sling-back dancing shoes or a self-adhesive brassiere alternative. The leopard-skin Lycra ensembles that would have given my mother fainting spells were traceable to my ill-fated attempts at putting together a cabaret act. They were very snazzy, but, objectively, if worn in real life, could give a girl a reputation for running a cheap escort agency. I tossed those to the back of the closet.

Ultimately, I walked out the door in a fitted white summer suit and the notorious crippling white heels. Every so often I forgot I was supposed to be young and breezy, and tugged at the irrationally short hem of the skirt.

Needless to say, I stuck out at the Blarney Rubble like a

pimple on Cindy Crawford's nose. Success. The outfit was one-half of my brilliant plan to be conspicuous.

The other half walked in the door shortly after I got myself seated at a relatively clean table. Shannon saw me the moment she entered, but walked the extra mile to stand squarely in the door and disbelieve everything from the decor to the beer selection.

She tossed her miniaturized gold-mesh fashion purse onto the faux-wood-grain table and glared at me.

"You," she pronounced carefully, "owe me—at the very *least*—one full lunch, not prix fixe, at Café des Artistes."

"Sit down, Shannon, and I'll explain everything," I whispered. I don't need to tell you that the entire bar was gaping. She stood her ground and gave the room another once-over.

"And cocktail hour at Bemelman's. What is this obsession you've developed about things Irish?"

"Done." Shannon sat, scrunching her coiffure with both hands and tossing the redo back. "I needed some bait," I explained.

"Yes, well, that would be me, but Victoria, do we have to *trawl?*"

"I'm fishing for something specific. This is where the big fish are," I explained. The bartender dropped two martinis at our table. "Thank you," I said, and handed him a ten and a five.

Shannon inspected the men in the bar over the rim of her martini glass. "Can you fake an Irish accent?" I asked.

"Aren't there enough in the room?" she asked back. "This martini is putrid," she announced. "You drink it. I'm going to order a margarita."

"Look at me, Shannon. I'm begging. Can you fake it?"

"Yes, yes, yes, I can do a very proper Irish accent, and I prefer 'faux.' Father wasn't nearly the purebred he liked to pretend. Certainly I can do better than that Mick pretender, Terrence, of yours. Now, may I get my margarita?

I have no intention of staying here unless suitably anesthetized.''

The martini *was* putrid, but I drank it anyway and got a start on Shannon's before she sashayed back to the table.

"So we're here to pick up men. All right. Now, you'd better tell me what flavor you have in mind because it won't be more than another minute before we have to start weeding them out."

"Really, Shannon, you're going to have to do something about that confidence problem of yours."

"Oh, wake up, Vic. Look over at the mirror behind the bar. What do you see?"

I saw two of the biggest tousles of golden red, curly hair ever to be crammed into a table for four. I had some idea, of course but, on the other hand, I had *no* idea.

"Two collies honeymooning?"

Shannon sat up straight, and pulled two curls down over her forehead. "No, funny woman. Here sits the earthly embodiment of the ultimate Doublemint Twin Fantasy." I felt eyes boring into me from all over the room. Yep, that was it.

"Okay, Shannon. I need a mercenary type, and an IRA agitator, just to be safe."

"Greedy. You already have your Terrence. How about one mercenary IRA type?"

"Shannon," I warned, "he is *not* my Terrence." I could sense warm bodies moving into our perimeter space. "Can we discuss this later?"

"Done." She tilted her head adorably, then turned to the man who had pulled up a chair next to her. "Oh, did I ask for company, or are you just being presumptuous?" Her voice lilted and trilled as though she were auditioning for *Finian's Rainbow*.

The man laughed long and loud as I sighed in relief. No doubt about it, Shannon had Celtic magic in her.

"Me buddies and me have a friendly wager over there."

He pointed to a gang of five standing near the back. "Which one of you is Shannon, the manager of McAleer's?"

"I knew it," I muttered into my drink. Shannon had slummed this path before me.

"And on whom did you put your money, boyo?" Shannon asked.

I realized I wasn't smiling encouragingly and rearranged my face.

"Why, on the real redhead, of course!" He wrapped his arm around the back of Shannon's chair. "But then, we have no way of proving I've won, now do we, darlin'?"

"Not during your lifetime, Paddy." Shannon knocked the man's arm off her chair and held up her hand to order another margarita.

I kicked her lightly under the table to subtly suggest that she behave more cooperatively. She cracked me a good one back with her designer ankle boots.

"Awww," the man intoned, "Shannon, it is Shannon? Forgive me for toying with ya, but I just didn't know how else to break the ice with two beauties such as yerselves. Can me mates and I buy you a round and apologize properly?"

Shannon continued to look straight ahead. Then, at what seemed the last moment, she turned to me, looking for my acceptance.

This time I remembered to smile. His "mates" looked to be a likely cross section of what I was seeking. With a nod from their fearless leader, they scraped empty chairs over to our table.

"Russell," he introduced himself. "And this here's Danny, and Greggy, and Michael, and Stew."

"Nice to meet you," Shannon said airily. "I will have a margarita, straight up with salt, and my cousin, Victoria, will have a vodka martini, extra dry this time, with a twist."

Cousin? I was thinking "evil twin."

By the bottom of my second martini I was on my way to blasted. Shannon, the one with the hollow leg, was doing fine. I assume she noticed the stupid glaze in my eyes, because after twenty minutes she dragged me off to the Colleens' Room.

On the way past the bar, she dropped a pile of cash with the bartender and ordered a round of shots for the men.

The bathroom was built for one, but that didn't stop Shannon. She sat me on the toilet lid and wiped my face with a damp paper towel.

"You have raccoon eyes," she said, rubbing. "Now"—she turned her attention to herself in the cloudy mirror—"Russell fancies himself the new Michael Collins, and the odd duck, Stew, has a lifetime subscription to *Soldier of Fortune,* or your name isn't Victoria." Somehow I'd missed all that, but I took her word for it. "Which one do you want?"

"What? Who's Michael Collins?"

"IRA activist at the turn of the century. Now, I think I've already gotten a jump start on Russell. And professional soldiers usually fall for the conservative woman in a suit, so that would be you and Stewart. All right? I have a late date, so let's wrap this up in the next ten minutes or so. I need to change into something flashy."

Okay, so now I knew that I had to charm the hand grenades off Stewart, and that Shannon did not think that a backless, sueded silk jumpsuit with matching high-heeled ankle boots was flashy.

The gents all stood when we returned to the table. I concentrated very hard and cast a thinly veiled appreciative look at Stewart. He must have noticed because he blushed.

It's a good thing that I trust Shannon's baser intuition, because I would not ordinarily have tagged the shy guy as the paid killer out of a group.

"So," I began.

"So," Shannon continued, "we have to be toddling off."

She handed a McAleer's matchbook to Russell and another to Stewart. "Give us a call, and we'll let you know if we're available." She tossed her hair one last time, lifted her micromini purse in two fingers, and walked away.

I followed with apologetic noises. Shannon had already flagged down a cab.

"What?" I protested, crawling into the backseat after her. "You got bored?" She directed the cabbie to McAleer's.

"Never waste more time than is necessary, Victoria. Don't worry; they'll call. Now, what is this all about?"

The taxi blew off the curb directly into the path of a Bronx-bound express bus. My horrified gasp of terror sucked saliva directly into my sorry lungs, causing me to cough my guts up.

Now you know. I do not travel by subway because I am cheap. I do so because I am chicken guano. It will never be possible for me to have so much money that I would voluntarily put my life in the hands of someone who passed his driver's license test in Farsi.

We broke the sound barrier during the straight shot up Tenth Avenue. I was still coughing at Seventy-seventh Street and Amsterdam, where Mohammed el Whoozits ran a red light and sideswiped a 1985 Chevy Caprice station wagon naïvely trying to cross the intersection on green.

Conscientiously, the driver threw the taxi into park immediately following impact where it sat in the middle of four lanes of traffic.

"Oh, for God's sake," Shannon groused, bullying her door open to the wail of oncoming horns. "If it's not one thing, it's another." She grabbed my sleeve and yanked me along with her into traffic. "If I wanted to walk"—she dragged me to the east side of the street—"I would have worn sneakers." The cab driver screamed at us. Probably for money, but I don't speak Farsi. "Aw, go drill for oil!" Shannon yelled back to the applause of the gathering crowd.

Since I'd lost a shoe, I limped along behind Shannon's long, angry strides back to the bar.

"Shannon, slow down. I thought you wanted to know why I dragged you downtown."

She slowed, but not much. "I thought it was a practical joke, actually, but go on."

"I'm being stalked," I shouted. She stopped and waited for me to catch up.

"Of course you are, Victoria. You're a bartender now. All bartenders have stalkers. If you couldn't attract stalkers, no one would hire you to tend bar. What happened to your shoe?"

"I guess I left it in the cab."

"Just as well."

"Shannon, I'm not talking about bar groupies. I'm talking about a real, lunatic stalker and I think he had something to do with Dave's death."

"Oh, well then. I have to close the bar tonight, what with Kerry in traction and all, so why don't you pop in at four and tell me all about it." It wasn't as though she cared, but at least she was curious.

"What if Russell or Stewart calls before I talk to you?"

"Silly girl. They'll call tomorrow, but I can assure you, those boys are much more interested in getting their green cards than in stalking anyone."

"I know who my stalker is," I protested.

Shannon walked into her building and up the stairs without so much as a backward glance. Even curiosity has its limits.

I felt very alone. So I returned to the man who loved me most in the world. Slasher seemed pleased.

"I tried not to care, Slasher. I really did." He seemed to understand.

We watched a Columbo Film Festival on cable between numerous catnaps.

Before I went back outside, I let Slasher haul every one

of his balls out of the drawer prior to upending it for another inspection. The fact that someone had gone to any trouble at all to eavesdrop on my personal life (ha) didn't make sense.

As an actor, I didn't have any groupies.

As a woman, I wasn't dating anyone important and/or political. Dan was out of town and would be for some time, so my surveillant would be wasting time waiting to hear from Duchinski within my walls.

As a bartender, I was just another nonthreatening member of the food-service profession. Of course, so was Dave. And he was dead. Of an intravenous overdose, even though Shannon adamantly insisted that he'd never used a needle.

Ergo, to wit, as Quillen Foster would say, "Trust your instincts." And mine had already directed me toward the Auld Sod. I would just stay pointed that way.

Outside, to my pleasant surprise, I spotted a uniformed cop standing in the circle of light at the end of my street, making 4:00 a.m. a little more palatable for walking alone. I waved as I passed on my way to meet Shannon at McAleer's.

The door was locked, so I rang the buzzer. Beau met me, mop in hand, and let me in. Timmy sat at the immaculate bar, holding a beer. The smell of Pine-Sol was everywhere.

"Herself is downstairs in the office," Timmy informed me. "Want a libation?"

Beau placed a chair upside down on one of the tables and said, "She doesn't drink."

"And I wear a dress," said Timmy.

"It's lovely you're lookin', too," I said as I walked downstairs.

Shannon was sitting at the old metal desk, two pencils stuck in her hair, a margarita at her right hand. "We're fourteen dollars short, and I can't find it. Here"—she handed me a wad of greenbacks—"count this and see what you get for a number."

I did. It was the same number she got.

"I'm scared, Shannon," I admitted at last.

"It's only fourteen dollars, Victoria."

"You're not listening to me, and I need you on my side right now."

"Is it your Irish stalker again?" She rattled around in a bag of rolled coins.

"I don't have an Irish stalker. My stalker is American, and I know who he is. We worked together at that theater in Maine last month. And I think you've talked to him."

"Me? When?"

"Remember when you asked me if my friend had come back after talking to you?"

"Clint Eastwood? I can't imagine why you'd want to avoid *him*. He's a lot better-looking than that Terrence guy groupie of yours."

"Wait a minute. You're never in the bar when Terrence is there. How did you even know that I have a regular customer named Terrence?"

"Sean mentioned it, I guess."

"You guess?"

"All right," Shannon harrumphed. "Sean asked me to warn you off him. It's not 'seemly.' It's very bad policy to date the customers, Victoria, and Sean wouldn't interfere if he didn't have a feeling about it."

"I'm not—" I started to deny a personal relationship with Terrence, and then decided it wasn't worth the time. Bar rumors only died of old age. It was Sawicki who concerned me. "Can you describe the man who asked about me?"

"I did." Shannon started counting money over again. "You worked with him, don't you have a picture of the cast that I could look at? That would settle it once and for all."

"He wasn't in the cast, he was the technical director," I said. I always take two disposable cameras with me when I go on tour, but they are to commemorate the actors, usually not the crew. Then I remembered.

Barry and Dan had visited me opening night, and I took several candid shots of the two men in my life just so that I would never forget how bizarre it was to see the two of them together in the backwoods of New England. Buck Sawicki had been ripping apart a defective set piece behind the barn theater as I snapped.

There was a good chance that I had a photograph. And I knew in my heart that if I showed it to Shannon, she would identify Sawicki as the man who had been asking about me.

That would teach me to unpack as soon as I returned from a show. The cameras were still in my luggage, on my bedroom floor, but the pharmacy on Broadway had one-day film developing, so there wouldn't be *that* much longer to wait.

Shannon looked up from her counting. "My, you *are* all atwitter, aren't you?" I nodded. "I don't understand, Vic. We are up to our rosy reds with the fuzz around here. You're *dating* one. Why don't you call him and get some protection from this madman?"

"One," I answered, "Dan is out of town at the moment. Two, he knows my stalker, and for some reason he won't talk about it. He said he checked and made sure Sawicki is still in New England, but he isn't. Dan lied to me. My God, if I can't trust the guy I've been dating for a year, how can I trust some stranger at the Twentieth Precinct?"

"He must have a reason."

"I'm sure. I just don't know what it is."

Shannon put her boots up on the desk. "Hmm. So what does that have to do with all the funny business earlier?"

She had changed into a snappy, long, peach-knit skirt and short cardigan for her late date. The boots, as always, matched perfectly. Without meaning to wander off the subject of my imminent doom, I couldn't help but wonder if we wore the same shoe as well as dress size. The color would be great for me, too, and I have never been able to justify paying money for shoes in any color besides black, white, or red.

"Well," I began feebly, pushing her feet from the furniture, "I've been thinking that with Dan out of town and with so much"—I pulled gently at the top left drawer—"time on my hands"—I stuck my hand under the wood and felt around—"I might as well"—I repeated with the top right—"do a little casual"—I repeated with the right bottom, *ah-ha*—"dating." Shannon watched me the way one cases out a dog with foam on the mouth. I put my finger to my lips. She leaned back and helped me pull the drawer from the desk.

I walked to the center of the room where the light was best and held the drawer over our heads. There, adhered to the bottom, was the twin sister of the device in my apartment.

The evil twin.

"So, what do you think?" I asked.

"I think getting out more is a good idea. You go upstairs, and I'll lock up the proceeds for the night. Sean can take them to the bank tomorrow morning." She took the drawer from my hands and put it back in place.

"Great. See you upstairs."

At last, I had a friend again.

After the brightly lit office, the basement seemed even darker than usual; I had to feel my way along the wall to the stairs. My dancing fingers caught on something unexpected along the smooth-paneled wall. It was an unhitched padlock. As I pushed, I realized that there was yet another door in the storeroom, and the door was ajar.

"Shhhh," Shannon hissed into my ear, and pushed me up the stairs. In the light of the bar, she explained, "Sean is sleeping down there. Nobody's supposed to know except Beau and me."

"Why would he do that? Do you think he knows about the bug in his office?"

"It's Kerry's office now, and you'd have to ask him. But if I were you, I wouldn't."

Timmy noticed my reappearance and slid a bourbon on the rocks down the bar. It stopped exactly in front of me.

"Thanks," I called. Then I asked Shannon, "Assuming that Kerry and I don't attract the same kind of sexual predator, what else could we possibly have in common besides no privacy?"

"Me," she suggested.

"How long has Sean been sleeping in the basement?"

"Oh, don't look so horrified. Kerry doesn't keep his father in the cellar. Sean has a beautiful home in New Jersey. And, as far as I know, he's only been staying down there since last, uh, week."

"Tuesday night?"

"Tuesday. That's right. The night Dave overdosed in the walk-in."

Or something, I corrected to myself.

TWELVE

THE TWO disposable cameras I had wedged into the edge of my wheeled carry-on were gone.

In frustration at my own lack of organization, I dumped the tangle of clothing and feminine hygiene products in a heaping lump on the unmade bed. The overhead light threw nasty shadows in the predawn gloom. As a last-ditch effort, I turned every pocket of the baggage inside out, then turned a plastic flashlight onto every corner.

The cameras had disappeared. My memory of packing them was precise. My costar, with whom I had sort of accidentally dallied, was a very famous star, and I had every intention of regaling my great-grandchildren with candid shots of the two of us horsing around on stage. In fact, the loss of my future bragging rights along with the film was much more upsetting to me than the lost chance that Shannon could identify Sawicki from one of the frames.

I *knew* Buck Sawicki was trailing me. And I was pretty damned sure that he was the one responsible for stealing my cameras. Perhaps his mother, like Duchinski's, is a Ryan, too.

Bugging my apartment and scaring the hell out of me in the dark was one thing. But destroying my great-grandchildren's faith in their great-grandmother's veracity and just leaving me with nothing but guilt was *way* over the edge. Not to mention the fact that I had spent two hours hunting for items that were already missing when I should have been asleep.

No more Ms. Nice Guy. I pulled a hair from my head and used saliva to apply it to the exterior crack of my apartment door. Thank you, Lieutenant Columbo. I was way past annoyed and on the fast track to reckless, but I still had enough composure left to be careful to pluck gray hairs only.

Security now documentable, I fumed my way to work.

Sean and Sleeping Bobby were planted, as I had come to expect, at the bar. Beau was enjoying a hearty Irish breakfast at a table near the brick wall. Sean's makeshift sleeping quarters appeared to be catching up with him. He definitely looked more frail than when we had first met, just a few days before.

"You look like you could use a good breakfast," Sean told me before I was five steps in the door.

"I haven't been sleeping very well," I said. "I'll just do with some coffee."

"Suit yourself," Sean said, and shook out his newspaper. "That big cop boyfriend of yours been keeping you out late?"

"Hardly," I answered sourly. "You know Dan?"

"Only just saw him the once," Sean said. "But he seems like a smart boy."

"Uh-huh." I carried my coffee to Sean's end of the bar. "I thought George and Dan were old friends. You know, the way they were hanging out here my first day." Sean did not look up from his paper. "Together," I added to no response.

"Budweiser," Sleeping Bob ordered.

I put a beer in front of him, took the money, rang it up, and moved back in for another assault.

"How's Kerry? Will he be out of the hospital soon?"

"Not if I have anything to say about it," Sean answered testily. He slapped his reading messily into the trash barrel behind the bar and stood. "And since you're here, you'd better get to work, hadn't you?"

I felt my face redden. "Right."

"I'll be in the office if you get yourself into any more trouble."

"Right," I mumbled. The old man shuffled around the corner and out of sight. Beau pushed his empty plate across the table and sighed in contentment.

"Mind if I get myself a Coke?" he asked.

"Go for it," I answered, still feeling sheepish from Sean's veiled reprimand.

Beau filled a plastic cup with soda. "The old man really likes you."

"Really?" I was not convinced.

"Oh, yeah. He got over his fit almost right away. That first day, I thought he was going to rip Kerry a new, uh, belly button. But then he settled down real good."

That was news to me. I thought Kerry was the screamer in the family. So much for female intuition. As far as I knew, Sean had been on my side from the get-go.

"What did George say?" I ventured.

"Well, you know George. He figured if they left you alone, you'd quit in a day anyway, so there was no reason to get you all upset and paranoid-like." Beau refilled his glass. "That George is one great guy."

"So I've heard."

"As a matter of fact," he leaned closer, "if you weren't Dan's girl, I think he'd maybe ask you out. But he's a great guy, and he wouldn't screw a buddy. You know."

"Yeah. They go back, those two." I slid a bottle of the house rum out of the speed rack, and sweetened Beau's cola, while keeping my expression bland.

"Some of my best friends I made during the war," Beau agreed. "Doesn't matter where we all ended up, when push comes to shove, you can always count on your army buddies. Family and friends, that's all you got in the end."

"Yeah." I leaned on my elbows to listen.

"Sean would never admit it," Beau whispered conspiratorially, "but he's been a lot less distracted since George got here from D.C. Kerry tries, but he's kinda hyper, himself, you know?"

"I know." I nodded. "When did George get back?"

"Oh, the day before you started. Dave was fit to be tied with so many McAleers in the room at once. I think he felt a little left out, too, what with not being a war veteran, himself."

"Lots of them, huh?" I slipped some more rum into Beau's plastic cup.

"Well, there was your boyfriend, of course, and George, and some other cops."

I wish I had been more surprised. But, with my deepest, darkest suspicions confirmed, it was time to go for the gold.

"How did you know they were veterans, Beau? Unless guys are swapping stories about it, I can never tell."

Beau smiled his cherubic grin. "Tattoos, Vic." He finished his spiked cola. "Look for the service tattoos."

Bingo.

Buck Sawicki again reared his ugly head, and in cahoots with Dan Duchinski. And Sean and George McAleer. The next thing I knew, I would probably discover that Slasher was plotting against me.

BRNGGGGGG.

"McAleer's, may I help you?"

"Victoria?" the unfamiliar male voice asked over what sounded like an outdoor pay-phone connection. I strained to make out the loud background noise. It sounded like a theater stage during opening week.

"Yes? May I help you?"

"Uh," his stammer was nearly washed out by the sounds of dropping lumber, "uh, this is Stewart."

Adding to my embarrassment of leprechaun gold, Terrence made his entrance into the bar with three buddies.

The bar was nowhere near ready for business, and I had a stutterer on a pay phone. My world and welcome to it.

"Stewart!" I enthused. "What can I do for you?"

"Uh," he said. "Uh."

"I have a rather full bar here, Stewart, and the connection

isn't very good.'' Terrence and his friends commandeered the table nearest the phone. "What can I do for you?''

"Uh, well, Russ and me, well, we're invited to a 'do' tonight, and, I know this is not proper notice, me and Russ were thinking that you and Shannon might be free to come along with us.''

"Tonight?'' I tried to listen to orders from Terrence and company while Stewart rambled on.

"I told Russ that you ladies would need more notice than just a few hours, uh, you know.''

"How many hours, Stewart? What time?''

"You mean you can? Shannon, too, because Russell is right here, and he needs to know, you know, uh—''

"When, Stewart? What time?'' I nodded at Terrence to assure him that he and his friends would not perish of thirst before I got off the phone.

"Six-thirty? If that's all right, I mean. We'll have to be driving up to Kingsbridge. That's where we're going for the 'do.'''

"That's fine, Stewart.''

"Shall we drop by your bar, then, Victoria? Uh, Russell thinks that would be best.''

There was the welcome CHUNG of the pay-phone time running out.

"Perfect. We'll both be ready.''

"Well, uh, good!'' CHUNG. "It's kind of a fancy party, so you—'' CHUNG. HMMMMMMMMM. We were disconnected, and not a moment too soon.

If I didn't give Shannon enough notice, my life would not be worth living. That is, assuming that I survived the initial notification, at all.

I served Terrence's table their first round and dashed around getting my side work finished before Sean reappeared and disapproved of me again. It ground away at my gut that Sean thought I was falling down on the job, especially now that I knew he hadn't wanted me working there in the first place. But why not?

"Where's the old man?" Terrence asked on his third stout.

Just because Sean had gone downstairs did not mean that was where he stayed, so I answered honestly.

"I don't know. He was a bit annoyed with me, and he left early." I emptied the brimming ashtrays and cleared empty cigarette and match packs. The men watched me in silence. "Do you need anything else right now? I have to make a call."

"You go ahead, darlin'. We're just fine," Terrence answered on behalf of them all. I patted his shoulder in thanks on my way to the pay phone behind the baffle wall that backed the jukebox. If Sean showed up, I wanted him to know that I wasn't using the business phone.

On the fourth ring, Shannon's machine picked up.

I don't like answering machines because they don't always allow for enough time for me to ease into a disagreeable message, so I blurted.

"Shannon, it's Vic, and Stewart called to invite us both to a fancy party in Kingsbridge tonight. They are picking us up here at six-thirty, so I guess we're driving. I'm sorry. I hope you don't have a date already, and I know it's your night off, and you don't want to be spending it in Kingsbridge, and I don't even know where Kingsbridge is, so, unless I hear—" The machine cut off.

I slammed the receiver down. Shannon was going to make me pay through the nose for screwing up her leisure time.

"Easy, Vic." Terrence held my hand on the phone.

"Terrence," I said, startled, and slid my fingers from beneath his. "Can I get you something?" I took shallow breaths in the enclosed corner, and tried to edge politely into open space, but he stopped me with an arm between me and freedom.

"Just on my way to the loo, and heard you mention Kingsbridge, of all places. It caught my attention, don'tcha know."

"And why is that?" I asked, thinking, And where is Sean? Or Silva? Or Sleeping Bob, or anyone?

"Why, because that's where I live, that's why."

"Ah!" I tucked down and squirreled under Terrence's arm. At the table I cleared empty pint glasses and returned behind the bar. "You boys all right there?" I asked. Terrence followed and leaned against the opening that served as a waitress station.

"I happened to hear that you're going to a party. Is that right?" Terrence persisted in his heavy accent. I remembered Shannon's firm opinion that it was an affectation, though it certainly sounded legit to me. Nonetheless, I found myself wary of the man.

"As far as I know," I answered carefully. "But it's a last-minute thing, and I'm not sure I'm up for a long evening. Especially in, uh, Knightsbridge."

"Kingsbridge. It's a far piece," Terrence agreed genially, his accent as thick as clotted cream. "Boys, our favorite bartender here is going to a party tonight in the neighborhood. I surely hope that you all got an invitation." The men laughed and shook their heads at such whimsy. Terrence turned his attention back to me. "Ah, but the Bronx is casual-like. Our parties are word-of-mouth invites for the most part, so"—he tweaked my lower lip between his right thumb and forefinger and pulled away—"I wouldn't be the least bit surprised to be seein' you later on, lass."

I forced myself to smile.

"That would be lovely," I told him. The men scraped their chairs back from the table. "So, maybe later."

"Don't disappoint, Victoria." Terrence pointed to me.

"Have I ever lied to you?" was past my bruised lips before I could choke the words down. When the men were safely out of sight, I sat on the nearest stool and balanced my forehead in the palm of one hand until my breathing slowed.

A nearly full cigarette burned in the ashtray on the table. I reached over three feet and snatched it to my mouth.

"I'm going to KILL you, VIC!"

A strong, male arm caught me as I lost my balance and fell off the stool toward the inviting floor. It was Quillen Foster, who stood between me and the enraged Shannon. Both of them were wearing sodden sweatpants and oversize T-shirts.

"Did you get my message?" I asked stupidly.

"Shoot her," Shannon instructed Quillen, pointing at me. She poured two coffees and set them on the bar.

"Maybe later," Quillen answered, setting me properly on my feet. "You ladies have a double date to get ready for." I looked quickly from the FBI agent to Shannon. She turned her back to me, so Quillen explained. "We went for an early-morning run. Your message was waiting before I even got a cup of coffee."

"Oh," I said into Shannon's ear. Under my breath, I added, "Never date the customers. Neverrrrrrr." She pinched my arm hard enough to leave a welt, but I needed her more than I needed cheap retaliation. "So, it's a date?"

Shannon pretended not to notice the smug expression on Quillen's disengenuous puss. Her snotty answer assured me that she had gotten a belly full.

"Why not? I deserve some *fun*."

Quillen knew when the getting was good. "I'll be running along, then, girls."

"You do that," Shannon and I answered in unison.

I was grateful that Quillen embodied the I-don't-care New York man.

Once in the enemy camp, I was sure all the pieces would fall in place—from Dave all the way to Buck Sawicki.

"All right," Shannon continued on her own. "I'll call Jack and have him come in an hour early. You look terrible.

If we're going to do this, let's do it with some élan. Wear a primary color and foof up your hair. Big hair is very 'in' in Little Ireland.''

"I wouldn't know how to achieve small hair."

"I know, Victoria. Now, if you'll excuse me, I have a pedicure appointment down the street. I'll meet you upstairs in my apartment at six sharp for a drink. I will not run the risk of being left alone with those Philistines. If you desert me for so much as one second, I'll have your guts for garters.''

"Thanks, Shannon."

"My pleasure. See you at six."

THANK YOU, Dan, for showing me the light. Thank you, Dave, for proving that I can't help but care.

Dan, George, Sean, and Buck all knew each other, no matter how much they lied about it.

Dave's death was suspicious enough to catch the attention of the emergency room doctor, but there was no investigation. Good work, Dan. Obviously, Dave had access to the secrets of Irish hell. *That, Sergeant Duchinski, is called motivation.*

Sawicki was the loose cannon. I supposed that would make me the cannon fodder.

Welcome back to the Big Apple, Vic, the home of "Trust nobody, no how, no way."

Yeah, well, I can still *care,* dammit.

I stewed.

IT WAS BOOZE business as usual until Sean thundered back into the bar at quarter to five close on the heels of my early replacement, Jack.

"Sorry, Vic," Jack apologized. "I had to tell him."

"I know," I answered. "It's not your fault, Jack. I appreciate your coming in early."

"I hope this Mick is worth it," Jack said, "because I've

never seen the old man so pissed. He looked ready to kill you.''

I noticed.

I seem to bring that out in men.

THIRTEEN

THERE WAS a single gray hair still adhering to the doorframe of my apartment when I got home at five. A quick inspection showed everything in the condition in which I left it early that morning, so I could devote an entire hour to primping.

The only brightly colored outfit I owned that wasn't red was a purple double-breasted suit I bought exclusively for my rare promotional appearances on television. Wardrobers seem to love the juxtaposition of gold/orange hair against plum. Personally, I think it's more than just a bit much. I dressed up the neckline with the spillover from a Wonder Bra, and let the high humidity coif my hair for me. The result was an interesting cross between Murphy Brown and Tina Turner. I liked it.

Slasher recognized all the signs of my deserting him for another man, and jumped from furniture to tabletop to get me to reconsider. All he accomplished was to spray fur through the air like shrapnel. I pushed him back from the door with my foot, and carefully closed it—making sure he hadn't left any pussycat parts in the way of closure.

In the hall I licked my palm and tried to roll the fur off my party outfit by swiping my hand down the fabric. Slasher had not succeeded in keeping me at home, but he'd done a masterful job of covering me with evidence of his existence. I believe I cursed the owners who did not spay his mother as I plucked hair after hair out of the weave of the cloth. If only I'd had the forethought to adopt a purple cat, so at least the mess wouldn't show.

And then I realized that the hair I had found still stuck to the doorjamb when I got back from work was not mine.

It was Slasher's. Mine was curly. The one on the door was shorter, and straight.

And I was going to be late if I stood around a moment longer in the hall.

"Guard the perimeter," I called to Slasher through the door.

As I hurried down the street, I managed to throw off the remaining cat hairs. Once inside Shannon's art-deco apartment, I asked her to wipe off my backside. She stood in her antiseptic kitchen and inspected the damage.

She wore a chamois floral-print slip dress with strapped-to-the-knee beaded sandals. African-influenced earrings dusted her tanned clavicles. Xena was underwhelmed by my fruit-bowl fashion statement.

"Blechhh," she announced.

"Don't hold back, Shannon, it will only give you gas." I accepted my criticism like a man.

"I am speechless," she said, looking me over like a dog who has been rolling around in roadkill.

"That's an improvement. I haven't even unpacked," I defended myself. "I did the best I could with what I had."

Shannon measured me by eye. "You can be fixed," she pronounced with satisfaction. "Strip." She whipped open her living-room closet and did a quick calculation of the array. The outfits were arranged in ascending tone value from bright white at the left to royal blue at the right. Matching shoes were shoulder to shoulder directly beneath their corresponding ensemble.

Now I know what it's like to shop at an expensive boutique with someone else's credit card. Shannon pulled two outfits from the closet and offered me my choice: peach or peach.

I chose the short peach, since my panty hose was still intact, but I was dubious, to say the least. The chiffon skirt and off-the-shoulders, ruffled top were my size, but a style I'd given up along with my marriage. Shannon unhooked my bra and pulled the blouse over my head. I tugged on the skirt, tucked what needed tucking in, and stood in front of the full-length mirror.

Not bad. It wasn't Shannon looking back at me, but a struggling Shannon doppelgänger. The real McCoy grabbed the back of my hair into her hands and secured it on the top of my head with an apricot-silk chrysanthemum—pulling ringlets out of the mass for full effect down the neck and cheeks.

"Here." She threw me a pair of delicate, heeled sandals in the precise peach of the chiffon. Naturally, they fit as though they were made for me. "For full impact, one of us was going to have to adjust our image, and you know it wasn't going to be me." She stood behind me in the mirror.

It was creepy. Same height, weight, color, and style. I had to give Shannon her due; it was an attention grabber.

"Wow," I breathed.

"When you go fishing, you have to have the proper bait, Victoria."

"I'm glad the blouse is double-faced."

"I'm glad you don't need a strapless bra." Shannon dumped the contents of my fanny pack into a spidery peach shoulder bag and flitted into the kitchen. I heard the refrigerator door close, and followed. She was pouring two shots of chilled Absolut into Lalique martini glasses. "Cheers!"

"Cheers!" I answered, and downed the cold vodka. "I feel funny without a bra."

"That's the point, Victoria." She refilled our glasses. "If you're going to let loose, go all the way. You'll feel sexier all night."

"Is that what I want?"

"It's what every woman wants," she said, finishing her drink and opening the apartment door to leave. I left my vodka untouched, and set my mind on the mission, following down the stairs behind the master.

To my chagrin, I seemed to be having a bad attack of

stage fright. Typically, I don't suffer from it onstage—it's only real life that makes me want to barf with anxiety. At the entrance to McAleer's, my stomach fluttered and my knees twitched. I stopped for a second to regroup.

"Well, well," Shannon twirped. "It's a funny old life."

"What?"

"Our dates are already here."

"Okay, give me a minute," I said.

"And so is your boyfriend—with George."

I sneaked my eyes up over Shannon's hair, still cowering behind her. Sure enough, Dan and George were ensconced at the bar two seats down from Russell and Stewart.

The *jerk*. Duchinski was supposed to be out of town. He *promised*.

"Shit. Shit, shit, shit, damn."

"I love a coincidence," Shannon glowed. I backed my way out to the street, tugging to get her to follow.

"Now what?" I asked. "Jeez. What is Dan doing here again? It's not even my shift. I haven't even really done anything, and he's catching me again. The scud. How does he *know* these things?"

"Calm down," Shannon soothed. "Don't feel so persecuted. You are not being followed. Think about it. Everyone in the bar knows you were going out tonight. Jack came in early, so you could get ready. No one could have expected we would be here. If anything, Dan is in there because he's sure you *wouldn't* be."

"True." I chewed the logic over for a moment. "The crud. Why is he avoiding *me?*"

"That is between you and your therapist. Now, you cool your jets out here. I am going to flit in, collect our dates, and we will slip quietly away out of the neighborhood without what's-his-name knowing any better."

"You are truly devious." I relaxed slightly. "I admire that."

"Everyone does." She accepted the compliment graciously, and went about doing as she promised.

Russell and Stewart were delivered to me within a minute, trailing behind Shannon like two freshly bathed golden retriever puppies. I stood as inconspicuously as I could in the late-afternoon sun, praying that the harsh light wasn't making my borrowed Sunday best completely transparent.

"Uh," Stewart began at seeing me, "uh, you look beautiful, Victoria. Uh, wow." He nodded to himself. He was so dear, that old black guilt washed over me. I promised myself that I'd ask Shannon later how she had hers removed.

"Car's right here." Russell pointed to a 1980-something, brown Dodge Aries parked directly in front of McAleer's damned, huge window. I felt as though my hair were a strobing light that read, VIC BOWERING, APPEARING LIVE AND UP TO NO GOOD THIS WAY!

I pretended to adjust the strap of one sandal as Russell unlocked the car and opened the door for Shannon. I prodded Stewart forward, telling him I'd be right there. I glanced at the picture window. The sun was angled low, reflecting blindingly off the shaded glass. With relief I noted that I couldn't make out anything through the window.

The second the back door was opened, I sprinted low across the sidewalk and into the backseat, turning my back immediately to the bar. If Stewart found my behavior peculiar, he didn't mention it.

In fact, he seemed utterly thrilled to be sharing a bench seat in the stuffy car with peachy, little old me. I wondered, for the ninety-four millionth time in my life, what I had gotten myself into.

Shannon filled the wind tunnel of the ride with charming chatter and adorable commentary. Not once did she let her phony Irish accent lapse. God bless her. I kept my ears open and my mouth shut all the way up Manhattan, and across the bridge to the Bronx.

Unlike the media view of New York's most maligned borough, the Bronx can be quite lovely. Well-kept row houses dotted stretches between larger apartment complexes. Trees shaded the sidewalks and streets, and the air smelled of newly mown grass. Elderly residents sat in lawn chairs in front of their homes and watched the traffic glide by. Fathers and mothers pushed babies in carriages and paused to visit with one another.

My hyperactive imagination shifted down another notch. The car turned off the residential strip and onto a more commercial avenue. The ribbon of pavement rolled up and down, far hillier than I had expected. Over the crest of one incline, I saw the remains of a block, decimated by the explosion I had witnessed on television.

The line of four, two-family houses had been nearly flattened. Though architecturally identical, each had been painted a different color: apple green, beige, white, yellow. From what I could see from the backseat, ground zero had been the house farthest away. There was a blackened chasm where the basement had once held cast-off toys and furniture.

"Murdering fools," I heard Stewart say to himself as we passed. Russell did not even glance at the rubble. Shannon was absorbed in applying lip gloss.

We pulled over and parked two blocks past the site of the explosion. It was a neat commercial section composed of an Italian catering hall, a video store, a pharmacy, and two Irish bars—one at either end, and each a bit less inviting than the other.

As a born New Englander, I am ashamed to admit that my first reaction was not that I was about to drag Shannon into a strange and potentially dangerous situation, but that she and I were unbelievably overdressed.

One of these days, I am simply going to *have* to restructure my worry list.

Russell pointed to the larger of the two bars, situated at the south end of the street.

"That's where we're goin'," he announced, opening Shannon's door for her. "The Blarney Rose!"

I smiled, sincerely, for the first time that evening. Somehow, through scheming and good luck, we were about to enter a place I'd only read about—on the back of a pack of matches shoved down a dead man's shorts. Dave directed from his grave.

The four of us entered from the street into a bar area much smaller than I had originally expected. The bartender was a slow-moving sixty-something man surrounded by a number of like-aged regulars. The television over the bar was blaring a soccer match and ignored by all. The digitalized jukebox blasted country and western music much enjoyed by a table full of younger men seated by the door.

"Hey, hey, hey," the patron with the skimpy ponytail announced Shannon's entrance. He waved an empty long neck in our direction, in case his duck-blind buddies didn't know what he was exclaiming at. "Nice wheels," he announced to my kneecaps. I waited for Shannon to disembowel the cracker on the spot, but she made a beeline to schmooze the bartender and left me on my own. Russell and Stewart were hashing something over on the sidewalk just outside the door and unavailable for my rescue.

"Hey, hey." Another man reached for me as I studiously ignored the table. "Polly want a green card?" I stepped aside, leaving him with a handful of smoky air. My impulse was to wipe the snake tattoo off his hand and shove it where the rainbow don't end—American to American.

I chose my accent carefully before firing. Best Little Whorehouse in Texas seemed aptly castrating.

"Listen to me, you little peckerwood," I spoke in a low voice so as to not draw undue attention to my citizenship, "you grab at me one more time, and I will blow your 'don't tread on me' ass into a Kmart wallet. *Comprende, amigo?*"

His companions burst into raucous laughter.

"Sorry, ma'am," Mr. Buzz Cut apologized. "I didn't know I was addressing Miss Annie Fuckin' Oakley."

I felt the door open behind me.

"Are you all right, Victoria?" Russell asked, shooting daggers at my table of erstwhile admirers. Stewart hung back, surveying the room.

Shannon, sensing misdirected attention, rejoined our group.

"Sure," I said. "I was just catching up on the news from the trailer park."

As a fancy party, it looked like a dud.

Shannon's powers of observation were as good as mine, but in the heat of dating she had apparently forgotten she was in the charming village of Kingsbridge for *my* benefit.

"I hate funerals," she said. "Let's blow this pop stand and find someplace to party with *homo erectus.*"

It's a good thing I don't travel armed, or I swear I would have shot her dead on the spot. I didn't want homo erectus; I wanted the thugs who were screwing up my life—and ended Dave's. I wasn't having fun. We weren't supposed to be having fun. I was supposed to be getting the information I deserved that was being kept from me by those nearest and dearest.

"I think it's cute," I said hurriedly.

"Oh, darlin', this isn't the party," Russell answered. "It's private-like. We're in the back room upstairs." He took the opportunity to place his hand on the small of Shannon's back and guide her farther into the building. Stewart and I followed, wordlessly, which seemed to be the basis of our relationship.

We left the dulcet tones of Patsy Cline behind us.

As with many of the old Irish bars, the establishment was a rabbit warren of rooms, spreading back and up. One bar for watching television, one for moving to the jukebox, one for conversation, the others for, well, whatever.

That thought gave me a second's pause.

There was a stairwell at the back of the second cocktail lounge leading both up and down. We started climbing, and as we climbed, Russell started singing.

"U2!" Shannon translated the noise. "Things are looking up." Indeed, Russell appeared to be looking up: up my skirt.

The stairs were narrow but well lit. Never an optimistic sort, I began to plot a fire exit. The walls were really far too close to the stair treads. There was no air-conditioning in the steep corridor, and my incipient claustrophobia began to squeeze at my lungs.

The tiniest part of my brain where I store my common sense throbbed.

Sure, Vic, smooth move. Why NOT go on a date in the middle of nowhere with two men you've met all of once in your life, whom you handpicked purely on the basis that they are probably DANGEROUS. Then I want you to LEAVE the crowd and isolate yourself in an enclosed space with no maneuvering area, you BOZO!

At the second landing, I saw light and felt the air move. In eight more steps, we were in the middle of a blare of ethnic music and a welcoming bank of cigarette smoke.

The floor shook with the bass of the sound system, and the pounding of Irish feet.

This room must be soundproofed, I thought. Ten feet down, it was as if there were no one there at all. It took some effort from me *and* my common sense to knock down the paranoia.

I was on a fact-finding mission. That was all. It wasn't as though I had accepted a double date with Charles Manson and Buck Sawicki. I had stuck purely to the periphery. Good for me.

"Good for you," Terrence shouted as we entered the party. "You made it! And," he added companionably, "lookin' wicked good."

"There's an expression I haven't—" I stopped myself. "You sound like my nephew," I finished.

"Lucky boy," Terrence answered, none the wiser.

To the best of my knowledge and vast experience, there is only one geographical region that commonly uses the colloquialism, "wicked good." New England. Specifically, the home of Margaret Chase Smith and my nephew.

Maine. Prison home of Buck Sawicki. Shannon was right, *ayuh.*

I surveyed the battlefield. A quick sweep of the room reassured me that Shannon and I had entered where we would make the greatest visual effect, for the benefit of the men. There was an exit at the far end of the room, with an exterior staircase at the end of the building. This particular room was used as a clubhouse of some sort by a bunch of people I did not know from Adam.

The trouble for me was, in Kingsbridge, if I *did* have to make an unannounced exit, I would not have the foggiest idea where the hell I was exiting *to*. At least back in Maine there were woods to hide in, and the nastiest things likely to be chasing me were hungry bears.

At that realization, my common sense apparently bade me bye-bye and left me on my own. As did Shannon, who was boogying up a storm with three dance partners, one of whom was Terrence. It was nice to know that she did not hold linguistic deception against him.

"Uh"—Stewart materialized at my side—"can I get you a drink, Vic?"

"Yes, thank you, Stewart. I'd like a"—what was I drinking before?—"uh, vodka. On the rocks, please."

"Lemon or lime?"

"Either. Both." I reorganized my brain and tried to concentrate in the incredible noise. "Whatever they have is just fine, thank you."

I watched him, on his way to the service bar at the street

side of the room, ask Shannon what she would like to drink.
For an alleged mercenary, Stewart was really very sweet.

The women in the room were every bit as overdressed as
Shannon had predicted, and younger than she might have
hoped. I felt naïve and foolish. There we were at a perfectly
jolly party, in a nice neighborhood that I would ordinarily
never visit, with two attractive enough men. It was all so
innocuous that I snorted a little laugh at my own expense
as I felt the muscles in my shoulders begin to relax and my
feet begin to tap to the music.

Don't get me wrong. Dave was still dead. I was still
pissed off at Dan Duchinski for running me around the rose-
bush, making me believe that I had lost my mind. And so,
far away from the muck and mire of life on the Upper West
Side, it occurred to me that I might actually be sane, and it
had to have been Dan who planted the surveillance devices
at my apartment and Kerry McAleer's office. It made mas-
culine sense.

After all, his woman had philandered not all that long
ago. And George McAleer was his friend. Maybe Dan
thought that Kerry had been diddling me. (Not mentioning
it was downright *sick*.)

And so what if Terrence was faking an Irish accent? He
hung out with immigrant laborers. In fairness, after just an
hour I had picked up Stewart's speech problem, and after
three tours of *Steel Magnolias,* I couldn't walk by a Southern belle without being infected with a drawl.

Yes, that made a perverse kind of sense to our Cleopatra.

Except, my better judgment reminded me, for Dave dying
in the walk-in.

Except I loved Dan and that would be crazy if he were
involved in murder.

Except that could have been plain bad luck, the Queen
of Denial argued. Accidents *do* happen. My grandmother
told me so.

I looked around the crowd for my date and my drink, not

necessarily in that order. The sun was beginning to truly set, filling the smoky room with a warm orange glow.

Backlit as though encased in flame at the exterior stair, stood Buck Sawicki, not thirty feet away.

Terrence waved to the ex-convict and opened the door to let him in.

FOURTEEN

MY CLAUSTROPHOBIA was back, and in a big way. The gang of revelers pressed in on me from every direction. Cutting through the crowd directly toward me was Terrence, looking ominously determined. Reflexively, I took a step backward onto the foot of an innocent woman.

"Ladies' room?" I asked, hoping against hope that the bathroom would not be one of those antiquated male bastion afterthoughts.

"Downstairs, past the main bar," she advised me.

Terrence reached toward me as I slid away, slicing my way through the late arrivals and down the worn back stairs.

Sawicki had been dipping in and out of my life for the entire week after I left him to play out his parole in Maine. I had no documentable reason to believe that this uncanny appearance would be anything more than his usual hit-and-run.

Bad choice of phraseology.

There was no railing in the stairwell, so I ran my right hand along the wall as I descended. Shannon's borrowed sandals had smooth leather soles that did not make the going any easier. My foot slipped over the worn steps edge as I approached the first landing, nearly landing me on my face for the rest of the trip down.

Settle down, I lectured myself. All you have to do is make yourself scarce for a half hour or so, until Sawicki looks around and leaves.

Then, the hell with Dan Duchinski and his lies. I was going to march myself straight to the Twentieth Precinct and let them know that they had a parole violator in the 'hood.

And if that didn't get me some protection, I would have a cheap, shallow affair with Quillen Foster and get the FBI involved. Ha!

That would teach Dan Duchinski to lie to me and make me believe that I was losing my mind. Again.

I reached the ground floor and peeked into the back cocktail lounge. It was deserted except for a young Hispanic couple who wouldn't have noticed a mass murder unless it happened on the table between their caressing fingers.

I headed downward again. The spring on the hinge was too tight, and the door slammed behind me with a nerve-shattering smack.

Carefully, I pushed the door back open to see if the noise had disrupted the Hispanic couple's concentration. It had not.

If Buck happened to have seen me upstairs and followed, I was confident that the young man and woman would not remember having seen me at all, let alone what direction I took. And since Sawicki was something of a professional, he would assume that I had escaped through the entrance lounge and out onto the street.

No one who was being trailed would corner herself in a basement.

Because that would be stupid.

I braced myself with my hand once again against the streaked wall of the stairwell. This final set of stairs was metal; rather than plummet to my immediate death, I removed Shannon's chic sandals and proceeded in my stockinged feet down to the basement corridor. All the while, I listened for the smack of the upper door to warn me of Sawicki's having a lucky hunch.

The stairs dumped me at the end of a long interior hall, punctuated with numerous doors on either wall. The ladies' room was the first to the right. I pushed the door open to inspect my temporary housing.

The six-by-six-foot cubicle was painted Pepto-Bismol

pink, as expected. To the right was a 1940s-vintage porcelain sink topped by a cheap mirror nailed through its plywood frame to the wall at a height of about five feet. A shoddy stall protected the toilet from view. The hook dangled sadly from the stall door with no eye to give it usefulness. Too typical.

SLAM! The door on the first floor announced a visitor. I stepped backward, into the basement corridor to listen for the sound of footfalls on the metal steps. There was nothing—no brushing of the walls, nor leather on steel.

If Sawicki was looking for me, he had fallen for my clever plan and exited through the first-floor rooms and out onto the streets of Kingsbridge.

Or, I reasoned with myself, some poor woman with a full bladder had decided that the trip was just too much for her and was asking the old bartender if there was another powder room with easier access, which I knew there wasn't.

If the second scenario was so, the bathroom was not big enough for the both of us, and to save my soul, I couldn't come up with a reasonable explanation for my loitering in the cellar. I made a quick inspection of the doors farther down the hall.

Judging by the size of the ladies' room, I guessed that the hiding cubbies on the left of the corridor would be the larger, and concentrated on them. All four of the storerooms were secured with heavy padlocks, but the room at the dead end on the right was locked with only an old cylinder.

It was an option, anyway, should I need one.

The stale air pulled slightly at the hem of my chiffon skirt in the direction of the stairs. Someone had opened the upper door again, pulling the stagnant air toward the first floor. I waited hopefully for the slam.

Instead, the hem of my skirt hung dead in the perfect silence. Listening for the telltale chung-chung-chung of a woman's dress shoes on the steel treads, I fished out my Swiss Army knife, which I kept on my key ring.

The basement hall was lit like a shopping mall, which was good news. The ancient screws securing the cylinder in the door were immediately visible. One of the three was already missing.

I laid my sandals on the hall floor so that I could muffle the keys in the palm of my hand as I worked the knife's screwdriver attachment. The harder I tried to make out the sounds of a man approaching, the louder the hum of quiet sounded in my ears. One screw fell into my waiting left hand as I worked the last impediment to my hidey-hole.

Years of New York air had deposited muck in the slot of the remaining brass screw. I pulled a blade from the knife's casing and scratched at the screw head. I heard the first dull clunk of a foot on the stairs. My hand froze in its position at the lock, and I waited to judge the interval between steps.

Clunk.

I jammed the blade of the screwdriver attachment as forcefully as I could into the dirty wedge and put my body weight behind it as I bullied the metal left. The screw held with all the perverse stubbornness of Dan Duchinski. I took a deep breath and leaned in for a last try.

The tarnished brass gave with a mousy squeak.

Clunk, came the footstep closer.

Clumsily, I twisted, causing my house keys to tinkle slightly. I cringed at my carelessness, and pried at the brass impediment with my fingernails. Ancient grease slipped at the sharp rim and cut my right forefinger, but at last, I had it.

Clunk.

The screw fell from my hand onto the cement floor with a heart-stopping ping and disappeared.

Clunk. Closer.

I held the brass plate against the door, jiggled the knob, and pulled the cylinder out of the solid, paneled door just far enough to stick the blade of my knife into the crack and pull. The backing plate inside the room clattered to the ground.

Clunk. Clunk.

The discarded sandals scraped slightly as I pulled them upward, and, grasping the rod on the inside of the closet door, I pulled and sealed myself in total darkness. Bracing my feet against the bottom of the door, I got a firm hold on the spiral, forged cylinder rod and leaned backward to force the door flush.

From fifteen feet away, I heard the stall door in the bathroom slam against the hollow sheeting of the enclosure. My shoulders punched into a wall of cardboard.

Smooth move, Bowering. You've locked yourself in a shoe box.

"Bowering?" Buck Sawicki called to me softly. "Bowering, I know you're down here." I heard him rattling the doorknob opposite the ladies' room.

Furiously, I pulled back on the metal stick, but the restricted space kept me from getting my full weight onto it. If I could pull enough pressure, Sawicki might believe that the door was still locked.

The second doorknob on the left of the corridor rattled. Unless, I thought, I was lucky enough to have found a room with a secondary staircase to the outside. The possibility of such a slight chance of escape broke a prickly sweat over my entire body.

Still leaning back, attached to the door by my left hand, I felt around the bottom of Shannon's peach purse for my lighter. Loose tobacco jammed beneath my fingernails.

The third doorknob refused to yield.

My bloody thumb and forefinger latched on to my trusty Bic. I pulled my hand from the purse and flicked as though my life depended on it. I knew I would have to let go of the remains of the lock to make my escape—that is, if I could even locate another door, so my inspection would have to be thorough and quick as a heartbeat.

"Bowering!" Sawicki called again from no more than two feet beyond my protective door.

The child-safety mechanism on my lighter was as good as advertised. The serrated plastic wedge dug into the raw meat of my thumb, once, twice. Three times was the charm. The flame shot from the nozzle in a deceptively telling chkkk, but I had my sight back in the flickering butane.

And the vision I had in those two seconds was enough to cause the lighter to fall from my grasp. It clattered to the rough floor in the crammed space, and I released the tenuous hold I had on the exposed interior latch.

My shoulders were wet where they had made contact with the sweating cardboard boxes that held the arsenal of poorly stashed dynamite.

Sawicki pulled the door from behind me and crushed my back to his hard chest. One arm compressed my diaphragm, forcing the air from my lungs, the other hand held my jaw clamped as though squeezing an orange from within its skin.

FIFTEEN

THE CALLUSED HAND slid upward over my face as I struggled. Sawicki's hold was so desperate that the only air I could inhale was in short, shallow snippets through the left side of my nose.

The temperature in the basement was easily hovering at a hundred degrees or more, and I was running out of fight faster than I would have liked to believed was possible.

"Give it up, Bowering," Sawicki urged, never letting up on a pound of pressure.

My field of vision encompassed my failed hiding space. The small closet was piled to the peeling ceiling with firepower. Besides the five boxes of dynamite, the floor was strewn with a hodgepodge of electrical devices and wiring. Rifles made sloppy teepees at the corners; handguns toppled from wooden crates. A triangular section of greasy Confederate flag eyed me from a high shelf.

As I fought my way through my negligible store of oxygen, the vista darkened, and I felt myself start to slump in Sawicki's arms. His faded tattoo disappeared into the peach chiffon of Shannon's blouse.

My last conscious thought was not of salvation, nor of my pathetic life flashing before my eyes, but that Shannon was going to kill me for destroying her outfit, and, if I wanted to live to fight her off, I'd better just give in to a very wussy faint.

It was a brilliant plan. I awoke a second later, when Sawicki laid me on the dirty concrete. His back was to me in the hall as he rapidly rifled the contents of the open closet. I was grateful for the fact that he could not seem to make up his mind as to which weapon he wanted to use to dispatch me to the big spotlight in the sky.

Gingerly, he pulled one of the sodden boxes of explosives from its shelf. As he slowly lowered it, I tucked my feet under my rump and jumped directly into a mad dash. Without jostling his cargo, Sawicki delicately placed the box on the floor before giving chase.

His consideration for his own skin gave me a head start the length of the stairs. I prepared to round the corner into the public first floor just as I heard Sawicki's first heavy thud onto the bottom stair. After that, all else was drowned out in screams from the floor above.

At the first floor door, I had to throw my weight against the wood to budge it; male fingers curved around the edge of the door and pulled it open against the noise.

Terrence used his wide back to block the human mass from slamming the door closed.

The near door from the club upstairs exploded in fleeing partygoers. Chivalry had died, and men rough-and-tumbled their way over the bodies of the slower womenfolk. Terrence was blessedly lost in the bedlam.

I rode the crest of the human tsunami through the front bar and out onto the sidewalk.

The waters stalled at the sidewalk outside, but I fled farther to the crowd congregating across the street from the Blarney Rose. I was careful to keep my head low, so that Sawicki wouldn't be able to spot me when he finally scrambled his way through the mob. I had no doubt that he was tenacious enough to fight his way back to me.

My kingdom for a subway station.

In the confusion, I no longer even knew north from south—not that it mattered. Shannon was nowhere to be seen, and I couldn't leave without locating my friend.

The wail of sirens approached from the distance. Before long, there would be no way out of the area, short of flying.

Still crouching, I poked an elderly man in the arm to ask what was happening.

"Bomb threat, I think," he answered without looking at me directly—his eyes glued on the mass exodus. "It usually is around here. I just hope no one is trampled to death."

Traffic crawled along the avenue. Drivers rubber-necked with the anxiety of those who know rescue vehicles are about to slam to a stop one inch from their back bumpers. I worked my way to the curb for one last-ditch attempt at locating Shannon. Sawicki wouldn't take long to appear, and I had no choice but to lose myself in the crowd one last time and hunt her down when it was safer. I felt like a spineless slug, cowering behind a very, very old man.

I pinched myself for courage and bobbed up at the curb for a rapid reconnaissance. If Shannon were outside, she'd be easy to spot. My eyes flew from left to right across the crowd, then down into blindness.

"Mrffff!" I protested. I lay flat on my stomach. It felt as though an elephant were standing on my back, and then I was propelled to my left side and I heard a door slam. Then there was the unmistakable electronic click of automatic door locks.

I forced one eye open into the crimson velvet upholstery, as a hamlike hand continued to force my face downward into the luxurious padding. From the front seat, I could hear self-satisfied whistling as the heavy car roared powerfully away.

Finnegans Wake.

I was being abducted by the nine-thousand-year-old man, Sean McAleer.

SIXTEEN

"YOU SHOULD HAVE listened to me when I told you that nice girls don't tend bar," Sean advised from the driver's seat.

I was not in a "nice girl" position. I was still facedown on the roomy backseat, my knees bent, calves and dirty-stocking feet waving in the air. The top of my head was slammed tightly against what I believed was a muscular male thigh. I sniffed.

Old Spice was the giveaway. I had been signed, sealed, and delivered—set up and paid off. There was only one man I knew of, besides my father, secure enough in his manhood to splash himself unashamedly with Old Spice, and that was Sergeant Dan Duchinski, NYPD. I wailed into the velvet.

"Dshnnnnskeeeeeeeeeee, yewlitgewameeee!"

"Nice talk," Dan commented, pushing my face down farther. I could envision him sitting behind Sean with his arm crooked out the open window while I suffocated. Rather than give him the satisfaction of smothering, I jerked my butt into the air, tucked my chin to my chest, and popped my head out from under his big old hand.

"You bastard," I said, smacking him ineffectually with my damaged right hand. "You rat bastard, Buck Sawicki almost killed me. I hope you're satisfied. Where are you taking me? Do you know that Shannon is still back there in Kingsbridge? Go back. GO BACK!"

"Don't worry about Shannon," Sean said as he accelerated to somewhere near the speed of sound south along the Henry Hudson Parkway. Duchinski shoved me back into the seat and buckled my seat belt.

"If she's hurt," I warned them, "I'm going to hold both

of you personally responsible. She's a woman alone in a fricking RIOT with a maniac on the loose!''

''Just goes to show,'' Sean narrowly avoided sideswiping a livery cab, ''what goes around, comes around, huh, Danny boy? It's about time she got a taste of her own medicine.''

If Sean slowed down, I planned to jump from the car.

''Where are you taking me?'' I examined the locking mechanism of the door and the clasp of my seat belt. Sean sped up.

''Where you can't do any more harm,'' Duchinski answered, wrapping his sausage fingers in a vise grip around the folded waist of my skirt and panty hose. ''Now, be quiet like a good girl.''

Dan's grasp was a fine deterrent. If I wriggled away, I would be naked from the waist down. And in New York City, that kind of display was certain to get a damsel in distress totally ignored.

We cruised past exits until Sean made a sudden turn, and our tires squealed ominously on the sharp exit onto the Seventy-ninth Street Boat Basin. We took the hard circle around the outdoor theater well at about forty miles per hour. I knew, however, that there was a four-way light coming up at Riverside, and no one ever made it.

Legally, that is. We scrambled through to the red light at West End Avenue, which turned to green in the nick of time. Sean careened around a bus to blast across four lanes at Broadway, then cut off a taxi for a left at Amsterdam. I don't think his foot ever came near the brake pedal until he slammed to a complete stop at Eightieth Street. I closed my eyes in terror.

When I opened them, we were neatly double-parked behind a Brunckhorst meat truck in front of McAleer's. Sean's nephew, Patrick, was tending bar. With his fist still clutching my clothing, Duchinski pulled me out of the car and hauled me through the bar. Sean conscientiously locked up his illegally parked Town Car and followed.

I would have screamed, but no one would have heard me over the jukebox. And you'd be amazed at how many women get carted through New York City bars in such an ignominious fashion. Dan carried me down the stairs to Kerry's office and pushed me down onto the sofa.

"You'll have to kill me to shut me up, Duchinski," I threatened, now that I knew he probably wouldn't.

"Where are your shoes?" he asked.

"Ask your friend Sawicki," I answered. Sean appeared in the doorway.

"Ask a stupid question..." Dan trailed off. To Sean he asked, "Can you lock Victoria the Secret in the office? I have to get back north for a while."

I was still unwilling to accept that Duchinski was at the center of a huge conspiracy just to "get" me.

"Wait!" I shouted, and ran to the metal desk. I yanked out the drawer with the listening device affixed, flipped it upside down, and displayed the evidence for the two men.

Dan smiled. "Buck does nice work."

"That he does," Sean agreed.

Sean reached into his pants' pocket, and pulled out a heavy ring of keys. He sorted through for a moment, and then nodded without acknowledging my exposé.

"My pleasure, Danny. I could use a nap myself, without having to worry about getting bashed over the head."

Dan stood in the door and shook his head.

"I'll be back to take care of you in a while, Vic." He stood aside as Sean closed and double-locked the office door. After a muffled exchange, I heard Sean click shut the door to his sleeping room as Dan's heavy steps quickly climbed the stairs. I chucked the desk drawer against the solidly locked door.

Then, though it's not my nature, I froze and counted to twenty. Then I counted to twenty in French, and then I counted to twenty in German, and then I listened for sounds of sleep from the tiny room on the other side of the common office wall.

Okay, so they are out to get me.

Either Sean was not a snorer, or he was still awake. For Shannon's sake, I couldn't spend all night waiting around for proof.

But, fortunately, I knew something Sean and Dan didn't know I knew—the presence and location of the old Prohibition exit door to the apartment building hallway. *Thank you, Shannon. I won't let you down.*

I flipped on the office's black-and-white television to cover any suspicious noise, and pried at the paneling with my ruined nails. At the first loosening of the hidden latch, I turned up the volume on the old set and changed the channel to New York One—all local noise, all the time.

Once again I was confronted by a door that would not budge. I tried to slide the barrier back throughout the local weather forecast, and pushed through the duration of the Straphangers' Report, periodically putting my ear to the wall to check on movement from Sean. At the News Update, I surrendered in a sweaty heap to take a breather.

The younger-than-springtime reporter stood in front of a fire truck and played with his earpiece. The camera drew back and the commentator fiddled. Fire department personnel jostled the bystanders and camera crew away from the action. The widened angle revealed the shamrock-bedecked entrance of the Blarney Rose. The ID strip rolled "Kingsbridge."

There was no sign of Shannon on the screen. I leaned back against the panel and felt it give. *Moron,* I cursed myself. The panel was designed to be pushed at the right side to expose the opening at the left. The light that spilled from the office was sufficient to see to the top of the stairs.

It was eight steps to the lift latch door. Rather than risk any untoward creaking sounds, I squeezed through the eight-inch opening and carefully pushed the panel closed behind me until I heard a click. There was still no sound from the old man in the room that was now beneath the steep stairs I climbed in the total darkness. I balanced uncertainly on the top stair, groped to locate the latch, lifted, and pulled the door inward. My eyes ached in the sudden attack of fluorescent lighting.

The great outdoors of the street was ten feet to my left, past the heavy security door. The damnable front window of McAleer's stood vigil directly left of that.

I listened for sounds of footsteps coming down the stairs from the apartments above. All was quiet, so I took a moment to think over my position.

A woman with any survival instinct at all would have taken a hard right and delivered herself to the Twentieth Precinct, two blocks north and another to the east, but obviously my survival instinct had hitched a ride out of town with my common sense.

Shannon was in danger *now*. And whatever Duchinski was up to, he was up to it in Kingsbridge, too.

Upon a moment's reflection, I realized that my nemesis, Sawicki, was actively occupied, far away from me. *Moron,* I accused myself again for good luck, as I sealed the stairway behind me and strode out into the summer night to enlist the aid of the cavalry.

Quillen Foster would do, since he was the only cavalry I could recognize from the doorway of the jam-packed bar.

"Quillen," I whispered in his ear as my eyes searched the room. He jumped, startled, then settled down into being picked up.

"Vic, good to see you," he responded. "Can I get you a—what happened to your shoes?"

"Long story." There was a suspicious reorganization at the far waitress station. "Do you have a car?" I kept my eyes glued to the spot where Sean would appear if he came into the bar from the basement.

"Sure." He looked puzzled but not entirely thrown.

"Let's go." I pulled at his sleeve.

"I just got my drink, Vic, can't it wait?"

The drinkers at the end of the bar parted to allow Sean McAleer a spot at the waitress station ten yards away. His rheumy eyes found me immediately.

"NO," I shouted, pulling harder. "Shannon's in trouble, and we have to get to her NOW."

Quillen responded with all the urgency for which his training had prepared him. We dashed out onto the sidewalk. Quillen took my arm and led me speedily to his silver Taurus, parked at a meter on the corner of Eighty-first Street.

"Where to?" he asked, not waiting for me to buckle up.

"North," I directed, looking behind me to McAleer's door. I didn't think Sean could have made it through the crowd so quickly, but the old man had surprised me several times already.

We got away clean, as far as I could tell.

"Talk to me," Quillen ordered, pulling a mobile blue light from beneath his seat. "Hold that." He thrust the emergency flash into my lap and rolled down the driver's window. He slapped the mechanism onto the roof of the Taurus and we were washed in strobing blue light as we careened up Broadway.

"Get onto the Henry Hudson," I pointed. "We're going to Kingsbridge."

"The Bronx?" Quillen asked, and lightened his pressure on the gas pedal slightly. "What is Shannon doing in Kingsbridge, of all places, tonight? I thought you two were going on a double date."

"It's a long story," I stammered.

"Yeah, well it's a long trip," he answered, pushing the pedal back to the metal. "Kingsbridge," he breathed. "Shit."

I began my tale of woe.

"You see—" I started, and was immediately interrupted by the FBI agent.

"Never mind, Bowering," he dismissed me. "I need to concentrate on my driving. You may not believe this, but we Feds don't do a lot of high-speed chasing. Just answer my questions yes or no, okay?"

"Okay." Quillen was right. Sean McAleer had more experience dodging Manhattan traffic, or at least, it bothered him less. I held on to the dashboard for dear life.

"Shannon's alone in the Bronx?"

"Well, we both—"

"Yes or no."

I closed my eyes as we tore up the tailpipe of a slow-moving Cadillac. "Yes." The Taurus veered sharply to pass on the right. I think I squealed like a girl.

"An Irish bar near where that explosion took place last week?" The tires screamed as we ripped onto the Grand Central Parkway.

"Yes." I was getting that doomed feeling again, and waited for the next question. It did not come.

Clearly, every person I knew on the Upper West Side knew the score except for Shannon and me.

Smoke billowed from over the street incline as we neared the Blarney Rose. Even with the aid of Quillen's magical emergency light, cars were locked end to end and would not budge to allow us closer. Quillen swore vehemently and threw the government car into park in the middle of the side street.

"You stay here," he ordered me. "I'll find Shannon and bring her back here. Right?"

I didn't doubt it.

"Right," I answered.

I just didn't trust his all-knowingness. Once he found Shannon, I had no way of knowing what he planned to do with her.

Or me.

The wind changed direction and smothered the car with smoke. Quillen slammed his door and disappeared into the noxious fog. I pulled the chiffon ruffle up from my bodice and held it to my nose. My eyes watered in protest to the airborne pollution the moment I opened the passenger-side door, but the chiffon filtered most of the smoke from my lungs.

Quillen had taken off in a straight line to the east, so I shot off due north. Any side street to the right should head me back to the commercial avenue and the Blarney Rose.

In uneven bursts, gusts of wind alternated clear sailing and total immersion from the nearby fire. I navigated primarily by the crowd noises emanating from the point of conflagration. Tears dissolved my mascara into gummy rivulets. I wiped my nose on Shannon's expensive shirt and ran to a position upwind, then cut over to get a clear look at the fire.

Supporting myself on a mailbox, I squinted and blinked in the direction of the smoke. The more my lids fluttered, the more grit carried on the wind ground into my eyeballs, and the more the mascara clotted and drizzled.

I was absolutely, clinically blind in the middle of I had no idea where.

A kind hand placed a linen handkerchief over the flood plane of my face as I hacked and wheezed.

And held the fabric tight against my mouth and nose.

"Damn you, Bowering."

I felt my battered feet being lifted from the pavement as Buck Sawicki hoisted me into his iron arms and carried me at a trot away from the crowd and emergency crews. This time he was careful to hold my arms down across my chest. I could only suppose that the sight of a powerful man carrying a disheveled, hysterical woman away from a raging fire wouldn't raise any alarms from onlookers.

Sawicki might even get a heroism award for abducting me in such a duplicitous fashion. I could envision the newspaper photo and the headline: "Valiant effort fails."

Life is funny.

I tried to make my weight as dead as possible, thinking that it might slow him down, or at least convince him that I was not an immediate danger. If anything, he sped up. Through the handkerchief I could not tell if my vision had cleared enough for me to make an escape, even if I should get the chance.

Cold air blasted across my wet skin. We were indoors. Sawicki dropped me heavily into what felt like an empty wooden container.

Free of his arms, I dragged the handkerchief roughly over my face and squinted into the light, but my eyes were too traumatized to focus properly, and all I could make out of my surroundings was a blur of yellow-orange. An expanse of wood cut into my side. As I flailed there was the sound of shattering glass.

"You're all right," a woman's voice assured me. I didn't think so. A wet rag dabbed at my ruined face. "Aw, Victoria," Shannon chided, "you spilled my martini."

Slowly, the world came into focus. Shannon plucked shards of glass from the table and dropped them into an ashtray. I squinted. The ashtray read "Harp and Ladle."

Sawicki had dumped me in a booth in an Irish bar with Shannon to stand guard. Nonetheless, I was relieved that I wouldn't have Shannon's demise on my conscience for whatever time I had left of my miserable life.

But, I'll admit, I hoped she would never get another night's peaceful sleep for her horrific, eleventh-hour betrayal of the poor, late me. And that it would leave furrows all over her smiling, self-satisfied face.

"You've been in on this from the beginning," I accused. Buck Sawicki leaned against the bar, four feet to my right, and handed Shannon a fresh martini.

"Have a drink," she urged. "You look terrible." I looked into the martini olive for a little wisdom.

"I'd prefer bourbon."

Sawicki nodded and gestured to the bartender, who was observing me as he would a two-headed goat.

"I don't suppose," Shannon mopped my cheeks with spilled vodka until she appeared satisfied with the way I cleaned up, "you packed any Valium?" she asked. Buck handed me my bourbon. I ignored Shannon's question.

"Just let me see if I've got this right," I said, watching Sawicki from the corner of my eye. "Dave was murdered because he was moonlighting as a munitions drop point. The walk-in at McAleer's was the perfect place to keep explosives that might become unstable in the heat."

Shannon leaned back in the booth.

"I don't know what you're talking about," she said.

Sawicki sat on a stool at the bar and casually crossed his arms across his chest.

"Go on, Bowering," he urged.

"Dave had a drug habit, cocaine, and the only way he could afford to maintain it was to be paid off in the stuff. Unfortunately, since everyone in the neighborhood knew what a mess he was becoming, it also made him a bad bet to keep his mouth shut forever, so the guys he was holding for gave him one big, final freebie."

"Okay"—Sawicki nodded over his ginger ale—"then what am I doing here?"

"You"—I sipped smugly at my bourbon—"are an armaments specialist in the paid employ of the Irish Republican Army. That's why you bugged my apartment. You were making sure that if I started to figure everything out, you could get rid of me."

"Then why would I bug Kerry McAleer's office, if this is an Irish plot?"

Shannon excused herself and toddled off to the ladies' room, giggling a bit at my powers of deduction.

"To make sure that Sean and Shannon weren't going to sell you out." Sawicki slid off his stool and into the spot left by Shannon. He leaned forward with a smile that might have been endearing if he weren't so intimidating. His tattoo rippled as he rolled his ginger ale and sloshed the ice cubes from side to side.

"So, Sherlock," he said, "how does Duchinski fit into all of this?"

I whispered bourbon breath into his face, "He doesn't. He never believed you were trailing me. You had him fooled, too?" I hoped. I cared.

"Wrong again," Dan corrected me from behind the high booth. "Let's go," he said. "My car is right around the corner. We'll meet George back at the ranch."

When I am wrong, I am so *wrong*.

"Why?" was all I could think to ask Duchinski as I followed him out the door.

"Because I like to see you suffer," he answered evenly.

SEVENTEEN

SOMETHING GOOD can come out of anything, my grand-mother used to say. The good part of having no one speaking to you is that it frees up a lot of time for self-abusive pondering. And, me being me, I did it out loud in the backseat stuffed securely next to my shadow, Sawicki.

"I know I'm right about Dave," I started. "The reason I know there was contraband in the walk-in was the missing case of Pabst. With the explosives removed, there was an empty slot which Bennie unwittingly replaced with a case of beer that had not been used or inventoried. Which," I rather surprised even myself, "incidentally, clears Kerry, who would not have made a stink over it if he had thought there was anything hinky about what was being stored in the walk-in."

Dan's poker face convinced me I was right, so far.

"Terrence," I continued, "must have been Dave's connection. He was adamant about convincing himself that I was Irish before he would relax around me, and then he tried to slip me cocaine to see if I would cause a stink or be amenable to taking Dave's place in the organization. The network is probably citywide"—I impressed even myself—"squirreled away in little cells in all kinds of Irish bars all over Manhattan."

"And the Bronx," Dan added.

"Right," I confirmed to myself. "Terrence had matchbooks from every Irish bar from the Battery to—"

The ah-ha principle struck again.

As a less-is-more actor, I should have recognized overkill when I saw it.

Terrence had gone to a lot of trouble to convince me that

he was something that he wasn't. Shannon spotted it right away. But I couldn't figure out why he would even bother to point me in the direction of an IRA conspiracy.

He wouldn't. I was a latecomer to the game. He had already set himself up in the immigrant Irish community as a fellow instead of the Maine native he accidentally revealed himself to be, so it was *them* he needed to fool.

And of all the fools I have known and loved, the least foolish of all the Irish ones would be Sean McAleer. If the old man smelled something rotten in Killarney, he would have naturally called his son, George of Alcohol, Tobacco, and Firearms. And George would notify the NYPD to protect his family, who would hook him up with a familiar senior officer to gather inside information.

Enter Dan Duchinski.

"Oh, God," I moaned in a wash of connective thought. Stashing explosives in the United States wouldn't do the IRA any good—they were thousands of miles away. Terrence was using Irish-American sentiment to double-blind a militia organization here in the States. "It was Terrence, all along. Sawicki was just a convicted felon, planted to infiltrate the militia who had their sights set on blowing a big bite into the Apple during tourist season."

"And to try and keep you from screwing up the works," Dan said as we arrived at McAleer's door. Beau was locking up early, but waved us in. I followed, meek and barefoot.

Sean shouted a hello from the door of the kitchen, saucepan in hand. I could smell eggs and bangers from across the room. George was pulling beers from behind the bar, and gestured to a large back table all set for dining. Beau brought a large tray covered with food into the bar. I took a place next to Shannon.

"I was right about Dave," I muttered to myself.

"Sort of," Dan conceded. He sat next to me and shook out his napkin. "But you were wrong about me."

"Only sort of."

"And Terrence."

"Kinda."

"And Sean, and Buck, and Shannon."

"Oh, for heaven's sake!" I surrendered. "All right, so I got myself a little paranoid, okay? But, you have to admit, it sure *seemed* like everyone was out to get me."

"Right you are, darlin'," Sean agreed. "We'll be missing that quality around here, for sure."

"I beg your pardon? What are you trying to tell me, Sean?"

"Why that you're fired, of course. Should have done it that day when I first saw you." He heaped my plate with eggs and sausage. "Nice girls don't belong behind bars."

The sound of the phone ringing barely penetrated my sensory overload.

"I don't know," Dan disagreed, digging into his meal. "Some do"—he chewed thoughtfully on a piece of white toast—"as long as the bars are in a maximum security facility."

Nice talk from a loved one. At least the worst was behind me.

"Victoria!" Shannon called to me, waving the phone in her hand. "It's Stewart. He'd like a raincheck!"

EPILOGUE

SHANNON AND I had our fancy lunch at Café des Artistes but, owing to my unemployment, she paid.

"I can't believe you stopped drinking," she admonished me over a glass of Perriér Joët.

"I just lost my taste for it." I shrugged.

"Yes, well, bartending cuts both ways in that regard." She toasted me. "Either you join in or give it up entirely. In many ways, the job has a better success rate than AA. Cheers!"

"Easy for you to say. Please tell me it wasn't Sawicki that etched that smile on your face." She tilted her chin innocently, which convinced me she had put another notch in her designer belt. But, far be it for me to expect a friend to do without, just because I was. "Terrific," I grumped, "I'm unemployed and obviously underloved. Which reminds me, how is Kerry doing?"

"Fine, I believe. He swears he's learned his lesson, but, as you know, some people just *can't.*"

"I know. Take responsibility for your own garbage, I say."

"What you need," Shannon said, "is a wee vacation to take your mind off your troubles."

"With what? My good looks?" I stared longingly at the ice bucket. "I'm broke. Even if Sean puts me in for my last week toward a claim, unemployment won't cut me a check for at least two weeks."

"Perfect!" Shannon signaled for another bottle. "I have enough frequent flyer miles to take us anywhere in the world! You won't even have to pack; I'll bring clothes for the both of us."

"I still can't afford it, Shannon." In my depression, I poured myself a glass of bubbly.

"Silly woman. It's FREE, Miss V!"

By my second glass of champagne, I had completely forgotten that nothing is ever truly free.

You know how I get.

Yeah. Life is funny.

I think Margaret Thatcher said that, and she *cared*.

CLEAN SWEEP

BARBARA PAUL

CURT HOLLAND and his second-in-command sat lost in their separate thoughts, both of them ignoring the muted television at the end of the bar. It was, Holland supposed, what passed for companionable silence among men with no connection other than work. Bill Tuttle had found this bar, the nearest to their offices that served Lagavulin, Holland's preferred scotch; now the barman knew them both by sight if not by name.

Tuttle was staring glumly into his glass. "Every time I look for pictures in ice, I see a skull. I used to see naked women, but now nothing but skulls."

"That's your libido complaining of fatigue," Holland said. "Telling you it's time to slow down."

"I don't have a libido. It ran away with Mary Sue Parkins thirty-one years ago. Fifth grade. Ah, Mary Sue of the Golden Curls. I wonder where she is now."

Holland looked for pictures in his own ice cubes and found a lopsided four-leaf clover. "Did you ever try to track her down?"

Tuttle grinned. "I've resisted the temptation. Mary Sue has become my icon for self-restraint. Let her live her life without interference from me."

Holland understood; curiosity without discipline was a child's game. Tuttle's restraint was especially commendable in view of the fact that he was in a better position than most to find out anything he wanted to know about anyone. Tuttle headed the team of hackers in Holland's employ that consistently fattened the bank account by running checks on job applicants, executives up for promotion, new companies that investors were interested in. It was what computer detectives did best.

Someone asked the barman to turn up the volume on the TV, and the sonorous tones of a newsreader floated through the air. Holland raised his voice and said, "We're not taking the Feuerbach account. That gang of starry-eyed idealists will never oust their CEO, and we don't back losing horses."

"A client is a client."

"And the CEO will be a better one."

"Okay, boss." Tuttle's Sergeant Bilko glasses had slid down his nose; he pushed them back up. "You're siding with the Establishment against the rebels? That's a first. Maybe something's telling *you* to slow down."

"Entirely possible," Holland said crisply.

"The last time we—whoa, hold on!" Tuttle was listening to the newscaster speaking of the death of a man named Gordon Lockerby, whose sole claim to fame was winning a million dollars in a magazine sweepstakes and then dying before he could cash his first payment check. "Huh," Tuttle said. "We investigated him."

"We did?"

"Just last month. Armstead Associates—the people who run the sweepstakes—Armstead sent us a bunch of finalists to check out."

Holland found that interesting. "Armstead screens its finalists? The winner isn't chosen by random drawing?"

"Never heard that," Tuttle said with a shrug. "But they use their winners in promotional gimmicks, so they want to winnow out drug dealers and cons on the lam and the like."

Holland smiled, mouth only. "And we all know how many escaped convicts stop running long enough to subscribe to magazines. I wonder how much other winnowing-out Armstead does."

Tuttle laughed. "You're too suspicious, Boss."

"There's no such thing as too suspicious." When they'd

finished their drinks, they parted company, Tuttle heading home to his wife and kids and Holland back to the building on Lexington that housed his offices.

A million dollars that hadn't been collected.

The door on the fortieth floor said only Holland Investigations, in deceptively modest lettering. Inside, the decor was deliberately and perhaps even ostentatiously upscale; the expanse of unused floor space alone told prospective clients this was no low-rent outfit they were dealing with. A light was on in one of the offices; someone working late.

The four computers in Holland's office were left running all the time. Holland sat down at one and called up Bill Tuttle's Armstead files. Originally the magazine promotional sweepstakes had been an annual event, but the response had been sufficient to warrant additional contests. Armstead had held three so far that year, and it was only the third day of September; time for one more before year's end. Was there that much money to be made selling magazines?

Evidently so. The range of magazines offered was astounding, from long-established periodicals like *Newsweek* and *Reader's Digest* to little-known publications for every specialized interest from glassblowing to marching bands. Armstead complied with the letter of the law by announcing no one was required to buy magazines in order to enter the sweepstakes. At the same time the entry form provided places for ordering *eight* subscriptions. The prize of one million dollars was to be paid out in ten annual installments of $100,000. No, you didn't have to buy magazines to enter, but Holland didn't give a fig for your chances of winning if you didn't.

He scrolled through the data collected by Bill Tuttle's team until he came to Gordon Lockerby, the winner who'd died before he could deposit his first $100,000 check. Lockerby had been a semiretired apple grower from upstate New York. Seventy-two years old, wife deceased, only living relative a great-niece who was a furniture buyer for Bloomingdale's. Holland clicked back to the contest rules. Prize money was not transferable; the niece had no claim on Lockerby's winnings. All those subscriptions coming in and no prize money going out—Armstead had won its own sweepstakes this time.

Suspicious, Holland ran a search on the ages of the finalists. Most of them were well on in years. But that alone proved nothing; Holland needed to know about previous winners.

He switched to the Internet and checked Reuters for any mention of Gordon Lockerby. There was a short item; Lockerby had run his pickup truck into a tree on a back road between his apple orchard and Schenectady. Cause of death was a broken neck. Lockerby was alone in his truck and no other vehicle was involved. Survived by his great-niece Selena Ross of New York City. In Lockerby's billfold were the sweepstakes check and a deposit slip for the Schenectady branch of the Amsterdam Savings Bank.

Holland logged off and headed down the hall toward the one lighted office. The late worker was André Flood, at twenty the youngest investigator at Holland Investigations. The youngest and arguably the best. André still needed some seasoning, but his intuitive approach to computers equalled and sometimes, Holland grudgingly admitted, surpassed his own.

It was after seven-thirty and the young man thought he was alone in the offices, but he was still wearing a tie. André Flood had his papers stacked neatly in sorted piles, his disks filed away where they ought to be, and not a Coke can or Twinkies wrapper in sight. Even his pens were lined up in a neat row. He didn't hear Holland come in and looked up only when he saw his employer's reflection in the monitor's screen. "Mr. Holland. I thought you'd left."

"Are you working on anything that can't wait?"

André rattled off a list of the projects awaiting his attention. "Nothing really high priority."

"Put it on hold. I have something I want you to do." Holland told him to find out who the decision-makers were at Armstead Associates, what their financial status was, what percentage they got back on each subscription sold, who the sweepstakes winners were the past two years. "Names, ages, how much they've collected, what they're doing now."

The young man's face brightened. "Is it a scam?" André loved scams.

"Could be. Start on it first thing tomorrow."

"I'll start on it now."

"Tomorrow, André. Go home. You do have a home, don't you?"

"I'll just make a start. It's only eight o'clock."

Holland checked his watch. "I'm supposed to be at the Four Seasons at eight."

"You'll be late," André said unnecessarily.

"*She'll* be late. I have a grace period." Nevertheless he was hurrying when he left.

THE NEXT MORNING a phone call to Bloomingdale's told Holland that their buyers' offices were not located in the store but at 919 Third Avenue. He found Selena Ross, Gordon Lockerby's great-niece and only surviving relative, on the fifth floor.

The woman herself was pure Noo Yawk. Dark-haired, intense, aggressively chic, with a voice that could pierce an eardrum if she raised the volume even a smidge. A true Manhattanite, she was instantly suspicious when Holland said he'd like to ask her about Gordon Lockerby. "Uncle Gordon? Why? And who're you?"

"My name is Holland and I'm looking into the Armstead magazine sweepstakes. If you—"

"Again, why? And 'Holland' tells me squat. Hey, you

could be out on parole for all I know. Why should I talk to you?''

Holland swallowed a retort and showed her his private investigator's license. A sympathetic approach, perhaps. "I'm sorry for your loss, Ms Ross." The unintentional rhyme took something off the sincerity quotient.

"What loss?"

She didn't know. Holland sat facing her across her desk. "Gordon Lockerby died yesterday, in an accident. No one notified you?"

Selena Ross looked startled. "Uncle Gordon's dead?" She was silent a moment. "Then I'm the last." She shook her head. "No one would know to notify me. My uncle and I weren't exactly in touch."

"You were estranged?"

"Look, Mr. Holland, I saw the man exactly twice in my life—the last time, I was eight or nine. After my parents died, I gave Uncle Gordon a call. Four years ago. The only two surviving members of a family ought to talk to each other, right?" She sighed. "He barely remembered me. And he was annoyed because I was keeping him from his TV program. That was the last contact I ever had with Gordon Lockerby."

Dead end. "Then I'm sorry to have taken up your time." Holland started to get up.

"Oh, no, you don't!" Selena Ross commanded. "You don't drop a bomb like that and then walk away. How did he die? What happened? Tell me."

Holland could hardly refuse such a gracious invitation. He told her everything—the sweepstakes winning, the first payment of $100,000, Lockerby's crash on the way to the bank.

When he'd finished, she burst out laughing. "The old coot won a million-dollar sweepstakes? And didn't get to spend a penny of it." There was a gleam in her eye. "He had the check with him when he died?"

"The prize money is not transferable," Holland said, amused at the way she was handling her grief.

"Yeah, but he was on his way to deposit it. That demonstrates intent. Did he leave a will?"

"That I can't tell you. But if he didn't leave everything to the Apple Growers Association, you now own a lot of fruit trees."

She grinned, and then suddenly sobered. "Hey, I'm not normally this greedy, but—well, maybe I am. All I know is that a disagreeable old man who gave me the cold shoulder when I tried to make friends is dead. And now I'll be able to pay off my credit cards. This is supposed to make me feel bad?"

"Not at all. But you need a lawyer."

"I need a lawyer," she agreed, and reached for her Rolodex. She barely noticed when Holland left.

AS HE WALKED BACK toward Lexington, Holland pulled out his phone and called André Flood. "What have you got?"

"I have the people stuff done," André's young voice replied. "I'm just ready to start on the financial stuff."

Holland had reached Lexington and looked uptown. Bloomingdale's was about midway between his offices and where he was standing. "Print out what you've got and trot on down to Bloomie's. I'll be in the coffee shop on the first floor or lower level or whatever it's called—I feel a sudden need for caffeine."

"What if there's more than one coffee shop?"

"Then *look* for me, André," Holland snapped, and broke the connection. Some detective.

ONLY FOUR OTHER MEN were in the Bloomingdale coffee shop, sitting three tables away from Holland's. One of the men was sporting a lime-green wig, another had on fishnet hose, and all four were wearing high heels, short skirts, and industrial-strength make-up. They were laughing and talking loudly, their eyes scanning the room to see out how much they were being watched.

Holland had started his third cup of coffee before André Flood showed up. André spotted him and headed toward his table—but then stopped when he caught sight of the cross-dressers. One of them waved a napkin in the air and called out, "Hi, Sweetie! Come join us!"

André's face turned pink and he hastily slid into the chair next to Holland's. The other customers were laughing good-naturedly at the drag queens' performance, but André was uncomfortable. "Why do they *do* that?"

"They need the attention," Holland answered. "Show me what you brought."

The young man opened his briefcase and pulled out a handful of printouts. "The president and majority stock-holder of Armstead is named Warren Winstead. His CEO is Cal Armstrong. They once ran an advertising agency called Winstrong but it went belly-up. Then twelve years ago they hit upon this magazine promotion scheme and struck a gold mine. They advertise that the winners are se-lected by an outside accounting firm to ensure impartiality." André was smirking. "A firm owned by Mrs. Warren Win-stead and Mrs. Cal Armstrong."

"What a surprise. Is that confirmed? The gold mine?"

"Not yet—I'll start on that when I get back. But if they've stuck with it for twelve years, they must be getting a good return."

Holland nodded. "It'll take me a few minutes to read through this. Get yourself some coffee."

"No, thanks. I'll…just sit here." Didn't want to be a target again. André had found that one of the year's earlier two winners had also died, a twenty-two-year-old leukemia victim in Indianapolis. The surviving winner was an eighty-nine-year-old woman in a nursing home in Seattle. Well, now. Armstead was handpicking winners who were not

likely to live long enough to collect their full million? He
read on.

The previous year's winners fit the pattern. An over-
weight, hard-drinking, chain-smoking fifty-year-old cop in
St. Louis who'd already had one coronary. A Los Angeles
party boy hooked on alcohol and cocaine. A race car driver
on the Florida circuit who'd crashed in three of his last four
races. A woman on dialysis in Houston. Only the cop and
the race car driver were still alive.

Holland raised an eyebrow at André. "Where did you get
all this detail?"

The young man looked pleased. "From Armstead's system." No one's computer system was safe from André
Flood. "They've been using a detective to check up on certain names just selected at random. As soon as the detective
found one with a short life expectancy, that person was
named the winner."

Holland's mouth tightened; what was more cold-blooded
than the human animal on the scent of a dollar? "But we
ran the background checks."

"Just started. Their detective became ill and had to retire,
so they contacted us."

"And made us an accessory to fraud." What had started
as an interest in a floating million was now becoming a
mission; Holland didn't like being played for a patsy. There
was no way he could allow Armstead to involve him in their
illegal sweepstakes. Ergo, Armstead had to go. Holland had
never wrecked a company before. He was looking forward
to it.

"There's only one winner that doesn't fit the profile,"
André was saying. "Gordon Lockerby."

"And?"

"He was seventy-two, but he wasn't sickly. And they
didn't know he'd crash his..." André's eyes grew wide.
"You mean they...?"

"Killed him. They couldn't wait for nature to take its course this time—find out why not. And fill in Bill Tuttle."

They stood up to leave, and a chorus of falsetto goodbyes trilled out from three tables away. "I *like* the older one," one voice announced. Holland smiled and blew a kiss toward the table, eliciting peals of laughter.

End of coffee break.

ARMSTEAD ASSOCIATES had its headquarters on South Broadway, in a building that had seen better days. The twentieth-floor offices were crowded, with rows of tables occupied by employees opening envelopes and feeding data into computers. Holland got in to see CEO Cal Armstrong by uttering three magic letters: IRS.

The most noticeable thing about Armstrong was that he had no neck. His head appeared to be resting directly on his shoulders—massive, linebacker shoulders that looked lumpy even under his custom-tailored jacket. Armstrong was in his late forties and thus ostensibly past his prime, but Holland would still hate to meet him in a dark alley. The first words out of Armstrong's mouth were a demand to see some identification.

Holland opened his billfold and flipped through half a dozen bogus IDs until he came to the one that said he was James Novak of the Internal Revenue Service. Armstrong looked at the photo on the ID and handed it back. "All right, Novak, what can I do for you?"

"You can file a supplementary quarterly return." Armstead Associates, Holland said, had undeclared income that was subject to interest and penalties. Two of Armstead's contest winners had died since the beginning of the year, and Armstead had to declare the unpaid prize money as additional income. New regulation.

Armstrong hit the ceiling. "What the hell kind of regulation is that? That prize money is money we earned—we already paid tax on it once!"

"Mr. Armstrong, we're trying to educate businesses to the new regulation—"

"Educate? Educate us to a new way of screwing us!" He reached for the phone and punched out a number. "Warren, better get in here. IRS." He turned back to Holland. "Our accountants said nothing about this new regulation."

Holland reminded him it was his and Winstead's signatures on the bottom of the tax forms. "Another thing—you can't expense funds you don't have. Unpaid prize money."

"But we do have it! It's on deposit. That's the law, Novak. Anybody running a sweepstakes in this country has to have eighty percent of the prize money on deposit before you can even announce the contest."

"We have no record of any such deposits."

Armstrong swore. "I'll show you." He went to the computer and started typing. "Here," he said. "Look at this."

Holland looked. The screen showed a year-to-date statement from Commerce Bank. Armstead had made four deposits, two payments and one withdrawal.

"That withdrawal was the money earmarked for our first winner this year," Armstrong said. "She died of leukemia, poor girl."

"I see," said Holland. "Could I have a printout of that?"

Armstrong printed it out. "So you're saying we owe tax on that withdrawal? That's double taxation, dammit. You can't do that."

Holland had just folded the printout and slipped it into a pocket when the door opened and a dapper, bearded man a few years older than Armstrong stepped into the room. "What's the problem, Cal?" he asked in a pleasant voice. Slim and graceful, Warren Winstead was as elegant as Cal Armstrong was thuggish; Holland wondered how the two had ever got together.

Armstrong gestured toward Holland. "This is Novak from the IRS. He says we owe them money." He stood driving one fist into his other hand while Holland explained the "regulation" again.

Warren Winstead was looking at Holland strangely. "Has this new regulation been challenged in court, Mr., er, Novak?"

Holland smiled. "Almost immediately. It held up. It's not retroactive, but you'll still need to include the unpaid prize money for this year in your next quarterly return. It's due on the fifteenth of this month, and that would be for both winners who've died since the beginning of the year."

Winstead gave him another odd look. "Good lord, man, it was only yesterday that one of our winners died. Don't you know anything about sweepstakes law? We can't touch that money for ninety days. Right now it belongs to no one. How can we declare it as income by the fifteenth if it's still frozen?"

"Earning interest?" Holland asked innocently.

Again, the odd look from Winstead. "Only two percent. And we declare it." On the defensive.

Holland pretended to mull it over. "Frozen assets will make a difference," he conceded. "I'll need to consult my supervisor. We'll get back to you."

"You do that," Armstrong said, and pointed at the door. Holland gave them an icy smile and left.

IT WAS A SIMPLE MATTER to lift Armstrong's fingerprints from the bank statement the CEO had printed out. It was equally simple to enter the FBI's computer system. A former FBI agent, Holland had discovered two back doors into the agency's system, created by the system designers to allow themselves access whenever crash repair was needed. Holland had seen no reason to share that information with anyone else at the agency.

Now the FBI's Automated Fingerprint Identification System told him Cal Armstrong had no criminal record. "He probably doesn't think of himself as a criminal," Holland said to Bill Tuttle, who was reading over his shoulder. "Just another businessman, trying to get an edge on the other guy. Fraud? Not a bit of it! Just sharp business practice."

"I wonder what he calls murder," Tuttle said. "Damage control? Do you really think they killed Lockerby?"

"They're picking winners on the basis of who's likely to die first. And Gordon Lockerby just happened to run his pickup into that tree at a convenient moment?"

"Yeah, well, put like that." Tuttle pushed his heavy-frame glasses back up his nose. "So what do we do now? Call the police?"

"Not yet." Holland thought a moment. "When a sweepstakes winner is announced—isn't that treated as an event worthy of the attention given a coronation? News releases, camera crews, the works?"

Tuttle was nodding. "Yep, lots of hoopla. I've seen some of those surprised winners in Armstead's TV commercials. Why?"

"I'm wondering if in the case of Gordon Lockerby either Armstrong or Winstead took part in the hoopla. Were they in the vicinity? There might be a tape at one of the Schenectady TV stations."

"I'll find out." Tuttle started out of Holland's office. "They might have hired someone to do it."

Holland had thought of that. If that were the case, he had virtually no chance of proving Winstead and/or Armstrong guilty of murder. He followed Tuttle down the hallway but turned in to André Flood's office.

"They're broke," André said by way of greeting. "They've got three million in the bank, but they need thirty million to pay off all the winners who are still living. They've been borrowing heavily and have a big payment due the first of October."

"So they needed cash before the end of the month. What went wrong? Why did they start losing so much?"

André lifted his shoulders. "Attrition. Magazine sales

have been slipping steadily for the past nine or ten years. People aren't reading as much."

"What percentage of the subscription money does Armstead get?"

"Varies according to the magazine, from ten percent to fifty. Big-circulation mags pay on a sliding scale—the more subscriptions Armstead brings in, the higher the percentage."

"And people are reading less," Holland said. "So the business is failing in spite of their thieving ways."

"What do you want me to do now?"

"Not a thing. That was nice work, André." Holland left without seeing the way the young man was glaring at him.

ANDRÉ'S REMARK that people were reading less reminded Holland of a book he'd been meaning to buy; that was as good an excuse as any to get out of the office for a while.

Holland didn't like the big chain bookstores and headed toward an independent shop on Sixty-seventh where he was greeted by name and left alone to browse as much as he liked. About a dozen other customers were in the small bookshop, none of them in a hurry. Holland ended up with four books in addition to the one he'd come to buy, not an unusual occurrence.

The bookshop owner, a middle-aged woman Holland knew only as Millie, took his credit card with a smile. "You're turning out to be one of my best customers, Mr. Holland," she said.

"I like your bookshop, Millie," he replied easily. "And I like buying from someone who knows books."

And Millie liked hearing that. She followed Holland out and stood holding open the glass door as they chatted about the books he'd bought. Traffic on Sixty-seventh Street was light, so Holland heard the car before he saw it.

A black sedan pulled up to the curb and paused long enough for Holland to spot the oversized nozzle pointing out the back-seat window. Without stopping to think, Holland dropped his books and threw himself at Millie. They hit the floor just as a tongue of flame shot in over their heads—a *whoosh* quickly followed by screams of fear and the crackle of burning paper. The car sped away.

A flamethrower. They'd come after him with a *flamethrower*.

One whole wall of books was burning; the fire arced to touch an aisle display, and then another…a second wall of books caught fire. The other customers were yelling and pushing their way out. Two of them had been burned. Millie had struggled to her feet and was trying desperately to gather up what books she could. Holland grabbed her and dragged her out to the street. "My books!" she screamed, struggling against him. "I've got to get my books!"

"They're gone, Millie," he said harshly. "Stay out of there." He held on to her arm with one hand as he fished out his phone and called 911.

A small crowd gathered, but the heat and smoke drove them to the other side of the street. Millie was crying softly; a couple of her frightened customers tried to comfort her. The life she'd built for herself had, literally, gone up in flames—and only because Holland had come to *her* shop to buy his book. He'd brought this on her.

The firefighters arrived, and an ambulance, and the police—who blocked off the street and started asking questions. The two burn patients were treated on the spot. A TV camera crew showed up and tried to interview Millie until Holland persuaded them they didn't really want to bother her; it took only one convincing threat.

Eventually the flames were out and the firefighters were satisfied the adjoining buildings were safe. The walls of Millie's store were still standing, but the place had been gutted. All that was left was one big, black, foul-smelling hole.

The police took Holland and Millie into the Seventeenth-Precinct stationhouse on East Fifty-first to make separate statements. They told the same story: they'd been standing in the open doorway when a car pulled up and someone fired a flamethrower at them. No, they didn't see who that someone was. No, they didn't get a look at the driver, either. It had happened so fast, you see.

Millie was telling the truth. But Holland had had a clear view of the dapper, bearded man behind the wheel; Warren Winstead had been driving. That meant No-Neck Armstrong was in the back seat manning the flamethrower.

Holland thought back to the odd looks Warren Winstead had kept throwing him in the Armstead offices. What Holland had assumed were querulous looks at the IRS's unwelcome interest in Armstead had been something else entirely. Winstead had recognized him, that was the only explanation. He'd simply gone along with the charade. Holland's face was not unknown to newspapers and TV news; going to the Armstead offices himself instead of sending one of his operatives had not been one of his brighter moves.

Cal Armstrong and Warren Winstead—so desperate that they couldn't take the chance on what a prying computer detective might turn up. *Amateurs,* Holland thought scornfully. So rattled by the mess they'd gotten themselves into that they didn't know anything to do but hit out.

They must have followed him to the bookshop—a simple tail job, since he'd gone on foot. And the result was that an innocent bookseller had lost everything she had. It was the reason Holland had not identified Winstead to the police. Seeing those two in prison wasn't enough.

He found Millie slumped in a posture of defeat on a wooden bench between two complaining hookers. "Come on, Millie," Holland said, "let me take you home."

She roused herself a little. "I called a friend."

"Then let's wait outside. You don't want to stay here."

Millie let him lead her out of the stationhouse. They stood on the sidewalk, impervious to the passersby who occasionally brushed against them. Holland asked if she had insurance.

"Some," she said shakily. "Not enough to restock. And I had a rent-controlled lease on that shop. I won't be able to find another place at that price. Not in Midtown." She turned an anguished face toward him. "I never thanked you. You saved my life, Mr. Holland, and I didn't thank you."

I also put you in danger in the first place. "You can give me a book when you open your new shop."

A sad little shake of her head. "There won't be any new shop. I'm done."

A Honda stopped. Another middle-aged woman climbed out and wrapped both arms around Millie without saying a word.

Holland watched the Honda pull away, thinking. According to André Flood, Armstead had three million in the bank. That would work out just right. One million for him, one for Lockerby's niece...and one for Millie.

By TEN O'CLOCK the next morning, FedEx had delivered the videotape from station WRGB in Schenectady. By noon, Selena Ross was standing in one of the conference rooms in Holland's offices watching it.

"So?" she said. "So the two guys who run the sweepstakes showed up when Uncle Gordon won. You said he was murdered. What's this tape got to do with that?"

Holland said, "Those are the two men who killed your uncle."

Her mouth dropped open. "But...*why?*"

Bill Tuttle said, "To keep him from depositing that check. The sweepstakes were rigged."

Holland explained that winners were chosen for their short life expectancies. "Armstrong and Winstead have money in the bank, but it's locked into special accounts payable only to previous winners. They figured some of those earlier winners were living altogether too long. They simply couldn't afford to pay off another one.''

"Then why not kill one of them? Why Uncle Gordon?''

"Geographical accessibility. Schenectady is closer than Los Angeles.''

"I think I'd better sit down.'' Tuttle moved a chair over for her.

André Flood was peering at the paused image of Cal Armstrong on the screen. "That man has no neck,'' he said wonderingly.

"It just happened to be your uncle,'' Tuttle told Selena Ross. "But *whoever* won that sweepstakes would be dead now. Armstrong and Winstead are desperate. They tried to kill Mr. Holland yesterday after he went snooping around.''

"I was investigating, not 'snooping','' Holland said testily.

"You shouldn't have gone yourself,'' Tuttle muttered.

"They tried to kill you?'' Selena Ross repeated.

"With a flamethrower.''

She slumped in her chair. "My god. My god.''

Holland said, "Tell her about their private detective, André.'' This time he did see the young man glaring at him.

But André did as he was told. "Armstead used a private detective to find likely prospects—that is, people who'd entered the sweepstakes who weren't likely to live long. That's the way they've been doing it for years. But they got into a financial crunch and needed someone to die right away. Your uncle was convenient.''

Selena Ross jumped up and yelled *"Jesus Christ!"* in her high-decibel Noo Yawk voice; André took a step back. "Why are we just standing here? Why aren't we calling the police?''

Holland gave her a sardonic smile. "Well, yes, we could do that. Or we could get your uncle's million dollars for you.''

Her eyes bugged. "What?''

"There is a way. But we need your help."

She looked from one to another of the three men. "What we're talking about here—it's not exactly what you'd call legal, right?"

"Not exactly."

"But ethical," André said. The others all looked at him. "You know. Punishment fitting the crime?"

"Thank you for that insight, André." Holland turned back to Selena Ross, ignoring the dirty look André was giving him. "I can take money from anybody's bank account, frozen or not. Every bank account in the world is vulnerable—all that's needed is ingenuity and patience. I can take the money, but I don't unless I have a damned good reason. Armstead has given me several. I can get your million for you. But you have to do something for me."

"Thought I might," she said. "What?"

"Make one phone call. I want you to call the Armstead offices and say boo. Speak to either Armstrong or Winstead and identify yourself as Gordon Lockerby's heir. Say that if they pay you the million your uncle won, you won't turn his letter over to the police. The one he wrote you right before he died."

"Uh-huh. And exactly what does this letter say?"

Bill Tuttle told her. "Your uncle wanted you to know that he was leaving everything to you...in case anything happened to him. He'd overheard Armstrong say something to Winstead about his truck—it probably meant nothing, but he was going to take a back route into Schenectady the next day just to be on the safe side."

She snorted. "They're never going to believe that!"

Holland said, "Oh, they'll believe it. They're already jumping out of their skins. They're wondering if I saw who it was attacked me yesterday and whether I'm coming after them snorting fire from both nostrils. Then you enter the picture with your hand out. They'll demand to see the letter, and you'll arrange a meeting."

"Do I wear a 'Shoot Me' sign at the meeting?"

"You don't go to the meeting. We do. Armstrong and Winstead won't risk meeting with a man they've just tried to kill, but you're a different matter. Get them to come out where we can reach them, and your part is done."

She looked dubious. "You're still making me a target. If not now, then later."

"There isn't going to be any later. Those two will be enfolded in the warm embrace of the New York Police Department before this day has ended."

"Oh, you can guarantee that, can you?"

"Yes." Holland said the one word in a way that permitted no doubt.

A moment for pondering. "That's all you want of me? One phone call?"

"One phone call. For one million dollars."

She agreed. André placed a phone on the table and the three men listened as she spoke to Warren Winstead. The conversation went as Holland had predicted; Winstead wanted to see the letter. A meeting was arranged for three o'clock by the fountain at Lincoln Center.

"Excellent," Holland said when she'd finished. "Now, if you'll tell André which bank you use so we can transfer the—André, why do you keep *glaring* at me like that? What's the matter?"

"Nothing." Still glaring.

"Don't tell me 'nothing'—what is this, post-adolescent sulks?"

"I said nothing was the matter."

"There must be some reason you're looking as if you want to kill me."

"I don't want to kill you."

"Well, that's comforting to know. But what is it?"

"Nothing."

Selena Ross looked at Bill Tuttle. "What's with these two?"

Tuttle waggled a hand in the air. "A little father-son adjusting. Don't worry about it."

"If it isn't too much trouble," Holland was saying icily, "would you please escort Ms Ross out? And don't forget to get the name of her bank."

Pink-faced, the young man gestured to the door and then followed Selena Ross out.

When they were gone, Holland made a sound of exasperation. "Tuttle, can you tell me why our young friend has suddenly taken to looking daggers at me?"

Tuttle grinned. "Because you call him André."

Holland stared. "That's his name."

"That's his first name. You just now called me Tuttle. You call everyone else here by their last names, even the women. André doesn't like being the only one called by his first name. He says you're treating him like a kid."

Holland stared harder. "He *is* a kid."

Tuttle's grin grew bigger. "I'm just telling you what he said, boss."

Holland threw up his hands and walked away.

THE MONEY WAS just sitting there, waiting to be taken. Holland broke the three million dollars into smaller amounts which he then diverted to accounts he'd set up in banks scattered around the globe. Each deposit was infected with a program that, after a specified period of time had passed, would redirect the deposit to a different bank. The programs that moved the money would then delete themselves, leaving no tracks.

Armstead had kept a separate account for operating expenses. Holland took that, too. Bonuses for Tuttle and André.

When he was finished, he headed toward Tuttle's office, where his second-in-command was busy getting himself wired. Holland cleared a space in the mountain of papers on a worktable and perched on the edge. "Almost ready?"

"Just about." Tuttle stayed motionless while the operative doing the wiring taped a backup microphone in place. "I still think we ought to dub out your voice when we're finished."

"It wouldn't do any good. Once Armstrong and Winstead learn they've been cleaned out, whose name do you think they're going to start yelling? No, I have to strike first."

"You're taking a gun?"

"Oh, yes. Winstead will be willing to talk, but Armstrong might take a little persuading."

The operative finished and gathered up his gear. Tuttle put on his shirt and said, "Ready when you are, boss."

"Let's get André."

The youngest member of their trio was waiting for them. "I've removed every mention of Holland Investigations from Armstead's system," he said. "And the program to scramble their password permissions files is set to activate at four o'clock—is that enough time?"

"Plenty. What's the new password?"

"*Steppenwolf.*" At four o'clock, Armstead's entire computer system would lock up. No one could make any entries, and—more important—no one could take anything out. All the incriminating reports their detective had filed on contestants with short life expectancies would still be there for the police to find, just as soon as Holland gave them the password.

"Are we ready?" Holland asked. "Then let us depart for Lincoln Center." He started out but paused in the doorway. "That was good work, Flood."

André's face lit up like a child's at a birthday party; he mumbled something that could have been *Thank you.* Holland rolled his eyes as he led the way out.

THEY'D CHOSEN the fountain at Lincoln Center because of its lack of hiding places. Sure enough, there at the rear of the plaza was Cal Armstrong pretending to be engrossed by a billboard in front of the Metropolitan Opera House. Warren Winstead was circling the fountain, looking for a woman who might be Selena Ross.

As planned, Tuttle and André split off to tell Winstead the bad news that Ms Ross would not be coming. Holland approached Armstrong silently from the rear and swiftly stuck his gun into the other man's armpit. "Do you know what that is, Armstrong? Don't move—stay very still."

Armstrong looked back over his shoulder. His face darkened when he saw who had the drop on him. "You!" he spat. "What are you going to do? You can't kill me with all these people around!"

"If you mind your manners, I might not have to kill you at all. Let's join your partner." Holland slipped the gun into his jacket pocket. "Slow and easy does it. Walk ahead of me."

For a moment Armstrong looked as if he was about to jump Holland. But then he started walking toward the fountain.

Winstead was waiting, flanked by Tuttle and André. "Well, Holland. Your nameless friend here tells me you have a proposition."

"Proposition?" Armstrong asked. "What proposition?"

Holland waited until Tuttle had moved to stand between the two killers and then stepped in close; he wanted every word on tape. "If you can convince me there'll be no more attempts on my life, I can get you out of your current financial difficulties. Do you understand? I can bail you out."

Winstead looked amused. "You're going to pay us to stop trying to kill you?"

Holland smiled coldly. "There's a little more involved than that. We need a front. A legitimate business—or at least one with the appearance of legitimacy—that will do a little laundry work for us. We pass sums of money through your accounts now and then, and each time we leave a little something behind for your trouble. It shows up on the bank records as interest. Legitimate income.''

Winstead folded his arms and chuckled. ''Well, well. The minute I spotted you posing as an IRS agent, I knew you were sussing us out. But I never imagined it would be for money laundering.''

Armstrong was eyeing André. ''Who's the kid?''

''My cousin from Paducah.'' Armstrong sneered. ''There's more,'' Holland went on. ''We meet your loan payment and make sure you have enough on deposit to end the year in the black. In exchange, we take half your profits from next year.

''Half!'' Armstrong roared. ''You're out of your mind!''

Winstead didn't even blink. ''Don't be hasty, Cal. They're offering us a way out.''

''But giving up half our profits—''

''Is better than going to prison,'' Tuttle finished with a growl. ''And that's where you'll end up otherwise. You think we won't expose your rigged sweepstakes? We don't like being told no.''

Holland raised an eyebrow; Bill Tuttle didn't often get the chance to play tough guy. ''And you've got to beef up your profits,'' Holland said to Winstead. ''We have some ideas on that, too. Well? What's it to be?''

''I accept,'' Winstead said.

''What?'' Armstrong yelled. ''Well, I don't!'' He turned to Holland. ''I'd like to break your damned neck!''

''But you won't,'' Holland said contemptuously. ''Unless you're even more stupid than you look.''

It took Winstead and Tuttle together to keep Armstrong from going for Holland. Winstead talked to his partner. It took a while, but eventually he convinced Armstrong that Holland was throwing them a lifeline. Armstrong still didn't like it, but he liked the idea of prison even less.

''Are we all calm again now?'' Holland asked, his cue to André that they were finished with the setup.

André spoke for the first time. "There's one condition." Holland could see Tuttle tensing; this was the important part. "No more killing," André was saying. "We just can't have that—it's too risky. You jeopardized your entire operation when you killed that apple grower."

Armstrong's jaw dropped, and even Winstead wasn't able to hide his surprise. "Yes, we know about that, too," Holland said impatiently. "You have no secrets from us. But it was a clumsy move, inexcusable."

André asked, "Why did you think killing that one winner would solve your problem? All it saved you was a hundred thousand dollars, and you need millions."

"Answer him," Holland commanded.

Winstead sighed. "We were trying to buy a little time. As long as the money stayed in the bank, we could borrow on it."

"And you've been borrowing for years," Tuttle said. "Getting in deeper and deeper. You'd have done better to sell the business."

"Nobody would buy it," Armstrong muttered. "We tried."

Holland said, "Let me make this clear. If you so much as come under suspicion for killing that apple grower, our deal is off. That back road to Schenectady—you could have been seen while you were doing the job."

"We didn't kill him there," Armstrong said. "Out in the open? No way."

"Where, then?"

"In his house. Nobody else was there—Lockerby lived alone."

There. He'd said the name. "So what did you do, hit him on the head?"

"I broke his neck. Old man, brittle bones."

"Then what?"

Winstead said, "Cal drove the pickup with Lockerby's body while I followed in our car. I stood lookout while Cal ran the truck into the tree. No one saw us, Holland. There is *no* witness. None. The police have no way whatsoever of connecting us to Gordon Lockerby's death.''

Holland nodded. "Very well. We'll go ahead and start transferring funds. But if you're wrong about no witness, expect all that new money to disappear overnight."

"I understand," Winstead said. "There won't be a problem."

"Then I think we're done for now. We'll be in touch."

There was a moment of awkwardness; then Winstead and Armstrong walked away without speaking. Even as Holland and the other two watched them head down toward Columbus Circle, they could see a spring starting to appear in Winstead's step.

"They think they've been rescued," Tuttle remarked. "Just when the night is darkest, Holland Investigations comes riding in to save the day! Ha."

"Mixed metaphor," André said.

Holland looked at his watch. "Twenty to four. That's close enough." He took out his phone and called the police.

BILL TUTTLE HEAVED A SIGH of resignation. "Another skull."

Holland peered into his own glass. "I seem to have a push broom."

"A push broom." Tuttle's head swiveled toward him. "Never in the history of ice-reading has anyone seen a *push broom* in the bottom of a glass. I don't believe it."

"Take a look." They switched bar stools in order not to disturb the ice.

Tuttle kept trying different angles until he saw it. "Well, I'll be damned. It *is* a push broom. You'll be written up in *The Ice Cube Imaging Gazette* for this."

"Such an honor," Holland murmured.

"Wait a minute…it's turning into a skull." Tuttle pushed the glass toward Holland and reclaimed his own drink. He paused a moment before he said what was on his mind. "We stole a lot of money today, boss."

"'Recovered' is the proper verb. Or 'redistributed', if you prefer."

"Still."

"You don't think Selena Ross is entitled to her uncle's winnings?"

"She has a valid legal claim. Law says you can't profit from a felony, and the only reason that check wasn't deposited was that a felony had been committed. No, that's her money."

"Then perhaps you object to our enabling Millie to open a new bookshop?"

Tuttle shook his head. "Winstead and Armstrong destroyed her old shop, they should pay for her new one."

"Ah. Then it's our share of the loot that has your nose out of joint."

"A million bucks for three days' work?"

"Hazardous duty pay." Holland placed his hand dramatically on his chest. "Only yesterday I faced death by fire— well, I ducked under it, to be exact. Don't you think my life is worth a measly one million dollars?"

Tuttle grinned. "Well, if you put it that way—"

"Oh, I do put it that way. Make no mistake."

"Then I guess maybe you undercharged."

"My own thought precisely." They finished their drinks and asked for refills.

Whether he'd undercharged or not, Holland was satisfied. Armstead was finished, and no more sweepstakes winners would die before their time. It had been a good three days' work.